I0677947

MIDNIGHT
QUEEN

MIDNIGHT QUEEN

WOLVES OF MIDNIGHT

BECKY MOYNIHAN

BROKEN
BOOKS

Text and cover design
Copyright © 2024 Becky Moynihan
All rights reserved.

This book is a work of fiction. Names, characters, organizations, places, events, and incidents are either products of the author's imagination or are used fictitiously. Any resemblance to actual persons, living or dead, or actual events is purely coincidental.

Published by Broken Books
www.beckymoynihan.com

No part of this book may be reproduced, or stored in a retrieval system, or transmitted in any form or by any means, electronic, mechanical, photocopying, recording, or otherwise, without express permission of the publisher.

ISBN-13: 979-8-9883737-2-8

Cover design by Becky Moynihan
Cover model by Ravven
www.depositphotos.com

To the broken:
May you find healing on the other side
of pain.

PROLOGUE

KOLTON

Insanity didn't claim me the way I thought it would.

I expected to fall into an endless abyss where no one could reach me. To forget who I was and everyone I loved. To simply exist in a void of nothingness.

But when I finally succumbed to the same fate my mother had, my consciousness wasn't reduced to nothing.

I was still aware. Aware yet irrevocably splintered—like the jagged remains of a broken mirror. I knew who I was. Where I was. But I was no longer myself. No longer *whole*.

I was shattered into pieces. Still breathing, yet unable to control my actions.

My body and mind were no longer mine.

They were held hostage by a pain too great to fathom. Too powerful to bear. It broke apart my sanity piece by piece, reducing me to a mound of useless rubble. Not killing me, but stripping my body of strength and sapping my mind of reason.

I hadn't been driven into madness. I was simply pain. Bone-crushing pain. Unable to speak or move.

Or so I thought.

I was still on the ground, desperately clinging to my wife. One second. One second more, and I would have lost her forever. Holding her was the only thing keeping me from completely falling apart. I could feel her, but I couldn't hear her. Couldn't hear anything besides the agonized thoughts piercing my skull.

You almost lost her. Almost lost them both. *You can't protect your mate and unborn child forever. They will die, and so will you. There's no escaping your parents' fate, a fate that is now yours.*

Fresh pain sliced through me, splintering my sanity even more. And then I felt it. A hand on my shoulder. A hand that was decidedly not my mate's.

An emotion suddenly ripped through my pain. Feral and raw, so fiercely intense that every thought, every instinct, switched off. Except for one.

Protect, protect, protect.

Like a demon possessed, I exploded off the ground and attacked.

CHAPTER 1

NORA

The attack happened so quickly that I froze, too shocked to react.

But when Kolton punched his second in command square in the face, I scrambled to my feet.

"Kolton!" I cried, staring in horror as he went after Jagger like he had the witches moments before.

Jagger stumbled back with a pained grunt. Surprise lit his expression, but he managed to duck in time to avoid another punch.

Releasing an unearthly growl, Kolton pursued him without mercy, delivering several punishing blows. When he drew blood, Jagger set his jaw like stone and fought back.

"Kolton, *stop*," I shouted, but he seemed deaf to my voice.

Panicking, I hurried forward to intervene. The second I did, a wall of tanned muscle blocked my path.

"Get out of my way, Griff," I ordered, desperate to break up the fight.

"Not going to happen, Nora," he tossed back, grabbing my arm when I tried to shove past him. "Something's wrong with Kolton."

"I know, but he *needs* me," I frantically argued, trying to wrench myself free.

He and Jagger were on the ground now, grappling for dominance. I'd seen them fight before, but this was different. This was *real*. Kolton was trying to *kill* his second. I could see it in his eyes. He wasn't looking at Jagger as a friend but as a threat. An *enemy*.

Something was definitely wrong. I couldn't reach him, and I didn't know why. Didn't know why this was *happening*.

"Vi, do something," I pleaded, still struggling to free myself.

Kolton's sister simply stared at the fighting pair, her olive complexion growing paler and paler with each powerful blow.

Unable to bear another second of this madness, I brought my heel down on Griff's bare toes. *Hard.* When he yanked his foot back with a sharp hiss, I used the distraction to twist out of his grip. Before I could slip by him, he whirled and latched onto me again.

"What the hell, Nora? That seriously hurt."

"Let *go*, Griff," I growled back, digging my nails into the arm he'd snaked around my middle.

"Let her go, Griff," Vi suddenly spoke, her voice a hushed whisper.

Griff snorted incredulously, his grip only tightening. "Are you two daft? There's no way I'm letting Nora—"

"Griff. Let her go. *Now.*"

At the slight tremor in Vi's voice, we both paused to look at her. She was still staring at Kolton and Jagger, but it was at that moment I realized how quiet they'd become. In fact, the only sound I could hear was the crackling flames still eating away at the Rivers' ruined mansion.

Griff swore under his breath. Confused, I glanced at the fight and immediately understood why. Kolton had stopped attacking Jagger and was now facing us. His focus was razor sharp, fixated on . . . Griff's arm around me.

Dread filled my stomach.

"Get behind me. Both of you," I said, trying my best to remain calm. Without a word, they obeyed. But when Griff slowly released me and took a step back, Kolton wasn't appeased.

I shivered as his gaze raked over me, devouring every inch. I was still naked. We *all* were. Which didn't help matters in the least.

A wave of possessive energy flooded our bond, stealing my breath. I'd felt the emotion from him before, but not like this. He was livid. Feral with rage. Every inch of him shook as he slowly lifted his gaze and set his sights on Griff.

Murder. Murder glittered in his dark amber eyes.

As he rose to his feet, the movement wholly predator, fear coursed through me. Reacting on instinct, I stepped toward him.

"*Nora,*" Griff hissed and reached for my arm to pull me back.

The second he did, Kolton exploded forward with a bellowing roar.

Instead of running for my life like a smart person would do, I planted my feet and screamed as loud as I could, "NO!"

Kolton faltered, but kept coming.

"Kolton, *STOP!*" I screamed again at the top of my lungs.

This time, he stumbled, nearly falling to his knees. The move brought him up short, and he paused, his gaze shifting to me again. For a split second, his expression cleared, and I saw him. The *real* him. My husband. My *mate.*

Emotion flooded our soulmate bond. Fear. Confusion. *Pain.* Overwhelmed by all that he was feeling, I gasped.

That small sound froze him in place. Distracted him.

A second later, a thick brown arm coiled around his neck.

I gasped again as Jagger squeezed Kolton's neck like a python, cutting off his air supply. Kolton grunted and fought to throw him off, but Griff was suddenly there, lending his support. Not to his alpha, but to *Jagger.* Together, they wrestled Kolton to his knees. Even then, he fought, his gaze still locked on me.

"Kolton," I whimpered, my heart twisting as I felt his desperation. His *agony.* Responding to it, I stepped forward, only for Vi to stop me. Her fingernails dug into my arm as I tried to break free. "Let me go, Vi. They're *hurting* him."

"I swear they're only trying to subdue him, Nora. It's not safe for you to be around him right now," she adamantly said, watching her brother slowly lose the fight.

Helpless tears filled my eyes. "But he *needs* me. I'm his soulmate. He wouldn't hurt me."

"I'm not so sure about that," she whispered back. Kolton continued to struggle, nearly breaking free of Jagger's chokehold. "That's not . . . that's not Kolton. I've seen this happen before, Nora. I just never thought it would happen to him."

As her words sank in, my heart stopped.

No.

No.

He was *not* going insane. Not Kolton. Not the strongest man I knew. Not the man who carried the world on his shoulders yet always managed to be there for his family. For *me*.

No. I couldn't accept her words. I wouldn't allow this to be his fate.

Still, I remained where I was as Kolton's best friends forced him into submission. As Griff placed a hand on his forehead and uttered a word. A *spell*. A sleep spell.

A tear slid down my cheek.

It's okay, I whispered to him through our bond, praying he could hear it. Praying the words were true. *Everything's going to be okay.*

Kolton's eyes rolled back, and he fell into unconsciousness.

They were looking at me like I had all the answers. In reality, I had no clue what to do.

Everything had happened so fast.

Only an hour ago, I'd been taking a shower and anticipating the dinner Kolton was cooking. And then it all fell apart. Arrow tried to lure me away. Storm and Zuriel almost fought. Brielle, my human best friend, got infected with werewolf toxin. The Blackstone Coven arrived. The house burned down.

At least we'd eviscerated the witches. Well, all except one.

Keisha had escaped, but not before Kolton had left his mark on her. He'd almost killed her. Almost. But Storm had been in the way. *I* had been in the way. If not for me, the entire Blackstone Coven would have been wiped out for good. The threat would have been eliminated.

We'd bought ourselves time, but I could still hear Keisha's final words.

You will pay dearly for this day. I will curse you. I will rain hellfire on your heads. My coven will be avenged. I will gather witches from every corner of the earth.

Despite the demise of her coven, I knew that she would return. I knew that with absolute certainty.

Which was why I needed to put on my big girl panties and come up with a plan. Well, the panty part I could do. Coming up with a solid plan would be the hard part.

"How long until Kolton wakes?" I asked Griff, presenting my back to him while I dressed. We'd all seen each other naked more than once, but I still wasn't used to it. At least the garage hadn't burned down. The vehicles inside were untouched, along with the stash of clothing we kept in them for emergency purposes.

"Two hours. Maybe three if we're lucky," Griff answered me, donning a bright neon t-shirt and board shorts. "A male his size won't take long to shake off the spell's effects."

Not far away, Jagger was already decked out in his usual black garb. The only thing on him not black were the diamond studs in his ears. He silently stood watch over Kolton where he'd laid him out in the backseat of the Rivers' white truck. I didn't fail to notice how careful he'd been, making sure Kolton's head hadn't hit the door on the way in. Even with a mess of fresh blood still covering half his face, Jagger continued to treat his alpha with respect.

A lump formed in my throat, which I quickly swallowed. Now wasn't the time for emotion. This was the time for *action*. I could process everything later when I didn't have an expectant audience and unconscious husband to take care of.

"Right," I said, slipping on a white, long-sleeved shirt over my bra. Despite my best efforts, my fingers left behind smudges of soot and blood on the material. "Then we need to find someplace safe for Kolton until he's back to his normal self."

Busy dressing in a purple shirt and dark designer jeans to my left, Vi paused to shoot me a sharp look. I ignored her.

Grabbing a pair of ripped shorts, I tugged them on before facing the guys. They stared right back, their expressions hard to read. Well, Jagger's was, but he didn't usually show emotion. Griff looked uncharacteristically solemn.

Unable to bear his sad, puppy-dog eyes, I focused on Jagger. "Well?"

He crossed his tattooed arms over his chest, the designs covered in a layer of blood and soot. "Well, what?"

"You're the second in command," I stated, as if that explained everything.

He slowly raised one dark eyebrow. "And you're the alpha female."

I impatiently shoved aside a clump of fiery red curls. "So that's it then? Kolton's unavailable, so I'm in charge?"

His blue-gray eyes remained steady on mine, but he didn't respond. He didn't have to.

Ah hell, this couldn't be happening. I was *not* prepared for this.

"We're here to support you, Nora. That's our job," Griff quietly spoke, no doubt sensing my panic. "Tell us what to do, and we'll do it."

Me? Tell *them* what to do? How had I gone from "pack disappointment" to being in charge anyway? Oh, yeah. I'd married an alpha. I'd passed my initiation test and had become the new alpha female. I'd earned the pack's *respect*.

It still felt unreal that I of all people had become the alpha female of the largest pack in the country. Still, rules were rules. If Kolton couldn't give the orders, then I was next in line to do so.

How freaking *terrifying* was that?

Storm, help, I silently communicated to my wolf familiar. She'd helped command an entire legion of *angels*, after all. If anyone was qualified to give orders, she was. *What should I do?*

I felt the warmth of her presence as she stirred and replied, *This is* your *destiny, Nora, not mine. You're strong and perfectly capable of making sound decisions all on your own. You were right earlier. Your mate needs you. He is lost, and I believe the only one who can find him is you.*

At her confident words, hope rose in my chest.

Lost. Lost but not *gone*.

I could cope with him being lost. That meant I could still reach him. I could help him find his way back. I *would* help him, and I would save him. Save him like he had saved me over and over again. I wouldn't give up hope. No matter how long it took, I would get my husband back.

As fresh resolve filled me, I raised my chin and calmly looked at my companions. "Okay, then here's what we're going to do . . ."

CHAPTER 2

NORA

The air was stale and musty, reminding me far too much of my time spent locked inside a cage in an abandoned church basement.

Still, I kept my shoulders back and refused to dwell on the horrific memory. This moment wasn't about me. This moment was about *him*. The man who'd go through Hell and back to keep me safe. It was my turn now. My turn to face my demons for the man I loved.

"This fallout shelter was built over seventy years ago, right after the Cold War started," Jagger said from beside me. "The previous alpha, Anthony Rivers, acquired it in the eighties and converted the space to contain feral werewolves. Because of its remote location, the shelter is able to best protect the werewolf, providing a safe environment for them to shift without fear of hurting someone."

I shivered, more from the thought of being forced to shift down here than from the chill air. The shelter was basically a bunker designed to withstand a nuclear attack. Unlike the beautiful home where Kolton's mother was being held, the cavernous space was underground, devoid of natural light.

A person could truly go mad down here.

Suddenly bombarded with doubt, I grabbed my wedding ring and began to twist it. "Are you sure this is the only place we can safely keep him?" My gaze remained on a spot across the room where Kolton lay on a cot bolted to the cement floor. The steady rise and fall of his chest reassured me, but only a little. What would happen when he woke up?

"It's too dangerous to keep him anywhere else," Vi responded from my other side. "This place rarely gets used anymore, and no one will think to look for him here. He can't be seen like this, Nora. If anyone finds out what happened . . ."

I squeezed my hands into fists. "I know."

They would put him down. His own pack—the people he'd grown up with and had protected for years—would turn on him in an instant. One werewolf's life, even their alpha's, wasn't worth risking the safety of the entire werewolf race. A part of me understood that, but a bigger part screamed at the unfairness of it all.

He'd risked everything for his pack, but they wouldn't do the same for him. One whiff of his current mental state and they'd tear him apart like a ravenous pack of . . . well, *wolves*. No wonder he'd faked his own mother's death, not even allowing Melanie to know about her to ensure she wasn't discovered.

A thought came to me then. One that nearly ripped my chest wide open.

Would I have to fake Kolton's death next?

Barely able to breathe, I shoved the thought aside. No. I would *not* go there. I was going to save him. I was going to help him get better. He would stay down here, but only for a little while. Only until whatever had broken inside him was mended.

Lost. He was *lost*. Not gone.

He suddenly stirred on the cot, uttering a low moan.

My body immediately responded to the sound, and I stepped forward. Hands shot out and stopped me. I almost pulled away, but doubt swirled in my gut once more. Did they really think he would hurt me? Remembering what had happened to Kolton's mom, I allowed the hands to drag me backward and out of the room.

But when Griff started to close the thick steel door, panic set in.

"He's going to be confused. I should—"

"He's *already* confused, Nora," Vi interrupted, her hands firmly keeping me from charging back inside. "Once he's fully awake, we'll use the intercom system to communicate. If he's lucid, we'll know soon enough. He wouldn't want you to risk your safety without knowing for sure."

I bit my trembling lip. They were right. I knew they were. But my soul . . . my soul *ached* to be reunited with its other half. Reason had nothing to do with its need to feel whole again.

The door closed with a thud of finality, and both Jagger and Griff made sure the lock was firmly in place. As miserable as this moment was, my one small consolation was knowing that Melanie and Brielle wouldn't have to witness this. They, along with Melanie's nanny, Miss Gabby, had made it safely to their destination. We'd planned ahead of time to meet up with them at the Rivers' penthouse in Albany. A fitting location, considering that Brielle's parents lived there.

They'd have to be told that their daughter was about to undergo a few . . . changes. I doubted she'd want to keep it a secret from them. We had many rules in the werewolf community, but keeping family in the dark—even a *human* family—wasn't one of them. Family, no matter the species, was everything.

The second the door was locked, I stepped toward the video intercom on the wall and pressed the button that would let me see and hear inside the room. When I saw Kolton slowly sitting up on the cot, relief weakened my knees. This wasn't so bad. I wasn't completely cut off from him. I could handle—

He suddenly shot off the cot like something had zapped him. Staggering halfway across the room, he stopped again and went ramrod straight. For an endless moment, he simply stood there. I couldn't even tell if he was breathing.

Growing concerned, I reached out to him through our bond. Everything was hazy. Static. As if the connection that bound us together had been damaged. *Broken.*

Not a single thought or emotion reached me.

Desperate to feel him, to *hear* him, I called out to his wolf familiar. *Shadow. Shadow, can you hear me? I can't reach Kolton. What's happening? Shadow? Shadow!*

Nothing.

It was like my connection to him had been broken too.

Storm, I can't reach Shadow. Can you?

She was silent for several beats. Then, *No. I think your mate has suppressed him somehow.*

"Oh, Kolton," I whispered, feeling the sting of tears against my eyelids.

Needing to speak to him the only way I could, I reached for the intercom again. Before I could press the button, Vi grabbed my hand.

"Wait. Just wait," she breathed. "I think he's about to speak. I think—"

An earth-shattering roar suddenly pounded my eardrums. So loud that I winced and covered my ears. I focused on the video feed again just as Kolton started moving. Started *charging* across the room. Faster and faster until he slammed into the thick steel door.

Wham!

I flinched as the door shuddered. A door strong enough to withstand a bomb.

Wham. Wham. *Wham.*

He slammed into it again and again, bellowing his rage, his sole focus on breaking down the door.

Speechless, I glanced at the others. Vi and Griff looked equally stunned, but Jagger simply said, "It'll hold."

Weakly nodding, I resumed watching Kolton throw himself at the door.

Hours. It felt like we watched him relentlessly try to break free of his cage for *hours*. Guilt gnawed at my gut. I knew how awful it felt to be locked up, yet here I was, imprisoning my own mate. I swiped at my face, not surprised to find it wet with tears.

Finally, after what felt like an eternity, Kolton backed away from the door and stopped. Through the monitor, I could hear his ragged breathing. See the confusion, the *anguish* on his face.

"No," he quietly groaned, reaching up to grasp the black t-shirt Jagger and Griff had put on him while he was unconscious. A ripping sound reached my ears as he tore the shirt in half. "No, no, no, no. I lost her, I lost her, I lost her."

He threw his head back and howled. The sound was gut-wrenching, the very definition of heartbreak. Peeling the shredded shirt off his body, he continued to howl as he fell to his knees.

The second he hit the ground, a tsunami of pain crashed into me.

I was suddenly falling as well, weak with devastation. Before I could hit the ground, Griff caught me. Unable to bear my own weight, I let him gather me into his arms. Arms that were strong and comforting, but all wrong. They weren't my mate's. I should be in my *mate's* arms right now, not his.

"He's ... he's in so much *pain*," I choked out. "It's too much. I can't ... I can't bear it."

Another arm wrapped around me as Vi joined us. "I'm so sorry, Nora," she whispered, her voice tight with emotion. "We'll stay and watch over him if you need to leave."

"No," I immediately replied, straightening as I forced my weak legs to hold me. "I can't leave. I need to be *in* there."

"We can't let you do that," Griff said, tightening his arms around me. "Kolton's gone feral. He'll hurt you."

I shook my head. "No, he won't."

"How do you know?" he asked, his skepticism clear.

"I just do. In *here*." I pulled back to place my hand on my chest, over the organ that was frantically pounding for its mate.

"Nora . . ." Vi started, but I quickly stopped her.

"Lock me inside with him."

When no one moved a muscle, I stepped back even more and squared my shoulders, my mind made up.

"Lock me inside with him," I repeated, my voice free of even the slightest tremor. "That's not a request. It's an order."

Griff's eyebrows shot sky high.

I took turns staring at all three of them, holding eye contact as I'd seen Kolton do many times before. I was dead serious, and I needed them to see it. To *feel* it.

The very last person I expected to listen to me was the first to move.

"*Jagger*," Vi sharply warned as he reached for the door's lock.

He paused, only to say, "Nora's right. Kolton has fallen. That makes her Midnight Pack's newest alpha. It's our duty to obey her."

I didn't know who looked more shocked. Me or them.

Vi was the quickest to recover, stepping forward to say, "That may be, but she's making a decision purely based on emotion, one that could get her killed."

"I disagree," Jagger calmly replied, watching me carefully. "I think we should trust that she knows what she's doing. Kolton put his faith in her. So should we."

At that, something in my chest loosened. With Jagger backing me up, I knew the others would listen, no matter their personal reservations. I silently nodded my thanks, and he dipped his chin in return. At the same time, his eyes burned holes into mine, the message in them crystal clear.

Don't let us down.

I swallowed hard, nodding once again in understanding.

They were trusting me, more than they'd ever trusted me before. I couldn't fail them. Too much was at stake.

Staring at me a moment longer, Jagger swung his focus to the others. "The second I open this door, be prepared in case Kolton tries to escape."

"And if he attacks Nora?" Griff asked, clearly still not okay with me going inside.

"Then we stop him by any means necessary."

Griff pursed his lips but refused to comment further.

"He won't attack me," I quietly assured, yet he and Vi still didn't look convinced.

Breathing a sigh, I faced Jagger again. "Go ahead and open it. I'm ready."

He nodded and grasped the lock, prying it open. But as I stepped toward the door, he placed a hand on my shoulder. I tensed, certain he'd changed his mind. Didn't matter. I'd force my way in if it was the last thing I did. Readying myself for a fight, I was surprised when all he did was say, "If you feel unsafe, just say the word. We'll get you out of there."

I threw him a grateful look. "I will. Thank you. And if there are any problems out here, let me know."

He dipped his chin again, then looked over my shoulder at Griff and Vi. Griff blew out a harsh breath, but they both joined us at the door without further argument.

"On my count, we open the door and let Nora in," Jagger

instructed, widening his stance in preparation. "Then close and lock it as soon as she's inside. Got it?"

Griff yanked an agitated hand through his spiky blond hair and muttered, "Got it. I just hope this doesn't end with Nora torn into a million pieces."

"Griff," Vi growled, but the sound was more worried than anything.

Despite my best efforts, I felt my heart trill with fear. Silently cursing, I shoved the fear down and focused on the task before me. This was Kolton. *Kolton.* My husband and soulmate. The kindest, most generous man I'd ever known. I had nothing to fear.

I'm here with you, Storm chose that moment to speak, immediately bolstering my confidence. *I will keep you safe.*

A pent-up breath shuddered from me. *Thank you, Storm.*

I could do this. I could *do* this.

"Ready?"

I nodded along with the others as Jagger began the countdown.

"Then get set to move in three . . . two . . . one . . ."

The door burst open. I lunged forward, just in time to avoid the door as it once again sealed shut with a resounding thud. Straightening, I immediately focused on Kolton. At what I found, I swallowed a surprised gasp.

His gaze was already locked on me.

Still on his knees, he studied me for several long moments. Assessing. Evaluating. As if sizing up . . .

Prey.

My heart started to thunder again, but I refused to show even an ounce of weakness. If I did, he would no doubt attack. I could see that clearly now. I was staring at a predator. A creature reacting solely on instinct. The slightest misstep could spell my doom.

Gathering every molecule of strength I possessed, I straightened to my full height and steadily held his gaze.

For what felt like an eternity, we simply stared at each other. Then, I opened my mouth and dared to whisper his name.

The second I did, he jumped to his feet and charged.

CHAPTER 3

NORA

He had me up against the door in two seconds flat, trapping me between his powerful arms.

All the air left me in a rush, and I held perfectly still as a growl vibrated his chest. It was a warning, a warning that I quickly heeded. Not exactly submitting, but not showing aggression either.

I was in his *territory*. A possible threat. The moments that followed were crucial, proving if I could be trusted. Or not.

I didn't speak. Didn't even breathe. Every inch of me wanted to reach out and touch him, to reassure and comfort him, but I didn't dare move a muscle.

This was *feral* Kolton, a version of him I'd never met before.

As much as I didn't want to believe he would hurt me, this version of him was a stranger to me. Maybe he thought of me as a stranger too.

So I held still. Held still while he continued to growl, his muscles bunching as if prepared to strike. When I didn't react, the growl gradually faded, until a deafening silence descended. Not daring to raise my eyes to his, I focused on his chest, on the dried blood still smeared there from his fight with the witches and Jagger. The cuts on his deep olive skin had long since healed, but I still itched to inspect every last inch of him. To make certain that he was okay—at least on the outside.

He suddenly moved, nearly making me jump. I focused all of

my willpower on holding still as he lowered his head an inch, then another and another. I felt something warm brush my cheek. His nose. He was . . . he was scenting me. His chest expanded as he dragged in air, inhaling me deeply.

Another growl vibrated his chest, but this one was different. Instead of a warning, the sound had a slight possessive undertone. My heart beat faster. Not with fear, but with *hope.*

Did he recognize me? Did he remember who I was to him?

As he slowly trailed his nose over my jaw, continuing to scent me, it dawned on me where he was headed.

His *spot.*

The spot between my neck and shoulder. The spot where he'd claimed me.

Sure enough, his head drifted lower as he scented a path down my neck. The pulse in my throat jumped, and he paused. One move was all it would take. One bite and he could sever my artery. I wouldn't be able to stop him. Not with him this close. I was all but helpless, and yet . . .

I slowly tipped my head back, exposing my throat to him. Expressing without words that I *trusted* him.

Another growl vibrated his chest. Pleased. He was *pleased.*

A thrill shot through me. Still, I made no other movement, not wanting to push my luck. He wasn't attacking, but that didn't mean I was in the clear.

When he finally reached his claim spot, my body thrummed with adrenaline. Being this close but forcing myself not to touch him was absolute torture. Energy whipped through me. Energy that was slowly causing me to tremble.

Kolton didn't seem to notice, though. He was too busy scenting his spot. He inhaled deeply. Greedily. Repeatedly brushing his nose over the sensitive skin.

He suddenly released a sharp exhale. My eyes widened as he tensed all over. As he began to uncontrollably shake. He gasped, again and again, as if struggling to draw in air. Each gasp hurt to hear, sounding more and more like sobs. Deep ones. Deep and soul-wrenching.

Just when I couldn't bear to hear one more sob—when I was about to risk everything and pull him close—he moved.

Not to attack, but to pull *me* close.

He slid his arms around me, burying his face in my neck. When a whimper escaped me, he shuddered and drew me tight against him. No longer able to hold still, I lifted my arms and clung to him with all of my might.

Tears of relief, of sorrow, burned my eyes, sliding down my cheeks. I silently cried as he trembled against me.

Neither of us made a sound for several minutes. We simply held each other, as if the contact was the only thing keeping us from falling apart. And maybe it was. Maybe this was the way to fix things. To fix *him*.

"I'm here, Kolton," I finally whispered, needing to reassure him. "I'll *always* be here."

He didn't respond, but having his arms around me was enough. He remembered me. To what extent, I didn't know. But he *remembered* me.

It was a start, one that made my hope bloom even more.

"I'll find you," I continued to whisper. To share my hope with him. My determination. "I promise I'm going to bring you back."

Kolton eventually settled enough to let me lead him away from the door.

As content as I was to remain in his arms, I was beyond exhausted.

Now that the adrenaline had worn off, my eyelids could barely stay open. Crossing the room, I encouraged him to lay down on the narrow cot he'd vacated earlier. But before I could claim a cot of my own, he tugged me down with him and wrapped himself around me. We barely fit, but he held me so close that we might as well have been one person.

Melting against him, I finally allowed myself to relax. We weren't out of the woods yet, but sleep would do us both good. I could only guess the time, but it was probably well past midnight. I hoped the others got some sleep too. They were no doubt still monitoring us over the intercom, but I hadn't heard anything.

Which was good. Kolton might not react well to the sound of their voices. He'd accepted me, but he still wasn't himself. Every move he made was reactive. Instinctual. And every attempt to reach him through our bond had ended in failure. It was as if he'd erected a protective wall around his mind to keep everyone out, including me. And I had no idea where Shadow went.

When Kolton's breathing finally slowed, I relaxed even more. Burrowing my face in his chest, I allowed the steady beat of his heart to lull me into sleep.

I was rooted to the spot, unable to stop the two males from fighting.

One had dark hair with a broader build, while the other had white-blond hair and a leaner frame.

I'd never seen them before, and yet my mind knew exactly who they were.

Anthony Rivers and Marcus Pemberton.

They fought outside the Rivers' family home, almost in the exact same spot where we'd confronted the Blackstone Coven. Blood coated their faces and bare chests, each blow they delivered brutal and efficient.

Death. They were fighting to the death.

But I wasn't worried. I knew who would win. He always won.

Pride warmed my chest, but it wasn't my *pride, I realized. It was Kolton's. This was his memory, not mine. His dream. I didn't know how I was here, only that I was.*

Two dark-haired females stood beside me, and I immediately recognized them. The younger one was Vi as a teenager, and the older one was Kolton's very pregnant mother. Sweat beaded her brow as she anxiously watched the fight. Every time her husband took a hit, she flinched and rested a hand on her swollen belly.

No one said a word. Despite their alpha's strength, even the slightest distraction could be deadly.

The family simply watched, silently supporting each other as the fight reached its climax.

Any minute now. Any minute, and we could finish celebrating Vi's sixteenth birthday.

We still hadn't touched her cake, and Mom's red velvet recipe was my favorite. Kolton's favorite.

Any minute now. Any—

A sudden cry of pain burst from his mother. I turned to see her doubled over, clutching her stomach. As she started to fall, Kolton lunged and caught her.

She suddenly looked up. Looked up and screamed.

Kolton whipped his head toward the fight, just in time to see Marcus Pemberton snap his father's neck.

His mom screamed again. Screamed and screamed as the light left her mate's eyes.

Her pain ripped through me, becoming my own. Becoming Kolton's.

He fell to the ground with her still in his arms, overwhelmed with grief for her loss. For his loss.

Her dark hair suddenly vanished, transforming into fiery red curls. Her face melted away until mine took its place.

My mouth opened and I screamed, consumed with sorrow. Driven mad from it. Lost in a sea of endless pain.

I awoke with a start, my heart still thundering from the horrific dream. When fresh pain hit me—pain that wasn't my own—I wrenched my eyes open to find that I was still tightly pressed against Kolton. Except that he was now trembling. *Shaking.* I peered up at his face and found it twisted in agony, his eyes still squeezed shut.

I gripped his shoulder and shook him. "Kolton. Kolton, wake up. It's just a dream. You're only dreaming. Kolton, wake—"

A startled squeak left me as he burst awake and pinned me beneath him in the blink of an eye.

"Nora, are you okay?"

At the sound of Griff's worried voice over the intercom, every inch of Kolton's body tensed. His lips peeled back in a silent snarl, and I froze, caught in his stare. I couldn't look away. We were too close. His lower half trapped mine against the cot. His chest heaved, each unsteady breath pushing us together. His arms were steel bands on either side of my head, keeping my face aligned with his.

I had nowhere to go. He was everywhere. *Everywhere.*

And yet, he'd never felt farther away.

As I stared into his eyes, all I could see was a wild creature consumed by pain. The man I knew and had grown to love was nowhere to be found.

"Nora, answer me or I'm coming in."

Swallowing the lump in my throat, I quickly responded to Griff,

"I'm okay."

A shudder rippled through Kolton. Otherwise, he didn't react.

"I'm okay," I repeated in a whisper, knowing he needed reassurance. "So are you."

He simply stared at me. Stared and stared until my eyes started to burn. Not from holding eye contact, but from seeing how vastly empty his gaze was. How *lost*.

What happened to you? I desperately wanted to ask him. *Where did you go?*

Before I could do something stupid like burst into tears, I once again swallowed the emotions demanding to be released. Breaking down wasn't an option. Neither was running away. I needed to stay strong and face reality, no matter how painful it was.

When I was about to coax him into letting me up, he moved. Refusing to flinch, I held perfectly still as he brought a hand to my face and touched my chin. Frowning, he began to rub at the spot. It took me a moment to understand what he was doing.

"It's not mine," I reassured him, but his frown only deepened. He tilted my chin up to inspect the skin of my neck. When he pressed his thumb to my throat, my pulse kicked up. His touch was gentle though, sweeping across the sensitive skin to remove the dried blood there. He made a sound of frustration, then abruptly lifted off me.

As he towered over me, I looked up at him with a question in my eyes, but he simply grabbed my hand and pulled me to my feet.

"Kolton, what—?"

Without a word, he turned and towed me after him. I obediently followed, throwing a confused look at the camera mounted on the wall near the door. No one responded over the intercom though, to my relief. It was as if the entire bunker held its breath in anticipation of what Kolton would do next.

He led me across the room past a small seating area containing a metal table bolted to the floor and two chairs. Nothing about this place was homey. But, considering its current use, I understood why. A feral werewolf would end up destroying anything in its path, so furnishing the space would be a waste of money. Still, I couldn't help but think that a couch or rug would be a cozy spot for an anxious wolf to curl up on.

Kolton didn't seem to notice any of it though. His sole focus was on the wide doorway straight ahead, which I'd been told earlier led to storage rooms and a communal bathroom. Once we were through the doorway, it became clear where he was headed.

"You want to clean up?" I quietly asked, watching closely for any sign of tension at the sound of my voice. He didn't respond, but he didn't stiffen either, which I took as a win. "I get it. I've never been in a house fire or a battle like that before, but it sure was messy. If you think *I* look bad, you should see—"

I swallowed the rest of my prattling words as he abruptly swiveled and reached for the hem of my shirt.

"Oh. Okay. You want me to—"

He had my shirt over my head before I could finish, leaving me speechless once more. Tossing it onto the bathroom counter, he dove right into unbuttoning my shorts.

"Um . . ."

He tugged them down, along with my underwear, making my face flame.

"I really hope there isn't a camera in here. If there is, turn it off, please. Like right now," I lightly said, hoping that the people I intended the words for couldn't actually hear them. It would mean they couldn't see me being *stripped* right now.

Kolton made no indication that he'd heard the words, his only focus on removing our clothes. Soon, we were both naked in the middle of the bathroom. He grabbed my hand again and led the way to one of the showers. Once there, he reached for the handle and cranked it.

"It's probably really cold—" I started, then yelped as, sure enough, the cold stream struck my face.

When I sputtered, Kolton pulled me into him and grasped the nape of my neck. I stilled, blinking up at him through wet lashes as he immediately got to work cleaning me up. Every movement was practical and efficient. There was no teasing. No heat. He simply wanted to clean me, nothing more.

I watched him as he thoroughly washed the blood and soot from my face, using body wash from the dispenser attached to the tiled wall. I didn't say a word, allowing him to clean me from head to toe. He even tackled my *hair*, God bless him. He didn't miss an inch, pausing more than once to inspect a spot before moving on. I let him ease his worries. Let him see for himself that I was uninjured and safe.

Only when he was done did I finally move. I lifted a hand and he tensed, snapping his gaze to my fingers as if they were deadly weapons. I paused for a moment, allowing him to thoroughly inspect the possible threat, then slowly resumed my course. He didn't stop me, silently tracking my hand as it reached for his face. When my fingers made contact with his cheek, a tremor shook him. I paused again, letting him adjust.

While I waited, he ever so slightly leaned into my touch. I swallowed a gasp, willing my fingers not to shake. "Kolton?" I whispered, my hope rising.

No response. His expression remained the same.

My hope plummeted. I swallowed again, this time in

disappointment. I wouldn't give up though. He wasn't communicating verbally, but he was still communicating in his own way. If I couldn't reach him through words, maybe I could through touch.

I started to clean him, doing to him what he did to me. From top to bottom, I paid attention to every inch, making sure to wash away every last soot streak and speck of blood. He didn't move, allowing me to touch him. To take *care* of him. When I reached his manhood, I paused, unsure how he'd react to being touched there.

So far, he didn't see me as a threat. But how exactly *did* he see me? As a possession? A caretaker? Or as his wife? His *mate*?

I didn't know, but there was only one way to find out.

Inhaling a quiet breath, I slipped my hand around him. When he immediately hardened beneath my touch, my eyes flew to his. Our gazes locked and my heart forgot to beat for a second.

Hunger. *Hunger* burned in the dark depths of his eyes.

Stunned, I stood stock still, barely able to breathe. I'd seen hunger in his eyes before. *Countless* times. But this time was different. This hunger was pure carnal lust, a predator's natural instinct to being aroused. My response was immediate. Instinctual. Even if I'd wanted to shy away from that hunger, which I didn't, my body was in charge now. It saw her mate's need and rose to meet it, growing wet and saturating the air with arousal.

A growl vibrated his chest as he inhaled my scent. His shaft hardened further, swelling against my grip. I squeezed without thinking, and he groaned embarrassingly loud. Holy hell. Even as my knees weakened at the sound, I prayed that no one was listening over the intercom.

When I searched his face, still unsure how to proceed, he growled again. This time, I could have sworn the sound carried with it a word. A single word that made my heart begin to race.

"Mate."

He knew who I was then. Knew that I was his and he was mine.

Clinging to that one growled word, I started to pump his shaft, overcome with a desperate need to make him feel good. He blew out a breath and braced a hand on the tiled wall, his eyes hooding. He didn't close them though, as if the predator in him still needed to keep a lookout for threats. I added more pressure, gratified when he grew so impossibly thick that my fingertips could barely touch. Another groan escaped him, making me even wetter.

His free hand shot between my legs, but I stopped him, firmly gripping his wrist.

"No. Just you," I said, surprised when he actually listened and dropped his arm. But when I let go of his wrist, he snaked his arm behind me and pulled me against him. My stomach did crazy cartwheels, but I managed to keep my composure. Mostly. A tear or two slipped free, but they went unnoticed, mixing with the water as it slid down the drain.

Resting my head on his shoulder, I continued to pleasure him. To communicate my feelings through touch. Each stroke sent a wordless message. *I love you. I'm here for you. You're okay. We're going to get through this.*

He pressed his mouth to my hair, each ragged breath sending tingles erupting over my scalp. As his pleasure built, his grip on me tightened. I swept my thumb over his swollen tip and he moaned, shuddering against me.

I squeezed my eyes shut, refusing to cry. Despite how intimate the moment was, it wasn't the same. *He* wasn't the same. I still couldn't feel him through our bond. The beautiful moment lacked the closeness I'd grown to love, to *crave*.

His thoughts and emotions were hidden from me. Locked away.

Even now, as he teetered on the edge of orgasm, I couldn't reach him.

His body was infinitely familiar to me. I'd explored every swell. Every dip. Every perfect inch of him. And yet, he felt like a stranger.

When he finally jerked against my hand and groaned his release, grief welled in my chest.

This moment should have brought us closer together. Should have *healed* the rift between us. But I could no longer deny the inevitable truth.

We'd never felt farther apart.

CHAPTER 4

NORA

My misery was momentarily lifted when we stepped back inside the main room to find an unexpected package on our cot.

"You guys are the *best*. Thank you," I gushed out loud, knowing the others could hear me through the intercom.

But, as I beelined for the cot, Kolton cut me off with a growl. I jerked to a halt so I wouldn't bump into him, glancing up in surprise. His stare was intense. *Fierce*. After a moment, he swung that gaze to the cot. Suspicion darkened his eyes, and he bared his teeth.

Oh.

"It's just food and fresh clothing," I told him, the words punctuated by a loud rumble from my stomach. When he didn't react—or move—I quietly sighed and stepped around him.

"*NO*," he barked, grabbing my hand to yank me into his arms.

I gasped, more from the fact that he *spoke* than from the mild whiplash.

"Nora?"

Jagger's voice over the intercom made Kolton tighten his grip on me.

"I'm good," I squeaked, trying my best to remain calm when what I really wanted to do was race toward that food and tear into it. Now that the smells were hitting me, I could barely think of anything else. *Hamburgers* and *fries*. And was that a strawberry milkshake? I hadn't eaten since lunchtime yesterday and my stomach was angrily reminding me of that fact. I thought I'd be too sad to eat, but apparently not. I was *famished*.

Despite knowing that Kolton might not understand in his current state, I spoke anyway. I *needed* food, and so did he.

"Look, I know that someone invaded your territory, but I promise the food is safe. Besides, I bet you'll feel better once you've eaten something." When he didn't react, it was all I could do not to scream. Trying a different tactic, I looked up at him and softly implored, "I'm really hungry, Kolton. The best way you can protect me right now is by letting me eat some food. Otherwise, I'm probably going to pass out or something."

I hadn't been serious about the last part, but the second I said it, his eyebrows slammed down. Oh, wow. Maybe he could understand after all. For several seconds, he simply scowled, a muscle thrumming in his jaw. Then, he abruptly released me. Relieved, I gave him a grateful smile. When his expression remained the same, my smile wobbled.

Don't give up hope, Nora, Storm said. *He's buried himself deep inside, but he's not gone.*

I know, I replied, grateful for her reassurance. *It's just hard seeing him like this. I don't know how to help him.*

That may be, but you are *helping him.*

How?

By showing him love. Love has the power to heal more than any medicine or magic. Be his light, child. Help him find his way out of the darkness.

I bit my trembling lip and nodded, sniffing back fresh tears.

Be his light.

I could do that. I could show him the way back by shining brighter. By giving him all that I had to give. I would give him everything.

Absolutely everything. He deserved it and so much more.

Straightening my shoulders, I put on a brave face and reached behind me for his hand. The second our fingers intertwined, I threw him an encouraging grin and tugged him toward the cot.

"Come on. I *know* you're hungry. And if you don't eat, I'll just end up scarfing it all down myself. I've done it before, and I'll do it again," I warned him with a light laugh. When he didn't respond, I forced myself to remain positive. He was allowing me to lead him toward a possible threat. That *had* to mean something. He was trusting me, which was a big step.

Arriving at the cot, I wasted no time divvying up the food. There was plenty of it, but I could seriously eat a whole deer right now. As I perched on the cot's edge with my hamburger and fries, my hands noticeably shook. Throwing one last glance at Kolton to make sure he was okay, I dove into the food with gusto.

"So *good*," I moaned a few minutes later when the last of my hamburger and fries had been demolished.

Licking my fingers clean, I reached for my strawberry milkshake, then froze when another hamburger slid into my line of view. I blinked up at Kolton, who was still standing beside the cot. He'd picked up his hamburger, only to offer it to me. My mouth started to fall open, but I quickly snapped it shut and wiped the shock from my face.

"Oh, no, I'm okay. This is yours," I told him and tried to give the hamburger back. But the second I nudged it toward him, he grabbed my hand and placed the burger into it. "Kolton, I don't need . . ." The words faded when I noticed his set expression. Wow. He *really* wanted me to eat this burger.

Searching his face a moment longer, I finally nodded and accepted the food. When I did, the stiff line of his shoulders noticeably relaxed.

"Thank you," I whispered, feeling self conscious as he watched

32

me take a bite, then another and another. It was awkward yet almost felt more intimate than the moment we'd shared in the shower. He watched me eat the whole thing, then made a sound in his throat. A *pleased* sound. I peeked at his expression again to find his face completely relaxed. Content, even.

Butterflies erupted in my full stomach. I should be taking care of *him*, and yet, he was still managing to somehow take care of me.

Love swelled in my chest. I wanted nothing more than to kiss him right now. Tamping down the need, I reached for my milkshake instead and stood. Kolton tracked my movements, holding still as I eased into his personal space. I met his eyes and paused for a long moment to simply stare at him.

It hurt. It hurt to look at his achingly familiar features and still not recognize him. But I *knew* he was in there. Every now and then, I'd catch glimpses. He might not be speaking or looking at me the way I desperately needed him to, but my soulmate was in there somewhere. It was my job to coax him out.

"I know you're trying to protect me," I started, forcing my voice to remain even, "but you need to let me protect you too. I don't know why this has happened or how to fix it, but I'm not going anywhere. I'm your wife, and I'm going to take care of you as best I can." Slowly reaching out, I grasped his hand and placed the milkshake into it. "You're mine, Kolton. Mine to keep safe. Mine to care for. As long as I live and breathe, that is my vow to you."

At the words, words he'd said to me not long ago, something flashed in his eyes. Recognition.

Biting my lip to keep it from trembling, I nudged his hand, encouraging him to drink the milkshake. He didn't move for what felt like an eternity. He just stared at me. Stared and stared. I didn't know what he was thinking, and I still couldn't feel him through our bond, but when he finally raised the drink to his lips and took that first sip, joy surged through me. I clasped my hands together, doing an internal victory dance.

Who knew that one little milkshake could fill me with so much hope?

They sent Vi in next. I made sure that Kolton was sitting on the cot before giving the green light, then held my breath as the door opened to allow his sister entrance. With her arms full of supplies, she took one look at Kolton and froze.

When I saw him tense, I placed a reassuring hand on his arm. "It's okay," I calmly said, communicating with my eyes for Vi to place the supplies on the floor and step back. "It's only Vi, your sister. She would never hurt either of us."

As she bent to put the supplies down, a warning growl rumbled in Kolton's chest. She stiffened, her face leaching of all color.

"It's okay, Vi," I tried to reassure her, firming my grip on Kolton's arm. "Just move slowly. That's it."

Her wide purple eyes darted to me, then back to her brother. I'd never seen her look so scared. I'd be afraid too if I were in her shoes. Her big brother had been the family's pillar of strength for the past six years. Against all odds, he'd kept them safe, facing challenger after challenger in order to keep them alive. Seeing him like this must be terrifying for her. Without him in charge, who would protect them?

A part of me wondered that myself. Without Kolton, who would keep this family from falling apart? Who would keep *Midnight Pack* from falling apart?

But a bigger part of me—a *louder* part—already knew the answer to those questions.

Me.

I would protect them.

I would keep this family and the pack from falling apart.

I didn't care how exhausting or challenging it would be to fill Kolton's shoes. I made him a vow, promising to take his place if something were to happen to him, and I would do everything in my power to keep it.

Anxiety tightened my chest, but I didn't show it. Didn't let it affect my voice as I said to Vi's retreating form, "Thanks, Vi. Be sure to keep me up to date on what's going on out there."

She nodded, throwing one last look at her brother before slipping from the room. The door thudded shut, the lock engaging.

I blew out a quiet breath, grateful that I hadn't needed Storm's help. But I would have. If Kolton had attacked again, I would have used every ounce of strength I possessed to stop him. With every fiber of my being, I wanted him better, but I knew he would be devastated if he ended up hurting his family. Which meant that I needed to protect him from *himself.*

When I felt the tension slowly drain from him, I gave him an encouraging smile. "See? That wasn't so hard. No one left any nasty presents in your territory. In fact, I can smell more food."

As my stomach loudly rumbled yet again, I snorted. It had only been a few hours since I'd last eaten, but my stomach was definitely ready for more.

"Let's go find out what they brought us," I said, hopping to my feet. Kolton made a sound of protest, but I ignored him, beelining for the supplies with a steady stream of dialogue to put him at ease. "I'm pretty sure I smell steak and potatoes. If so, you guys are seriously getting a raise. Wait, Kolton pays you, right? Or do you all just have your own credit cards to the family fortune? Speaking of, I wouldn't mind having one of those credit cards. Not that I'm much of a shopper, but now that winter's approaching, I'd love to have some plants inside the—"

I stopped dead, the realization of what I was about to say hitting me like a sledgehammer.

Kolton was off the cot in a flash. Before I could collect myself, he had his arms around me, wrapping me up so completely that I could barely breathe.

"Nora!"

Kolton growled at the sound of Vi's shout through the intercom. One of his hands cupped the back of my head, pressing my face to his chest. I could *feel* his heart, racing impossibly fast as he curled himself around me like a shield. I tried to speak, but the words came out muffled.

"We need to get her out," I heard Vi shout again. I tried to shake my head, but Kolton's grip was too tight.

Not knowing what else to do, I closed my eyes and focused inward on our bond. On the invisible connection we shared.

It still felt damaged. Broken. But I reached out anyway, pushing a dose of calm toward it.

It's okay, I whispered into the void where we had once so easily communicated. *I'm fine. There is no threat here. We are safe.*

Kolton's breath hitched, his fingers spasming.

I slipped my arms around him and splayed my hands on his back, continuing to push calming energy toward our shattered bond. *I'm here. We are safe*, I said, repeating the words until I felt his heart slow. When his desperate hold on me started to relax, I blew out a relieved sigh.

"I'm okay, guys. Don't come in," I called, turning my head so that my ear was pressed to his steadily-beating heart.

"What happened?" Jagger asked.

Kolton tensed, but when I rubbed comforting circles on his back, his muscles loosened.

"It just hit me that we no longer have a home," I confessed, feeling sorrow well up again.

It was Griff who spoke next. "It's just a house, Nora. At least we're all still together."

I nodded, blinking back tears.

"We'll rebuild, better than ever," Vi added. "Besides, I've been wanting to remodel my room anyway."

I huffed a shaky laugh, beyond grateful for their presence. Without them here, I probably would have fallen apart a long time ago. I'd never been more relieved to rely on someone other than myself.

"I love you guys," I whispered, allowing myself to rest in Kolton's arms.

"We love you too," Vi whispered back.

CHAPTER 5

KOLTON

Something had changed.

My reality was becoming clearer. Sharper.

My movements were less instinctual and more . . . intentional.

Ever since my latest freak-out, I felt less like a prisoner in my body. I still couldn't speak or react the way I wanted to, but I didn't entirely feel like a feral *beast* either.

After a hearty meal of steak and potatoes, one where Nora had made certain I ate my fair share this time, we sat down at the metal table for a game of cards. When it became clear that Nora had no clue how to play, I tried to take charge. Tried and failed. A sound of frustration left me as my fingers refused to cooperate, pausing inches from the deck.

I might not see every little thing as a threat anymore, but my body was still not fully mine.

Nora quietly took in the scene, then reached across the table and placed the cards in my hand. The moment her fingers brushed against mine, some of the haze freezing me in place lifted. I gripped the deck and began shuffling the cards. Sloppily, but at least my hands were obeying my commands.

"Good," she said with a quiet laugh. "I know how to play *Go Fish*, and that's about it. My parents were never really into cards. Or games. Or any kind of bonding activity, really. They were too busy taking care of the farm and running errands for Alpha—for Hendrix."

When she looked down, I tried to sense her emotions. Tried and failed. The ability to feel her, to communicate with her through our bond, had vanished the second I'd lost my mind. Not being able to access our connection left me feeling untethered, like an astronaut lost in space. Every time I tried to find it again, the connection slipped through my fingers like water.

Not only could I not connect with my mate, but I'd somehow lost Shadow. I couldn't feel or speak to him. Couldn't even *shift*.

I was still trapped. Trapped inside myself. And yet . . . every time Nora touched me, I felt a little more lucid. A little more *sane*. I could fully hear her when she spoke now. And when I'd freaked out earlier, I'd heard flashes of her voice inside my head.

I'm here, she had said. *We are safe.*

Just like that, I'd felt a sense of calm, almost as if she'd shared the emotion with me. As if she'd *healed* a shattered piece of myself.

I opened my mouth to reply to her, to comfort her, but nothing came out. Frustrated once more, I gripped the deck too hard and the cards flew out of my hands.

"That's okay, I'll get them." Nora quickly jumped up from her seat to collect the scattered cards.

I watched her, unable to do anything else. Never in my life had I felt this helpless. This *weak*. How could she stand it? How could she even *look* at me?

I was practically a ghost, barely even there. I didn't fail to notice how distraught that made Nora. Despite my fragmented mind, I could see her sorrow. Her *pain*. She was devastated, but no matter how desperate I was to comfort her, my hands and voice wouldn't cooperate.

Was this how my mother had felt for the past six years? Like a prisoner in her own body?

The thought threatened to send me into another tailspin of despair, so I forced my focus on the present once more. Namely, on my strong and resilient mate who had no clue that she was pregnant with our child. I needed to find a way to tell her somehow, but all my efforts thus far had been in vain. Without me able to lead Midnight Pack, she would have to take my place as alpha. I knew Jagger, Griff, and Vi would support her, but they didn't know about her pregnancy either.

It was too early. Too unexpected. If it hadn't been for the blankets she'd left on our bed, I never would have even suspected. Female werewolves cycled differently than humans. Outside of the one or two times they went into heat every year, the chances of becoming pregnant were low, barely even existent.

Still, I should have known better. Should have realized my body was knotting her because she was fertile and emitting readiness pheromones.

But beating myself up over it wasn't going to fix things. She needed me now, more than ever. Besides the exceptional challenge that being alpha of Midnight Pack posed, Keisha and Arrow were still out there. Both were still a threat to Nora in different yet equal ways. And if either of them learned of her pregnancy . . .

The chair I was sitting on abruptly clattered to the floor as I jumped up and grabbed the metal table. With a violent roar, I yanked it free of the screws bolting it to the floor and threw it across the room. When the table crashed into the wall, Nora sprang up with a gasp, dropping the cards. At the startled look on her face, remorse hit me hard. I tried to apologize, but no words formed on my tongue.

Seconds later, the room's door burst open. At the sight of Jagger, my protective instincts went haywire. Despite knowing who he was, I couldn't control the growl that ripped from my throat. In a flash, I had Nora pressed against me, my arms tightly banded around her.

"No, *don't*," she cried, throwing up a hand as Jagger stepped toward us.

He paused, but I could see the trail of black fur rippling up his arms and the flash of yellow in his eyes. He was done with my erratic behavior, and I couldn't blame him. If I were in his shoes, I would have taken Nora from me a long time ago.

Still, my lips peeled back in a silent snarl, warning him away.

I might not be able to speak, but the message was clear.

MINE.

No way was I letting him take her from me.

"Please," Nora continued, calmer than she had any right to be. How was she not *terrified* right now? "He didn't hurt me."

"But he *could* have," Jagger said, his gaze set like flint. *Give her up*, it clearly demanded.

Never, I shot back, puncturing the message with another growl.

Jagger glared for a long moment, then focused on Nora. I tensed, but he ignored me. "We need to talk."

"Um, okay," she said.

"In private."

She was silent for a beat. Then, "You can tell me here. I don't want to exclude him."

A muscle thrummed in Jagger's jaw. I thought he would leave then, but he surprised me by saying, "The pack has caught wind of what happened to the house. They're asking questions and growing worried, even though I've assured them everything's fine."

Nora stiffened in my arms. "The witches. We didn't—"

"I contacted Buck early this morning. He's already taken care of the bodies and cleaned up the yard. It's his job to discreetly dispose of evidence and not ask questions."

She relaxed again. "Okay, that's good. Thank you. Would it help if I called the pack's influential members and told them that Kolton and I are perfectly safe?"

Jagger shook his head. "They'll need proof. They always do."

"So they need to *see* us? But Kolton isn't ready."

"You, Nora. They need to see *you.*"

"But it's too soon. I'm not—"

"Ready to become alpha? To *lead?*" he interrupted, his voice firm and unyielding. "If you don't do this, we're all screwed. Rumors will fly, challengers will come forth, and the first ones they'll target are us. They'll have no qualms killing you, me, Griff, Vi, and even Melanie. That's how this works. That's what will happen if you don't show your face to the pack and announce your intention to become the new pack alpha."

"But Kolton isn't *dead.*"

"It's safer for him if the pack thinks he is. Make them believe he died in that house fire. Telling them that he had a psychotic break will only incite panic, and we have enough on our plates right now. Make them think he's dead, Nora, then crown yourself the new pack alpha. It's the only way to keep Kolton alive."

At his harsh, unforgiving words, anger trembled through me. At the same time, I knew he was right. The pack wouldn't understand my weakness. It was better to announce my death and let Nora take over my position. She was strong and of sound mind, two things that werewolves respected in a leader. As much as I hated the idea of her carrying such a heavy burden, I knew she could do it. She *had* to, for the sake of us all.

Still, I worried she wasn't prepared for this monumental task. She'd only just found her voice and confidence, and was now being told that several lives depended on her. I knew how scared she must be feeling. Knew how daunting this responsibility was.

So, it was with utmost shock that I heard her say, "Okay, then. Set up a meeting for tomorrow morning. Tell them I'll be there."

Even Jagger looked shocked, then relieved and the slightest bit proud. As he should. I couldn't even begin to describe how proud of her I was in this moment, but I did nothing to show that. I was a stiff, emotionless wall, proving just how right they were to hold a conversation as if I wasn't there.

Jagger left soon after, sealing the door shut behind him. It took me several minutes, but I eventually convinced my arms to let Nora go. When I did, she silently turned and began cleaning up the mess I'd made. As I watched, fresh pain tightened my chest. She would have to leave me soon, and I'd have to let her.

Problem was, I didn't know if I could.

Several hours later, we finally readied for bed. The afternoon and evening had dragged by slowly. Each hour that passed, Nora had grown more and more pensive. Subdued. I could tell that tomorrow's meeting weighed heavily on her mind, but she didn't talk about it. She kept her one-sided conversations light, as if she didn't want me to feel bad for putting her in this position.

But I did. The guilt was eating me alive. She needed her husband. Her *mate*. And he was nowhere to be found. I might as well be dead, for all the good I was.

As she slipped inside the bathroom to wash her face and brush her teeth, I stood stock still in the middle of the main room and listened. Simply listened. I hadn't been able to hear properly before. To think rational thoughts or even pick up a deck of cards. But I could now, thanks to Nora. It had to be her presence, her *touch*, that had brought me back to a semblance of reason.

Maybe that's what I needed. To be closer. To breathe her in. To taste. To touch her.

If I did, maybe the broken pieces would finally start to mend. If I did, maybe this *nightmare* would end.

All on their own, my legs started to move. When I saw where they were headed, anticipation shivered up my spine. For once, my mind and body were fully cooperating. We wanted the exact same thing: to be close to her. We entered the bathroom and saw her in front of a sink brushing her teeth. We didn't slow, striding right up to stand behind her.

She froze, glancing at my reflection in the mirror. "Kolton, what—?" she started, then stopped when my chest brushed against her spine.

Slowly, she straightened and set down her toothbrush, still staring at me in the mirror. Whatever she saw made her breath catch. My body immediately responded to the sound, pressing even closer until I could feel her along the length of my front. My groin bumped against her backside, the contact effectively making me harden. I ignored the feeling, focused solely on her.

Reaching up, I grabbed a handful of fiery curls and swept them aside. She shivered but held perfectly still, which encouraged my body to keep going. Just like I wanted it to, my head lowered, pausing so I could inhale the sweet flowery scent of her hair. Gently fisting the mass, I tipped her head back and resumed my course, feathering my lips down her vulnerable throat. Her pulse jumped, and I paused again to nuzzle the spot, inhaling deeply once more.

She gasped, her neck slightly arching as I dragged my mouth to the spot where I'd claimed her, then softly growled in satisfaction against her skin. My scent was still strong, but I needed it to be stronger. I didn't bite her though. Instead, I lifted my other hand and palmed one of her breasts.

"Kolton," she breathed, trembling as my thumb rubbed her hardened nipple through her thin top. I played with it for a moment, then slid my hand south. When her breathing sped up, my body went haywire. Unable to slow my hand, it dove straight down inside her pajama bottoms. As my fingers slipped between her folds and found her clit, she arched against me with a breathless cry.

Her backside pressed against my stiff cock, and I groaned into her neck, the need to take her riding me hard. Every instinct I possessed wanted me to yank down her pajama bottoms and slam my cock inside her, but I somehow resisted. Somehow forced my body to obey my commands, to focus solely on pleasuring my mate.

She leaned more fully against me as I pressed my middle finger against her sensitive flesh and began to move it in a circular motion. As always, she responded beautifully to my touch, softly moaning and trembling while I worked her body into a pleasurable frenzy. Every sound, every reaction, made me thrum with satisfaction. Her pleasure was mine, and I felt myself gain more and more control the longer I touched her.

I'd been right. Contact with her made me feel better. A single touch lifted the fog and brought me that much closer to reality.

She gripped my arm, dissipating even more of the fog. I stroked her harder. *Faster.* Desperate to be free of the wretched weakness holding me prisoner. Nora bucked against my hand, trembling violently as she teetered on the edge of orgasm.

Without slowing, I bit down on her neck, wringing a cry from her. I bit down harder and she stiffened all over, her body shuddering as she orgasmed. She dug her nails into my arm and groaned her release, then went limp against me. I slid my hand from her underwear, holding her to me as I finished claiming her. With her heart still pounding and her breathing labored, she allowed me to take my time. To make sure my scent was buried deep within her. Only when I was thoroughly satisfied did I finally pull away.

As I did, I heard a hitch in her breath. A gasp. Not from the orgasm I'd just given her, but from . . .

I jerked my head up to look at her reflection in the mirror and immediately saw the tears on her face. Panic squeezed my chest. Had I hurt her? Had I—?

"I'm sorry," she choked out, her lips trembling. "I didn't mean to cry. I'm just so scared. I didn't want to burden you, but . . ." She drew her bottom lip into her mouth and bit down *hard*. Hard enough to draw blood. "You said I would never have to do this alone, Kolton. You said you'd be right beside me every step of the way. You *promised*."

She heaved a sob, then another and another, covering her face with her hands. Her pain and sorrow tore my heart to shreds, but what really gutted me was the anger I'd detected behind her words. She was mad. Mad at *me*.

"I'm sorry," she sobbed, again and again, clearly feeling guilty for her anger.

Without a word, I picked her up and carried her from the bathroom. She continued to cry and apologize every few seconds, only quieting when I laid her down on our cot and wrapped myself around her.

It's okay, I tried to convey with my actions, brushing a curl back from her damp cheek. *Everything's going to be okay*.

But it wasn't enough. She needed *more*.

Squeezing my eyes shut, I focused on my mouth. On forming words on my tongue. For several long minutes, I fought with my body and mind, wrestling them for control. *Begging* them to let me do this one small thing.

Finally, when I was exhausted—when I'd just about given up

hope—a single word tumbled from my lips.

"I."

Nora softly gasped.

Inhaling a breath, I forced more words to tumble out. "I'm here. I'm . . . still here, sweetness."

She burst into tears again, each sob coming from deep within her, as if wrenched from her very soul. I held her impossibly close, silent tears tracking down my own face.

It wasn't much, but it was something.

Something that I clung to with all of my might.

CHAPTER 6

NORA

I had the dream again. The nightmare of being in Kolton's body as he witnessed his father's death and his mom's broken screams. And, once again, I ended up taking his mother's place.

But the dream didn't end there.

It switched to a different scene, one with a dark figure hovering over a pregnant woman clearly in labor. At the glimpse of ginger hair, I knew the pregnant woman was me, but the dark figure above me was definitely not Kolton. He was several yards away, unable to reach me. Fear, agony, and desperation consumed him as he helplessly watched from afar. As the dark figure revealed her face to him.

Keisha.

She grinned sadistically, then knelt beside me. Kolton roared his fury, but there was nothing he could do as she placed a razor sharp nail against my swollen belly. With one brutal stroke, she gouged it in deep and began to savagely cut.

Kolton screamed. Screamed and screamed and screamed.

His pain eclipsed my own, stealing my breath. Unable to bear it a moment longer, I reached out to him through our bond. My touch was like a phantom mist, wrapping invisible fingers around our damaged connection.

This isn't real, I spoke to him in the dream, infusing my touch with love. With strength. With healing energy. *This won't be our fate.*

I didn't expect him to respond, so it was with utmost shock that

I heard him say, *I can't lose you, Nora. I can't live without you. If you die, I die.*

I won't let anything tear us apart, remember? Not even death itself. My pain vanished as I focused solely on him. On pushing healing energy toward him through our bond. *Rest, Kolton. Let the dream go. I promise you'll never lose me.*

A great sigh shuddered from him, and the dream slowly melted away.

The next morning, I awoke to the most beautiful sight.

Eyes of darkest amber stared back at me. There was so much love brimming in their depths that my breath caught.

I blinked, expecting the image to vanish. I must still be dreaming. There was no way this was real. The eyes were so clear. I could see him. Truly *see* him.

When the image didn't go away, every inch of me froze. This couldn't be real. I had to be hallucinating, seeing only what I desperately wanted to see. This couldn't—

A hand—a very *warm* hand—touched my cheek, causing me to jolt. Okay, that definitely felt real. I'd had realistic dreams before, but this one was—

The beautiful eyes winked out, and I panicked for a second. Then sucked in a breath as warm lips feathered across mine. When I froze in shock again, the lips pressed against mine more firmly. Undeterred by my catatonic state, they continued to kiss me, growing more urgent by the second. When a tongue slid along the seam of my lips, coaxing me to open, I pulled back with a sharp gasp.

The eyes opened again, carefully searching my face.

I stopped breathing, then whispered in a trembling voice, "Kolton?"

He didn't respond, but his eyes. His *eyes*. They spoke a thousand words with a single glance.

A cry burst from me.

He captured my lips again and swallowed the sound. This time, I responded. Eagerly. Desperately. I kissed him hard, reaching up to grip his hair with trembling fists. He wrapped his other arm around me and pulled me close, peppering me with kisses while I continued to cry.

This was real. *Real*. Kolton was kissing me. The *real* Kolton. The man I'd hopelessly fallen in love with.

Tears slid down my face, but he kept brushing them away, kissing me like a man starved for air. I opened my mouth, and he greedily dove in, tangling our tongues together. My body filled with overjoyed bliss. The grief I'd been carrying in my soul was soon washed away by a wave of contentment.

I could kiss him forever. Could happily stay like this for an eternity, because *this*. This was the only thing I wanted. Only thing I needed.

My mate had come *back* to me.

But I'd made a promise, one I couldn't break. This moment had to end, which made me want to cry all over again.

Somehow finding the strength, I pulled back enough to breathlessly whisper, "How? How are you better?"

His eyes softly caressed my face. Untangling one of my hands from his hair, he placed it on his cheek. "You."

"Me?"

He leaned into my hand and nodded. "Your touch."

My eyes widened. "My touch has been healing you?"

He nodded again. "Especially in my dream."

"Your dream . . ." My mouth fell open. "Wait, that was *real*? Hold on. Is your favorite cake red velvet?"

He nodded a third time.

Holy crap. What did this mean?

Responding to the question in my eyes, he said, "It's called dreamwalking. The ability to enter another's dreams is something that all soulmates are able to do. You subconsciously reached out to me and formed a connection while we both slept."

Before I could fully digest his words, Jagger's voice interrupted us over the intercom. "We need to get on the road soon, Nora."

Kolton stiffened, as did I.

"I don't want to go without you," I said, fresh panic tightening my throat. "I could reschedule the meeting. Maybe in a few days or a week, you'll feel better enough to come with me. That way, we won't have to tell the pack that you're dead."

Sorrow lined his face. He shook his head and pointed at himself. "I'm broken. A failure."

The words were like a punch to my gut. I couldn't sense what he was feeling through our bond, but the pain in his eyes told me everything.

"No," I said, my voice gentle yet firm. "You're not a failure. You are Kolton Rivers, the most powerful alpha of the largest pack in the country. You are selfless, kind, and the best husband and soulmate a girl could ever ask for. You give me courage and *strength*. You might feel broken, but I'm going to fix you. To *heal* you. I accepted all of you, remember? Every single piece. Even the broken ones."

He stared at me for a long moment, then sighed and rested his forehead against mine. "I can't go. It's still not safe. *I'm* not safe. Leave without me. I'm just a liability."

"Did you abandon me when *I* was just a liability? I won't leave you."

He sighed again. "You have to, sweetness. The pack needs you."

"*You* need me."

Capturing my hand, he pressed a kiss to the back of it. "They need you more."

I pursed my lips to stop myself from arguing, knowing what was really troubling him: his family's safety. His mother and sisters were vulnerable without his protection. It was *my* responsibility to protect them now. I also had Brielle and my parents to think about. Although they weren't currently pack members, they were in Midnight Pack territory. What happened to them was on me.

But to fake Kolton's death when he was *so close* to getting better? How would the pack react when he suddenly came back from the dead a month from now, or even sooner?

We could lose their support. Their *trust*.

Either way, we could end up losing everything. But, despite the odds stacked against us, I had to try. Had to keep this pack together after all the sacrifices Kolton had made for it.

Somehow, I managed to drag myself to the bathroom and take a quick shower. I might not have a fancy business outfit like last time, but I was at *least* going to smell good. Untangling my hair as best I could, I decided to leave it down. Dressed in dark jeans and a flowy, forest green top, I didn't exactly scream "alpha female of the wealthiest pack in America," but they'd seen me *naked* at my initiation last month, so this was a step up.

Staring at my reflection in the mirror a moment more, I squared my shoulders and tipped up my chin. "Leave your doubts at the door, Nora Elizabeth Finch," I murmured, trying to psych myself up. I'd faced Midnight Pack's influential members before. I could do it again.

Except that I'd had *Kolton* by my side before. This time would be different. *Much* different.

Before I could do something stupid like hide in a corner, I turned on my heel and marched out of the bathroom. The second I entered the main room though, I slammed to a halt.

Kolton was standing in the room's center, and I immediately knew something was wrong.

"Kolton?" I questioned, daring to take a step toward him.

He gave his head a sharp shake, gritting out, "I can't let you leave."

I stopped again, staring at him in confusion. "But you just said that I should go."

"Lied. I lied," he said, jerking both hands through his hair. The movement was agitated, and his fingers noticeably shook. "I can't. Can't let you go. I'm sorry."

"It's okay," I said, softening my voice to put him at ease. "I can cancel the meeting and go another time. I—"

"NO!" he shouted, startling me enough that I jumped. With a muttered curse, he started to pace, gripping the back of his neck so hard that the skin reddened. "Can't lose you. Can't lose you. Can't lose you."

I stayed where I was, uncertain what to do.

Before I could make up my mind, he jerked to a stop and growled, "*Griff.*"

"What's up, Kol?" Griff immediately replied through the intercom.

"I need you to . . . to stop me."

"Sure thing. What did you have in mind?"

Kolton clenched his teeth. Then blurted, "A freezing spell should do it."

"I can do that."

"Kolton," I started, stepping toward him again.

He stiffened all over and snapped, "Jagger, get her out of here before I lose it again. *Now*. And don't you dare let her out of your sight or there'll be hell to pay."

Before I was ready, the door burst open. As Jagger and Griff dashed inside, Kolton whirled toward them and roared.

"*Rigescunt indutae!*" Griff yelled at the same time. Magic flared bright at his fingertips, just as Kolton charged.

Suddenly, everything stopped. Or, rather, *Kolton* stopped. Dead in his tracks. Completely still like a frozen statue.

"Hurry. The spell won't hold him for long," Jagger said, moving toward me. When I continued to gape at Kolton in shock, he sighed in exasperation and grabbed my arm. "Come on. He'll be fine."

"But . . ." I said, still staring at Kolton while he led me toward the exit. "This could set him back. This could ruin all the progress I've made."

"It probably will, but we'll deal with that later. Right now, your focus needs to be on the meeting and what you're going to say."

When we reached the door, I looked back at Kolton and found him staring right at me. Griff blocked my view of him as he helped Vi shut and lock the door behind us. But I could have *sworn* in that final second that Kolton's expression changed to one of pure terror.

A moment later, the emotion pounded into me through our bond.

I stumbled from the sheer force of it, clutching at my heart as it started to race. Jagger steadied me, and soon Vi joined us, peering into my face with concern. She opened her mouth to speak, only to be drowned out by a deafening roar.

Griff strode to the intercom and slapped a hand to the device, just as the video showed Kolton regaining use of his limbs.

"No!" I cried, but it was too late. The video went dark and the sound switched off.

Still clutching my chest, I stared at the device, willing it to turn back on.

"Sorry, gorgeous," Griff said, blocking my view once again. "We can't have you charging back in there."

I glared at him for a second, then quickly looked away. It wasn't his fault. It wasn't any of their faults. They were just trying to help.

Still, I nearly ran to the door and ripped it open when I heard the first *wham!*

"Get me out of here. Please," I choked out, tearing my gaze from the door.

Vi took charge then, grabbing my arm to lead me away. Still reeling from the terror flooding the soulmate bond, I blindly followed her. As we made our way up the incline leading to the stairwell, a faint cry reached my ears.

"Nora, *NO!*"

At the sheer desperation in Kolton's voice, my legs buckled beneath me.

Griff caught me before I could hit the ground, hoisting me into his arms. "I've got you, gorgeous."

I fisted his shirtfront and held on tightly, trying to slow my thundering pulse. I couldn't handle much more of this. If it didn't end soon, I was going to break.

"Nora, don't leave me! I can't lose you. I *need* you."

"Oh, Kolton," I sobbed, the words bursting from me before I could stop them. I'd told him I wasn't going anywhere, yet here I was, doing just that. Guilt threatened to tear me wide open.

"Walk faster, Griff," Jagger ordered.

I gripped his shirt harder as he practically jogged up the incline, then took the stairs two at a time. Seconds later, we were bursting outside into the clear morning. I greedily gulped down the fresh air, still struggling to control my tears.

"I-I'm okay," I stammered as the others joined us, relieved that I could no longer hear Kolton's cries. "You can let me down now."

"You're not okay, Nora," Vi said, even as Griff gently lowered me to my feet. "None of us are. We're all struggling to cope, and I won't pretend otherwise."

"Yeah, but I can't fall apart right now. You all need me to be strong."

"We do, but you're still allowed to feel. Don't suppress your emotions, Nora. Believe me, that never ends well."

I snorted. "Oh, they've been coming out whether I want them to or not. I can't seem to stop crying." At the sudden frown that creased her brow, I asked, "What is it?"

"It's just . . ." She grabbed the end of her sleek ponytail and wrapped it around her finger. "When you were in the shower earlier, I could hear Kolton muttering something over and over. At first, I thought he was talking about *us*, but now, I'm not so sure."

"I heard it too," Jagger said. When he and Vi shared a look, panic crept up my throat.

"What did he say?"

Instead of answering, Vi asked Jagger, "Don't you find it weird that Kolton suffered a mental break while Nora is still alive and well?"

"I guess," he responded, crossing his arms. "I'm assuming he was triggered after almost losing her to that witch. Probably reminded him of what happened to your parents."

She waved a hand in the air. "Yes, yes, but there has to be more to it."

"Like what?" Griff questioned. "What more could there be?"

Vi darted a look at me. "I didn't put the pieces together until now, but Nora bought a bunch of blankets about a week ago."

Jagger shifted on his feet impatiently. "So?"

"So, Kolton said 'I can't lose them.' *Plural.* I know he cares about all of us, but I doubt he's thinking about us much right now. His sole focus is on protecting Nora and—"

Everyone fell silent. They simply stared at each other, yet each glance managed to speak volumes. Problem was, I had no clue what they were saying.

"Me and *who?*" I said, trying not to freak out. "Seriously, guys, what's going on?"

"No way," Griff whispered, shooting me a look. One that quickly fell to my stomach.

Jagger went poker straight, then quietly swore.

"Vi?" I implored, pleading with her to explain.

When she finally focused on me, her eyes were suspiciously wet. "I could be wrong," she said in a trembling voice, "but I think you might be pregnant."

CHAPTER 7

NORA

Jagger never once took his eyes off the road, but I could somehow still feel his gaze on me.

It was definitely a skill of his, one that was particularly annoying right now.

"Just spit it out," I said from the front passenger's seat beside him. "I know you want to say something."

Griff shifted in his seat behind me but remained silent. Shockingly, he hadn't said a single word during the hour-long car ride to our destination. Despite wanting to come with us, I'd asked Vi to stay behind with Kolton. We weren't going far, but if he somehow escaped while we were gone, at least she'd be there to give us a heads up. So far, she had nothing to report, though. The door had withstood Kolton's latest assault, and he was now pacing the main room's length, muttering "I can't lose them" over and over.

Finally, Jagger responded, "You should eat."

I looked down at the untouched breakfast sandwich he'd ordered for me at a drive-thru in Saranac Lake, the small city they'd been picking up supplies at for the past day.

My stomach growled, greedy for the egg and sausage sandwich. At the same time, it roiled with nerves, warning me that eating right now might end badly.

At the thought of throwing up, Vi's shocking statement once again invaded my mind. Snorting, I glibly replied, "Why, because I'm eating for *two* now?"

They couldn't possibly believe that I was pregnant. A pile of blankets couldn't confirm that. Sure, Kolton had reacted strangely when he'd seen my creation on our bed, but . . . but *no*. I couldn't be pregnant. I would *know* if I was.

Right?

"Because you need to appear strong in front of the pack," Jagger evenly said, ignoring my sarcasm. "Even if they expect you to be grieving, you can't show any sign of weakness."

Grieving. Right. Because I was supposed to pretend that my husband was *dead*.

Sighing, I unwrapped the sandwich and took a huge bite. "Why can't all werewolves be like you guys?" I muttered around the food, wishing for the umpteenth time that I didn't have to do this. "I've shown weakness plenty of times around you, and you haven't attacked me."

"We aren't ordinary werewolves. You know that," Jagger responded to my rhetorical question. "Most werewolves struggle to control their animal instincts, even the submissive ones. If we were like them, Kolton would be dead right now. As the alpha female, you might even deliver the killing blow."

"*Never*," I snapped, swallowing so fast that the food lodged in my throat. When I coughed, Jagger thrust a water bottle at me. After guzzling enough water to clear my throat, I added, "I really hate how readily our kind attacks weakness. One little flaw and they're quick to shun you. And God forbid if you're *different* from them in any way."

"That's true." He fell silent for a beat, then, "I was five years old when my parents shunned me."

I blinked, caught off guard by his confession. "I . . . I didn't know that. I'm so sorry."

He shrugged. "I started to shift early without the aid of a full moon. Most werewolf parents would be freaked. My pack kicked me out, but I wasn't on my own for long."

"Wait, you weren't originally a member of Midnight Pack?"

"No, I was born into a small Canadian pack just over the border. When they cast me out, I managed to wander into Midnight Pack territory. It was a wonder I survived at all. My wolf familiar kept forcing the shift on me. Not all the way, but I was spotted by more than one human in a half-shifted state. Anthony Rivers caught wind of an adolescent wolf-boy wreaking havoc in Buffalo and went to investigate.

"At first, he didn't know what to make of me, but he took me home anyway. I immediately formed an attachment to his son and Griff soon after. To this day, I believe that friendship is the only reason Anthony let me stay. He convinced a family in his pack to adopt me, and a few months later, all three of us experienced our first full shifts—without the aid of a full moon. Suffice it to say, all three of our families were shocked. Anthony and Charlotte Rivers swore our families to silence though. Very few in the pack know that we're different, and the ones that do have also been sworn to secrecy.

"I owe my life to the Rivers' family. We both do," Jagger continued, flicking a glance at Griff in the rearview mirror. "Not many werewolves would have done what Kolton's parents did for us. They were an exception to the rule, and we've strived to follow in their footsteps ever since. Which was why we so readily accepted you when you first came here."

I snorted a laugh, almost spitting out a piece of egg. "Yeah, you were *so* welcoming. Your first words to me were 'She doesn't smell right.'"

What looked like a smile twitched his full lips. "In my defense, I'd never met a werewolf with a dormant *angel* familiar before."

"Yeah, but I was plucked off the streets the same way you were. A little empathy would have been nice."

I wasn't mad. Still, he finally looked over at me and said, "I'm sorry it took me so long to come around. I shouldn't have judged so quickly. All I saw was a potential threat, and I'd do anything to protect the family that found and accepted me."

Unexpected tears formed in my eyes, and I quickly blinked them away. "So would I."

A look of understanding passed between us, something I never thought would happen between me and Midnight Pack's grumpy second in command.

After that, a comfortable silence filled the truck's cab. Busy preparing my speech for the upcoming meeting, I was startled when my stomach gave an unexpected lurch. I rested a hand on it and inhaled a few steadying breaths. Nerves. It was just nerves. When it lurched again, my skin broke out in a cold sweat.

For the first time, Griff spoke up from the backseat. "You okay, Nora?" He leaned forward to better see me. "You look a little pale."

I nodded, only for saliva to rush into my mouth.

Ah, hell.

"Pull over," I said, so quietly that all Jagger did was glance at me with a quizzical frown. My stomach heaved. I frantically slapped a hand over my mouth, blurting, "Pull the hell over, Jagger."

He did as instructed, just in the nick of time. I scrambled out of the cab and immediately chucked up my breakfast onto the grass. If that wasn't embarrassing enough, I heard both guys jump from the truck. Before I could wave them away, my stomach heaved again.

Hands grabbed my hair and held it back as I curled forward and threw up once more. "You'll be okay, gorgeous. It's perfectly normal,"

Griff crooned, gently rubbing my back.

When the bout of nausea subsided, I sputtered out, "W-what is?"

"Morning sickness."

I groaned, gratefully accepting the water bottle that Jagger handed me. "You can't be serious, Griff," I muttered, rinsing out my mouth before carefully straightening.

"What?" He sounded genuinely confused.

"You think I'm pregnant too." I slowly faced him, and he let go of my hair.

"Well, you've been having a lot of sex lately. It's not that far-fetched."

Trying and failing not to blush, I hurriedly replied, "Yeah, but I wasn't in heat."

"Maybe not, but female werewolves can still become pregnant under the right conditions. You could have unknowingly been giving off signals."

"Signals?"

"Pheromones. That you were ready to breed."

My jaw dropped.

Ignoring my shock, Griff asked point blank, "Did Kolton knot you, by any chance?"

"Whoa!" I loudly said, feeling my face burst into flames. "I am not discussing this with you, Griff."

When I skirted around him to reclaim my seat, he trailed after me. "Nora, I'm the pack healer. None of this is weird for me."

"Well, it is for *me*." I climbed back into the truck, slowing when my tender stomach threatened to rebel again.

"I'm sorry if this conversation makes you uncomfortable, but my concern is only for you and the baby."

Baby. *Baby*.

Holy hell, this couldn't be happening.

Covering my face with my hands, I moaned, "It's too soon."

"Actually, werewolves have a very short gestational period compared to humans. The sooner prenatal care starts, the better."

I shook my head. "I know, but that's not what I meant. It's too soon for me to be having *babies*. I'm only twenty-two and just out of college. I haven't even started my *career* yet."

"That's the past you talking," he gently said. "The present you that agreed to marry an alpha is the one you should be focused on now."

Crap. He was right. I might not be ready for motherhood, but this was what I'd signed up for. My *body* apparently already knew that, but my brain was still struggling to accept it.

I lowered my hands. After a few deep breaths, I looked over at him. "So you really think I'm pregnant?"

A slow smile overtook his face. "Yeah, gorgeous. I really think you are. And I think you're going to be an *amazing* mother."

When my chin wobbled, he laughed and bent down to draw me into a hug. I clung to him, needing all the support I could get. To say I was overwhelmed would be an understatement.

First, I was supposed to become the new pack alpha. And now, I was *pregnant*? Talk about emotional overload. I wanted nothing more than to curl up in Kolton's arms and listen to his quiet reassurances, but I didn't have that luxury right now.

At least I had Griff and Jagger with me. I was understanding more and more why Kolton had made them his second and third in command. They didn't take charge, but their unwavering support gave me the strength to stand up and face the task before me.

With their help, maybe I could do this after all.

Less than ten minutes later, we finally reached our destination.

Spotting the wide open gates, panic tightened my chest.

"Are you sure we should be having this meeting here?" I questioned Jagger, doubt assailing me.

He drove through the gates without hesitation. "Why, are you afraid the witch will return?"

"No. At least, not right now. She's vulnerable without her coven and will need to gather forces if she plans to attack again. But what if the pack questions our motives for inviting them here?"

"I'm already expecting them to question us, which is why they need to see the destruction for themselves. It's the only way they'll believe that someone like Kolton could possibly perish in a house fire."

I chewed on my lip in thought. That made sense. It would take a lot to kill Kolton, but if they saw how the house had collapsed, leaving all three stories reduced to rubble, maybe they would believe that he'd been buried beneath it all.

"Okay," I said with a sharp nod. "Then let's do this."

A minute later, the house came into view. Or rather, the smoking mound of rubble that used to be the Rivers' majestic mansion. All on their own, my eyes began to water. I'd only lived there for a short time, but I'd started to consider it home and had already acquired several fond memories. I focused on those memories as we slowly approached, allowing sadness to line my face. At least I wouldn't have to *fake* tears over the death of my husband. They were readily available at the slightest prompt.

Several vehicles were already parked in the roundabout, and I immediately stiffened when twelve figures came into view.

It's not the witches, it's not the witches, I silently reminded myself, relaxing a little when I started to recognize faces.

I still didn't know all of their names, something I'd have to rectify soon. Kolton had made them the pack's most influential members, which meant that he trusted them. I would trust them too, even though the hairs on the back of my neck were starting to stand on end as they all turned to face the approaching truck.

Show no fear. Show no fear.

No one said a word while Jagger parked and hopped out. I carefully watched their faces for any reaction, not surprised to see a few frowns. They'd been expecting Kolton to be at the wheel.

"You can do this, Nora," Griff murmured, squeezing my shoulder. "We've got your back."

Nodding, I shoved down my nerves and opened my door. The second I emerged from the truck, several of the pack members looked relieved. That would change though. I took a step toward them, then another and another. Jagger and Griff joined me, but stayed a few yards back. The moment the pack got a good glimpse of my tear-stained face, their relief vanished.

The brown-haired male in his late twenties that I recognized as Carter stepped forward. He darted a glance behind me as if expecting to find Kolton, then focused his concerned gaze on me. He opened his mouth, only to swiftly snap it shut. Audibly inhaling, he bluntly said, "You've been mated."

"Yes," I confirmed. "Almost two weeks now."

Approval shone in his gaze, but he quickly grew serious again. "I'm surprised to see you here without Alpha Rivers."

Okay, then. We were getting right to it.

"Yes. As you can see," I said, gesturing to the smoldering ruins behind us, "there's been an accident. We all managed to get out in time . . . except one."

Shocked gasps filled the air.

"You can't mean . . ." the only female in the group said, covering her mouth with her hand.

Focusing on the memories once more, my tears came faster. "Yes," I replied, raising my chin a notch, even as my voice quavered. "Alpha Rivers has fallen."

Silence settled over the group. Then several voices were speaking at once, each louder than the last.

A burly middle-aged man with a thick beard spoke louder than the rest, booming out, "I don't believe it! We need *proof*."

Straightening to my full height, I said, "That's why we invited you here. So you could see for yourselves how devastating the fire was. Kolton sacrificed himself so we could all get out alive. Despite his strength, even *he* couldn't survive a collapse this huge. He was . . . he was crushed beneath the weight. I can only hope that he went quickly."

Not all of them looked convinced by my tearful speech, but Carter looked ashen as he said, "And his sisters?"

"Safe. Grieving the loss of their brother."

He nodded, then turned to the others. As they all shared a look, I held my breath. Did they believe me? Was my grief convincing enough?

After a long moment, he finally turned back to me and said, "So this meeting is about your intention to become the new pack alpha."

It wasn't a question.

"Yes. As Kolton's wife, it is my right to claim his position, and I have every intention of doing so."

He nodded again. "And it is our duty to respect that right."

At that, I released a quiet sigh of relief. This had been easier than I thought.

"One question though," he abruptly added, gesturing at the ruined house. "Why do I smell magic?"

CHAPTER 8

NORA

I was silent for too long.

The question completely threw me for a loop. I hadn't even *thought* about the possibility of lingering magic. Buck, the pack's cleanup man, had removed any physical trace of the witches' presence here. Even the grass had been scrubbed clean of blood and gore from the battle. But the house fire . . .

The fire had been *magic*. A faint metallic scent still drifted from the smoking wreckage.

When I finally opened my mouth to speak, it was too late.

"You said the fire was an accident," Carter went on, suspicion slowly darkening his gaze, "but it looks more to me like arson. And by someone who can perform *magic*."

Ah, hell. This had been a bad idea. A *really* bad idea. They were too smart to be fooled—which was a good thing. But in this case, not so much.

Jagger took a step forward. "Are you questioning the integrity of your new *alpha*, Carter?"

When Carter stiffened at Jagger's menacing approach, I held up a hand. "Stand down, Jagger."

It was like the entire group collectively held its breath, waiting to see if the pack's second in command would obey the quietly-spoken order. I already knew what would happen if he didn't. I'd lose them. I'd lose them all. My one minute as the new alpha would end in epic failure.

Forcing my expression to remain calm, I waited for it all to come crashing down. But the moment never came. Jagger stopped. Stopped and *obeyed* me.

I could barely contain my shock, but it was clearly written on several of the pack member's faces, including Carter's.

Capitalizing on the moment, I spoke before anyone else could. "I don't blame you for your suspicion. We all have questions, including me. It isn't a secret that being alpha of Midnight Pack is a highly-coveted position, one that comes with many enemies. I'm prepared to face those enemies as Kolton and his father before him did, proving to you that I am worthy of the alpha position, but I won't tolerate being disrespected. If you have questions, just ask them. Don't try to trap me with words."

Carter might as well be throwing daggers at my head, his stare was *that* hard. I held his gaze, refusing to panic. He was a dominant male, no doubt about it, but I was an alpha female. I would *not* cower before him, and under no circumstances would I look away first. This was a test—a *challenge*—one that I had every intention of winning.

Without a word, the male stepped forward, slowly erasing the space between us. A familiar warmth stirred within me as Storm grew alert at his approach.

It's okay, I quickly reassured her. *I've got this.*

If he attacks, I'm taking control, she warned, protectiveness pulsing through the connection we shared. *I won't let him harm you or your unborn child.*

I inwardly groaned. Storm thought I was pregnant too? Instead of arguing with her, I replied, *He won't. I won't let him.*

Because I suddenly knew what to do. Either my alpha instincts were kicking in or I'd learned from watching Kolton, but when Carter was inches away from invading my personal space, I bared my teeth and growled.

I didn't speak a word. I didn't have to. That one sound said everything I needed him to hear.

Back off. Take one more step and see what happens.

He immediately stopped, his hands slowly forming fists. For a long moment, he simply stared at me, assessing my strength. I let him, standing tall as he openly scrutinized me. He could stare at me all *day* if he wanted. I wouldn't show an ounce of weakness. Finally, his gaze wavered, as if unable to bear mine a moment longer. Blinking rapidly, he looked away.

Internally, I did a little victory dance, until he cleared his throat and said, "The pack will want a funeral."

It was my turn to blink. "Oh."

"It'll give them closure. They didn't react well when Kolton refused to have a public funeral for his parents six years ago. He nearly lost their respect and support. Since you're brand new to the pack, withholding a funeral could make you extremely unpopular, something you can't afford right now."

Oh. Oh, wow. He was actually *helping* me. I'd expected begrudging tolerance at most and outright hostility at worst.

This was . . . this was more than I deserved, truth be told. Especially since I was clearly withholding information from them.

Swallowing the lump of guilt in my throat, I nodded and murmured, "There might not be much left of his body, if anything at all. We haven't found it yet."

"We could send in a team to look for him," the sole female said, looking far more sympathetic than the rest.

I offered her a small smile before shaking my head. "No, that's all right. I'd like to do it myself." Turning to Carter again, I added, "But

I'd like help with the funeral preparations."

He dipped his head. Not much, but enough to assure me he wasn't going to attack. "I'll see to it personally. We'll also need to discuss the Alpha Ceremony."

I blanked. "The Alpha Ceremony?"

"It's a public handing-over of title and powers to the new alpha. The event often brings forth a few challengers, so we'll need to prepare you for that as well. There aren't many challenger rules, but you should be aware of them."

Ah crap. I didn't know about *that*.

Sweat beaded my brow, but I didn't dare wipe it away. "Of course. Anything else I should be aware of?"

His eyes narrowed slightly. "This is a delicate time. Rumors will run rampant, and you'll do well to stay in front of them. If the pack suspects foul play in the death of Alpha Rivers, they could mutiny. Tread carefully over the days to come, Nora. Being alpha of this pack isn't for the faint-hearted."

At that, I tensed. The threat in his voice was subtle, but it was still there. He might be helping me, but that help was clearly a double-edged sword. He knew something wasn't right, and I didn't doubt for a second that he'd turn on me if he found out that I'd been lying to him.

When the meeting finally ended, I knew my problems were only just beginning. The influential members of Midnight Pack might be treating me like their newly-appointed leader, but not a single one of them had bothered to call me "Alpha."

I should have felt relieved that I was returning to my mate, but I couldn't have been more nervous.

"How is he?" I asked Vi, hurrying toward the intercom. Before I could reach it, she pulled me into a tight hug.

"You're okay. Thank God," she breathed, immediately pulling back to give me the once over. "Are you hungry? Thirsty? Have the guys been taking good care of you?" She paused to shoot Griff and Jagger sharp looks.

"I'm fine," I said, surprised by the overprotective energy pouring from her. "How has Kolton been?"

"Settled down after the first hour. He's been sitting on that cot for like two hours now. I couldn't get him to speak though. Not a single word. Except for the occasional blink, he hasn't moved a muscle." She stopped to peer more closely at me. "How did everything go? You look a little pale."

"She threw up," Griff spoke before I could. "Morning sickness."

Vi's eyes bugged out. "You *threw up?* Do you feel dehydrated? Weak? Here, sit down. Let me get you some water."

I sputtered a protest, but she dragged me over to a folding chair and plopped me down. A second later, she shoved a water bottle into my hands.

Jagger quietly snorted. "This is going to be fun."

"Vi," Griff groaned, "chill out. You're worse than I am."

Vi whirled to glare at him indignantly. "*Chill out?* She's carrying my little niece or nephew! It's my job to make sure she's taken care of."

At the fresh reminder that I might—and probably *was*—pregnant, I jumped up from my seat. All three of them snapped their gazes to me, as if expecting me to pop out a baby right then and there.

"Okay, look," I said, handing the water bottle back to Vi. "I appreciate your concern. Really, I do. But the meeting didn't go as well as I'd hoped, and pregnancy is the last thing on my mind right now. All I want to do is see Kolton and get him better, because the thought of going to his funeral is utterly *terrifying*, and—"

"Wait, *funeral?*" Vi squeaked, throwing Griff a horrified look. His expression immediately softened. When he went to her, she didn't stop him from pulling her into his arms.

"We'll explain everything," he said, resting his cheek on top of her head. "But first, let's put Kolton out of his misery." At the sharp look I gave him, he rolled his eyes. "Not like *that*. I can tell you've been making him feel better, Nora, so whatever you've been doing, keep doing it. Sex would probably help too, and don't worry about it harming the baby. Even Kolton's dick isn't large enough to—"

"*Griff!*" Vi snapped, shoving him back. A laugh burst from him, and he unapologetically winked at me.

I sighed. "You'd better not be spying on us in there, Griff."

He placed a hand to his chest in mock offense. "Me? Spy on my alpha having hot, passionate *sex?*"

"You mean *alphas*," Jagger corrected.

Vi blinked at me. "They accepted you then?"

"More or less," I replied, hiding a grimace. "I don't think they believed my sob story though."

"You handled them well under the circumstances," Jagger spoke again, surprising me with his praise. "You were calm and unflappable. Even if they have doubts about the fire and Kolton's death, they'll respect you for standing your ground."

I nodded, throwing him a grateful smile. "Thanks. I seriously couldn't have done this without you guys."

He inclined his head. "We don't believe in doing things alone in this pack. No matter what happens with Kolton in the days to come, we won't leave you to face the rest of the pack by yourself."

Ah hell. He'd totally gone and done it. *Jagger*, of all people. When tears promptly filled my eyes, Vi enveloped me in another hug. Griff joined in, lifting us both clean off our feet, and I couldn't help but laugh. Then I laughed harder when Griff reached back and dragged Jagger into the hug.

"Dude, you're too much of a lone wolf," he said when Jagger tried to pull away. "Just accept it for once. One hug won't kill you."

"It might," Jagger muttered, but he settled into the embrace with a resigned sigh.

Unused to so much close contact, the hug was a little overwhelming for me as well. But in a *good* way. Even Storm seemed to accept it, despite the fact that she was surrounded by demon spirits. Maybe because it felt good to be around people who cared. Who accepted all that you were, no matter how different you were from them. Who enveloped you in their comforting warmth and scent.

What else could feel better than that?

Being held by your soulmate, Storm suddenly said, surprising me. When longing trickled through our connection, my heart went out to her.

I'm so sorry for what happened between you and Zuriel.

Me too. But I doubt that's the last we'll see of him and his host.

My eyes popped open. *Do you know something?*

Only that Zuriel has always been single-minded in his mission to eradicate the world of demons. Now that we know his host shares that mindset, he won't stay away for good.

Great. Just one more thing to add to my already heaping plate.

But before I could start stressing about yet another problem, the hug ended. I immediately beelined for the bunker door, desperate to see Kolton.

"I won't stay in there too long," I hurriedly reassured the others, grasping the lock. "I know the funeral needs to happen soon, then the Alpha Ceremony. And I'm sure Brielle's pissed that I haven't personally called her back yet. When is the next full moon again? We'll need to get her out of Albany before then. And then there's the house to think of and where we'll all stay until it's rebuilt. And—"

"*Nora.*" Vi grabbed my shoulders and turned me toward her.

"Sorry," I said with a grimace. "I've never been much of a planner. This will take some getting used to."

Vi shook her head while still managing to keep her perfect bangs in place. "I know you're not used to receiving help, but that's what we're here for. Forget about all of those things for now. Let me, Griff, and Jagger worry about them, and you just focus on getting Kolton better, okay?"

At her words, some of my panic melted away. "Okay," I said, silently cursing when tears tried to emerge again.

As I turned and finished unlocking the door, Vi stopped me once more. "And, Nora? Don't forget to take care of yourself. Being alpha is a stressful job. It'll bury you if you let it, so please. Don't let it."

"I won't," I said, more to myself than to her. One of my biggest flaws was the need to prove myself at the cost of my own health. I couldn't go there again. Couldn't let this pack define who I was like my old one had. I wanted them to accept me as their alpha—albeit temporarily—but I wouldn't harm myself to make that happen. Doing so would only hurt the ones I loved . . . including the unborn child that might be growing inside my womb at this very moment.

Nervous all over again, I fought to calm my racing pulse as Jagger and Griff helped me open the door. Pregnancy should be the *last* thing on my mind, but it was suddenly all I could think about. How would Kolton react when I told him? Did he even *want* a child? We'd never discussed children before. We'd consummated our marriage less than two weeks ago, and I thought we'd have plenty of time before kids came into the picture.

By the time I entered the room and the door thudded shut behind me, my emotions were everywhere. I'd hoped to do Kolton proud by confidently waltzing inside and announcing how well his pack had accepted me as their new alpha. I'd hoped to leave any worries and doubts at the door so he could focus solely on his own health. It was *my* turn to carry the burden of being alpha. *My* turn to fix things. To fix *him*.

But the first thing that came out of my mouth when I saw him still sitting on the cot was, "I screwed it all up. I'm so sorry, Kolton. You've worked so hard to keep this pack together, but I'm pretty sure I just ruined that today. I wasn't strong enough. Wasn't *confident* enough. They saw straight through me to the weak and pathetic girl I used to be."

As I dumped my fears and uncertainties onto him, he slowly rose to his feet and quietly approached. I stayed where I was by the door, unable to stop the words from tumbling out.

"I mean, they might have *outwardly* supported me, but I know they didn't believe me about the fire and your death. They're going to look into it and find all the holes in my story, and when they confront me, I'll end up telling them the truth. I *hate* lying. I was lied to my whole life, and I don't want to be a controlling, manipulative leader like Hendrix was."

Kolton was feet away from me now, silently watching as I word-vomited everywhere.

"I want to be firm yet fair, honest yet kind. I want to be open and understanding, earning respect by listening before speaking. I want to . . . I want to be like *you*, Kolton. I want to be—"

My words ended in a gasp as his mouth found mine. He cupped my face and tilted my head back, kissing me thoroughly. *Deeply*.

I was suddenly drowning in him. In his warmth. His scent. His *taste*. He caressed my tongue with his, and I grabbed onto his shirt to keep from falling. When I released a needy moan, he backed me against the door and pressed his body to mine, delving his tongue even deeper into my mouth.

Butterflies erupted in my stomach, and I held on for dear life as he ravaged my mouth like a man possessed.

Just like that, every single doubt, worry, and fear evaporated into thin air.

All that existed was him and me, our bodies saying more than words ever could.

Still, I couldn't help but whisper through our bond, *I missed you.*

I missed you too, came his immediate reply.

A startled sob burst from me. He continued to kiss me, gently wiping my cheeks when they grew wet with tears.

How? I asked into that special place where only he and I existed. Reaching out, I searched for our invisible bond, shocked to discover that it felt almost normal. A few spots were still frail, but the damage was mending. *Healing.* Another sob left me.

I'm sorry, Kolton's voice rumbled through my mind, the sound instantly soothing the hurt its absence had caused. *I'm so sorry for shutting you out. For hurting our bond. But I'm trying. I'm trying to heal. To let you in. I've spent the entire morning preparing for this moment.*

A relieved laugh slipped free, followed by a hiccup. *What, kissing me senseless?*

Oh, I plan to do a whole lot more than kiss you, sweetness, he purred. My core instantly heated at his words, and I shivered with anticipation.

Griff had *better* not be spying on us right now. Not that I would stop this from happening even if we *were* being watched. This moment was everything. Everything I'd hoped for. *Prayed* for. Kolton was healing, and I'd do everything in my power to help him become whole again.

God, you smell so good, he inwardly groaned, pulling his lips from mine to kiss my jaw, then my throat. Unlike the last time we'd been in this spot, there wasn't an ounce of fear in my veins. I immediately melted against him, arching my neck to give him better access. He paused to nuzzle and kiss his claim mark, then abruptly stiffened.

My eyes fluttered open. *What's wrong?*

"Too many smells," he said out loud, his voice a low growl. "Too many *males*."

I bit my lip, trying not to laugh at how possessive he sounded. "What are you going to do about it?" I asked, not quite able to hide my amusement.

"This." In one swift movement, he reached down and whipped my shirt off.

I gaped up at him in shock. And then something came over me. A feeling that rushed through my veins and filled my mind with naughty naughty thoughts. I didn't know if the feeling was his or mine, but I didn't care.

I was suddenly moving and so was he. We came together in a clash of lips and limbs, our only goal to consume each other. I grabbed his shirt and wrestled it off, moaning loudly when he pressed our flushed skin together. Our kisses were out of control, hot and desperate and needy. Each time we pulled away to remove clothing, our mouths came together again in a frenzied rush, nipping and biting and sucking.

With one swift yank, Kolton snapped my bra off and lifted me, curling my legs around his waist. I clung to him as he tangled his hand into my hair and pressed me against the door once more. The cold metal did nothing to cool my overheated skin, rapidly growing slick with sweat. The second he rocked against me, revealing how hard he was, any remaining embarrassment over being overheard vanished.

"Kolton," I whimpered, reaching for the button of his jeans. He shuddered at my touch, grinding himself even harder against me.

I need you inside me. Right. Now, I told him through our bond, demanding in my need.

I felt his lips curl into a smile against mine, making me ache for him even more. "Is that an order, *Alpha?*"

My eyes flew open to find him already watching me. He pulled back a little to reveal that devilish smile still curling his mouth. God, I'd missed that smile so much.

"Alpha?" I repeated breathlessly, still trying to undo his pants. "I was hoping to hear that word today, but not from *you*."

His smile widened. *I'm secure enough in my manhood to let you take control, sweetness*, he crooned through our bond, sliding a hand up to toy with my hardened nipples. When I sucked in a gasp, he added, *Tell me to call you Alpha, and I will.*

At that, my whole body shivered with pleasure. I was surprised by my reaction, not expecting to enjoy the thought of being in control so much.

When I didn't respond right away, he bent down and sucked one of my nipples into his mouth. My spine arched off the door, and I moaned, closing my eyes. As he sucked and nibbled on the sensitive flesh, I released the button to grip him through his jeans. He hissed, his hardened length swelling beneath my touch.

Tell me what to do, and I'll do it, Nora, he spoke mind-to-mind, driving me crazy with desire. *Tell me to get on my knees before you, and*

I will. You've earned it. You've earned my submission. My unwavering devotion. You've earned the right to be called Alpha.

I was seriously going to come on the spot if he kept talking like this. I'd never thought of myself as having an ego, but the more he stroked it, the more it craved his attention.

Unable to speak, I expressed with touch what I wanted, grabbing his hand to place it between my thighs. A growl rumbled in his chest, and he readily honored my request by rubbing my clit through my jeans.

"Holy hell," I groaned, letting my head fall back against the door as pleasure rolled through me. So much pleasure that, seconds later, I couldn't hold back my orgasm. It ripped through me, stealing the breath from my lungs. Still, I managed to cry out as ecstasy slammed into me.

Kolton released my nipple to raise his head and gently kiss my neck. But when he started to ease back, I blurted, "*No.*"

He froze.

Still trying to catch my breath, I gasped, "Strip. Now."

Amusement filled our bond. I bit my lip to keep a grin at bay. Being in control like this was heady. I didn't think I'd ever been this turned on before. My body was beyond sensitive, overwhelmed by the simplest touch. And when he reached for his jeans to quickly tug them off, I was immediately hungry for another orgasm.

"Now me," I ordered next, shivering as his fingers brushed my bare stomach. They slid down my skin, then slowly unbuttoned my jeans, clearly trying to torture me. "*Faster.*"

His soft chuckle warmed the side of my neck. "Yes, Alph—"

"No 'alpha,'" I interrupted. When I felt a flicker of confusion through our bond, I silently added, *I'm not your alpha, Kolton. Not now. Not ever. You're* my *alpha. Don't ever forget it.*

He was quiet for a long moment, but I could feel him. Feel his emotions. Feel the gratitude and love pouring through our bond. Finally, he kissed my neck again and resumed his task, his voice a bare whisper as he said, "I won't, sweetness."

CHAPTER 9

KOLTON

It was torture allowing her to command my movements. *Exquisite* torture.

I could feel how hungry she was, nearly eclipsing my own hunger. She was enjoying this role reversal and, surprisingly, so was I.

When she'd left this morning, it had been pure agony. I'd thought for certain that my mind would break again, that terror and pain would consume me once more. But, as time had passed, a fierce determination had gripped me instead.

If Nora was brave enough to take my place as alpha, then I would be strong enough to face my pain. It wouldn't consume me again. I wouldn't let it.

So, instead of raging and destroying the room like my instincts were demanding I do, I'd settled onto our cot and become perfectly still. It had taken all of my strength to keep my body from moving, but I'd won. I'd wrestled it into submission.

And then came the harder part. Getting my *mind* to cooperate. I'd spent hours silently talking myself off the ledge, ordering my brain to remain calm, to slowly lower its defenses. There were still barriers. Still jagged pieces that needed mending. But I'd finally repaired my bond with Nora. A patch job, really, but I could feel her now. *Speak* with her. And my overwhelming relief at having the connection restored was absolute.

The moment she'd finally come back to the bunker, I'd sensed her stress and panic and guilt. I'd quietly listened to her words, knowing that she saw herself as a failure. But she couldn't be more wrong. She was *alive*. Alive and well, without a single scratch on her. If she had failed, then she would have come back bruised and bloodied—if she'd come back at all.

The pack might still have their suspicions, but they respected her enough to follow her lead. As they should. She deserved their respect. Deserved to be followed.

Despite how terrified I'd been for her safety, I knew she had it in her to lead.

When she told me to strip, I'd inwardly howled with excitement. I liked when she took charge. *Loved* it, actually. She didn't make me feel like less of a man as she told me what to do. In fact, I somehow felt stronger. Her strength was my strength, and I marveled at her courage as she ordered a male twice her size to take off his pants.

I'd readily complied, then eagerly removed her own pants. When I moved to press our naked bodies together again, she stopped me with a hand to my chest. I stilled, waiting for her next command.

I couldn't have been more shocked when she looked up at me and whispered, "Touch yourself."

At the soft order, my cock swelled to the point of pain. Needing to ease the pressure, I immediately obeyed, reaching down to grip myself. As endorphins rushed through me, I quietly groaned, "You're going to be my undoing, sweet flower."

She lowered her gaze to watch me grip myself, darting her tongue out to lick her full bottom lip. I bit back another groan.

"I know," she continued to whisper. "But I'll put you back together again. I promise."

My breathing sped up as she reached between her own legs and touched her clit. A quiet moan escaped her, and wild desire swept through me. I gripped my shaft harder, gratified when her breath caught. As she started to stroke herself, I pumped my shaft, my gaze glued to what we were doing.

This was new for me. New and thrilling. I'd never let myself experience something like this with a female before. I'd simply taken control and ensured both of our pleasures, not allowing the moment to go beyond what I was willing to give.

But *this*. This was far beyond anything I'd ever done. I'd never allowed a female to so thoroughly control the outcome. To so beautifully *show* me what she desired.

I was wholly enraptured. Undone and remade as I experienced exactly what this incredible female wanted me to.

When our breathing grew ragged, our movements becoming frantic as we chased after our pleasure, she suddenly withdrew her hand from between her legs. Before I could prepare, she slid those same fingers, now slick with her arousal, over my swollen tip. At the feel of her wetness coating my sensitive skin, mixing with my own arousal, all the air fled me in a rush.

Her other hand gripped mine, ordering me to release myself. I did, but my eyes shot up to hers, wild with desperation. The need to come was all-consuming. So powerful that I found myself pleading with her. *Begging.* "Please, Nora."

Her eyes held mine, bright with understanding. She reached between us again and gripped my rock hard shaft. I jerked against her fingers, releasing a sharp groan of relief. Then panicked again when her hand didn't move.

"Nora. I need—"

"I know exactly what you need," she crooned, guiding my hand to pick up one of her legs. The move brought us closer together, so close that the engorged head of my cock brushed against her slick folds. Moaning, I tried to press against them, but she squeezed me sharply, ordering me to stop. "You'll move when I want you to move. Now, be a good boy and hold still while I impale myself on you."

A harsh breath escaped me, the sound filled with disbelief. And arousal. How was this woman mine? She was too good to be true.

Reacting to the sound, she tilted her lips in a wicked smile—one that I found far too fascinating. Unable to help myself, I dipped my head to kiss her. Before I could make contact, she barked, "*Behave.*"

At the sheer dominance in her voice, pleasure rolled through me in waves. "Yes, sweetness," I managed to say, trembling from how badly I wanted to plunge my dick inside her right now.

But I was entirely at her mercy. She was calling the shots, and it was my job to obey. As she slowly eased my cock toward her entrance, I thought I would die from the torture of it all. Torture I wouldn't have survived if I hadn't been enjoying it so much. She took her time, rubbing her peaked nipples against my chest before allowing my tip to slide through her wetness. I released another harsh breath, gripping her thigh tightly.

So close. I was *so close* to where I desperately needed to be.

Barely able to contain myself, I held perfectly still as she slowly allowed me inside her. Inch by inch, I slid in, feeling more and more at peace as I did. It was like coming home. She *was* my home. The only home I needed.

Finally, when I was fully inside her, fitting perfectly like a sword made for its sheath, she ended the torture.

"Don't hold back," she said, sounding as winded as I did. When I didn't move, she said it again, the command in her voice unmistakable. "Don't hold back, Kolton."

Something in her eyes nearly made my heart stop. It was like she knew. Knew that I hesitated because . . . because she was pregnant.

Because I didn't want to hurt her. Hurt *either* of them.

But how? How could she know?

"You won't hurt me," she said, rocking forward to seat me even deeper within her. "It's okay, Kolton. Let yourself go. It'll help you. *Heal* you."

I struggled to breathe, continuing to desperately search her eyes for confirmation. As frantic as I was to take her, I had to know. Had to know if she—

There. A flicker in those beautiful ocean-blue depths. A *knowing*.

"Nora," I said in a strangled whisper, staring at her a moment longer. Needing to be sure. When that flicker brightened in confirmation, I choked out her name again and crushed her to me. Burying my face in her hair, I squeezed my eyes shut and let go. Let everything go and allowed my instincts to take over.

They readily took control, fitting Nora's body against mine. Molding us until we became one. I held her impossibly close, lifting her leg higher so I could ease out of her, only to slide in deep once more. She wrapped her arms around me, pressing her face to my neck as I slowly thrust in and out, enjoying how tight she was. After a while though, she said, "Faster, Kolton. Harder."

When I made a sound of protest, she released a growl.

A laugh burst from me. "Did you just growl at me?"

"*Yes.* And I'll do more than that if you don't screw my brains out right this instant, Kolton Anthony Rivers."

I laughed again, then groaned as she dug her nails into my back. "What a naughty little mouth you have, wife."

"The better to suck you with, husband," she said sweetly, making my cock grow rock hard again. "Which I won't be doing later if you don't screw my brains out."

Finding it hard to breathe again, I managed to say, "Is that a threat?"

"A promise. Now, give me the ride I want or suffer the consequences."

Well, she truly had me by the balls now. Not that I minded in the least. Letting the last of my control go, I pulled out of her, then firmly gripped her thigh and slammed in deep.

In reply, she threw her head back against the door, crying out my name. The sound whipped me into a frenzy of lust, and I pounded into her again, groaning at how good it felt. How *right*. Using the door to brace us, I set a punishing pace, slamming into her so hard that the metal shuddered beneath my assault.

She spurred me onward, shouting "Yes!" over and over at the top of her lungs. If the others could hear us, she'd no doubt be embarrassed later. But right now, she didn't seem to care about anything but getting her "brains screwed out" by me. I gladly did just that, giving her a ride worth remembering.

It wasn't every day that you had wild sex against a blast door, after all.

And wild it was, just short of being feral. As our pleasure built, she clawed at my back, hard enough to break the skin. When I repaid her with a sharp nip to her earlobe, she bit into my neck. Not hard enough to draw blood, but I suddenly wanted her to.

"Do it," I hissed, angling my cock so I could drive it in deeper. When I hit the sensitive bundle deep within her, she screamed against my neck, her walls viciously clenching me. I saw stars, nearly blacking out from the bliss. When I could speak again, I groaned out, "Claim me, mate. Claim me as I have claimed you."

She shuddered against me and whimpered a little, as if afraid that she'd hurt me. But when I slammed into her again, she bit into my neck with the force of a pitbull.

I roared, pain and pleasure overloading my senses. She held on, digging her nails into my back for good measure to keep me in place. I trembled as my balls tightened, my release building and building. It was too much. I couldn't hold on any longer. I tried to slow my thrusts but Nora rocked against me, increasing the pace. Driving me to the brink of insanity.

An insanity that I wanted. *Needed.* An insanity that I'd gladly lose myself to over and over.

Unable to hold back my orgasm a second longer, pleasure whipped through me like a gale-force wind. I jerked against her with another roar, spilling my hot release. It came and came, filling me with indescribable bliss. A moment later, Nora's walls mercilessly squeezed me as her own orgasm shot through her. She released my neck with a cry, stiffening at the pleasurable assault. I held her tightly, her orgasm continuing to milk my own, leaving me trembling and utterly spent.

When the high slowly started to fade, I gathered her to me and kissed her damp brow, basking in the afterglow of the absolute perfection we'd just shared.

As our breathing slowed, I finally found my voice. Finally said what I'd wanted to say ever since I'd seen the beautiful nest she'd made on our bed.

"You're pregnant, sweetness."

She was silent for a long moment. Then she softly replied, "I know."

CHAPTER 10

I'd underestimated the intimacy of eye contact.

Combined with soft, lingering touches, it was almost too much.

Each look and gentle caress imprinted on my soul.

Somehow, even though we were barely touching, I'd never felt closer to my soulmate. After Kolton had confirmed what I'd already known in my heart, he'd tenderly wrapped me up in a blanket before laying down with me on our cot. The significance of the gesture wasn't lost on me, now that I knew without a doubt that I was pregnant.

A nest. My blanket creation had been a *nest*.

I knew that female werewolves instinctively made them earlier on in their pregnancy. Knew that they felt the need to create a safe space, one they could retreat to before and after their child was born. I'd unknowingly made that spot on our bed, my instincts guiding my movements before I'd realized what they meant.

The need to mourn the loss of my nest would come, no doubt soon, but I was currently too content to grieve. With the blanket still tucked around my naked body, I was facing Kolton on the narrow cot, marveling at how clear his gaze was. For the past hour, we'd simply stared at each other, taking comfort from each other's closeness. Every few seconds, he'd reach out and touch me. My cheek. My lips. My hair. Trailing soft caresses down my neck and bare shoulder. I touched him in return, paying close attention to the warmth of his skin, the prickle of his unshaven jaw, the softness of his mouth.

He might have flaws, but to me, he was perfection. *My* perfection.

His lips beneath my fingertips suddenly moved as he whispered, "Thank you."

My eyes met his again. "For what?"

"For this." He kissed my fingers. "For saving me. For not giving up on me. I was lost and couldn't find my way back to you, but every time you touched me, I felt a little bit more like myself again."

A small, satisfied smile pulled at my mouth. I let my fingers wander, trailing them down his neck to rest on the spot where I'd marked him. *Claimed* him. His skin was smooth now, healed of the bite mark I'd inflicted, but my scent was still there, buried deep within him.

My smile widened, then abruptly fell. "Did all of this happen," I hesitantly began, not quite able to look him in the eye, "because you found out I was pregnant?"

He was silent for a long moment, then quietly said, "Look at me, Nora."

I did, suddenly nervous of what I'd find there. Unmistakable sorrow lined his eyes, but I couldn't tell if the guilt I was feeling came from him . . . or me.

"When Keisha almost took you, my world shattered. I couldn't handle the thought of losing you both. The pain was too unbearable, so I . . . so I broke." He paused, then said, "I allowed fear to lock me away. To control me. It's why you couldn't reach me through our bond. I cut myself off from everything, including you, because . . ."

"Because?"

"Because reality became too much. I couldn't face a world without you in it."

I searched his eyes, my heart twisting at the grief I found there. "But I'm still here," I softly reassured, sliding my fingers up and into his hair. His eyes drifted shut. "We both are."

He sighed and reopened his eyes. "I know, but I couldn't convince my mind of that. All I could think about was how close I'd come to losing you. One second. One second more and you would have been gone forever. You and our unborn child."

My throat tightened with emotion. "Is that why you wanted me to leave with Melanie and Brielle? Because you were afraid something like this would happen?"

He stroked my cheek for a moment before admitting, "Yes."

"I'm so sorry," I burst out, my chin quivering. "I didn't mean to get pregnant."

"Oh, sweetness," he quietly groaned and pressed a kiss to my forehead. "This isn't your fault. *None* of this is. I'm the one who failed you."

I shook my head. "Don't be so hard on yourself. You've done so much for your pack and family. For *me*. You had a breaking point, and there's no shame in that. We all fall apart sometimes."

He heaved a sigh. "Not me. Alphas can't afford to fall apart."

I snorted softly. "Even superheroes fall on occasion."

His lips twitched into a smile against my forehead. "Have I mentioned how perfect you are for me?"

"Once or twice. But I don't mind hearing it again," I said with a laugh, then quickly sobered. "So you're . . . you're okay with this? With me being—"

"Pregnant with my child?" he finished for me, pulling back to meet my imploring gaze. "I thought loving you was terrifying, but this is somehow more. More *everything*. I look at you now and can barely contain all that I feel. I'm scared and elated and so desperately in love that I can barely stand it."

He cupped my cheek to gently wipe a tear away.

"So if you're wondering if I'm okay with this," he went on, his voice growing husky with emotion, "then yes. I'm more than okay. I'm thrilled beyond words and honored to have been given the task of protecting this miracle we've made."

He slipped a hand inside the blanket to rest it on my bare stomach. The move was so protective, so gentle, that I whimpered. At the sound, he gathered me into his arms and pressed a kiss to my hair.

"I vow to protect you both with my very life, Nora, but I need you to know that I'm not fully healed yet. There's something inside me. Something dark and feral. Its only goal is to protect you, no matter the cost. When it senses a possible threat, eliminating that threat is its only mission. I can feel it even now, ready to attack at the slightest provocation."

I rested my cheek against his steadily beating heart, surprised that I didn't feel even the slightest bit afraid by his confession. "Is that why you attacked Jagger right after the fight with the witches?"

"Yes. I knew it was him, but it didn't matter. This thing inside me . . . it's dangerous. *I'm* dangerous. I'm afraid of what I'll do the moment I'm released from this place. It's why I needed you to go without me this morning. I'm sorry for putting you in this position, but I'm not fit to lead. To be alpha. The pack isn't safe around me right now, not even my own family."

"And Shadow? I haven't been able to reach him. Neither can Storm."

Pain and guilt flickered through our bond, the emotions decidedly Kolton's. "He's still there, but I . . . I repressed him. So deep that I can't even feel him."

I blinked in alarm. "Why?"

"When I broke, I couldn't tell friend from foe. Everyone was a threat to you, including him."

"Oh, Kolton." I pressed a kiss over his heart, hoping to soothe away some of his guilt and pain. "He's a *part* of you. You know he wouldn't hurt me."

"I know, but I couldn't think clearly. My mind and actions weren't my own. I've never done that to him before, and I don't know how he'll react when I manage to undo the damage."

"Is there anything I can do to help?"

He hesitated for a long moment. Then, "I think he needs to see Storm."

"Oh. Is she . . . is she safe around you?"

"Besides you, she's the only one who is. The darkness inside me doesn't recognize you two as separate beings."

"Well, that's good." I wiggled in his arms until he released me. The second he did, I sat up and swung my legs over the cot's edge, popping to my feet. "Okay, then. Let's do this."

He blinked up at me in confusion. "Do what?"

I unwrapped the blanket and playfully tossed it in his face. "Let's free your wolf, silly."

The blanket plopped onto the cot to reveal his stunned expression. He rolled into a sitting position. "Here? *Now?*"

I smirked at him. "You know how ironic this is, right?"

He shook his head with a semi-amused grunt. "I noticed. What do you want in exchange for freeing my wolf?"

My smirk grew. Sidling up to him, I leaned down and whispered a mere inch from his lips, "You."

Before I could pull away, he grabbed the back of my head and crushed our mouths together. Only when I was thoroughly weak-kneed and trembling did he break the kiss to whisper back, "Deal."

Holy hell, would I ever get enough of this man? Probably not. Selfishly, I loved being alone with him down here. Ironic, since this place had reminded me of my time with the witches. But there were so many terrifying unknowns outside this room, ones that I would have to face all too soon. In here with my mate though, things were simple. *Safe.* The world couldn't touch us now that he'd begun to heal.

It wasn't going to be easy leaving this place, but once Shadow was freed, I had a funeral to prepare for. Now that I knew about the inner turmoil Kolton was still facing, I worried that his healing journey would take far longer than I'd thought. We couldn't let him out of here if his first instinct was to attack anyone who came close to me.

Maybe we needed to have sex again. He said that my touch helped him feel better, so maybe—

I think you forgot, wife, that I can hear your thoughts again, he suddenly purred inside my mind. *And I'd like nothing more than to have sex with you again, but if we do that, I'll want to do it again and again and again. Shadow will be beyond upset that he missed out on all the fun.*

I sputtered out a laugh, feeling my cheeks heat. "Well, we can't have *that* now, can we? I know how important our sex life is to him."

"Exactly," Kolton said, kissing my lips again before rising to his feet. "Plus . . . I don't feel right without him."

I gave him a sympathetic look. "I know exactly how you feel. Now that I've formed a connection with Storm, I can't imagine being cut off from her again."

Guilt flooded our bond once more.

Kolton opened his mouth to speak, to no doubt apologize yet again, but I quickly placed my finger over his lips to silence him. "I *forgive* you, Kolton. It was awful not being able to reach you, but it wasn't your fault. Shadow will come to realize that too when we set him free. So no more apologies, okay?"

His guilt continued to linger between us, but after a lengthy moment, he simply nodded.

"Good. Then let's get Shadow out of there. Storm, are you ready?"

Familiar heat stirred within me. *I'm ready, but are you sure this is a good idea? Shadow is a violent spirit and could be angry that his host repressed him. He might take out his anger on me, which could in turn harm you and the baby.*

At that, Kolton went stiff as a board.

Crap. He could hear Storm again too.

Before he could get all ragey protective on me, I hurriedly replied to Storm, *That won't happen. He absolutely adores you. There's no way he would hurt you.*

Still, I sensed her doubt, along with a fierce wave of protectiveness from Kolton.

"*Enough,*" I abruptly snapped. "Both of you. We are all bonded, including Shadow. He's one of us and deserves our support, not judgment. For all we know, he's confused and scared from being cut off from us. He's *alone*. We need to set him free. Right. Now."

I could sense their surprise at my outburst, but I wouldn't apologize for it. Shadow was family, and he needed us.

After a long moment, Kolton finally said, "You're right. He deserves the benefit of the doubt. I won't stop him from taking over, but if he threatens either of you in any way, do whatever it takes to subdue him."

"We can help too, if need be," Jagger said through the intercom, startling me. Who knew how long they'd been listening. So long as they hadn't listened to us having *sex*, I was okay with it.

"It won't come to that," I replied. "Storm's got this."

I could feel her surprise again, this time at my unwavering confidence in her. After how Zuriel had treated her and being cast from Heaven, she probably didn't have much confidence in herself anymore. Well, *I* believed in her, even if she didn't believe in herself. I'd wasted too much time doubting myself, and so had Storm. This was her moment to show us what she was made of.

Taking a step back, I locked eyes with Kolton and said, "I'm ready when you are, Storm."

I didn't have to wait long.

Seconds later, heat blasted through me and I began to shift.

CHAPTER 11

STORM

When I shook off the last of the shift, Nora's mate slowly crouched before me.

I could sense how nervous he still was, an emotion that I too shared. The only one who seemed completely at ease with this plan was Nora. Not because she hadn't thought it through, but because she truly believed it would work. She truly believed that *I* could free a demon spirit from his hellish prison.

More times than I could count, I'd helped send demons back to Hell. Not once had I tried to rescue one from it.

The irony of the situation wasn't lost on me. An angel trying to *save* a demon. I shouldn't want to. I shouldn't even care what happened to him. And yet he'd come to my rescue more than once these past couple of weeks. He'd saved Nora and his host's family, proving that demons were capable of more than wicked deeds.

Yes, he was violent and crude, but there was no mistaking his loyalty. The same couldn't be said for my own kind, for the spirit who had once called me his. Ever since the argument I'd had with Zuriel a few nights ago, I'd begun to question our bond. To wonder if it was even real. After witnessing the connection that Nora and her mate shared, how could I not?

"So, how do you want to do this, Storm?" Kolton said, breaking me from my thoughts.

I cocked my head to the side, considering. He hadn't shown

any aggression toward me, confirming his earlier words to Nora. Whatever dark thing that had possessed him to attack a member of his own family didn't see me as a threat. I might as well be Nora.

With that in mind, I stepped toward him. When he didn't so much as twitch, I dared to take another step. Then another. He watched me carefully, his curiosity plain. Without a word, I extended my muzzle toward his hand . . . and licked it. At the gesture, he flipped his hand palm up—an invitation to continue. I licked it again, stepping even closer. The move brought my head within touching range, and . . . he did just that.

Touched me. No, *petted* me.

I stiffened, nearly pulling away. A part of me still chafed at being treated like an animal. I'd once been a majestic being made of magic and *light*. No one would have *dared* pet me in that form.

But this was who I was now. A fallen angel made flesh. A *wolf*. Petting came with the territory. And now that I *was* being petted, I didn't mind it so much. I even kind of liked it. The sensation was unlike anything I'd felt in spirit form. Kolton's hands were steady. Diligent. Strong. No wonder Nora inwardly simpered about them so much.

Allowing myself to enjoy the moment, if only a little, I leaned into Kolton's hands as he continued to pet my head with sure strokes. When he began to scratch the side of my neck though, an embarrassing moan rolled up my throat.

Storm. Focus, Nora barked inside my head, clearly having heard the sound.

Kolton chuckled.

What's so funny, Mr. Handsy? Nora snapped at him.

Kolton chuckled again, making the situation worse by continuing to scratch my neck. All on its own, my hind leg lifted, beating at the air. What was this sorcery?

"Are you jealous, sweetness?" Kolton crooned at his mate, enjoying this moment of teasing far too much. So was I, but I wouldn't let Nora know that.

Kind of. Which is really weird, Nora admitted with a huff. *Can we just focus, please? You can touch each other, but no more moaning, okay?*

Kolton smirked but stopped scratching my neck. At the loss, I bit back a disappointed whimper.

"I don't feel Shadow's presence yet," he said after a moment, his worry clear. "Maybe I buried him too deep."

Touch isn't enough, I finally spoke. *Nora didn't heal you with touch alone.*

Nora's surprise flared through our connection. *What do you mean? How did I heal him then?*

Kolton stared into my eyes, understanding slowly dawning on his face. "With magic," he answered for me.

I simply nodded.

But I didn't even try *to do magic*, Nora said, her tone one of disbelief. *I barely know how.*

Doesn't matter, I replied. *Intention is often more powerful than knowledge when it comes to magic. You wanted to heal your mate, so you did.*

And you're only telling me this now?

The frustration in her voice was clear. I was silent for a long moment before quietly admitting, *I didn't know it was possible. I thought . . . I thought I'd lost that ability. When Zuriel finally noticed me about a century ago and realized my potential, he helped me turn my healing magic into something altogether different. Something deadly. What was once used to give was used to take away. Instead of healing, he taught me how to . . . to burn.*

"The light that engulfed Nora when she woke from a nightmare," Kolton said. "It burned me when I touched it."

Yes. My instinct was to protect her against the witch Keisha. To defend. Zuriel taught me how to use my magic for fighting purposes, so when I faced a demon in battle, I could burn them into oblivion.

Kolton's hands on my head stilled.

Wait, into oblivion? Nora questioned, not noticing how preternaturally still her mate had become. *Like, send them back to Hell?*

I kept my gaze trained on Kolton, knowing that my next words could damn me. He already knew though. I could see the understanding in his eyes. The flicker of *fear.*

No, I finally answered Nora, deciding to admit the truth despite my precarious position. *I could burn them into nothingness. I could obliterate their spirit until it no longer existed on this plane or the next.*

Nora gasped in shock. Kolton remained frozen with his hands still on my head. If it wasn't for Nora, he probably would have snapped my neck by now.

Nora finally noticed how quiet he'd become and quickly said, *But you wouldn't do that to Shadow or the others. Right, Storm?*

A sudden bout of sadness consumed me. Sadness that she'd even have to ask. *They are part of your family, Nora*, I softly replied. *I would never harm them, especially not like that.*

Nora was silent for a beat. Then, *Kolton? Are you okay?*

He continued to stare at me, his expression now unreadable. The air thickened with tension, but neither of us moved. I wouldn't shy away from his judgment. There was a very real possibility that I'd fought others like him during my time as an angel. That I'd ripped their familiars from them, just like the Blackstone Coven had wanted to do.

In truth, I wasn't much different from the witches, maybe even worse. I was a hypocrite. I'd done terrible things in the name of justice. I'd blindly destroyed without knowing all the facts. I'd never seen myself as a killer, but as I stared into Kolton's eyes, I was suddenly ashamed of all that I'd done.

It was on the tip of my tongue to apologize when he heaved a tired sigh and shook his head. "That's in the past. I won't hold it against you, Storm. I understand that angels and demons are programmed to hate each other. I can only hope that you don't feel that way now."

I was silent for a long moment. Did I? Did I still hate demons? Or did a part of me, a very small part, actually respect them?

I blinked, confused by my conflicted thoughts. Demons had been my enemy for so long. How could I ever hope to redeem myself if I no longer hated my enemy? If I *shunned* my purpose?

A whine pressed at my throat, but I shoved it back down. I could worry about my state of purgatory later. Right now, I had a job to do, one that Nora had entrusted me with. I wouldn't let her down.

Setting my confusion aside, I said, *The only thing I feel now is a desire to help. I thought I'd lost my ability to heal, but Nora proved me wrong. The ability is still there. I'd just forgotten how to use it.*

Kolton's eyes narrowed. "And you want to use it now? To set Shadow free?"

Yes.

But what if you accidentally hurt him instead? Nora spoke up, suddenly worried.

I won't. My intentions are perfectly clear. I want to heal, not burn.

Kolton blew out a sigh and gave his head another shake. "Okay, then. Do it. But know that I'm trusting you to honor your word, Storm. Shadow's life depends on it."

I know, I quietly said, grateful that he was giving me this chance. I admired him even more for it. Despite the darkness inside of him that he was afraid of, Nora's mate was far from corrupted. And if he wasn't corrupted, then perhaps his demon familiar wasn't my enemy after all.

Somehow reassured by that thought, I closed my eyes and reached inside of me for the magic that I hadn't touched in far too long. The magic that had once been pure goodness, meant to fix and mend. Somewhere along the way, I'd unknowingly lost my purpose. My *gift*. I was created to heal, not to hurt. But I'd allowed Zuriel to twist me into something I wasn't.

A killer.

No wonder I had fallen. If anyone here was corrupted, it was me.

Resolved to fix what I had broken, I focused on the task before me. On finding the nurturing light within. Normally meant to heal the weary souls of mortals, I used it now to coax a trapped demon from his cage.

At first, all I saw, all I *felt*, was darkness. It was like falling into the black pits of Hell itself, devoid of all light and hope. Every instinct in me recoiled, resistant to going somewhere I was never created to be. But I pressed on, not allowing fear to control me. I'd allowed myself to be controlled for far too long. Allowed Zuriel to strip my innocence from me. My *goodness*.

If I was ever going to find my goodness again, then I would start here, helping someone in need.

Redoubling my efforts, I urged my magic to light up the darkness. To guide my path. Almost immediately, a glow surrounded me. Relieved, I began my search in earnest, using my inner senses to track the demon familiar. It felt like forever that I searched the empty void. All was still and silent. Nora's mate had spoken true. He'd buried

Shadow *deep*.

I pushed more light before me, cutting through the darkness. Carving a path deeper and deeper. When I found nothing, I decided to speak. To let him know that I was here.

Shadow.

Still nothing.

Shadow, it's . . . it's Storm. Are you here? Kolton and Nora are worried about you.

No answer.

Sighing, I added, *Fine. I'm a little worried too. This isn't like you. Where's the rage? The violence? I expected you to be fighting down here. To be clawing your way out of this prison with everything you had.*

At the silence that greeted me, sudden anger boiled up.

Okay, be that way, I snapped, my voice echoing through the vast pit. *It's not like I care what happens to a demon anyway. You were born in darkness, so you probably* like *it here. Go ahead and stay here then. I hope you enjoy being alone and forgotten!*

A sudden sob burst from me, startling me into silence. The anger faded as a new emotion welled up. One that I never expected to feel about a *demon*.

Hurt.

I tried to push the emotion away, but it wouldn't leave. It was the only thing in this hellhole that wanted to be around me. The only thing that hadn't abandoned me after all these years.

But I was tired. So tired of being miserable. Of wallowing in my pain. I wanted to be free of it. Free of the guilt and regret and self-hatred. Free of my *past*.

I wasn't that same being anymore. My eyes had been opened. My opinions had changed. I no longer thought that all demons were bad and all angels were good. I no longer saw in black and white.

I wanted to grow. To be better. I wanted to think for *myself.* And right now, I wanted nothing more than to make amends for all the wrong I'd done, starting with the demon who'd done nothing but protect me and my host from the start.

I'm sorry, I began, surprised by how much I meant the words. *I'm sorry for trying to kill you the first time we met. I'm sorry for treating you like you were beneath me. For judging you before I knew you. You're not at all like I imagined a demon would be. You're honest and loyal, and you care deeply. A being like you doesn't deserve my blind hatred. I was wrong, and I want . . . I want to make it up to you. But that means breaking free of this cage. I can't help you if you won't let me. You have to want it just as much. You have to want to be free.*

Each heartfelt word was punctuated by a burst of my magic. My *healing* magic. It pulsed from me in waves, illuminating the darkness. Pushing it away. Until I finally felt it. A warm presence. A familiar one. One that filled me with renewed hope.

I surged forward, shouting, *I'm here, Shadow. I'm going to get you out. Just hold on.*

My magic led the way, guiding me closer and closer to his dormant presence. It felt like he was asleep, curled up in a den like I had for the past twenty-two years. Hiding from the pain of being rejected.

Shadow, I'm here, I continued, reaching out to touch him with my magic. *You're not alone. Wake up. Wake up!*

The second my magic touched him like an invisible hand shaking him awake, a blast of heat shoved me back. Back, back, back, until I wrenched open my eyes with a startled yelp and scrambled away.

Kolton's crouched form suddenly exploded upright. He threw back his head and roared, the sound quickly morphing into a howl as his body began to change. To *shift.* Within seconds, Shadow's demon form—his *true* form—towered above me. Standing nine feet tall with dark fur covering his massive body, he heaved in breath after breath, slightly swaying on his hind legs.

I waited for a beat, allowing him to adjust. To realize he was no longer a prisoner. He wildly looked around the room, his gaze swinging my way. But he looked right through me. Like he couldn't even *see* me.

Shadow, I began, but that's as far as I got.

With a mournful-sounding howl, he stumbled across the room and threw himself at the door. It shuddered on impact, making the ground beneath my paws tremble.

What's wrong with him, Kolton? I heard Nora say through our connection.

I don't know, he immediately replied. *I tried speaking to him, but he's not responding.*

Shadow backed up, only to rush the door again. When he slammed into it, the door groaned loudly. The cement wall around it cracked.

"Nora, what's the plan here?" Jagger shouted over the intercom. "The door's not going to hold."

Storm, what should we do? The panic in Nora's voice was clear.

I watched Shadow closely, studying the way he moved. His heart trilled dangerously fast, his breath coming in short spurts.

He doesn't realize, I finally said, watching as he backed up once more. *He doesn't know that he's free.*

Storm, we need to do something, Nora desperately cried as Shadow tensed, prepared to rush the door again. *He's going to break through!*

A sudden calm settled over me. *Let him*, I said. *I've got this.*

When he lurched forward, I looked at the camera and barked a warning. A second later, Shadow crashed into the door. Metal squealed as it caved under his massive weight, unable to contain him. He plowed through the exit, and I immediately raced after him. When I burst into the hall, he was already loping at full speed up the ramp. Kolton's family moved to go after him, but I stopped them with another warning bark.

Not checking to see if they listened, I shot after Shadow. I knew he was fast, but he practically flew up the incline, hitting the metal stairs at a dead run. They shrieked under his weight, but thankfully held as he charged up them. I doggedly pursued, keeping him locked in my sights. I couldn't lose him. Couldn't let him get away. If I did, there was no telling what havoc he would wreak on the world in his current state.

Hearing him crash through the door above, I put on a fresh burst of speed and lunged up the stairs. I would only get one shot at this. One moment to reach him. If I failed, I didn't want to think of what the consequences would be.

But I wouldn't fail. This was my *purpose*. My true purpose. Thousands of years of conditioning were rushing back to aid me as I tore after the confused demon. In his true form, he could outrun me. I was no match for his great speed and strength. Once he made it into the trees, I'd lose him for sure.

But there was a small clearing around the bunker, one large enough to serve my purpose. Even with the afternoon sun illuminating the clouds overhead, I knew I could reach him. The moment I burst outside, I started to change. To shift. To reveal who I *truly* was.

Within seconds, I transformed in a blaze of brilliant light.

CHAPTER 12

SHADOW

An explosion of light blinded me.

Disorientated, I dropped to all fours and slowed my charge toward the trees. Shaking my head, I blinked to clear my vision. As my eyesight slowly returned, I prepared to run again. To escape this prison I'd been transported to. But before I could, a gust of air brought with it a familiar scent. One that had me greedily inhaling.

Impossible.

I shook my head again. I was *alone* in this prison. Alone for the first time in my very long existence. It was terrifying. So wretchedly awful that I must be conjuring her scent to make this sad existence more bearable.

Blinking away the last of the bright spots, I surged forward again, only to hear a voice. *Her* voice.

"Shadow."

Now I *knew* I was hallucinating. I'd heard her voice *out loud*, not inside my head. And the usual rough edge was missing. Her voice was almost melodic now, dancing along my senses like a summer's breeze. Still, I hesitated, wishing I could hear it again, if only to replay it in my mind over and over when I once again succumbed to loneliness.

"Shadow, look at me."

I closed my eyes, shuddering at how good it felt to be graced with her voice once more. This might not be real, but I would cling to it for as long as I could.

"For heaven's sake, would you look at me already? I'm not going to stand here all day."

At the annoyance in her voice, my eyes snapped back open. The spots had cleared, but the world was still bathed in white light. Except, the white light was now moving. Forming a shape. A graceful one at least seven feet tall.

When I realized what I was looking at, the air froze in my lungs.

She was beautiful. The most beautiful creature I'd ever laid eyes on. Her body was shaped like that of a lupine, standing upright on slender hind legs. I could barely stand to look at her, the glow emanating from her almost painful to behold. When I lifted a clawed hand to shield my eyes, the glow noticeably dimmed. Enough that I could make out her other features. Like her eyes, so brilliantly blue that they sparkled like a faceted jewel.

But that wasn't all. Behind her stretched a massive pair of *wings*. So bright that I couldn't look at them directly. Still, curiosity got the best of me. I stepped toward her, surprised when she didn't pull back or even growl. She simply watched me with her keen gaze, tipping her head back when I rose to my full height.

She was so small compared to me. Small and delicate. But I seriously doubted there was anything weak or helpless about her. She exuded power, a power that drew me in like a moth to a flame.

When I was close enough to touch her, I stopped and simply stared. She unflinchingly met my gaze, not moving a muscle as I reached out to touch one of her wings. Expecting to feel soft feathers, I almost jerked my hand back when heat engulfed my clawed fingers instead. The intensity wasn't enough to burn me though, so I allowed my hand to wander, marveling when it caught nothing but air.

Light. Her wings were made of pure *light*.

"You've been holding out on me, angel baby," I gruffly whispered, wishing with everything in me that this was real. But there was no way she was here. Storm would never reveal her true form to me.

She didn't think I was worthy of it.

"I had to get your attention somehow," she replied, still allowing me to play with her wings of light. "Your wolf form is scary enough. *This* form would surely get noticed by the human populace."

I huffed a laugh. "No need to worry about that. There's no one here but me."

Storm cocked her head to the side. "You still believe you're imprisoned?"

"Yes. Although, this conjuring of you is definitely a welcome distraction."

She glanced down at herself as though unimpressed. "This form is still made for the earthly plane. In the spirit world, I'm made entirely of light."

"And I'm made of shadow. You know what they say about opposites."

She looked back up at me through narrowed eyes.

I ignored the warning. "Whatever form you take, you're more beautiful than I could have imagined."

Proving my point that this was indeed a figment of my imagination, I leaned down and brushed my muzzle against hers. Delicious warmth rippled along the fine fur on my face.

"You feel *heavenly*," I groaned, continuing to nuzzle her. To inhale her scent. But when I darted my tongue out and licked the corner of her mouth, she shoved me back with a growl. I blinked at her in surprise.

"What do you think you're *doing?*" she barked, reaching out to shove me again. I winced as her form brightened once more. "We might be connected, but we're not *mates*. You can't just *lick* me like that."

Stunned, I simply stared at her irate face. When she met my gaze again, her anger suddenly fizzled out.

"Shadow? What is it?"

I continued to stare at her in disbelief, then whispered, "This is real."

Her expression noticeably softened. "Yes, Shadow. This is real. You've been set free."

My breath caught. "How?"

"I . . . I found you and used my magic to awaken you."

I stared at her for the longest time. Long enough that I could tell she was uncomfortable. Then my lips stretched into a wolfish grin. "I knew you cared about me, angel baby."

She bared her teeth at me in a silent snarl. "Insufferable demon. Don't think this means that I like you. I was only trying to help Kolton and Nora."

A chuckle rolled up my throat. "Resist all you want. I can be patient when it's something worth waiting for. And you are definitely—" I paused, suddenly realizing what was missing. It was silent. *Too* silent. Panic tightened my chest once more. "Why can't I hear them? Why can't I *feel* them?"

"Calm down," Storm said, her voice softening again. "Your connection to them was damaged when Kolton repressed you."

"Repressed?" I growled, stumbling back in alarm. "He *repressed* me?"

"He didn't *mean* to," Storm said, eyeing me sharply. "He doesn't deserve your wrath."

I dug my claws into my palms, still struggling to control my anger. My *hurt*. Kolton had never tried to repress me before.

"I trusted him. *Trusted* him. After all that we've been through. After all that I've *done* for him. How could he do this to me?"

"He's *sorry*," Storm barked, her magic flaring. "The thought of losing his mate and unborn child was too much for him."

My jaw dropped. "What did you say?"

"He's sorry."

"No. The other part. You mentioned a child."

"Yes. Nora's pregnant."

I blinked. Blinked again. When her words finally sank in, I threw back my head and released an ear-splitting howl. I *knew* Kolton had been knotting her for a reason—not that I was going to tell him that. He'd thought it was the mating frenzy, but I'd suspected his instinct to breed her had kicked in. About time too. I still couldn't understand why it took him so long to mate her.

When the echoes of my howl faded, I grinned at Storm once more. "Run with me."

She gaped at me like I'd lost my mind. "You're no longer mad?"

"Oh, I'm still hurt by what Kolton did to me, but this pregnancy needs to be *celebrated*. Come. Run with me in wolf form. I'm not ready to give up control just yet."

Storm shivered, as if the invitation to run filled her with excitement. Not waiting for a reply, I dropped to all fours and began to shift into my wolf form. Normally, I only shifted when Kolton asked me to, but I was feeling like a rebellious teenager at the moment. A *horny* one.

My angel baby had come to rescue me from my forced solitude. That had to mean something. She'd almost attacked her past lover a few days ago, so maybe she was ready to move on. To be properly pursued by a *real* male. A male who didn't want her simply for her power.

110

Despite the painful shifting of my bones, I grinned like a fiend. The breathtaking angel couldn't resist me forever. My plan to bring Kolton and Nora together had succeeded. Now it was my turn to get what *I* wanted. I'd continue to wear her down for as long as it took. And then . . .

She would be mine.

Seconds later, I shook off the shift and glanced back to see that she'd done the same. No longer in angelic form, she looked like a wolf, albeit a large one.

Ready to run, angel baby? I internally said, disappointed when she didn't respond. Our connection must not be fully restored yet. No matter. I could communicate just fine as a wolf. It would give me an excuse to get closer to her anyway.

Turning, I trotted up and boldly rubbed against her side. She allowed it, which sent a thrill of excitement through me. Pushing my luck, I rounded her backside and rubbed up against her other side. She growled quietly, but I chose not to heed it. Coming even with her, I brazenly licked her cheek, then her snout.

She snapped at me and I danced away. Only to slide forward and lick her nose. Her ears flattened against her skull, but she didn't snap this time. So I went for it. All the way. Showing my clear affection by nipping and licking at her mouth. She froze, no doubt in shock. She didn't reciprocate, but she didn't pull away either.

Before I could push my luck even further and possibly ruin the moment, I gave her one last lick and took off like a shot. Listening closely, I howled with pleasure when I heard her follow. She yipped in reply, and I slowed, allowing her to run beside me. Unlike her past lover, I had no intention of putting her second. She would be my equal in every way—if she accepted me.

But I knew the road ahead would be difficult. She wasn't going to give herself to me without a fight. She'd been rejected and didn't easily trust. Not to mention the fact that she was an angel and I was a demon. We might both be in the same predicament for the time being, but we wouldn't be this way forever. A day would come when our spirits returned to the plane that created them.

I wasn't going to think about that day right now though. All I wanted to focus on was how good it felt to be running beside her. To not be *alone* anymore. She'd freed me from my cage, and I was indebted to her.

To show my gratitude, I put my nose to the ground and began to hunt. The woods surrounding the bunker were teaming with prey, and it wasn't long before I picked up a trail. Minutes later, a rabbit burst from a nearby bush and the chase was on. I charged after it, but so did Storm, yipping her excitement. I slowed, just a little, realizing that the best way to show her my affection was to let her have the kill.

She took the lead, gaining on the rabbit in no time. It didn't stand a chance against her. With a leap, she pinned it beneath her claws, delivering the killing blow with one swift bite. I looked on with pride, admiring how she managed to be brutally efficient yet graceful at the same time.

Expecting her to hoard the rabbit for herself, I was stunned when she shifted to the side—an open invitation for me to join her. My grin returned. Nothing said affection like sharing a fresh kill. I *knew* she secretly liked me.

The meal was over far too quickly, but I capitalized on every moment, making sure to give her the best pieces. When I'd swallowed my last bite, I looked up and caught her staring at me. Before she could look away, I stepped forward and licked the blood from her chin. *Slowly*. Taking my time.

And she let me.

I allowed myself to thoroughly enjoy the moment, making sure to clean every last fleck of blood from her snowy white coat. When I was finished, I reluctantly pulled back. She stared at me a moment more, then darted forward and licked my nose.

I couldn't have been more shocked.

Before I could recover, she took off into the woods again. I watched her go, trembling as I felt an instinct roar to the surface.

Chase, chase, chase.

Giving in, I tore after her. Adrenaline pumped hotly through my veins as I unleashed the animal in me. This moment was for *us*, no one else. I finally had her all to myself, and I was going to enjoy every last second of it.

When I finally caught up to her, I playfully nipped at her hindquarters. She abruptly whirled and our limbs tangled. We rolled across the ground, kicking up dirt and pine needles. I tried to protect her from the fall, but she was up again in a flash, shaking the dirt from her fur. The moment I skidded to a halt, she attacked.

With a leap, she pounced right on top of me. I landed flat on my back, blinking up at her in surprise. She pinned me beneath her, her maw opened wide to bite my face off. I made a lame attempt to defend myself, and our mouths collided in a clash of teeth and tongues.

My warning growl abruptly cut off as I suddenly realized what was happening. She was play-fighting. Play-fighting with *me*.

Delirious with excitement, I scrambled to my feet and trounced her back, making sure to be careful as I wrestled her to the ground. She nipped me, and I nipped her back, pausing to nuzzle her neck. She stilled, allowing the affection for a few moments, then lunged to her feet and took off again.

For *hours* we did this. Chased and played. Teased and flirted. We enjoyed the simplicity of existing as animals while the world continued on without us. Time lost meaning. Day turned to night. Still, we frolicked in companionable silence until, at last, exhaustion caught up with us.

Finding a small cave, I made sure it was unoccupied first, then led the way inside. Storm followed, watching as I turned in a circle, then plopped down with a tired sigh. She silently approached me, her movements suddenly shy. Nervous. I held still, leaving the decision up to her.

For a long moment, I didn't breathe, certain she would find a spot against the cave wall. A spot as far away from me as she could.

But, once again, she shocked me. Despite her nervousness, she came right up to me and laid down by my side. At the feel of her warm body pressed to mine, I shivered with contentment. When I felt her relax, I curled my body around hers, resting my chin on her neck. After a moment, she snuggled against me and released a sigh.

With a happy grin twitching my mouth, I let my eyes drift shut. Today had been pure magic between us. I didn't know what tomorrow would bring, but I did know one thing.

Without a doubt in my mind, I was falling head over heels for an angel.

CHAPTER 13

NORA

I awoke to the sensation of warm hands on my bare skin.

Moaning sleepily, I arched my body in a languid stretch, which only encouraged the hands to roam more. They slid over my breasts and stomach, drawing me further awake. I let out another soft moan, keeping my eyes closed as I enjoyed the way those roaming hands made me feel. When one swooped down to tease the sensitive area below my belly button, I jerked, my backside bumping up against something hard.

A grin stole across my face. "Well, good morning to you too, husband," I said, my voice still husky with sleep.

"Morning, wife," he replied in that sexy rumble I loved so much. "I don't know about you, but I woke up extremely horny."

To prove his words, he pressed on my lower belly, aligning my backside with his thick arousal. My grin widened. I wiggled my butt against his stiff cock, and he groaned.

"Do you want to play, wife?" he purred in my ear, sliding his hand lower, but not low enough.

I softly hummed and rubbed up against him. Slowly. Teasingly. "After the evening our familiars had, I do indeed want to play. I'm just surprised they finally shifted back. I must have been pretty tired, because I barely remember it."

"Me neither. I don't think Shadow's ever run and played that hard before, not even when I was an adolescent."

"He was excited. I could sense Storm's excitement too, surprisingly. She genuinely enjoyed his company yesterday. I can't believe she exposed her true form to him. And *wings?* Wow."

"It was incredible. The form didn't hurt you?"

"No. The light was intense, but not like the times I felt it in the past. It was kind of warm and comforting, actually."

"Shadow seemed to have the same experience when he touched her wings. She must be able to wield her form as she does magic, depending on her intent."

Neither of them contradicted our musings. Maybe they were still asleep after their horny romp. At least they hadn't humped each other. I wasn't sure how I felt about that.

"I can scent your growing arousal, sweetness," Kolton said, slipping his fingers down a few more inches. One of them was *almost* there, the tip pressing lightly against my pubic bone. "Did you want to finish what they started?"

"Yes," I breathed, gasping when his other hand tweaked my nipple. There was something extremely erotic about this moment. Maybe it was the secluded cave or the fact that our horny wolves had made *us* horny. Either way, I wasn't going anywhere until we were both completely satiated.

I was just about to arch back so that his hand slid further south when he said, "Then sit on my face."

My eyes flew open. "What?"

His amusement trickled through our bond. "You heard me. Sit on my face."

"Sit on your . . ." My cheeks burst into flames as I figured it out. "Oh."

He chuckled quietly. "*Oh*, indeed. Now be a good girl and straddle my head. Daddy is hungry."

Daddy?

I would have burst out laughing if I wasn't so turned on. I could practically feel his tongue on me already, making me almost drip with anticipation.

"Nora," Kolton growled, giving my nipple a sharp tug. "Face. Now."

At the bite of pleasure-pain, I swallowed a moan and scrambled to obey him. When I turned to face him, he was already on his back, waiting for me. I got distracted by his dick though, hard and saluting the air.

"Eyes up here, wife," he commanded, and I reluctantly lifted my gaze to his. His lips twitched in amusement. "You can suck on me all you want later, but right now, it's my turn."

Holy hell, I couldn't wait to have that wicked mouth on me. I was practically burning up with desire, seconds away from combusting. I moved toward him before I could, not wanting to miss out on this new experience.

"Good girl," he crooned as I crawled toward his face. When I was close enough to grab, his hands shot out and dragged me on top of him. I let out a squeak and braced myself against the cave wall, tensing my legs so I wouldn't plop onto his face. He tutted softly and said, "I can't have you tense like this, sweetness. If you're going to ride me, I need you to be relaxed."

"Ride?" I glanced down between my legs and immediately froze, stunned at how starved he looked. Ah hell, I wasn't going to survive this.

"Yes, Nora," he patiently said. "You're going to ride my face like a pony."

My eyes bugged out and I sputtered, "A-a pony? But I'll *smother* you."

He barked a laugh. "You won't smother me. I promise. Just focus on enjoying the ride, and I'll do the rest."

My thighs began to quiver as excitement rushed through me. "Okay, I can do that," I breathlessly said. "So, what should I—*Aah!*"

My words ended in a startled cry as he grabbed my hips and pushed me down. His tongue immediately found my clit, and pleasure shot through me. I moaned, firming my grip on the cave wall. As his tongue licked at the bundle of sensitive nerves, I saw stars. The pleasure was intense in this position, allowing him to thoroughly tease and flick my center. When he pushed me down even more so that he could suck on the nub, I cried out his name, my entire body shaking.

Ride me, sweetness, he said through our bond, continuing to suck until my breath came in short spurts.

Giving in to the moment, I began to rock, gasping as my pleasure only heightened. His mouth tugged on the sensitive flesh with each movement, sending sparks of bliss shooting through my body. His unshaven stubble created the most delicious friction, making each nerve-ending hyperaware. Just as I began to find a rhythm, he shifted me forward a bit and broke our connection. My whimper of disappointment turned into a shuddering gasp as his tongue suddenly delved into my entrance.

"Holy hell," I moaned aloud, and he chuckled quietly.

Keep riding my face, wife. Use me to find your pleasure.

Oh, I would. Face-riding was my new favorite thing.

I started to rock again, concentrating on the way his tongue slid in and out of me. Every few seconds, he'd curl the tip against my walls, bringing me even more pleasure.

Before I knew it, I was riding his face with abandon, bouncing like I was on the back of a bucking bronco. With each movement, his tongue thrust in deeper, just the way I liked it. As my pleasure built, I clung to the cave wall for dear life, feeling my thighs tense in anticipation.

Responding to my growing desperation, Kolton pulled his tongue out and rapidly swirled it over my clit. Barely able to breathe, I forced my eyes open and glanced down at him, wanting to watch what he was doing. At the sight of his mouth working between my legs, I released a breathless whimper. Kolton opened his eyes and met my stare.

Do you like to watch, wife? he purred, his eyes darkening with lust. *Do you like to see me eating you?*

Unable to speak, I weakly nodded.

With a wicked grin, he sucked me deeply into his mouth and bit down. Ecstasy ripped through me, and I cried out, orgasming hard against his mouth. He continued to suck, making me spasm and shake with each pull. When my legs turned to jelly, he positioned me to sit on his chest, holding me steady while I slowly came down.

"That was," I gasped out, still trying to catch my breath. "That was amazing."

He gave me a self-satisfied smile. "Glad you liked it. My turn now."

As he sat up, I slid down his front, my arousal leaving a trail on his skin. *Marking* him. A pleased growl vibrated his chest.

"So wet and ready for me," he purred, guiding me straight on top of his waiting cock. He easily slid inside, my walls already slick and relaxed for his arrival. When he was fully sheathed inside, he softly groaned, "So perfect. Made just for me."

Even though I was still coming down from my high, I settled more firmly on top of him, marveling at how whole he made me feel. How *complete.*

Suddenly overwhelmed, I leaned forward and pressed a trembling kiss to his lips. He cupped my face and immediately pulled back to look at me with concern.

"What's wrong, Nora?" He wiped at the tears sliding down my cheeks. "Did I hurt you? Is the baby okay?"

When he moved to lift me off him, I tightened my legs around his waist. "No, I'm fine. We're both perfectly fine," I said with a sniffle. "I'm just so . . . so *grateful.* I was so lonely before you came into my life, and now I'm just . . . You've given me so much. A home. A family. Love. And now a baby? I'm overwhelmed, but in a good way. Sometimes, I still can't believe that this is real. That I was lucky enough to be chosen for this. That you're my soulmate."

At my tearful words, his worry slowly faded. "I wish I could give you more. You deserve the world." Sudden guilt pulsed through our bond, and he looked away. "My weakness forced you to face the pack alone. I put you and the baby in a dangerous situation, and I can't forgive myself for it. I don't know how you can even stand to be with me."

"Kolton, look at me." When he didn't, I grabbed his face and forced his gaze to mine. "You are the strongest person I know, and I have nothing but respect for you. I know how hard it must have been to let me face the pack without you, but you *did*. Because you believe in me and care deeply for your family. You could have told me to hide from the pack, but that's not you. You're loyal and honorable, and you don't run away from your duties. That's what I *love* about you. That's why I'll gladly take your place as alpha until you're able to return."

Sighing, he closed his eyes and rested his forehead against mine. "I still don't know how I'll react around others. I don't want to lose control like that again. I can't. I can't go back to that dark place. I can't leave you to handle things alone."

120

"I won't be alone, and I won't let you go back to that place," I said. "Your family has my back when you can't, and I have the power to *heal* you, remember? In fact, I plan to heal you right now."

Curiosity flickered through our bond. "Oh? And how will you do that?"

I slowly smiled and dropped one of my hands between us. "With touch, of course."

His stomach flexed as I slid my hand down each hard muscle, deliberately using my nails to scratch him. He sucked in a sharp breath, gripping my hips when I teased the trail of dark hair beneath his navel before slipping lower. When I reached the place where we were still connected, I lifted up so that I could wrap my fingers around the base of his shaft. It immediately swelled, and I grinned.

"Griff said that sex would help and that it won't harm the baby."

A low growl vibrated Kolton's chest. "I don't want to talk about *Griff* right now."

My grin widened. I squeezed Kolton's shaft, and his growl turned into a groan. Lifting off him some more, I teased his swollen head, swirling it around my entrance before allowing it inside once more. When I continued to tease him, his base thickened, forcing my fingers apart.

"Mmmm," I hummed, squeezing him again. "I miss this."

"Miss what?" he asked, already winded.

"Your knot."

He huffed a laugh.

"I'm serious. I know it already did its job . . ." Kolton laughed again. ". . . but I still want it."

He pushed me down on him, and I released his shaft. "So, you like to be *bred*, mate?"

Biting my lip in thought, I slid my hands to his shoulders, then softly admitted, "Yes? Is that weird?"

He made a pleased sound in the back of his throat. "Not at all. It excites me." As if to prove his words, his length grew impossibly thick, just short of knotting me.

"Kolton," I gasped, my walls eagerly spasming. Wanting to see, I looked down and caught a glimpse of his huge cock stretching me wide.

"You forever surprise me, sweetness," he rumbled, releasing one of my hips to slide a hand between my legs. When I saw his fingers touch my clit, a moan burst from me. "You like to watch, you like to breed, and you like it rough. I can't wait to find out what else you like."

When he began to pleasure me in earnest, I squeezed my eyes shut and surrendered to the moment. His touch and thickened length were pure heaven, filling me with utter bliss. If my touch healed him, the same could be said for his. There was nothing in the world that compared. Moments like this mended my wounds and fixed my hurts more than anything else could.

It was like we were feeding each other. Nurturing. Giving life through the act of making love.

I opened my eyes again to see that I practically glowed, my skin outwardly radiating what I was inwardly feeling. No, I *was* glowing. Truly glowing as we gripped each other, our breaths growing frantic and our bodies slick with sweat. I glanced up at Kolton to find him already staring at me.

"You're glowing, Nora," he said, his voice filled with awe.

I was too far gone to respond back. He continued to watch as I slowly came apart, each thrust driving me closer to the edge.

When I couldn't hold on any longer, he crushed our mouths together and kissed me deeply. Pleasure exploded through me, and I screamed, a sound that he thoroughly swallowed. Seconds later, he slammed into me once more and groaned into my mouth, expelling his release.

Our bond flooded with euphoria, almost more than I could take. The feeling was his and mine combined, making us experience twice the pleasure we normally would. I spasmed around his cock as a second orgasm hit me, suddenly aware of how tight the fit was.

He'd knotted me. He'd knotted me *good*. His cock completely filled me up now, stretching me impossibly wide. When I felt the ridges along its length lock us together, I sighed in contentment.

Is this what you wanted, wife? he purred, still kissing me.

Yes. So much, yes. I wasn't even embarrassed to admit it. I loved how his knot made me feel, like we were one being. Not just in body, but in mind and soul.

"You can have it whenever you wish," he said out loud, pulling back to rest his forehead against mine once more. "Whatever I have, sweetness. All that I am, every last broken piece, is yours. Never forget that."

"I won't," I whispered. "Not ever."

CHAPTER 14

NORA

After hours spent tangled in each other's arms, we finally left the cave, only for Kolton to halt in his tracks.

I opened my mouth to question him, then snapped it shut as a voice filled my head.

Well, that was incredibly satisfying. Thanks for the show, especially the pony ride. I wanted to shout 'yeehaw' but didn't want you to get distracted and fall off.

I would have blushed with embarrassment if I wasn't so elated to hear him again.

Shadow! I inwardly cried, my face splitting into a grin. *I'm so glad you're back.*

Thanks, little one. Congrats on the baby, by the way. Are you sure it's not mine?

You wish, I replied with a snort, peeking up at Kolton's face. His skin was ashen. Reaching out, I laced my fingers through his. He rapidly blinked, as if coming out of a trance. When he glanced down at me, I mouthed, *Talk to him.*

Nervous energy pulsed through our bond. Swallowing, he gripped my fingers tightly before saying out loud, "Shadow."

Silence filled the connection we all shared. Then, *Did you hear something, little one? No? Me neither. Being forced into a cage of solitude by someone you trusted messes with your mind a bit. I must still be hallucinating.*

Kolton's grip on my fingers almost turned painful. "Shadow, I'm . . . I'm sorry. You have no idea how sorry I am."

More silence.

My heart ached for them both, but I kept quiet. The rift they were experiencing was one I knew all too well. But to experience that rift for the first time in two decades must be extra painful.

"You know how gutted I was after what happened to my parents," Kolton continued, his hand starting to tremble. "I was only nineteen when my entire world flipped upside down. After I became alpha, I had to quit school. Vi and Melanie needed me, as did the pack and family business. I gave up my life for them.

"You more than anyone know how that changed me. My carefree days were over. The weight of my new responsibilities was almost more than I could bear. But I did. I bore it, never daring to hope that I'd be more than my duties. Never believing that I could have what my parents once had.

"So when I was gifted that very thing, I could feel myself changing once more. I no longer lived solely for my duties but for a love so vast that I'm consumed by it. And when that gift was almost taken from me, my world didn't just flip upside down. It was *shattered*. I couldn't fathom a life without that precious gift, so I destroyed myself. I destroyed *you*, Shadow.

"And I'm sorry. I'm so sorry for betraying the one person who's kept me strong all these years. I should have turned to you for help, because you've always been there when I needed you. I know that what I did to you is unforgivable, but I *still* need you, Shadow. I might not be able to live without Nora, but I can't *survive* without you. You're a part of me. A *gift*. And I'm not complete without you."

Overwhelmed by Kolton's impassioned speech, I silently wiped the tears from my face. He might have hurt Shadow, but he sure knew how to apologize. I only hoped that Shadow was the forgiving type. If he held a grudge for too much longer—

Okay, okay, I forgive you, Shadow groaned. *I think you thawed the darkest corners of Hell with that speech.*

Isn't Hell hot? Storm chose that moment to speak up.

Why, angel baby, I'm appalled, Shadow exclaimed in mock offense. *As a celestial, you should know that Hell is nothing like the storybooks portray.*

Well, I haven't exactly vacationed there, she replied, dead serious.

When Shadow boomed with laughter, relief flooded the bond. I glanced up and caught Kolton's smile, returning it with one of my own. As Shadow and Storm continued to lightly bicker, Kolton pressed a kiss to my hair and whispered, "Come on. There's a few more people I need to apologize to."

My eyes widened in alarm. "Do you think you're ready to see them?"

"I don't know. But now that I have you, Storm, and Shadow to help me, I have to try."

Nervous but hopeful, I didn't protest when he began to walk back toward the bunker. We could have shifted and made better time, but the long walk allowed all four of us to reconnect. Shadow dominated the conversation, chatting away with mostly me and Storm. I could tell that he was still hurt and trying to process his emotions, but that was to be expected. At least he was talking and not bottling it all up.

Kolton listened intently, calmer than I'd seen him in days. Being separated from his familiar must have made his condition worse. Despite how different their personalities were, they really did need each other to survive. Now that their connection had been restored, it was clear that they fed off each other's energy and also balanced it. If Kolton hadn't repressed Shadow, maybe none of this would have happened.

He must have been thinking the same thing, because a fresh wave of regret suddenly flooded our bond.

"I know," I said before he could say anything. "I wish it hadn't happened either, but we're going to get through this. Please don't beat yourself up over it."

Well, maybe a little, Shadow unhelpfully said, and I rolled my eyes.

Before I could respond, Kolton stiffened. In a flash, he pulled me into his arms, his hold nearly cutting off my air supply. Confused, I tipped my head back to study his tense face.

"What is it?"

"The others," he ground out. "I can smell them."

Still confused, I searched the area and finally spotted something on the ground not far away.

"They left us clothing," I said with relief. Traipsing around naked with my husband was one thing, but I still preferred to be dressed around everyone else. Wiggling in Kolton's grip until he loosened it, I added, "It's okay. You don't have to see them yet if you're not ready. Now that the bunker door is broken, we could just hang out in the woods until—"

When I paused, his arms tightened once more. "What's wrong, Nora?"

At the sharp tone of his voice, I winced. So much for him being calm.

"It's just that I can't stay out here with you," I replied, forcing my voice to remain even. *One* of us needed to be calm.

"Why not?" he demanded with a feral edge.

Sighing, I said, "Because I need to prepare for your funeral."

Deafening silence. Not even Shadow made a sound.

Then, "Tell me everything."

So I did. I told him about the car ride, including my bout with morning sickness. Told him about the pack's reaction to his death in the house fire. Told him about their recommendation for a funeral to gain the pack's favor. But when I told him about the Alpha Ceremony, he went rigid like stone.

"No. Not happening." He abruptly released me and began to pace through the trees. "I can allow the funeral, but an Alpha Ceremony is too dangerous. In a pack this size, there will be no avoiding challengers."

I watched his agitated movements, struggling to remain calm. "But what other choice do I have? They're not going to wait until you get better. They want the funeral and ceremony to happen within the week."

"Then I'll get better *now*," he barked, whirling to face me. "Because I'm not letting my pregnant wife fight *my* battles."

I pursed my lips. "But they're my battles too, Kolton. They became mine when I agreed to marry you. So, if you're not fit to lead Midnight Pack, then I'll face whoever challenges me for the alpha position. I won't let you down."

At that, his expression fell. "Oh, sweetness. You could never let me down." Heaving a sigh, he shook his head and murmured, "I've really screwed this up."

Yes, you have, Shadow agreed.

Kolton barked a laugh. "Thanks, Shadow."

You're welcome.

"No, really. Thank you. Your blunt honesty has always kept me from wallowing in self pity. Whenever I've messed up, you've made sure I owned it. I lost a father when I needed his guidance the most, but you've filled that role more than I give you credit for."

Shadow was silent for a long beat, then said, *You can call me daddy, if you want. Maybe not in the bedroom though. We don't want to make your mate jealous.*

I threw my head back and groaned, "*Really*, Shadow?"

He snickered. *You can call me daddy too, little one. But that will definitely make Kolton jealous.*

Storm snorted. Actually *snorted*. Like the conversation amused her.

Giving up, I headed for the clothing piled in a neat stack at the base of a tree. Despite Kolton's misgivings, I really couldn't stay out here with him. Someone had to lead Midnight Pack. There was no way around that. No *hiding* from it. My new duties were waiting, and I had no intention of running from them.

While I tugged on a royal blue top and dark jeans, all was quiet. I was just slipping on a pair of white Converses when Kolton quietly said, "You've changed so much."

I looked over at him, pausing to shove my unruly hair back. "Oh?"

"You're decisive and confident. You've *bloomed*, Nora. Into something that takes my breath away."

At the unmistakable awe in his expression, I felt a blush rise up. Straightening, I self-consciously cleared my throat. "Well, I bloomed because of you, Kolton. And I know you still want to protect me, but I need you to let me go."

Panic flashed in his eyes.

"I will *always* come back to you," I quickly added, "but I need the space to grow. To become who I'm supposed to be. You sacrificed your life for this pack, and now it's my turn to do the same. Let me go, Kolton. Let me go and trust that I can take care of myself."

He watched me for several moments, then slowly stepped toward me. When he was directly in front of me, he reached up to tuck a stray curl behind my ear. "I do trust that you can take care of yourself. You've already grown so much since I met that wild, desperate girl in my club a few short months ago. You're strong and capable, and I couldn't be prouder. But I will always be terrified of losing you, and I will always feel the need to protect you. You're my wife. My *soulmate*. You are precious to me, and the very thought of someone trying to hurt you makes me want to set the world on fire."

A swallow got stuck in my throat. "Is that something you can do? With your magic, I mean."

His lips twitched. "Darken magic is very different from Elemental magic. If yours was born from light, then mine was born from darkness. My magic wasn't designed to heal; it was created to *cut*. To destroy. If I wanted to burn the world, then yes, I have the ability to unleash hell. The fire that consumed the family estate would look like child's play in comparison."

A shiver racked my body from head to toe.

He noticed and slowly grinned, ducking his head to whisper in my ear, "But I don't think my mate is afraid of the darkness. I think she's drawn to it. Maybe even likes it."

"Maybe," I whispered back. Probably. Definitely. Especially if that darkness was used to protect. I'd never once seen Kolton wield his magic with evil intent.

Maybe light and dark magic were neither good nor bad. Maybe it was all about the user's intention. If that was the case, the same could be said for angels and demons. Which meant that Storm definitely deserved a second chance at redemption. She'd used her magic to save someone. Sure, that someone was a *demon*, but still.

I tucked the thought away for later, adding yet another thing to my to-do list. Right now though, I needed to meet up with the others.

Hopefully Carter hadn't called while we were frolicking around in the woods. He was already suspicious enough.

With a sigh, I pulled back and met Kolton's gaze. "I have to go now."

His grin faded. "Then I'm going too."

I blinked at him in surprise. "You almost went off the rails at a mere *scent*."

"I know, but I won't get better by staying in these woods. If I can't keep it together, then I'll let Shadow intervene."

Shadow didn't respond, but he didn't need to. Even *I* was struggling to accept Kolton's words. He might mean them, but I couldn't forget how feral he'd been only a few shorts days ago. I couldn't be careless with the safety of others just to protect his feelings.

"Please, Nora," he said, shocking me with his humility. To me, he would always be the alpha of all alphas. But right now, he was following my lead. The lead of his alpha female.

For whatever reason, that majorly turned me on.

Blinking away the sudden haze of lust, I replied, "Okay, I'll let you try. But if you threaten any of them, you're done."

He nodded. "Okay."

"I'll protect them from you, got it? I won't hesitate to stop you."

He nodded again, somehow looking submissive and proud at the same time.

God, I loved him.

Resisting the urge to kiss him senseless, I stepped aside so he could change into a white t-shirt and black jeans. Even though he'd been naked for the past several hours, I couldn't help but admire how the clothing hugged his powerful frame. When he caught me ogling, that wicked grin of his returned.

"Lead the way, wife," he deliciously rumbled, letting his own gaze

131

travel the length of my body.

Holy hell. How did he manage to make submissive *hot?*

Clamping my mouth shut so I wouldn't start to drool, I turned and led the rest of the way to the bunker. Kolton followed in my wake like an obedient puppy. I could feel his gaze on me, practically burning holes through my clothing. Seconds later, desire spiked through our bond.

"You're enjoying this *way* too much," I muttered, forcing myself to keep going so I wouldn't turn around and jump his bones.

His answering chuckle sent a pleasant tingle up my spine. "I do enjoy it when my mate takes charge. Especially during sex."

I nearly tripped over a root. "So you like when I dominate you?"

"Yes."

Oh. Oh my. The most powerful alpha in the country liked when I dominated him. *Focus, Nora.* Now was *not* the time to be getting wet and horny.

"In fact, if you threatened to collar and tie me up, I'd probably come on the spot."

My knees weakened. It was all I could do to keep myself from melting into a puddle on the forest floor.

Oh, I'd love to see that, Shadow purred. *Maybe with a little flogging.*

When Kolton had the audacity to laugh, I threw back my head and yelled, "Okay, *enough.* I'm seriously going to orgasm right now if you don't stop."

"Did Nora just say *orgasm?*" a voice called through the trees.

Kolton immediately lunged for me. Faster than I could blink, his arms coiled around me like a python. Feeling a growl build in his chest, I focused on remaining calm.

"It's okay," I soothed, placing my hand on his slightly trembling arm. "It's just Griff."

"Everything good, Nora?"

"Yes," I called back to Griff, praying that I spoke true. "We'll stay here so you can approach. Just go slowly."

Please be okay, please be okay.

I'm trying, Nora. I promise, Kolton responded to my silent plea, even as his trembling increased.

Relieved that he was at least communicating, I focused on the approaching footsteps. It wasn't just Griff heading our way, but Vi and Jagger as well. Which could be a good thing or a really bad thing. We already knew Kolton wasn't above attacking his second. Of the three, Jagger was the most dominant—and therefore the biggest threat. Trying my best not to panic, I pushed calming energy toward Kolton. My fingers warmed, and I quickly glanced down, surprised to see them faintly glowing.

Magic really *was* all about intention. I wanted to heal Kolton, and so I was. I could only hope that it was enough.

Before either of us was ready, Griff, Vi, and Jagger materialized through the trees. At the sight of them, Kolton stiffened even more. He didn't growl though, which I counted as a win. They each took in the protective way he held me, then wisely stopped a safe distance away.

"Do we need to subdue him again?" Jagger said, focusing on me instead of Kolton. His stance was ready, prepared to defend at the slightest sign of aggression.

"I won't attack you," Kolton replied before I could, his voice almost guttural.

Vi made a startled sound, her eyes impossibly wide as she stared at him.

"Good to know, bro," Griff said, looking the most relaxed of the three. "But I won't hesitate to take you down again if you come at any of us."

"As you should." Kolton paused for a moment, then said, "I'm sorry for the mess I've made. I didn't . . . I didn't expect this to happen. It never should have. I've broken your trust, so I wouldn't blame any of you if your loyalties have shifted."

Griff scoffed. "Kol, it's *us*. We've followed your lead for twenty years. We're not about to stop now just because you briefly went AWOL."

"But I *attacked* you."

"You did, but we understand why now." Jagger slowly relaxed his stance. "Past trauma isn't easily healed, something that I know all too well. You've been under a lot of stress for a long time, and it finally got the best of you. What matters is that you're facing it now and learning how to cope. We have your back, boss. We always will."

Emotion swelled through our bond. Sensing a shift in Kolton's demeanor, I gently pulled free of his hold so I could turn and snuggle against him. He heaved a sigh and cradled me close, his trembling slowly fading.

For several moments, no one said a word. And then, without warning, Vi moved. Not away, but *toward* us.

"*Vi*," both Griff and Jagger barked at the same time, lunging for her. She evaded their hands, slipping past as she beelined toward us with determination.

Kolton stiffened at her approach, but not like before. I could sense his fear. Not fear that she would hurt me, but fear that he would hurt *her*.

It's okay, I softly assured through our bond, keeping my arms around him in case he reacted badly.

When she was a handful of feet away, Vi stopped. I searched her face, stunned at how tired she looked, like she hadn't slept in days. I'd been so focused on Kolton that I hadn't noticed before. Hadn't seen how her brother's condition was affecting her.

With sudden realization, I knew what she'd come for. Knew what she needed. What they *both* needed.

I pulled away from Kolton again, this time releasing him completely.

Nora, he called through our bond, his fear spiking.

You can do this, I told him, standing just out of reach. *I believe in you, Kolton. I know you won't hurt her.*

He held perfectly still, so still that he didn't even blink. He stared at Vi, and she stared back. I waited, holding my breath. Clinging to hope. Daring to believe.

Please be okay, please be okay.

And then, without a sound, she threw herself at him. He froze as she squeezed him tightly, her face scrunched up like she was trying not to cry. He didn't react. Didn't do a thing.

For several long moments, he simply stood there and let her hug him. Simply stared at her in dead silence. No one moved or spoke. We watched and watched. And then he slowly lifted his arms. Slowly lifted them and . . .

Hugged her back.

The moment he did, she burst into tears. Great sobs left her, the sounds so heartbreaking that I couldn't hold back my own tears. Just like that, Kolton's fear and tension melted away. He clutched her to him, a lone tear sliding down his own cheek.

"I'm so sorry, Vi," he said in a strangled whisper. "I'm so very sorry."

"I thought you *left* me," she cried. "I thought you left me like *Mom* did."

"I'm so sorry," he repeated, kissing her brow.

"Never leave me again, Kolton."

"I won't, Vi."

"*Promise.*"

"I promise. Never again."

CHAPTER 15

NORA

The day of the funeral came all too quickly.

Werewolf funerals weren't anything like human ones. At least, not modern day ones. The bodies couldn't be stored in a morgue on account of our genetic differences. Traditional burial and cremation was too risky. The only way to keep our society hidden from humans was to care for our own, from birth to death.

Which was why funeral pyres were the way to go. Held in remote locations far from prying eyes, the deceased's pack watched over them while they burned, assuring there was nothing left for humans to find.

Problem was, we didn't have a body to burn today.

For all the pack knew, Kolton's body had been completely decimated by the raging house fire. Nothing remained, not even his teeth. Whether they believed the story I'd told the influential members was still uncertain. I was about to find out though.

"This is a bad idea," Jagger muttered under his breath, sticking close behind me as more and more members arrived.

I knew he didn't mean the funeral. We'd spent the past twenty-four hours preparing for this moment, hoping that Kolton would recover enough so we could call this whole thing off. But, despite the heartfelt embrace he'd shared with his sister, being around other males was still too difficult for him. Every time Griff or Jagger got too close to me, his protective instincts went haywire. True to his word, he'd managed not to attack them, but I could feel how hard it was to keep himself in check.

If his instincts were still triggered by his two closest friends, then being around the rest of his pack would be catastrophic. So we'd gone ahead with the plan, except for one minor adjustment—or rather, *major* adjustment.

We'd brought Kolton with us.

Long before the first members had started to arrive, we'd canvassed the area and found a spot far enough away that no one would pick up on his scent but close enough that I could still easily communicate with him through our bond. I knew allowing him to come was dangerous, but he'd been right earlier. Cutting him off from everyone wasn't going to help him heal. He had to learn control again, and keeping his distance from the funeral would be a great test of that.

I was about to remind Jagger of that when he added, "She's only six."

Oh. *That.*

Despite the growing darkness, my night vision allowed me to pick out each face. Vi and Griff had left earlier to bring Melanie and her nanny, Miss Gabby, to the funeral. Letting the youngest Rivers sibling attend was also a huge risk, but not having her here would raise all sorts of questions.

My eyes finally found her in the distance, rounding the secluded lake to join the rest of the gathering pack. She was sandwiched between Vi and Griff, who were holding her hands, and wearing a little black dress. I squinted to better see her face and was relieved to find her expression solemn. No tears, but at least she wasn't grinning and chattering away like usual.

"She's smart," I finally answered Jagger, making sure to speak so only he could hear. "She knows how to keep a secret."

Jagger grunted. "Let's just hope no one tries to talk to her."

Yeah. That could be bad. Considering what had happened to her mom, it would have been doubly cruel to keep the truth from her. She knew Kolton was alive but had been warned not to tell anyone. To her, this funeral was a game. If she pretended to be sad, she'd win the game. The prize? A new stuffed unicorn to replace the one she'd lost in the fire.

Refusing to stress over what the six-year-old might say during the funeral, I focused on the other arriving members. Miss Gabby wasn't too far behind them, and behind her was the Rivers' previous nanny, Mrs. Bailey. Not surprisingly, I could see the middle-aged lady chatting away with a young woman. One close to my own age, wearing a stylish pencil dress and a little black hat over her wavy, honey-brown hair. When she lifted her head, I immediately recognized who it was.

Jagger swore under his breath.

I glanced over my shoulder and found his gaze glued to the spot where I'd just been looking. His jaw was rock hard, his eyes faintly glowing yellow.

"Jagger," I murmured in warning.

With another soft curse, he blinked and the yellow faded. "What is *she* doing here?" he said, flicking me a glance as if I had something to do with it.

I shrugged and turned back around. "Brielle has always been very independent. She also doesn't like to miss out on stuff. I'm not all that surprised to see her here."

A quiet growl vibrated Jagger's chest. "But we *explicitly* told her that this was a pack-member-only event."

Stifling a laugh, I replied, "All the more reason for her to come.

She doesn't like being told what to do, and in her eyes, she *is* a member. Even before Arrow cut her, she thought so."

"Well, the pack won't look too kindly on an outsider attending Kolton's funeral. She might be on the verge of her first shift, but that doesn't automatically make her pack. Even if you tell them she's your best friend, they might try to test her. And if she doesn't submit, a fight could break out."

I chewed on my lip, suddenly nervous for my stubborn friend. "Hopefully it won't come to that, because she won't submit."

Jagger didn't respond, but his tension was palpable.

Everything okay?

The voice in my head immediately helped soothe my fraying nerves.

Melanie and Miss Gabby are here, I replied to Kolton, nodding as a few pack members walked past me. To my surprise, they dipped their heads in return, an open sign of respect. *And so is Brielle.*

Brielle? How is the pack handling her presence? Kolton didn't sound nearly as concerned as Jagger had.

Mrs. Bailey is talking to her.

That could be a good thing, if she makes a good first impression.

That's what I was thinking. And Brie is great at making friends.

Kolton chuckled. *Werewolves aren't the same as humans.*

No, but she won over you guys pretty easily.

True.

I won't ask her to leave. If the pack gets restless, I'll announce her intention to be initiated. And if any of the males bother her, I'm sure Jagger will intervene.

Amusement trickled through our bond. *You noticed that too?*

I fought to keep a straight face, nodding at another pack member. *He's hardly spoken two words to her, but there's no denying how attentive he is.*

Which is very unusual for him. Females don't often hold his attention.

A quiet snort left me. *Well, it's kind of hard to ignore Brielle.*

"Care to clue me in?" Jagger muttered.

My lips twitched, but I managed not to laugh. "Just keeping a certain someone in the loop."

"Well, tell him that you're kind of busy. We're about to start soon."

Just like that, any traces of humor vanished. Sure enough, I scanned the clearing and saw that roughly two hundred members had arrived. Even the youngest children were accounted for. I spotted Carter in the crowd and straightened when he looked my way. He nodded, confirming that we were about to start.

My nerves took a nosedive again. Thankfully, Vi and Griff arrived with Melanie then. The little girl broke free and ran the rest of the way toward me. I bent and scooped her up, relieved when all she did was fiercely hug my neck. After a moment, she buried her little face in my curls and whispered, "Am I doing good?"

"You're doing great, Melanie."

"I want my new Princess to be blue. Like your eyes. It's my favorite color now."

My heart warmed, and I hugged her a little tighter. "You got it."

Apparently satisfied that her demands had been heard, she pulled back and made grabby hands at Jagger. He immediately leaned forward and took her from me. As soon as my arms were empty, Vi stepped into them. She squeezed me tightly, murmuring, "How is he?"

"Good. Better than I expected. I didn't expect to see Brie here though."

Vi pulled back with a snort. "That girl is *definitely* not an omega."

"Tell me about it."

When she released me, Griff took her place, enveloping me in a bone-crushing hug. Good thing Kolton wasn't close enough to witness it or Griff would be losing his arms.

"He'd be so proud of you," he croaked, sniffling loudly.

I stifled an eye roll. "Seriously, Griff?"

"What?" Sniffle. "Just trying to sell it." Sniffle sniffle.

"Thanks, but you can let go now."

With one final squeeze, he stepped back, but not before loudly sniffling again. When he went to stand beside Vi and Jagger, I focused on the approach of my best friend. Mrs. Bailey and Miss Gabby had veered away to mingle with the gathering crowd, leaving Brielle to stand before me alone.

I didn't fail to notice the hush that fell over the clearing, their curiosity over the newcomer plain. Hopefully Brielle remembered that werewolves had excellent hearing. Then again, she *was* a werewolf now. Although she hadn't shifted yet, her senses should have begun to heighten.

Searching my face, she quietly said, "Are you okay?"

I nodded, feeling the sudden burn of tears against my eyelids. "Are you?"

She blinked several times, clearly struggling herself. "Yeah. I'm . . . I'm adjusting okay. I haven't felt the pull of the full moon yet."

"You still have a couple weeks."

"That's what Miss Gabby said." She fiddled with the gold cuff on her wrist, then blurted, "Are you mad?"

I immediately knew what she meant. She'd refused to leave when I'd asked her to, and the price had been her humanity. It could have been worse, but I'd never wanted this for her. Life as a werewolf wasn't easy.

"No," I said, meaning it. I just wanted my best friend back. "Are you?"

She quickly shook her head. "No. But I'm sorry that all of this happened. I wish . . . I wish I could have done something to help."

"Oh, Brie," I said when her lip quivered. Stepping forward, I pulled her into a hug. At my open acceptance of her, hushed whispers filled the air. They weren't hostile though. Just curious.

"There's quite a few teary-eyed females here," Brielle took the moment to whisper. "Which one's Barbie?"

I pressed my lips together so I wouldn't laugh. "Behave," I whispered back. "She's not a threat to me."

Not after I'd broken her nose.

"Still, I have this crazy itch to put her in her place. Is that a werewolf thing?"

Oh, boy. Brielle was definitely not an omega. Finding out where she fit into the pack's hierarchy would be interesting.

"Later," I said, kissing her cheek before pulling back. "But seriously though. Behave."

She flashed her dimples at me and went to stand beside Vi. When she walked past Jagger, she threw him a haughty look. He took her in without a word, his expression unreadable. Apparently, she was still upset at him for making her leave with Melanie and Miss Gabby during the fire. Not that he would apologize. He'd just been following orders, after all.

Setting aside their little drama for later, I focused on the other pack members. Most of them looked genuinely grief-stricken over the loss of their alpha. Only a few of them openly glared at me with suspicion, one of them being Jasmine Deveron, of course. Her broken nose had long since healed, but mascara now ran down her perfect face.

Sheesh. If looks could kill, I'd be dead many times over. There was no doubt who she blamed for Kolton's "death."

Thankfully, Carter approached me then, providing a welcome distraction. "Are you ready?" he asked, gesturing at the lake.

I glanced to where the pyre floated in the shallows. A rope kept the wooden structure from drifting away, tied securely to a stake buried in the grassy bank. Instead of Kolton's body resting on top, flowers decorated the surface. I'd picked them out myself, arranging them on the pyre with loving care.

The center was empty though, reserved for the body that should have been there. It reminded me of the nest I'd created, one that had so easily been consumed by fire. This one would too.

Releasing a shaky breath, I nodded at Carter that I was ready. He glanced at Jagger and Griff behind me, then dipped his head and stepped back. With a whispered word, Jagger set Melanie down and moved toward the lake with Griff. Despite both of them being fully clothed, they entered the frigid water, heading straight for the pyre. When they reached it, Carter pulled the stake free and released the rope. They grasped the wooden structure, one on each side, pushing it out onto the lake until they were waist-deep in the water.

As they stopped and faced the shore, I turned to Vi. She already held the torch that would light the pyre. She reached out to ignite the end and it lit up with a *whoosh*, bathing the faces around it in an orange glow. Stepping toward me, she offered me the torch. As I accepted it, her purple eyes misted, revealing that she too was feeling the emotion of the moment.

Did they perform a private funeral like this for their father? Was she thinking about him now?

Inhaling, I carefully lifted the torch and picked my way toward the water. Not bothering to remove my black ballet flats, I walked right in, my hot-blooded genetics allowing me to quickly acclimate to the cold temperature. When the water reached my knees, my flowy black skirt began to fan out around me. It soon sank beneath the surface, undulating against my legs like seaweed.

I kept going, keeping the torch above water level. When I neared the pyre, the water nearly reached my chest. My wet hair pulled at my scalp, and I reached up to remove the daisy I'd tucked into it earlier. I paused to stare at it, gently twisting the stem between two fingers. My eyesight suddenly blurred as tears filled my eyes.

Fiercely blinking them away, I said through our bond, *This is too real. It truly feels like this is your funeral.*

I know, sweetness, Kolton immediately replied. *I'm so sorry.*

Sniffing back more tears, I rose onto my tiptoes and carefully placed the daisy in the center of the pyre where his body should have been. *I need you to hold me after this.*

For as long as you need.

For some reason, that only made me more emotional. Biting my trembling lip, I glanced at Griff and Jagger. They both nodded their readiness. I blew out a shaky breath and took a step back, then tossed the torch onto the pyre. In seconds, the greedy fire spread across the wood, eating up my flower creation.

Jagger and Griff shoved the pyre out into deeper water, swimming with it for several moments before finally letting go. The structure continued to drift away, the flames now raging across its surface. I stayed where I was, caught in the fire's snare. It burned and burned, filling the air with acrid smoke. Reminding me of the house fire. Of the *witches*. Of how close this had nearly become reality.

Griff and Jagger swam back to join me in watching the pyre burn. They stood by my side like faithful guards, and I took comfort from their steady presence, reassuring myself that we'd all made it out alive. We hadn't walked away unscathed, but we would help each other heal, however long it took.

When the fire ran its course and started to die down, we finally turned and headed back to shore. As I emerged from the lake, I glanced up to find two hundred werewolves staring back at me, not a single dry eye among them. The expectant looks on their faces was unmistakable. Their leader was gone, and they needed reassurance. Needed verbal confirmation that I intended to fill his shoes. An impossible task, but one that I would rise to meet anyway.

With my wet dress still clinging to my body and water dripping into my shoes, I lifted my chin and said, "I know Alpha Rivers' death was sudden, and you're struggling to make sense of it. None of us could have foreseen this, and I share your grief over his tragic loss. But know that I'm here for you and will do everything in my power to be a good alpha. I—"

"You could *never* replace him, you man-stealing *whore!*" a shrill voice screeched, cutting off my speech.

Stunned, I watched as Jasmine pushed her way to the front of the crowd, her pretty face now twisted in ugly hatred. Vi growled and moved toward her, but I yanked up my hand for her to stop. She did, but still shook with barely-restrained anger.

"Really, Jasmine? You're going to disrespect Kolton's memory by causing a scene at his funeral?" I coolly said, hoping to defuse the moment before it could escalate.

But she was too far gone. Too *incensed*. She pointed a finger at me and screamed, "This is *your* fault. He wouldn't be dead right now if it wasn't for you. I know you forced him to marry you somehow. He only claimed and *mated* you because he felt obligated to. But he really wanted *me*. I've known him since we were children, and it was only a matter of time before he made *me* his wife. But then you came along and ruined *everything.*" She turned to the other pack members and spat, "I don't want her as my alpha. I *won't* call her alpha."

As several of the pack members began to restlessly stir and whisper amongst themselves, I knew that I had to act fast.

Nora, what's wrong? Kolton chose that moment to speak, no doubt picking up on my sudden influx of emotions.

Nothing. I've got this, I quickly replied, gesturing at Jagger and Griff to stay put as I strode forward.

At my approach, Jasmine whirled back around. Her eyes widened and she noticeably flinched, no doubt remembering our last altercation. But before she could retreat, I was in her face.

"Are you challenging me, Jasmine?" I said, speaking loud enough for everyone to hear. "Is that what this pathetic rant is? A challenge for *alpha?*"

She blinked rapidly, struggling to hold eye contact. "N-no," she stammered, her pulse racing with fear. "I'm not challenging you." I was about to relax a little, until she said, "But *he* will."

She looked to the left and I followed her line of sight. Rounding the lake was a lone figure, lean and tall, with a shock of white-blond hair.

Ice filled my veins when I recognized who it was.

Arrow.

CHAPTER 16

NORA

I was almost in too much shock to react. When Griff and Jagger stormed toward Arrow, I was barely able to stop them in time.

"Stand down," I barked, ignoring their sharp looks. "This isn't your fight."

As I stepped away from the crowd to await Arrow's arrival, Jagger changed direction to stand beside me. "It isn't yours either," he hissed in my ear, his worry clear.

"But it is," I quietly replied, keeping my gaze locked on the back-stabbing alpha I'd once stupidly trusted. "I'm the only one standing between him and his goal to destroy this family. I won't let him become Midnight Pack's new alpha. Not without a fight."

Jagger opened his mouth to say more, then stepped back with a muttered curse as Carter hurried up to me. "Is that Arrow Pemberton, the alpha of Northwood Pack?"

"Yes."

Carter clicked his tongue in disapproval. "We haven't finished preparing you for the Alpha Ceremony, but we can't turn him away if he wishes to challenge you."

A swallow got stuck in my throat. "We're doing the Alpha Ceremony *now?*"

"The timing is unconventional, but with challengers already arriving, we have little choice. At least this way, you'll only have to face one challenger today. Unless more arrive, of course."

More? Okay, I was officially starting to freak out now. How did Arrow even know we'd be here? Already guessing the answer to that question, it took everything in me not to turn around and break Jasmine's nose all over again. If I did, I'd no doubt pummel her until every bone in her body was broken.

The pack probably wouldn't respect me as their new alpha if I did that, despite how good it would make me feel. Their restlessness grew the closer Arrow came. They were no doubt sizing up their possible new alpha. I couldn't help but wonder how many of them were silently rooting for him instead of me.

Shoving the unsettling thought aside, I focused on maintaining a calm demeanor. Anything less could be construed as weakness. Arrow appeared calm as well. Almost *too* calm. There was a slight swagger to his steps, as if his confidence had been restored with the news of Kolton's death.

I kept my hands loose at my sides, when what I really wanted to do was ball them into tight fists. After how he'd played us and stolen Brielle's humanity, the desire for revenge was strong. The witches might have been the ones to attack us, but he was the one who'd sold us out to them.

When he neared, a familiar heat inside of me surged up.

It's okay, I told Storm, feeling her anger ripple through our connection. *Let me handle this.*

You mean to fight him?

I'm hoping it won't come to that, but, yes. If I have to.

You will need me.

The pack can't see us shift. Most of them still don't know that we're different.

I don't care. Your safety is more important.

Arrow arrived before I could say more, coming to stand a little closer than what would be considered appropriate. Carter backed up a step, but Jagger did the opposite, surging forward to growl at Arrow.

Arrow didn't even glance at him. "Call off your guard dog, Nora," he said, keeping his ice blue eyes trained on me. "I've only come to talk."

I lifted a skeptical brow at him. "Talk? Maybe you failed to notice, but we're kind of in the middle of a funeral right now. If you wanted to talk, you should have asked Jasmine to pass me her phone."

My accusation was clear. A wave of fresh whispering swept over the pack.

Arrow's lips twitched with faint amusement. "She's been very helpful to me these past few weeks. I plan to raise her status in the pack once I become alpha."

I barked a laugh, and his amusement vanished. "You're still as delusional as ever, I see. You can't become alpha. Not with me still alive."

Pushing past Jagger, Arrow stepped even closer to me, crowding my personal space. I raised a hand, silently asking Jagger to stand down. He obeyed, but he didn't back away. As Arrow peered down at me, I lifted my chin and stared him dead in the eye, refusing to back down.

After several tense moments, he quietly chuckled, his amusement returning. "That's where you're wrong, Nora. I don't have to fight you, not if you willingly submit to me. My intentions haven't changed. You know what I want. Even though you still reek of *him*, I will take you as my mate. We can lead this pack together as a bonded pair."

I stared at him, utterly floored that he still thought I would accept him as a mate. Curling my lip back, I quietly growled, "That will *never* happen, Arrow. I'd rather die than become your mate."

His mouth pulled down into a heavy frown, but I wasn't finished yet. Stepping closer so that we were nearly nose-to-nose, I hissed, "I know you still want to hurt this family—*my* family—and I won't let that happen. What's more, I'm pregnant. Kolton's seed, his *child*, is in my belly. You can't cleanse me of him. He will always be a part of me, and I will ensure his legacy lives on. So either fight me or get the hell out of my territory, because my answer is *no*. No to you. No to your agenda. You threatened my family, and I want nothing to do with you."

With my confession, the pack's whispering reached a crescendo. I caught several surprised exclamations but didn't dare look away from Arrow. His shock was quickly morphing into furious, deep-seated disgust. I'd hoped to catch him off guard with the news of my pregnancy. To deter him from pursuing me. But I was pretty sure that plan had just backfired.

He looked about ready to kill me now.

"You're pregnant?" he seethed, noticeably trembling. "You're pregnant with that devil's *filth?*"

At that, Jagger lost it. With a roar, he charged Arrow before I could stop him. Lightning quick, Arrow whirled and whipped out his hand. The move was so unexpected that Jagger couldn't block him in time. He came to a dead halt as Arrow grabbed his throat in a vicious hold.

My calm facade shattered.

"Arrow, *stop!*" I yelled. Out of the corner of my eye, I saw Griff surge toward him. When Jagger made an awful choking noise, he froze.

A manic laugh burst from Arrow. "You shouldn't have done that, Nora. You shouldn't have allowed him to *impregnate* you."

Nora? Tell me what's happening. Something doesn't feel right.

The urgency in Kolton's voice threatened to undo me, but I kept my sole focus on the madman before me. "Let Jagger go, Arrow. Your fight is with *me*, not him."

He whipped his head around to look at me, and I nearly gasped at the intense glow in his eyes. "You forget what my *mission* is," he snarled in a voice I'd heard only once before. *Zuriel.* "My fight will always be with *them*."

True panic beat at my chest then. Arrow was losing it. He was going to reveal his secret—*our* secret—in front of the whole pack. And if I didn't do something, he could very well kill Jagger, then go after the others. Maybe even me.

I had to shift. Had to reveal Storm's true form. It was the only way.

NORA! Kolton bellowed this time, picking up on my panic.

Right as I made my decision and was about to call on Storm, she blurted out, *Arrow is here and about to unleash his fury on your family. We need you here right away, Kolton.*

"Storm!" I cried in dismay, but it was too late.

Kolton's roar filled my head, so loud that I gasped and covered my ears. But apparently, I wasn't the only one who had heard it. Arrow's face went white as a sheet. The burning fire in his eyes flickered and dimmed, before sputtering out completely. He blinked as if coming out of a trance.

"What have you done?" he whispered, his expression now one of abject horror.

Another roar filled my head, this time even louder. I flinched and so did Arrow. A flurry of voices suddenly rose into the air.

"Alpha Rivers. That was *Alpha Rivers.*"

Cries of confusion and excitement bombarded my senses, but I kept my gaze locked on Arrow. Despite my growing fear, I forced my lips into a wicked smirk. "That's right, Arrow. Kolton's still alive.

I would run if I were you. My mate has been *extra* protective lately."

He violently shook at the news. I stopped breathing, all of my focus on stopping him if he tried to kill Jagger. One swift jerk of his hand was all it would take. With Zuriel so close to the surface, his strength was amplified. Jagger was strong, but he wasn't allowing himself to shift. Arrow had the upper hand. Literally.

Unable to hold still a second longer, I hissed, "Kill him and I will make your life a living hell, Arrow. I don't care what it takes. I will *end* you."

His trembling increased. Sweat beaded his brow, the lines of his body stretched taut. He looked ready to explode. I stared and stared at him, burning my threat into his retinas. Demanding he stand down. After a moment that lasted an eternity, his gaze finally wavered. In a blink, he released Jagger. As Jagger stumbled back, Griff rushed forward to lend his support.

"This isn't over, Nora," Arrow said, nervously glancing at the woods behind me. "I will get what I want, one way or the other."

With that, he whirled and took off. Every inch of me ached to go after him. To eliminate the threat he posed to my family. But the sound of someone crashing through the woods behind me kept me rooted to the spot. Any second now. Any second and Kolton would come flying from those woods like a bat out of hell.

Normally, I'd be relieved. But there was nothing normal about this moment. This moment was pure pandemonium, and it was about to get worse. So much worse. Two hundred werewolves stood between me and him. It didn't matter that they were his pack. If the darkness inside him saw them as a threat, then he could attack. He could go *feral* again.

I had to stop him somehow. Had to—

Too late.

He materialized from the trees like a dark phantom, all fury and power and deadly intent. Dressed in black, he blended into the night, except for his eyes. His eyes were yellow, bright and piercing as they burned a path through the crowd. Several of the pack members shrank back with startled cries, while the rest froze, struck dumb by the sight of their alpha come back to life.

When he kept coming, clearly on the warpath, I stepped forward. "Kolton."

Like a heat-seeking missile, his gaze shot to me and locked on.

That's it, I softly coaxed through our bond. *Keep your eyes on me. Only me.*

A great shudder racked his large frame. He prowled forward, his focus solely on me as he cut through the pack. They scrambled out of the way, creating a path for him. I held still as he approached, pushing calm energy toward him through our bond.

Don't worry about the others. Just focus on me, I continued to quietly soothe. *You're almost there. Almost—*

"Hey," I said when he finally reached me. His hands lifted and began to thoroughly inspect me for injury. "I'm okay. We're all okay."

He continued to run his hands over my body, reassuring himself that I was indeed unscathed. No one moved or spoke. They simply watched in shock and bewilderment as their alpha feverishly checked over his mate like a man possessed. Despite the attention, I didn't stop him. Knowing for himself that I was safe was the only way he would calm down. At least he hadn't attacked anyone. Yet.

After a long moment, his frantic movements slowed, then stopped completely. He blew out a ragged breath and straightened, but the fierce glow in his eyes remained. "Where is he?"

"Gone. He ran when he heard your approach."

Frustration and anger pulsed through our bond. "How did this happen? How did Arrow know about the funeral and this location?"

"Jasmine told him," Vi spoke up. "She's been in contact with him, feeding him information. Even before this."

Kolton went preternaturally still.

"Kolton," I quietly warned, laying my hand on his arm. It began to tremble under my touch. *Stay calm. If you confront her, you could lose control.*

Despite his trembling, he didn't move, keeping his gaze locked on me. But then Jasmine made the terrible mistake of speaking.

"I did this for you, Kolton," she had the audacity to say, daring to take a step forward. "Nora doesn't belong in this pack. I tried to make you see that, but she blinded you. I wanted to honor your memory by having her removed, but Arrow tricked me. He only wanted *her*, the little slut who made you impregnate her. I—"

"*Enough.*"

The loudly spoken command echoed across the clearing like a shot. Before I could stop him, Kolton twisted around and stalked toward Jasmine. Catching sight of his glowing eyes, she shrank back with a startled gasp. The pack members behind her retreated, leaving her alone to face their irate alpha.

She blinked up at him, her blue eyes round with fear. "Kolton, I—"

"Not another word." His voice was like a slap. She flinched back, then snapped her mouth shut. He stared at her for a long moment, long enough that she lost the ability to hold eye contact and dropped her gaze. Only then did he quietly say, "You knew that Arrow couldn't be trusted. You knew what he did to my sister and what his father did to my father. You knew that we broke ties with his pack, and yet, you still chose to work with him. You didn't do this for me, Jasmine. You did this for the only person you truly care about. Yourself."

She made a pathetic whimpering sound, but he wasn't finished yet.

Lowering his voice another octave, he said, "It's *you* who doesn't belong, Jasmine. I've allowed your self-entitlement and jealousy to go unchecked for far too long, but no longer. You've insulted my wife for the last time. Pack your bags. I want you out of my territory by morning. You are no longer welcome in Midnight Pack."

When he turned, effectively dismissing her, she fell to her knees with a loud wail. Kolton's expression was set like stone, his eyes still burning fiercely as he set his sights on Carter next. The dominant male went poker straight, but to his credit, he didn't flinch under the alpha's intense gaze.

"See to it that Jasmine Deveron follows through with my order," Kolton told him. My confusion over why he would give Carter this task and not Jagger or Griff didn't last long. It was a test. A test of *loyalty*. He wanted to see if the influential members of his pack would still follow him.

After a tense moment, Carter finally dipped his head and said, "Right away, Alpha." Before heading toward Jasmine though, he sent me a look. The message was clear. I had a *lot* of explaining to do. A gut feeling told me that we could just as quickly lose their support if we didn't give them the answers they sought.

As Carter led a still-weeping Jasmine away, the rest of the pack nervously shifted on their feet. Kolton took the time to scan the crowd, making sure to meet the eyes of every single one of them. Most of them quickly ducked their heads, cowed by his intensity. I doubted they'd ever seen him like this before. He was barely in control, seconds away from snapping if anyone dared step out of line.

The air thickened with tension. Only when it was stifling did he finally cut through it, saying, "Does anyone else wish to challenge me or my mate?" He stood tall, allowing the silence to stretch. Then, "Good. Then go home. The funeral's over."

They immediately began to disperse, returning the way they'd come without a sound. I watched them go, making sure none of them tried to talk to him. He was clearly done. I could feel how tense he was through our bond, like a rubber band stretched to its breaking point. One wrong move could set him off.

Waiting until the majority of the pack was a safe distance away, I quietly said without taking my eyes off Kolton, "You all right, Jagger?"

"Yeah. Already healing."

With his back still facing us, Kolton didn't move a muscle.

"Good. I think you all should leave, then."

"Is the game over?" Melanie piped up, oblivious to the tension.

"Yes, Mellie," Griff replied. "The game's over."

"Did I win?"

"You definitely won," Vi said. "Let's go get your prize. You wanted a purple unicorn, right?"

"No, *blue.*"

"Are you sure? Because purple is the best color."

The two continued to banter as the group moved away, effectively blocking Kolton from Melanie's view. Discussing her new unicorn did the trick though, and she didn't once ask for her brother. In no time, their voices faded, until it was finally just the two of us.

As soon as the coast was clear, I called out to him. At the sound of his name on my lips, he full-body shuddered. "Kolton," I called again, but he didn't turn. I approached him, watching for any signs of aggression. There was none. He was frozen, as if he'd lost the ability to move. "Kolton, it's okay. They're all gone. You can let go now."

When all he did was shudder again, I carefully placed my hand on his back. Nothing happened. He didn't even flinch. Growing worried, I went around him and peered up at his face. His eyes were tightly squeezed shut.

"Hey," I whispered, reaching up to touch his cheek. The second I made contact, his hand jerked up and caught my wrist. The hold didn't hurt, so I lifted my free hand and touched his other cheek. He caught that wrist too but didn't pull my hands away. With them still touching his face, I focused on pushing healing energy toward him. After a moment, my fingers began to glow, lighting up the night.

His eyes flew open, locking onto mine. They still burned yellow, but not as brightly as before.

It's okay, Shadow, I said through our connection. *You can let him go now. Thank you for helping him.*

Just like that, the fiery glow dimmed to a dark amber. Kolton blinked several times before refocusing on me. His breathing suddenly sped up, along with his heart rate.

He opened his mouth to speak, but nothing came out.

When his panic flushed through me, I started murmuring soft words of comfort, reassuring him that everything was fine. That no one was hurt. That he'd done good. When his panic remained, I pulled his head down and kissed him. Gently. Using the connection to infuse him with calm.

Within seconds, he was kissing me back. Not gently, but with a desperation that took my breath away. One moment, I was standing, and the next, I was pressed against the nearest tree. As I felt his arousal through the delicate material of my dress, my own desperation kicked in. I reached between us and wrestled with the button on his jeans. When I felt him spring free, I eagerly grabbed his hardened length.

He groaned against my mouth and reached for the hemline of my skirt, hiking it up to my waist. With one swift move, he tore off my underwear and positioned himself at my entrance. As he thrust in all the way to the hilt, I threw back my head and moaned. He didn't waste any time. He began to thrust in and out like a madman, sending pleasure rocketing through me.

I didn't dare slow him down. Didn't *want* to. I was as desperate for him as he was for me. This evening could have gone so horribly wrong, and the need to reconnect was all-consuming. I clung to him as he drove inside me over and over. Each thrust was like a balm, soothing our frayed nerves better than any words could.

Even when I felt his panic begin to fade, he didn't slow. His need for me was powerful, and I gladly gave myself to him, keeping up with his feverish pace. Faster than I thought possible, my body tensed, on the verge of release. Kolton felt it and pumped even faster. Harder. Until I couldn't hold on any longer.

My orgasm ripped through me, and I screamed into the night. Kolton joined me a second later, roaring so loudly that the tree at my back shook.

Afterward, as we struggled to catch our breath, Kolton nuzzled my cheek and whispered, "Again."

I huffed a weak laugh, then nodded and whispered back, "Yes. Again."

CHAPTER 17

KOLTON

My hands shook while I sat on the closed toilet lid, unable to move.

Some moments, I could function just fine. While others, I could barely string two words together. The nightmare came and went like a raging fever, leaving me weak and dazed.

She's okay, she's okay, she's okay, I reminded myself, a mantra that I'd repeated more times than I could count over the past week.

I could hear Nora in the adjoining bedroom, getting ready for the day. She'd wanted to head back with the rest of the family to our Albany penthouse. Brielle still had unfinished business here, and Nora wanted to support her friend when she met with her parents. I'd agreed, if only because I couldn't bear to be parted from her, even for a few hours.

I had business of my own to tend to. Business that couldn't be put on hold for much longer. The others had tried their best to do damage control this past week, but there were some things that only I could handle. Now that I'd come back from the dead, those responsibilities had once again fallen squarely onto my shoulders. Words couldn't describe how grateful I was to Nora for carrying the load while I couldn't, but it was time for me to reinstate myself as the alpha of Midnight Pack.

"Kolton?"

At the sound of her concerned voice through the closed bathroom door, I fisted my hands to hide their shaking.

"I'll be out in a minute," I called, forcing my tone to remain light. Collected. Calm. The exact opposite of how I was feeling.

She was silent for a long moment, then, "Do you need anything?"

"No, but thanks for asking. Go on ahead to breakfast without me. I'll just be a minute."

Worry flitted through our bond. She wasn't fooled by my words. Still, she said, "Okay, but don't forget that I'm here for you. We all are. We know you still need time to heal."

"Thanks," I managed to say before my throat sealed shut. A big part of me still couldn't believe that they'd chosen to keep following me. That they'd brushed off this past week as a mild inconvenience.

I didn't think the rest of the pack would be so understanding though. I'd already received several calls since last night's funeral, enough that I'd had to turn off my phone. But I couldn't ignore them forever. I owed them an explanation, as well as an apology. What I would tell them, I didn't know. They would want to know more about Arrow Pemberton's arrival, that was for sure. But explaining what had caused the house fire and my disappearance wouldn't be so easy.

I'd already screwed up last night by exposing a hint of Shadow to them. Eyes that glowed yellow without a full moon present weren't normal. But if I hadn't allowed him to help me, my control would have definitely snapped.

The dilemma of safeguarding our secret versus keeping the pack's respect weighed heavily on my mind. I didn't know how to juggle both anymore. Something had to give, and I didn't know which one to choose.

Several minutes later, I finally found the strength to leave the bathroom and face my immediate dilemma: joining my family for breakfast like a normal person. The bedrooms were on the second floor of the penthouse, so I was able to listen to the chatter below while I quietly slipped into the hallway and made for the stairs.

Nora and I had arrived later than the rest, staying beside the lake until well-past midnight. I'd filled myself up on her, becoming drunk on her touch and luscious body. We'd made love several times, until she'd grown exhausted and could barely hold her head up. My instincts had screamed at me to keep her in those woods all to myself. To ignore life's responsibilities in favor of protecting my pregnant wife.

It was she who had talked some sense back into me. Who'd reminded me that our family needed protecting too. It was clear to me now that Arrow wasn't going to give up trying to tear this family apart. He'd already convinced one pack member to betray us. Who knew what he planned to do next.

And then there was Keisha. I couldn't forget her parting words. Her *threat*. I'd ignored her threats once before. I wouldn't make that mistake again. She might be weakened without her coven, but she was still a danger to us, especially Nora.

She's okay, she's okay, she's okay, I recited as a fresh wave of panic rose up. I could hear her down below, laughing at something Griff had said. I took a moment to savor the sound, knowing that it would end the second I arrived.

Sure enough, when I started to descend the open staircase, the conversation died a sudden death. Even Melanie stopped chattering away about her new stuffed unicorn at the sound of my approach. My hands began to shake again. By sheer force of will, I made it to the bottom, then turned to face the six individuals sitting at the dining table.

They were already watching me, their expressions varying. Besides Nora, I hadn't spoken to any of them since before the funeral. Overwhelmed by their expectant looks, like they wanted me to say something, my trembling increased.

Without a word, Nora rose from her seat and approached me. I focused solely on her, like I was drowning and she was the life raft. Glancing at my shaking hands, she reached out and laced her fingers through mine. With a reassuring squeeze, she said, "Come on. We saved some breakfast for you."

Swallowing, I nodded and allowed her to lead me toward the table. So focused on her, I didn't notice the seating arrangement right away. But as she directed me toward the head of the table, I saw that Vi and Brielle were seated on either side. I breathed a little easier, grateful for their forethought. When I pulled out the chair and sat, Nora immediately positioned herself on my lap.

I blinked at her in surprise, but she simply handed me a plate of food as if sitting on my lap at mealtimes was completely normal. Picking up her own plate, she settled against me and began to eat without missing a beat.

"Now that we're all back together," she said around a mouthful of scrambled eggs, "I thought it would be smart to hold a meeting. Things have been a bit chaotic lately, and I want to make sure we're all on the same page. So, what are your most pressing thoughts and concerns?"

I continued to blink at her, struck dumb by how effortlessly she'd taken charge.

"Our phones have been ringing off the hook," Vi was the first to speak, directing her words toward Nora. "I'm pretty sure every member of the pack has tried to contact us in the last twelve hours."

Griff barked a laugh. "Yeah, because Kolton crashed his own funeral. So epic."

Nora nodded. "We'll have to answer them soon, but I was hoping we could pay a visit to Brielle's parents this afternoon. They need to know about her upcoming transition and what to expect."

"Good idea," Jagger replied from across the table.

Quiet until now, Brielle straightened in her seat as if she'd been poked. "Yeah, I should get that over with. I'll call them and make sure they're home first."

Nora picked up a sausage from her plate, then abruptly set it down. When she placed her plate back on the table with a quiet moan, my instincts went on high alert.

"Nora." I set my own plate down and shifted her on my lap so I could see her face. Alarm bells rang in my head when I saw how pale she looked. "Nora, what's wrong?"

She didn't respond, except to purse her lips and place a hand on her stomach.

"Morning sickness, bro," Griff said with a snort. "It's your turn to hold her hair back this time. I don't handle puke very well."

Nora threw him a glare. So did Vi, who said, "You're the pack *healer*, Griffin."

"So? I can heal and still be grossed out by certain bodily fluids. Not all of them, of course." He threw Vi a wink, and her mouth snapped shut with a *click*.

"I still can't believe you're going to have a *baby*," Brielle said to Nora, excitement replacing her nervous energy from moments before.

Mellie looked up from her big blue unicorn. "What baby?"

"Nora and Kol are pregnant," Vi quietly explained to her.

Mellie's face scrunched up in confusion. "Boys can have babies?"

Griff guffawed and leaned forward in his chair. "Has no one told this child about the birds and the bees yet? You see, Mellie, when two people love each other very much—"

"*Griff*," Vi snapped. He stopped with a laugh. Sighing, she said to

Mellie, "Nora is the one who's having the baby."

Mellie's eyes widened. "Am I going to be a big sister?"

"Aunt, actually."

Her face scrunched up again.

As conversation continued to circulate the table, I felt myself slowly relax. Everything about this moment was familiar to me. It was comforting. *Safe.* And as Nora's nausea subsided and she settled against me once more, I relaxed even further. Maybe my mate's touch wasn't the only thing that could help me heal. Being around family again felt good. Felt *normal.* Maybe that meant I was returning to my normal self as well.

With that in mind, I let the last of my tension go and focused on enjoying this precious moment with my family.

Not surprisingly, Brielle's parents didn't take the news of their daughter's impending werewolf transformation very well.

"What is this? Some kind of *cult?*" her father sputtered, glaring at me like I had personally recruited and brainwashed his daughter. "Give me one good reason why I shouldn't call the cops right now."

If he'd been a werewolf, I would have taken this moment to put him in his place. To remind him of who he was talking to. But since he was human, I had to follow *human* protocol and ignore my instincts. Maybe Nora had been right. Maybe I should have remained in the truck. The walls of the Lacroix's charming suburban home were slowly closing in.

Before I could speak and possibly make things worse, Brielle said, "You're not going to call the police, Dad. If you did, they might take me in for questioning and find out what I am."

"What you *are* is our daughter. Our *human* daughter!" he shouted. Brielle's mom placed a hand on her husband's arm, only for him to pull away in frustration. "I know we raised you to think for yourself, Brielle, but this is utter nonsense. Werewolves don't exist, just like *BigFoot* doesn't exist. I believe in facts, not fantasy. I thought you felt the same."

"I *do* feel the same," she cried, clearly upset that her parents didn't believe her. "But this isn't fantasy. This is *real*."

"Then show us," Brielle's mom cut in, trying her best to keep the peace. "Prove that you are indeed a . . . a werewolf."

Brielle shook her head. "I *can't*, Mom."

"See?" her dad butted in, his face alight as if he'd won the argument. "You can't prove it. That means it's not true."

Brielle threw Nora a helpless look. Quiet until now, Nora calmly said, "I know this is a lot to take in, Mr. and Mrs. Lacroix, but the reason why Brie can't show you is because it's too dangerous. The first few times a werewolf shifts are when they're most feral. Humans will look like prey to them, even their friends and family. But with time, they learn how to control their instincts. Brielle will too. I'll make sure of it."

Brielle's father stared at Nora like she'd lost her mind. I felt a growl push at my throat, but quickly swallowed the sound. Shadow would usually be encouraging a little violence by now, but he was still fairly subdued. He'd come to my aid when I'd needed him at the funeral, but I knew he was still licking his wounds. I never thought a day would come when I actually missed his radical notions, but I did. I truly missed having his nonsensical thoughts banging around in my head.

Mr. Lacroix's attention left Nora and focused on Brielle once more, allowing my instincts to settle a bit. "You're moving back home with us. You're clearly caught up in something, and we're going to help you get out of it. We'll hire the best therapists. I don't care how expensive it will be. We're not going to lose our only daughter to an insane group of fanatics."

When he reached for her, she yanked her arm back. "No, Dad. I'm . . . I'm not coming back home. That's why I'm here today. To tell you that I'll be staying with my new pack. I'm not quitting my job or anything, but I can't stay here on my own. Not right now, at least. Nora's right. I've seen firsthand what a newly-shifted werewolf is capable of. It would kill me if I hurt either of you, so I need to go somewhere safe. Somewhere I can learn how to control my new instincts."

Her parents gaped at her in shock, too speechless for words.

After a moment, Brielle moved forward and pulled her mother into a fierce hug. "I love you both. *So* much." Sniffling, she released her mom and turned to her dad. At the lost look on his face, she whispered, "Oh, Daddy," and wrapped her arms around him. "Don't worry about me. I'll be okay, I promise. You can call me day or night. As soon as it's safe, I'll come back to visit."

She pulled away again, sniffing back tears. Staring at them both as if memorizing their faces, she turned for the door.

Nora quickly followed her, but I lingered to say, "I'll keep her safe. You have my word."

Unfortunately, my words had the opposite effect I was going for. Panic filled Mr. Lacroix's eyes and he shoved past me to dash after his daughter. "Brielle, *no!* Don't do this!"

Mrs. Lacroix hurried after her husband, and I slowly followed with a weary sigh. Allowing humans to know of the supernatural world always posed a risk, but most cared about their transformed loved ones enough to stay silent. Exposing them to the authorities would only hurt them, and instinctively, humans seemed to understand that.

Most of them, anyway.

I'd had to put out a few fires over the years, but I was used to extinguishing rumors. Being a notorious billionaire also helped, but I tried not to use my money as a weapon. My only goal was to keep my pack safe, even if doing so severed the connection to their past lives.

For Brielle's sake though, I hoped her parents eventually came around. If not, we would become her new family.

Despite their dismayed cries, neither of her parents stopped us from entering the truck. As we started to pull away though, their pleas finally got to Brielle. She curled forward in the backseat with a sob, placing her hands over her face. From beside her, Nora wrapped her arms around her best friend, murmuring soft words of comfort.

I focused on the road again, emotion tightening my throat as a desire to see my own mother hit me. She might not be the same person anymore, but I still loved her deeply. Still longed for the connection that only a parent and child could have. And now that I'd experienced a taste of the brokenness she lived with every day, that longing had only grown.

What if her condition could be reversed somehow? What if she could begin to heal like I had?

I understood how fragile the mind was now. How easily it could be broken. But with the proper care, it could be mended. Maybe not the same as before, but the shattered pieces could be put back together again, forming a new awareness. A new appreciation for life and all it had to offer. My mother may have lost her mate, but she still had her children. Still had *family*.

Maybe I could somehow remind her of that. Maybe I could help her see that life was still worth living. That she could feel love again, feel *whole* again, if she only allowed herself to.

When we arrived back at the penthouse, Jagger was the first to greet us. At the grim look on his face, my instincts went on high alert.

"What's wrong?" I questioned, unconsciously reaching for Nora. The moment she was tucked against my side, my instincts started to settle.

Until Jagger replied, "There's been an attack."

CHAPTER 18

NORA

He was struggling.

Just *talking* to Jagger was hard for Kolton, let alone focusing on the dire news. But it had only been a week. One week since he'd shattered into pieces. All things considered, he was doing amazing.

I could feel his frustration at himself though. He wasn't used to being anything but calm, cool, and collected at all times.

When his hands began to shake, I silently slipped my fingers through his, lending my support. The news was awful. A member of Midnight Pack was dead, and another was missing. The victims were an older mated couple that had been with the pack for years. As with a large majority of the pack, they lived just outside of Lake Placid. No one had witnessed the attack, but according to Buck, it looked like the male had died trying to protect his wife.

"There's something else," Jagger said, a hesitant edge to his voice.

"What is it?" I asked, drawing his gaze to me.

He pursed his lips. Then blurted, "Buck smelled magic at the site. We think a magic-user was responsible for the attack."

Kolton went still as stone.

I felt the blood drain from my face, but managed to whisper, "Keisha?"

"Or Arrow," Griff said, joining us while still giving me and Kolton plenty of space. "He was pretty upset when he left the funeral, and we don't know if he's still on pack land. He could be out for revenge."

"But why would he attack a random couple from the pack?" I questioned. "He doesn't have anything against normal werewolves."

Griff shrugged. "He's insane. You never know with him."

True. He was unpredictable. But this seemed more like something Keisha would do. It had only been a week since she'd lost her coven though. Could she really have recovered this quickly? Gained *allies* this quickly? She was blind, after all. Even with her third eye, she'd need help getting around, especially through portals.

There was always a chance that this was simply a random attack, but I doubted it. Too much had happened recently for this to be a coincidence.

Before I could speculate too long, I said, "I want to visit the crime scene. See if we can find some more clues as to who did this."

Kolton's fingers tightened around mine, but he didn't utter a sound.

Jagger crossed his arms over his chest, a furrow bisecting his brows. "I'm not sure that's a good idea. Whoever the killer is, they could be waiting for an opportunity to get you out in the open."

A low growl vibrated Kolton's chest. Through our bond, he said, *You're not going alone.*

I looked up at him and met his intense gaze. "I won't be going alone. I think we should *all* go. The pack needs us. They're no doubt confused and scared, and it's our duty to protect them. What better way to regain their trust and support by personally trying to find out who did this?"

He searched my face, no doubt feeling how calm I was. Sure, I would much rather hide from a killer than track one down, but after all that had happened this past week, we needed to earn the pack's respect again by showing them that we still had their backs. Personal problems aside, we couldn't afford any more rumors. We were already swimming in them as it was.

After a long moment, Kolton released a quiet sigh and nodded, the intensity in his eyes fading. "Okay, then. We'll go right now. And someone should tell Carter and the other influential members to meet us there. It's time I answered a few questions."

Word of the attack had spread like wildfire.

By the time we got to the site, there were at least a couple dozen pack members milling about the grounds. Carter and the other influential members had arrived before us, and it was clear that they were as shaken up by what had happened as the rest of them.

The second they saw the Rivers' truck and Jeep pull onto the rural property, they hurried over to us.

Let me know if things become too much, I spoke to Kolton through our bond, watching as he slowly released his grip on the truck's steering wheel and killed the engine.

He nodded without looking at me, his gaze on the approaching pack members. *I will. As long as you remain by my side, I should be okay.*

With that, he shoved his door open and jumped from the truck. Before I could do the same, he strode around the vehicle and opened my door. The second I hopped out, he snagged my waist and tucked me against his side. Jagger and Griff joined us, along with Vi, Brielle, and even Melanie. We had no intention of letting the six-year-old see the dead body, but we didn't want to leave anyone behind either.

The pack needed to see us as a united front, now more than ever. Showing up all together like this was more reassuring than words ever could be.

When several of the pack members were only a few yards away, Kolton surprised me by saying, "My mate is pregnant with my unborn child. I would ask that you all keep your distance from her during this time."

Like magic, every single one of them halted in their tracks. I blinked, even more surprised to see the understanding on each of their faces.

Smart. The old "my wife is pregnant" trick, I praised Kolton through our bond, hiding a smirk when I felt his amusement.

"I know you all have questions, and I'll do my best to answer them," he continued, "but I want to see the body first."

Several nodded and stepped aside, but a few hesitated. I couldn't blame them. They'd thought their alpha was dead less than twenty-four hours ago, and now he was demanding their obedience as if nothing had happened. Kolton apparently didn't feel the same though. When he stepped forward and they didn't immediately create space, a warning growl rumbled in his chest.

That did the trick. They scurried out of the way, their eyes wide as he stalked past with me still glued to his side. I didn't mind—for now. But I didn't want to be attached to him like a barnacle forever. At least he wasn't attacking anyone. Baby steps.

We'd just made it past the hovering crowd when one split off from the rest and began to tail us.

"Oh, my dear boy." I recognized the boisterous voice of Mrs. Bailey without turning around. "The surprises never cease. My heart can barely take it. A *baby*? Heaven be praised, there is no better news. A pity that it was followed by such sorrow. Daisy Wickham is a close friend of mine. We were supposed to meet for breakfast this morning. When she didn't show, I came by the house and found Robert's body in their front yard. Poor man. I can only imagine what happened to

Daisy, but I don't think she's dead. The only blood I could smell was her husband's. I didn't believe you were dead either, truth be told. Even at your funeral, I said to myself, 'Marianne Bailey, that boy is *not* dead. He's too strong to be taken out by a measly house fire.' And I was right. I knew you couldn't possibly—"

"Thank you, Mrs. Bailey," I gently, yet firmly interrupted when it became clear she wasn't going to stop anytime soon. "We appreciate your concern and thoughtful words, but we need to focus on finding out who attacked Mr. and Mrs. Wickham. I think it's best if you return home now. It would be most helpful if you could encourage the others to do the same. If we find out anything, we'll let you know."

I heard her stop, but Kolton kept on walking.

"Oh, yes, sweet girl. Right away!" she called after us, not the least bit upset that she'd been dismissed. "I'll make sure to do just that. You can count on me."

I looked up just in time to see Kolton's lips twitch. *What?* I asked mind-to-mind, nudging his side.

You handled her perfectly. I couldn't have done it better myself, and I've known her my entire life.

A blush rose to my cheeks. Before I could look away, he gripped my chin and lowered his lips to mine. Still walking, he breathed against my mouth, "I adore you."

The world disappeared for a moment as I unashamedly basked in his warmth and scent. But it returned all too quickly when he pulled away, revealing the crime scene up ahead. At the foot of the house's front steps lay a prostrate body. Blood spattered the stairs and sidewalk around him. The front door of the house was ajar, as if he'd come outside to investigate a noise.

Beside the body stood a male about the same age as Kolton. He had shoulder-length brown hair and a short beard, looking for all the world like a hot lumberjack. He even wore a red-and-black plaid shirt.

"Buck," Kolton acknowledged him with a nod, stopping several feet away.

"Alpha," Buck replied in return and threw me a curious glance. When Kolton noticeably stiffened, the male's heavy eyebrows ticked up.

"Don't mind him," Griff said, striding past us to give Buck a friendly clap on the shoulder. "The poor guy is dealing with a wicked case of pregnancy hormones."

Despite the situation, a short laugh escaped me.

Don't encourage him, Kolton scolded me while glaring at Griff.

Sorry, I replied, biting my lip so I wouldn't inappropriately laugh again.

Jagger and Brielle soon joined us, but Vi remained a safe distance away with Melanie.

"Anything new?" Jagger said to Buck by way of greeting.

"No," Buck started, then paused when he caught sight of Brielle. She had a hand tightly pressed over her mouth, and her face was leached of all color.

Jagger noticed and subtly shifted to block her view of the body— or Buck. Maybe both.

"I'm fine," she shakily said, waving him away. "I've just never seen a dead body before."

Buck raised his eyebrows again. As the pack's cleanup guy, I could only imagine how many dead bodies he'd seen. Crouching beside Mr. Wickham, he said, "There's something about this murder that I didn't mention over the phone. His eyes." He reached down and carefully rolled the body face up. "They've been gouged out."

At the sight of the poor man's mutilated face, Brielle stumbled away and retched. If I hadn't already seen a face exactly like this one not too long ago, I would have joined her. Still, nausea swirled violently in my belly as I took in the grisly sight.

"I don't think the killer used a knife either," Buck went on, clearly not affected by the carnage. "This was a hack job. There are several thin abrasions surrounding the sockets, as if from—"

"Fingernails," I whispered.

He looked up at me in surprise. "Exactly."

When I swayed, Kolton steadied me, all but carrying my weight.

It's her. It's really her, I silently told him, not bothering to hide my panic. *Keisha's sending another message.*

A low growl vibrated his chest. He curled himself around me like a living shield, as if he expected her to appear at any moment.

Jagger saw and quietly swore. "Thanks, Buck, but you should probably leave that part out of your public report."

"No problem." Buck rolled the body face down again and stood.

"What about the wife?" I managed to say, the words half-muffled by Kolton's chest.

Buck didn't even miss a beat. "My guess is that she was kidnapped, though I couldn't find evidence of a struggle. There aren't any fresh footprints leading away from the house and their cars are still here. But then I caught the scent of magic . . ."

Portalled. She was portalled *away*, I told Kolton.

Looks like it, he grimly replied.

"Another attack involving magic?" a new voice said, causing Kolton to stiffen once more. "That can't be a coincidence."

I turned as best I could to face Carter, who'd wisely stopped several feet away. As the other influential members trickled in behind him, a tremor shook Kolton. Trusting that he'd speak up if the situation became too much for him, I focused on the dozen varying expressions before me. Nervous. Confused. Sad. Afraid. Their emotions ran the gamut, but the most glaring emotion was suspicion. I couldn't blame them, and apparently, neither could Kolton.

Before I could speak, he cleared his throat and said, "No. It's not a coincidence. The house fire was a premeditated attack, and so was this."

"Kolton," Jagger quietly cautioned, but Kolton just shook his head.

"No, we can't keep them in the dark any longer. Not after this latest attack. They need to know that Midnight Pack is under siege and what we're up against."

I stopped breathing. Was he really going to tell them everything?

Sensing my nervous energy, he gently ran his hand down my arm. *Trust me, sweetness.*

I do, I replied without hesitation. *I trust you with my life.*

Love pulsed through our bond.

"What do you mean 'under siege'?" the lone female—who I now knew was named Rebekah—questioned.

"A group of witches called the Blackstone Coven attacked Nora a few months ago. We kept her safe until they attacked again about a month ago and managed to kidnap her."

Carter's eyes grew round in sudden understanding. "That was when you went missing for a week."

Kolton nodded. "I had to find her, so I dropped everything to track her down. I ended up saving her and killing the coven's leader, only for a new leader to rise up—a diabolical one who will stop at nothing to get what she wants. A week ago, the coven came to my family's estate and attacked. We were prepared and defeated them, but the house was lost under their assault."

Several of the influential members shook their heads in disbelief, including Carter. "Why didn't you tell us? Why *lie* to us and take such great pains to cover up the truth?" The more Carter spoke, the more angry he sounded.

We were in for it now. There was no going back.

Calmer than I expected him to be, Kolton answered, "Because it was the only way I could think to keep the pack safe. These witches are powerful and merciless. Most of the pack aren't equipped to handle an enemy like this. I'm sorry for the lies and subterfuge, but you know how quickly rumors and chaos spreads in this pack. The witches were only targeting my family, so I kept the rest of you out of it."

Carter's lips thinned. After a long moment, he said, "If you defeated the coven, then why has there been another attack?"

"I injured the leader, but she managed to escape."

Whispers and exclamations of dread filled the air.

"What does she want? Why is she attacking werewolves?" a male of hispanic descent asked, struggling not to panic.

I tensed, but my worry was needless.

"She wants to experiment on us. She covets what we can become and wishes to harness the power of the wolf for herself," Kolton smoothly replied.

More whispers. Carter's eyes narrowed, but he didn't comment.

"I know that this news is alarming," Kolton went on, "but I have every intention of defeating this witch once and for all. She's lashing out to get our attention, but her goal isn't to destroy the entire pack. When she focuses on her target again, we'll be ready."

Carter tilted his head in thought, then slowly dropped his gaze to me. "Her. The witch's true target is your wife."

Kolton tightened his arms around me, but honestly answered, "Yes."

A dozen gazes hit me all at once. I straightened, refusing to flinch under their intensity.

"So you're saying that Daisy is experiencing what the witch wants to do to *her?*" the hispanic male said, jabbing a finger at me. "That Robert was simply collateral damage, all so this witch could get *her* attention? The blame rests on her then. She's responsible for this."

"*Hugo,*" Kolton barked, so forcefully that several of the pack members jumped. "This is my *wife* you're talking about. The pack alpha female. The woman who will bear my *children.*" He placed a protective hand on my belly. "She's carrying my son, the future heir to Midnight Pack. You will show her respect or face my wrath."

A shiver raced up my spine, but not one of fear. I didn't need him to defend me—not anymore—but I still found it incredibly sexy when he did. Not to mention the whole "protecting my belly" move was super adorable.

Also, *son?* Did he think we were having a boy?

Hugo immediately ducked his head in submission. "Apologies, Alpha. I spoke out of turn."

After a long beat of tense silence, Kolton gave a curt nod. "Apology accepted. I know you're all upset by what happened today and the news I've shared, but the last thing we should do is turn on each other. Nora is a member of this pack and deserves our protection, not judgment. None of this is her fault, and blaming her will only cause division when we should be banding together more than ever. Other supernaturals have gone to war with each other over the years, but werewolves have always stood united. This *witch* is our enemy, and taking her down should be our sole focus."

Several of the pack members lowered their gazes, properly chastised by his impassioned words. Only Carter was still staring at me, seeing far more than I wanted him to.

Noticing his stare, Kolton said, "Whatever you have to say, Carter, say it now. I explained and apologized for what happened. If you have a problem with anything I said, let's hear it."

Oh, man. If I was Carter, I'd be quaking in my boots. But I didn't give the male enough credit. He might not be an alpha, but he remained stoic all the same.

After a lengthy moment, he released me of his gaze and focused on Kolton once more. "Out of respect for the Rivers family legacy and your stalwart leadership of Midnight Pack, we will continue to follow you. But remember that loyalty is given and can just as easily be taken away."

The warning was clear. A warning that Kolton didn't take lightly.

Inclining his head, he replied, "Understood. Now let's get back to business. We have a lot to discuss."

CHAPTER 19

NORA

Two days later, we received another troubling report.

A second body had been found. Daisy's.

Apparently, Mrs. Bailey had been keeping an eye on the Wickham's house and had discovered her that morning. She'd been tossed onto her front porch like discarded trash, but that wasn't the most disturbing part.

She'd been gutted.

Buck had created quite the vivid picture over the phone, explaining how her stomach looked like a wild animal had torn into it. I'd promptly raced to the bathroom and thrown up my breakfast.

The image was too real. Too *personal.*

Keisha wasn't leaving a doubt in our minds who was behind the murders. But, just like last time, catching her was proving to be impossible. We couldn't track her without a scent trail, and she continued to use portalling as her mode of travel.

She might ultimately want *me*, but who knew how many more wolves would die before she decided to contact me again. Even then, Kolton wasn't going to let her anywhere near me, and that included my mind. Our soulmate bond seemed to be a deterrent for her, but when I was away from him . . .

I stopped the thought from forming, not wanting Storm to pick up on it. She didn't want Keisha anywhere near me either. I understood why, of course, but this was the third death I felt responsible for. First my old alpha, and now this innocent couple. Keisha had slaughtered them because I hadn't turned myself in. I knew I wasn't responsible for her actions, but I still felt guilty.

I'd been the one to contact her in the first place. It was only right that I should try to fix this.

Kolton wasn't going to like it though. He *really* wasn't going to.

I felt the familiar warmth of Storm's presence and quickly thought of something else. By the time evening rolled around, I knew what I had to do. It wasn't hard. We'd spent another exhausting day driving to and from Lake Placid, doing our best to remain a calm, united front as more and more panic spread throughout Midnight Pack. Mrs. Bailey had been inconsolable, and we'd spent a good chunk of time discouraging her from talking too much about what she'd seen.

We'd decided to allow the influential members to spread news of the Wickham's deaths so the pack could be on their guard, but had cautioned against revealing the sordid details of their murders. It didn't seem to matter though. The pack was unraveling, demanding that their alpha stop the killer before they could strike again. We'd returned to the Albany penthouse late in the evening, wiped from another stressful day.

I watched as Kolton paced down the hallway off the living room to take yet another phone call, trying his best to defuse the panic despite the personal toll it took on him. Cuddled on the couch with Vi, Melanie, and Brielle, I suddenly yawned and muttered, "Okay, bedtime for me."

"Since when have you gone to bed this early?" Brielle questioned, poking my side. "Even Melanie is still up."

I shrugged and untangled myself from the fuzzy blanket we'd been snuggling with. "Since I became pregnant?"

She made a face at me. "You've been preggers for all of two

seconds. You can't possibly be this tired already."

"Actually," Griff piped up from the kitchen where he was making a sandwich, "the gestation period for werewolves is only four months, so Nora is already well into her first trimester. It's normal at this stage to experience tiredness, nausea, and heightened emotions. Other hormones are heightened too, especially the libido. I'm assuming that Nora has been very horn—"

"*Griff*," Vi loudly groaned, then chucked a couch pillow at him. It zipped through the air so fast that it struck Griff square in the face, making him almost drop his sandwich. From his spot at the kitchen island, Jagger released a quiet snort.

"On that note," I said, good-naturedly shaking my head, "I'm off to bed. Goodnight, everyone."

They murmured their farewells, not the least bit suspicious of my departure. I felt kind of guilty for using my pregnancy this way, but I didn't know how else to get a few moments alone. I was constantly being watched and not just by Kolton. They were *all* acting overprotective, treating me like a fragile doll. It somehow warmed my heart and felt stifling at the same time.

I couldn't blame them though. We'd been through a lot lately, and werewolf pregnancies didn't happen every day. Emotions were high and were undoubtedly going to be even higher once I followed through with my plan. I didn't hesitate though, my mind made up. I climbed the stairs to the second floor and quietly closed myself inside the master bedroom.

Calmly getting ready for bed so as not to alert anyone, I waited until I was certain everyone was still downstairs before slipping into bed and shutting my eyes. My mind fought against the notion of falling asleep for several minutes, but it eventually lost the battle. I drifted away with one word flitting around in my head.

Keisha, Keisha, Keisha.

At first, I struggled to open myself up to the connection.

Our forced blood bond felt wrong. Violating. Subconsciously, my mind knew that I needed to remain guarded against it, not vulnerable. But allowing Keisha access to my mind was the only way I could gain access to *hers*.

I could sense that Storm still didn't know what I was up to. Her mental shields were up out of habit, which allowed the stirrings in my mind to go undetected.

My only worry was that Keisha was too busy being evil to notice how vulnerable I currently was. I still didn't really understand the connection we shared. It wasn't like a green light turned on every time we were both available for a telepathic chat. And so far, only she had initiated contact. I wasn't even sure if this mental thing worked both ways.

Just as I was beginning to doubt my plan, I felt her presence like a malevolent fog, slipping past my defenses to croon inside my head, *So we meet again, little wolf. I'm surprised to find you so unguarded, especially after the last time I invaded your mind.*

Instead of replying, I poured all of my concentration into slamming my shields down, making sure they were airtight. The second I did, I felt her presence expand inside my mind, pushing against the barrier I'd erected. Against the *cage*.

After thoroughly testing my mental walls, she released a low laugh. One that slowly built in volume, filling my mind with its malicious echo.

So, the little wolf has learned a new trick. You think you can keep me trapped in here? she said, almost sounding amused.

You're going to pay for murdering those people, Keisha, I replied. *I'm done letting you mess with my pack.*

Let me? She laughed again. *It's funny that you think you have any control over what I do. I'm the one with the mental abilities, not you. You're simply a parasite that's hitched a free ride through the bond I created. I could take over your mind right now and force you to let me go.*

Try it, I seethed, preparing to defend myself. *Try it and see what happens.*

Oh, the little wolf has grown claws, she purred approvingly. *Too bad I want what you have so badly. We could have made a great team.*

It was my turn to laugh. *You're crazy if you think I would ever work with you.*

Perhaps, but you will work with me, willingly or not. I have foreseen it. I know about the babe you carry. He will be mighty. Powerful. I will take him from your womb. He will be mine to wield and control. It's a pity that you will die while giving him to me, but I already told you that sacrifices must be made in order for witches to become powerful again. But don't worry. I'll take great care of your son, so long as he cooperates with me better than his mother did.

Every word she spoke was like a knife being plunged into my chest. A sudden emotion rose up, so intense that it took my breath away. I could barely control it. Barely *contain* it. The emotion grew and grew until a scream built in my head. A scream that burst from me in wave after pulsing wave, pounding into Keisha.

You will not take him from me!

A blast of searing heat followed the forceful statement. A heat so intense that the dark void of my mind became a blinding sea of white.

I continued to scream. Continued to direct the force of my

fear and rage toward Keisha's presence. After an endless moment, I became aware that I wasn't the only one screaming. Keisha's cries were terrified and filled with pain. I'd heard those cries before, when Storm's magic had burned away her eyes. Recalling the terrible memory, my concentration slipped.

Just like that, the screams ended, including mine. I was suddenly falling. Convulsing. Writhing.

Too much. The heat was *too much*.

"NORA!"

I would know that booming voice anywhere. It was Kolton, trying to reach me. Trying to pull me back to reality.

Nora, let it go! another voice roared. Storm. *It will kill you!*

Well, *that* got my attention.

Dragging air into my lungs, I focused on letting go of the pain and anger. The frantic voices calling out to me helped speed along the process, until the searing heat inside me slowly faded away.

The second it did, strong arms scooped me up and held me impossibly tight. "I've got you, sweetness. I've got you," Kolton croaked, his breathing ragged as he cradled me against him.

I listened to his thundering heart, using it to anchor myself back in reality.

After a moment, I whispered, "It's okay. I'm okay." I expected my voice to be raw after all the screaming, then realized I must have only been screaming in my head.

"What happened?" Kolton questioned, nuzzling his face in my hair.

Before I could speak, Storm snapped, *You foolish girl.*

Kolton stilled. "What did she do?"

She went after the witch!

Ah, hell. I was in so much trouble.

I opened my eyes, relieved when the room came into focus. For a moment there, I thought I'd accidentally burned out my eyeballs.

"Thank heavens," I murmured. My gaze landed on the door and I grimaced. They were all here. Jagger, Griff, Vi, Brielle, and even Melanie. I threw them a lame wave. "Hi, guys."

"*Nora.*"

I grimaced again. Kolton was already sounding less worried and more upset. It was only going to get worse. Might as well enjoy our little cuddle session while I could.

"I can explain," I said, snuggling closer to him. "You see, I realized that no one can find or reach Keisha but me. We're still connected, and now that I know more about bonds and mental shields and magic, I decided to contact her. I knew you wouldn't approve, so I—"

"Like *hell* I wouldn't approve," Kolton barked, yet he still held me with infinite care. I chanced a peek at his face, then wished I hadn't. His eyes were pure yellow. Trembling with barely-restrained anger, he hissed, "That was *reckless*, Nora."

Guilt lodged in my throat. "I know, and I'm sorry. But people are dying, and I couldn't sit back and watch it keep happening when I knew I could do something about it."

"But that wasn't your decision to *make*," Kolton replied, his voice rising once more. "Do you not understand yet that I would cease to exist if something happened to you? What you did was incredibly selfish. Not only could you have been hurt, but the baby could have been hurt as well. We're a *family*, Nora. We make decisions *together*. Do you understand?"

I lowered my eyes. "Yes, Alpha."

You should punish her.

At Shadow's words, I nodded and whispered, "Maybe you should."

"Yes, I *should*," Kolton said. Then, to the rest of our silent audience, "Everybody out. My wife needs to be disciplined for her wrongdoings."

Griff made a choking noise.

I glanced up in time to catch the horror on Brielle's face. "It's okay, Brie. I'll be perfectly safe."

Kolton scoffed. "Have you forgotten who I am, *wife?*"

At the dangerous edge to his voice, I shivered from head to toe. "I know exactly who you are, husband," I quietly replied, making sure to keep my tone submissive.

Kolton growled, and Brielle's eyes widened further.

"Come on," Griff said, nudging her toward the exit. "Our alphas need a little alone time. I think we should all go out for some late-night ice cream. Right now, it's safer out there than it is in here."

Truer words had never been spoken. I could feel how tense Kolton was. He was going to explode any second now. Sure enough, the moment they all filed out into the hallway and Jagger shut the door, Kolton set me down and stalked several feet away. I tracked his jerky movements, watching as he clenched and unclenched his fists.

When we heard the others leave the penthouse, he finally turned to me and said, "You will tell me if what I do becomes too much for you. You will tell me if I frighten you or if you experience unwanted pain."

Holy hell. He really was going to punish me. Not only that, his eyes were still a bright yellow. He'd never done this before. Never allowed Shadow to be a part of our intimate moments. Although, for all I knew, he simply planned to bend me over his knee and spank my butt raw. I was pretty sure Shadow would love a piece of that action.

"Nora," Kolton pressed when I took too long to answer.

Swallowing, I quickly nodded.

"Use your words, Nora. Give your consent out loud."

"Yes, Alpha. I will."

His eyes flashed even brighter. "Good. Then come here."

I did, moving toward him on silent feet. When I reached him, I stopped and stared up at him expectantly. He held my stare for a long moment, his gaze almost too much for me to bear. I wasn't just looking at Kolton right now. I was looking at them both. I didn't know if this was a new experience that Kolton wanted me to have, or if he was simply too angry to handle this moment without Shadow's help. Either way, I wasn't going to question it.

I'd scared him, and he had every right to be mad at me. Whatever he planned to do to me, I would remain submissive.

"Hold still," he ordered, reaching out to touch the short hem of my nightgown. When he grabbed a fistful, I glanced down and gasped at the sight that greeted me. My nightgown was on *fire*. Purple flames ate at the delicate material, disintegrating it to ash. "Hold. Still."

At the repeated command, I froze, not even daring to breathe. Inch by inch, the purple fire slowly traveled up my nightgown. Kolton was clearly controlling the blaze, keeping a firm grip on the material. A normal fire would have burned up the nightgown within seconds and then gone after my flesh. But, although hot, the fire didn't hurt me. It carefully burned away the nightgown, leaving my skin untouched.

Up, up, up the fire went, destroying the material until the last bit vanished in a little puff of acrid smoke. I swallowed, impressed by his level of control. The flames hadn't singed even a single hair. I looked over in time to see Kolton's deadly black claws emerge. My eyes rounded as the claws hooked the front of my panties and tore it down the middle. A few swipes later and the satin material floated in pieces to the floor.

Okay, that undressing had been *hot*. Literally.

When Kolton started to back up, I met his eyes again.

"Stay," he ordered, slowly sweeping his gaze over me from head to toe. Knowing that he wasn't the only one staring at my naked body, I blushed. Deep down, I knew that Storm and Shadow experienced whatever Kolton and I experienced, but there was no hiding from that fact this time. Kolton was making it perfectly clear who he was. Man. Demon. Feral beast. They were all a part of him, and they were all on prominent display as he continued to eye me with lust.

By the time he stopped again, my face wasn't the only thing that was warm. As if he could sense my growing arousal, a wicked smirk slowly tilted his lips. Uh oh. He wasn't going to make this easy for me.

Whatever you do, don't beg, I firmly told myself, then uttered a curse when Kolton quietly chuckled.

"Oh, you will beg, sweetness. Mark my words. Now kneel."

At the shocked look on my face, his smirk widened.

"You heard me, wife. *Kneel.*"

I did, lowering to my knees on the carpet. He watched me for a moment, then issued another command, one that nearly had me choking on my spit.

"Crawl to me."

Holy *crap*. What kind of bedroom kink was this? And had this been Kolton's idea or Shadow's? If I had to guess, probably the latter's.

Before he could repeat the order, I dropped to all fours and began to crawl his way.

"*Slowly*. And don't take your eyes off me."

Oh boy. He was enjoying this way too much. I knew that even without the aid of our bond. All I had to do was glance at his groin to see the hard erection straining through his pants.

"Eyes up here, wife."

Biting my lip, I raised my gaze to his and slowly crawled forward. He tracked my every move, focusing on my breasts more than once. Growing bolder, I added a little sensuality to my movements, gratified when his nostrils flared. When I was in front of him once more, I paused and waited for his next command.

He prolonged the moment, clearly intending to torture me. I sat like a dog at his feet, surprised that I didn't feel an ounce of humiliation. He might be punishing me, but his intent wasn't to hurt me. Even now, I could feel his love for me. His devotion. If I asked him to, he would end this moment in a heartbeat.

But I didn't want him to. I was enjoying this just as much as he was. Which he seemed to realize. He smirked again, but it quickly vanished.

Reaching for the buttons on his shirt, he slowly began to undo them. "Any number of things could have gone wrong, Nora. She could have accessed your whereabouts again. She could have trapped your mind."

I watched him undress, trying not to drool. "But she didn't. I trapped *her*."

He paused, then resumed his task. "How?"

"After I dreamwalked with you, I started to wonder if my connection with Keisha was a two-way thing, so I tried to trap her inside my mental shields. If they could keep her out, then they might also be able to keep her in, and they did."

The last button came undone, exposing a sliver of his deep olive skin and delicious six pack. "She still could have hurt you. She's powerful."

"I know, but I'm powerful too. It's why you found me the way you did. I used my magic to blast her. I *hurt* her, Kolton. Really hurt her. I might have even caused some permanent damage, like when Storm used magic to burn out her eyes."

He paused again, then shrugged off his shirt. Holy hell, I would never get tired of this man's pecs. They were so well-defined and broad, with a light smattering of dark hair across the powerful expanse. Noticing my stare, he chuckled again. "Like what you see, wife?"

I bobbed my head in reply.

The shirt fell to the ground, and he reached for his pants. When I tensed in anticipation, he paused once more. Evil, evil man.

"I appreciate that you want to help, Nora, more than you could know. You've been invaluable to me this past week and have proven how strong and capable you are, but I can't break again. What you did scared the hell out of me, and I don't want you to contact her anymore. Promise me."

"But—"

"*Promise* me, Nora."

I pursed my lips, but eventually gave in. "I promise."

"Good," was all he said, then unbuttoned his pants and allowed his erection to spring free. At the sight, I immediately grew wet. Slowly removing his pants and shoes, Kolton paused to inhale my scent. Humming, he said, "Are you hungry for me, mate?"

I nodded.

"Too bad, because I'm not done punishing you yet."

Frowning, I watched as he kicked his clothing aside and grabbed his hardened shaft. A whimper pushed at my throat, but I shoved it back down. Still sitting on the floor before him, I was nearly eye level with his cock as he began to stroke it. I forced myself to remain still, quietly watching as he pleasured himself. As he made a show of blissfully moaning and fisting himself harder. His pace increased, and the head of his shaft swelled. A bead of arousal glistened at the tip, making my core light on fire. I squirmed in place, desperate to relieve the ache.

"How badly do you want it?" he breathlessly asked, continuing to milk his pleasure.

"Badly," I admitted, squirming again.

"Then beg." More arousal leaked from the tip. "Beg me for it."

Ah, hell. He completely had me, and he knew it. I couldn't resist. I wanted him too much, and I'd do anything to have him. Even beg.

The cocky bastard had planned this from the start.

Willing the acid out of my voice and filling it with sugary sweetness, I batted my lashes up at him and whispered, "Please, Alpha. I want to suck on you. I want to make you come in my mouth."

He released a loud groan. It lasted so long that I thought he'd orgasmed at my words. But when I glanced down again, he was even more engorged.

"Come here, sweetness," he ordered, and I eagerly popped up onto my knees once more. "Lick it. Lick it good and clean."

When my tongue darted out to wet my bottom lip, he softly groaned again. Without touching him, I leaned forward and licked the tip's wet seam. His rich, salty taste exploded on my tongue, and I immediately licked him again. When the tip was thoroughly cleaned, I pushed my luck and took the whole head into my mouth.

With a growl, he grabbed a fistful of my hair and halted my movements. But when I swirled my tongue over the tip, he released a shuddering exhale and thrust his cock inside my mouth. So deeply that I almost gagged.

He paused. "Can you handle it?"

"Mhmm," I muttered around his length.

"I won't go easy on you. Stop me if it becomes too much."

In reply, I swallowed more of him. Another groan escaped him, and then he was thrusting. Like *really* thrusting. As if my mouth was a vagina. I did my best to relax my throat, allowing him full access. But he was so *huge*. I could barely breathe under the assault, unable to pull away as he grabbed the back of my head to control the thrusts.

Somehow, I managed not to gag as his swollen tip hit the back of my throat again and again. His pace grew feverish, and right as I felt him swell so big that I could barely contain him . . .

He pulled away.

My lips released him with a wet pop, and I dazedly blinked up at him in confusion. He looked equally dazed, yet he clearly said, "Did you think I would make this easy? We're nowhere near finished yet, sweetness. Now get on the bed."

CHAPTER 20

NORA

My weak legs were barely able to carry me, but I made it to the bed and crawled on top. The moment I did, an unseen force flipped me onto my back, pinning my arms and legs to the mattress. For a split second, panic filled me. Keisha used to pin me down like this while she cut me open.

"Are you okay?"

I looked up and found Kolton hovering over me, not Keisha. At the sight of him, my panic started to fade. When I nodded, he took a moment to carefully search my face.

"If it's too much, just say the word."

"I will," I whispered, testing the strength of his magical hold. It felt like my wrists and ankles were shackled to the bed by invisible cuffs. I could move my head and body, but only so far as the restraints would allow. When I stopped struggling and peered up at him expectantly, his eyes flared bright.

He was excited. Excited to see me vulnerable before him. Not in a malicious way, though. More like he enjoyed bondage play. Which made sense, since he liked to dominate and see me willingly submit.

Leaning over me, he brought his head down to whisper in my ear, "I'm going to torture you now. Nice and slow. I'm going to give you what you want and then take it away. I'll bring you to the edge of orgasm over and over but won't let you fall. You will scream. You will beg. But you won't find relief until you've served out your punishment. Then and only then will I put you out of your misery. Do you understand?"

A tremor shook my entire body. I'd never felt more raw. More exposed. Goosebumps erupted over me, yet my skin felt flushed. I didn't know if I could survive this, but I sure as hell wanted to try. I *desperately* wanted to.

Kolton was showing me a side of himself I'd never seen before, and I needed to know all of him. Every nook and cranny and dark corner. If he took pleasure in torturing me this way, then I wanted to experience it with him. To take pleasure in it as well.

I nodded, whispering, "I understand."

At my consent, he emitted a pleased rumble. The sound curled my toes and shortened my breath. I felt something sharp prick my thigh. The tip of a *claw*. It slowly scraped a path upward, dragging my nerve-endings awake. I held my breath as it curved inward and headed for my aching center, only to change course at the last second. I released a disappointed sigh, then inhaled sharply as it trailed up my stomach. At my reaction, the claw slowed even more, but didn't pull away.

I hadn't asked him to stop, so he didn't.

Until now, I'd always associated claws on my stomach with pain. But I wasn't in any pain at the moment. The sensation felt good, the rush of pleasure making my stomach muscles involuntary flex. My core began to tingle, and I instinctively tried to squeeze my thighs shut. But I couldn't. When I squirmed against the invisible restraints, Kolton chuckled in my ear.

"We're only getting started, sweetness. Don't start begging yet."

"I won't," I promised, even as I gritted my teeth.

He chuckled once more and resumed his torture. Lightly grazing the claw over my ribs, he circled it around my right breast, then the left. When my nipples hardened, desperate for some attention, he moved on.

I swallowed another disappointed sound, refusing to cave so easily. He wanted to torture me? Fine. I would show him just how strong I was. Whatever he had to dish out, I would take. I wasn't going to fall apart just because he—

"Oh!" I sharply exclaimed, promptly losing my composure as he circled back around and started the torture all over again—but this time faster. He did it again and again, until I couldn't help but tremble beneath him.

"Have you had enough yet?" he purred.

I started to shake my head, then stifled a gasp as he sucked my earlobe into his mouth and bit down. Not gently either. When I didn't pull away, he rewarded me by soothing the bite with his tongue. I arched my head back, urging him to use that tongue on other areas. He obliged, kissing a wet trail down my neck to his claim spot, then paused.

His heart suddenly began to race. Before I could wonder why, he pulled back and met my eyes to say, "I want to bite you."

My stomach went crazy with drunken butterflies. I liked it when he claimed me, so I didn't really understand his hesitation. "Okay," I simply said.

He shook his head. "Not like I have in the past. I want to bite you as a wolf."

When a feral light entered his bright eyes, a swallow got stuck in my throat. "Oh." He wanted to *bite* bite me. Not with teeth, but with *fangs*. When he suddenly looked uncertain, I quickly said, "I'll tell you if it hurts too much."

His heart pounded even harder. I could tell he was excited by the green light, and yet he continued to hesitate.

"Werewolf, remember?" I quietly reassured, giving him a small smile. "I can deal with a few puncture holes."

He swallowed hard, darting a needy glance at the spot between my neck and shoulder. "I'll ease your pain," he roughly whispered, beginning to shake.

"I know you will. I'm not afraid of you."

He blew out a harsh breath and nodded, focusing on my neck again. When I arched it to further expose the spot, he finally gave in. I didn't see the moment when his canines elongated, but I definitely felt all four sharp points puncture my flesh. As they sank in deep, I couldn't hold back a cry. I might be a werewolf, but being bitten still hurt like hell. Responding to my pain, he slipped a hand between my legs and began rubbing my clit.

At the pleasurable assault, my back bowed off the bed. I released another cry, but not one of pain. Kolton bit me harder but continued to stroke me, filling my body with ecstasy. I moaned, chasing the delicious high. Just as the pleasure began to make me shake, he pulled his fingers away. Pain came rushing back in and I whimpered, "Please, Kolton. Don't stop."

A satisfied growl rumbled in his throat.

Crap. I'd totally begged.

Still, I was too far gone to stop now. Tugging against my invisible restraints, I pleaded, "Just let me orgasm once. That's all I need, Kolton. Just—"

He lowered himself and rubbed the head of his cock against my slick entrance. I bucked from the contact, desperate for more of it. He continued to tease the entrance, filling me with aching want and frustration.

"Kolton," I snapped, trying to thrust my hips upward. He pulled his cock just out of reach. "I need more. I need—*Oh*." My vision splintered as he rubbed the tip over my swollen clit. Grabbing his shaft for better control, he massaged the sensitive nub in a circular motion until I was trembling and panting beneath him.

As the pleasure almost reached a tipping point once more, I begged him not to stop. Only a little more. A little—

He pulled away again.

I screamed my frustration, calling him a few choice names. I felt him smile cruelly against my neck.

Have you had enough yet? he said through our bond, running his fingers teasingly over my inner thighs.

"Yes!" I ground out. "I need you to put me out of my misery. *Now.*"

He teased me a moment longer, clearly amused with my anger. Just when I was about to chew him out for real this time, he unlocked his jaw and carefully slid his fangs from my neck. One look at the damage, and he bent his head again to gently lick the wounds. After a moment, the throbbing of the bite faded as my supernatural healing kicked in. He stopped licking and tenderly kissed the spot.

Despite how ramped up my body was, I patiently waited for him to finish. Claiming me helped calm him. I could already feel how content he was, and when he pulled away to look at me, the feral gleam had left his eyes. In fact, they were no longer yellow. I blinked in surprise, then blinked again as I felt the pressure on my wrists and ankles disappear.

"You've served out your punishment," he said, lifting off of me to stand beside the bed. "You're free to go."

I gaped at him in shock. "Are you kidding me right now? After all that, *this* is what I get? You said you'd put me out of my misery, you bastard!"

Scrambling off the bed, I lunged at him. As we collided, he

stumbled against the bedside table and a vase crashed to the floor. Ignoring it, I pushed him up against the nearest wall and dragged his head down for a bruising kiss. He immediately responded in kind, flipping our positions to press me against the wall. A painting clattered to the floor. When he ground his hard erection against me, I groaned into his mouth.

Yes. This was what I wanted. Our feverish bodies pressed together, frantically seeking release. And I needed release. *Bad.* I was almost in tears, the ache was that fierce. But a wicked sense of vengeance for what he'd just put me through hit me then. Sucking his bottom lip into my mouth, I bit down without warning. *Hard.* So hard that I tasted the coppery tang of blood.

He jerked back with a growl, breaking the kiss to narrow his eyes at me. "What was that?" he demanded, raising a hand to wipe the blood from his lip.

Shrugging, I pushed him back and stepped away from the wall. "Punishment."

When I sauntered off, leaving him high and dry with a rock hard dick, he growled a warning, which I completely ignored.

"*Nora.*"

I bent over, giving him a clear view of my backside as I began to pick up his discarded clothing. "I think I'll just go to bed," I mused. "It's been a long day."

He growled again, the sound more insistent this time, *demanding* to be heard. When I continued to ignore him, he stormed over and picked me up with one strong arm. I yelped and struggled to get away, but he easily carried me to the bed and tossed me onto the mattress. I scooted backward, only for him to grab my legs and drag me back. Prying them apart, he leaned over the bed and growled, "You're not going to bed until I've pleasured you senseless. You thought what I did earlier was torture? That was only a taste of what I will do to you, wife."

With that, he delved between my thighs and found my aching center with his tongue. The swift rush of euphoria stole my breath, and I gripped the sheets for dear life, letting my eyes blissfully roll back. Already on the brink of release, I could only endure a few licks before an orgasm was barreling through me. I threw back my head and screamed, shooting so high that I nearly blacked out.

Barely giving me time to recover, he flipped me over and dragged me to the bed's edge. Still gripping my thighs, he drove himself inside me balls deep, stealing my breath once more. In this position, I had no control. All I could do was grip the sheets and moan into the mattress as he took me hard from behind. In no time, we were both panting and slick with sweat, our bodies trembling as our pleasure built.

He suddenly smacked one of my butt cheeks. *Hard*. Hard enough to leave a mark.

I screamed as another orgasm slammed into me, fisting the sheets so hard that they tore. Kolton pounded into me a few more times, then spilled his release with a bellowing roar.

When he slumped forward to rest his elbows on either side of me, I thought he was done. Nope. He somehow had the stamina for another round. Joining me in bed this time, he made love to me so passionately that the bed frame cracked. After that, he still wasn't finished. We ended up on the floor, driving each other wild with teasing touches and playful looks.

The anger, fear, and tension from earlier had completely disappeared, and all that remained was our desperate love for each other.

As we filled the night with endless passion, our problems seemed a lifetime away. It allowed me to pretend, just for a moment, that

Keisha hadn't left her mark on me as well, leaving me utterly terrified that her foretelling would come true.

That she would take away our son . . .

And I would die.

Storm knew something was up. Not that I was doing a very good job at hiding it.

When I stubbornly avoided her probing questions the next morning at breakfast, she went for the jugular.

Kolton, your mate is keeping something from us. Something important.

I inwardly scowled at her, making sure she felt my annoyance. *Are you going to snitch on me every time I do something you don't like?*

If it gets me the results I seek, came her matter-of-fact reply.

"Ugh," I groaned aloud, earning me several curious looks. I waved them away. "It's nothing. Storm is just being a *pest.*"

Hey, don't talk about my angel baby that way.

"Don't you start too, Shadow," I warned, hating that they were ganging up on me. I almost missed the days when the only person inside my head was me. It was much easier to ignore things that were bothering me that way.

When Kolton lowered his fork to stare at me expectantly, I stifled another groan. He was doing so much better today. More at ease after how intimate we'd been last night. He'd even surprised me by making a steak and eggs breakfast this morning for everyone. Brielle had asked him to make her steak rare and had gobbled it up in record time. I'd noticed a restlessness in her this morning that I'd never seen before and had just been about to ask if she was okay when Storm had swung all the attention my way.

Thanks a lot, I inwardly grumbled at her, pretending I hadn't seen Kolton's expectant look by focusing on my plate. Crap, no wonder she'd been suspicious. I hadn't eaten a single thing yet.

Worry trickled through the soulmate bond. "What's wrong, Nora?"

Suddenly queasy at the thought of telling Kolton, I jumped to my feet and carried my plate to the kitchen. "It's stupid, really." I placed my plate on the island to rummage in the drawers for plastic wrap. "I don't know why I'm even worried. It's not like we can trust anything that comes out of her mouth. She was just trying to scare me."

"She?" Kolton slowly rose to his feet. "She who?"

Ah hell, I did *not* want to have this conversation. Finding the plastic wrap, I focused on sealing it over my plate. When my hands shook, making the plastic bunch up, I blew out a frustrated sigh and wadded it into a ball. "Plastic wrap is *so* annoying. I like that press and seal stuff much better. Do we have any? We should get some."

"Nora."

"We should go shopping today. There's some stuff I need, and I could really use some retail therapy after all the stress we've been under. We could also start packing up Brielle's apartment today. Have we decided where we're going to stay while she transitions?"

"Nora."

Growing frantic, I ripped off another piece of plastic wrap and wrestled it over the plate. "Obviously we can't stay at the estate," I blathered on, cursing under my breath when my hands continued to shake. "The guest apartment over the garage is too small for all of us, but the cabin at Ampersand Lake is only an hour away from Lake Placid. Staying there would allow us to be closer to the majority of the pack and give Brielle the seclusion she needs for her first shift. It would also be a shorter drive for when we start rebuilding the house. Which we're going to do, right? Because it had started to feel like home to me, and—Ah!"

As the plate I was wrestling with slipped off the island and crashed to the floor, Kolton surged toward me.

"I'm *fine!*" I shouted, throwing my hands up. He froze in his tracks. I made the mistake of looking at him then. His gaze saw *right* through me. He knew I was stalling. Even worse, he knew that I was utterly terrified. Suddenly finding it hard to breathe, I bent and started cleaning up my mess.

"Nora," he said again. Softer this time, as if trying to calm a spooked animal.

"I'm fine," I repeated, continuing to pick up the broken ceramic. "It was that stupid plastic wrap. We really should replace it with something better. I'm sorry about the steak though. I'm sure it was delicious. I'm just not feeling very . . ."

When my words ended in a muffled sob, Kolton was there in a heartbeat, pulling me into his arms. He sat on the floor next to my mess, leaning against the island as he held me on his lap. I tried to compose myself but failed, unable to stop the sob that wrenched from my lungs.

"I'm sorry," I choked out, fisting my trembling hands into his shirt. "I didn't want to . . . didn't want to worry you. But I . . . I can't stop . . . can't stop thinking about it. About what she said."

"Tell me," he said, gently running his fingers through my curls.

I shook harder. "I-I can't. I'm supposed to be helping you get *better*. This will . . . will ruin everything."

Even as I felt him tense, he quietly said, "I'm not going anywhere, sweetness. Whatever you have to say, I can handle it. With you by my side, I can handle anything."

"But that's just it. If this premonition comes true, I won't *be* by your side."

Ah hell, I had *not* meant to say that. But it was too late. I couldn't take back the words, and Kolton certainly wasn't going to drop the matter now.

Sure enough, alarm flared through our bond. "What do you mean?" he asked, the tension bleeding into his voice. When I didn't respond right away, the tension only grew. "*Nora.*"

I bit my lip hard enough to break the skin.

Nora, Storm said, her voice filled with calm reassurance. *Don't carry this on your own. Let us help you.*

Inhaling a trembling breath, I finally nodded and whispered, "Keisha foretold my death."

There was a flurry of movement as the others left the table to join us in the kitchen. Kolton, on the other hand, didn't move a muscle. He wasn't even breathing.

Lies, Shadow growled inside my head. *She was only trying to frighten you.*

Storm, like Kolton, remained silent.

"What else did she say?" Jagger questioned when Kolton didn't.

I peeked up at their solemn faces. Even Melanie looked worried. When I lifted a hand toward her, she hurried over and crawled onto my lap. Kolton still didn't move. Drawing strength from the support surrounding us, I found my voice again.

"She knew I was pregnant," I began, then paused, waiting for Kolton's reaction. Nothing. He was still as stone. I couldn't feel a single emotion or hear any thoughts from him. Not good, not good, not good. Still, the others were staring at me expectantly, so I continued, "She said he would be powerful."

"He?" Vi asked. "She thinks you're having a boy?"

I nodded. "She seemed pretty certain of it, and she seemed pretty certain that . . . that she would take him from me. From my *womb*, was what she said."

Griff released a low growl. "Over my dead body."

"Mine too," Brielle said with surprising ferocity.

"Same," Vi replied.

Jagger just nodded and crossed his arms over his chest. Melanie grabbed one of my curls and snuggled closer to me.

Kolton remained motionless.

My worry for him grew, but I forged ahead anyway, recounting what else Keisha had said. When I explained how I'd possibly hurt her with magic, Storm perked up.

Was your intent to harm her?

I think so. I was angry. Really angry. The thought of Keisha taking my baby away made me wild with rage, so I lashed out, I answered her.

Good. I'm glad, Storm said. *You might have injured her third eye. This might make her even more dangerous though. A wounded animal will always attack when threatened. You must guard your mind at all times.*

I will.

Whether Keisha's premonition was a lie or not, I wouldn't be letting my guard down again. I'd found so much love and acceptance in this family, and I wouldn't let her take that away from me.

Despite my resolve, I couldn't help but continue to worry about Kolton. The news hadn't broken him, but his mind and emotions felt distant, like he'd erected a barrier between us. I knew he'd heard every single thing that I'd said, but our connection was silent.

When I reached out to him several minutes later, all I felt was a chasm. A *void.*

An endless pit of darkness.

CHAPTER 21

KOLTON

I knew I was scaring her.

Truth be told, I was scaring myself too.

I'd never felt a rage like this before. A rage that was quiet. Focused. Balanced on the tip of a knife with deadly precision.

To unleash that rage was to unleash death, so I hid from her. I protected my beloved mate from the darkness that crouched inside me like a predator about to strike. If I let the darkness emerge, it would destroy everything. It would kill without mercy, slaughtering anything it considered a threat to the woman who carried my child.

My *son*.

In my core, I knew the witch's words hadn't been false. She meant to take my son and wife from me. She meant to destroy my *world*. Which was why the darkness inside had reared up, prepared to destroy her first.

But it didn't understand that the threat wasn't in this room. It didn't understand anything but rage. A rage that would stop at nothing to protect the one thing that kept me sane. But that rage would consume me if I let it. That rage would *control* me, undoing everything that Nora had helped me fix these past several days.

I couldn't give into it. Couldn't even reach out to her. Not with the darkness this close to the surface.

So I stayed silent. Stayed silent when I should have been comforting her. Stayed silent while the others offered her their

support instead of me. I knew she was worried. Hurt. Scared.
But silence was far better than unleashing hell on earth.

CHAPTER 22

NORA

Over the next several days, I grew to expect Kolton's silence.

He spoke only when spoken to, his sentences clipped and matter of fact. I tried my best to accept it, to remind myself that he was still struggling. Still *healing*. Setbacks happened, and there was no greater trigger for him than being told that his wife and child would be taken from him.

I took comfort in the fact that he was still here. Not all of him, but enough that he could function and tend to his responsibilities. When we weren't busy packing and relocating our stuff to the cabin at Ampersand Lake, he was on the phone. Besides the pack needing him more than ever, he still had a billion-dollar business to run.

We all did our best to help him carry the load, but he seemed to need the work. To *thrive* on staying busy. It distracted him from obsessing over Keisha's premonition. At the end of each long day, he poured just as much of himself into showering me with love. There was no lack of intimacy, and I fell asleep every night with his arms tightly wrapped around me, but he barely spoke a word. Not only that, his mind was still closed off from me, as if he was hiding. As if he didn't want me to discover what dark thoughts lurked inside him.

I'd tried to reach out to him again and again. Tried to reassure him that I was okay. That *he* was okay.

Despite his silence, I could feel the darkness brewing just beneath his calm surface. He hid it well, but he couldn't hide it from me. I knew he was struggling to control it. Knew he was doing everything in his power to keep it from me.

But that was the problem. I didn't want him to. I wanted to *help* him. I wanted to *face* it with him so we could conquer it together.

He was still here, but his need to protect me made it impossible to reason with him. There had been no more attacks, and Keisha hadn't tried to reach me through the blood bond, but I was never far from his side. Every time he took a call in another room, he made sure that Jagger or Griff were watching me. I was under constant protection, and yet, it wasn't enough for him.

Despite his calm outward demeanor, he was always vigilant. Every little thing was a possible threat. He'd backed me away from windows on several occasions, certain that someone would see me and report back to Keisha. I knew he meant well, but I was starting to feel like a prisoner. If he didn't relax soon, I was going to explode, which would only make things worse.

Thankfully, the moment we all moved into the Ampersand Lake cabin, he seemed more at ease. The woods were familiar and offered protection, and the cabin itself was filled with happy memories. Our scent still lingered in the air, a fact that Griff had bluntly pointed out while cracking open a few windows. The space was cramped compared to what we were used to, and we all had to share bedrooms, but at least we were together. At least we hadn't needed to make use of the fallout shelter again.

With the approach of another full moon came a new set of distractions. It was almost October, and the fall leaves were in full color. The air held a constant chill, but it wasn't truly cold yet. Not that the approaching winter had any affect on us, something that Brielle noted often. Her restlessness had increased, along with her heightened abilities. Normally an indoors kind of girl, she was spending more and more time exploring the woods.

Her transition to werewolf had turned into a blessing, really. It kept me from constantly stressing over Kolton's behavior. She had dozens of questions which I readily answered, wanting to prepare her for what was to come. She was still sad over her parents' refusal to face the truth, but otherwise, she was handling the transition well.

Aside from the occasional fixation on raw meat and insatiable need for fresh air, she was still herself. Still my loyal, accessory-loving, occasionally boy-crazy best friend. I hadn't wanted this life for her, but a selfish part of me was glad that she was no longer human. Being my best friend was dangerous, and at least I didn't have to worry about her safety as much anymore. She might not have magic or a spirit familiar, but she was about to grow a wicked set of fangs and claws.

Once she experienced her first shift, we would officially initiate her into Midnight Pack, along with my parents. Kolton had asked Buck to occasionally check in on them, and they seemed content in their new location. I mean, who wouldn't? They'd scrimped to make ends meet for the past thirty years and were now situated in a brand new home in upstate New York. Kolton had practically given them an all-expense-paid vacation for life.

I hadn't visited them yet, still worried that Keisha would use them as leverage against me, but I was glad they were adjusting so well after what had happened to Hendrix. Hopefully sooner than later, it would be safe enough to work on repairing the damage they'd allowed their old alpha to wreak on our relationship.

In the meantime, I would focus on my relationships with the people who'd included me into their family. Ominous death premonitions aside, I wanted to live life to the fullest. My stomach was still flat as ever, but it wouldn't be long before a baby bump appeared. Now was the time to be active before motherhood took all my energy and attention. I was already winded far too easily, and I would only slow down more the bigger my belly got.

When the first night of the moon's pull finally arrived, I was more than a little excited. Not for Brielle to feel the inevitable pain that came from wolfing out, but because I would get to shift tonight. I could feel Storm's excitement too. I was pretty sure she secretly wanted to run with Shadow again, although she'd never admit it.

Both Griff and Vi had left earlier today to stay with Charlotte Rivers. Vi had wanted to help Brielle with her transition, but Kolton didn't want anyone to travel alone. Although nothing bad had happened for several days, he wasn't going to take any chances.

The moon was high and bright in the sky, the air crisp and clear, when Brielle started to spike a fever.

"Whew, I bet this is what hot flashes feel like," she breathlessly said, pulling off her sweater. She kept her pale pink camisole on, but probably not for much longer. Luckily for her, she wasn't shy about nudity. It was like she was born to be a werewolf or something. We hadn't moved outside yet, and when she lifted her honey-brown hair to cool her neck, I caught Jagger staring at her from across the room.

The plan was for me and Kolton to help Brielle before and after her shift, making sure her wolf stayed in the woods and didn't seek out human prey. Jagger would remain in the cabin to watch after Melanie, who was already tucked in bed. He hadn't argued against the plan, but I hadn't failed to notice him watching Brielle more and more. They'd barely spoken to each other in two weeks, and she was clearly still holding a grudge against him, but there was no mistaking the looks he gave her.

Midnight Pack's enigmatic second in command had eyes for my best friend.

"Do werewolves get menopause?" she asked me, clearly not aware that Jagger was listening—or simply didn't care. "I know that we don't get periods as often, which I'm super excited about. I'm not so sure about this 'in heat' thing though. All I can picture is me yowling and rolling on the floor like a cat. But if a hot werewolf male offers to help me with it, I won't say no. *That* part I'm okay with."

I looked over at Jagger again to see his cheeks darken. Holy hell, was he actually *blushing*?

From his spot across from us on the living room's loveseat, Kolton abruptly stood and strode toward the front door. I froze, worried that he'd heard something outside. Or someone. Then relaxed again as he paused at the foot of the stairs and quietly called up, "Mellie? Are you awake?"

I heard a sniffle. Then a little voice replied, "I don't feel so good."

Kolton was silent for a beat. "Is your familiar trying to come out?"

"I think so. She likes the full moon."

Sighing, Kolton glanced at Jagger.

"On it, boss," he said without waiting for instructions, hurrying toward the stairs as if glad for the distraction. Couldn't blame the poor guy. Brielle was practically stripping and saying she wanted the first available guy to bang her.

When he'd carried Melanie outside, Kolton took up guard beside the door. He'd barely said anything all evening, but he didn't need to. I remembered my first shift like it was yesterday. Brielle had already found a pond nearby that would be perfect for her to submerge in during the transformation process. It could take another hour or two before she was ready for that though.

A normal werewolf couldn't shift as quickly, especially on the first try. Sometimes, it took them hours. In the worst case scenario, days. But Brielle was young and strong. I was certain her transition would go smoothly.

Just like I predicted, she doubled over in pain an hour later.

"Crap," she groaned, her skin slick with sweat. "If labor pains feel like this, I'm never having kids. Remind me to tear off Arrow's balls if I ever see him again."

"We should go," I said, directing the words to Kolton. Not surprisingly, his only response was a nod.

When he came forward to pick Brielle up, she waved him away. "That's okay. I've got this."

She stood from the couch and immediately collapsed to the floor. I rushed forward, wincing when I touched her arm. Her skin was boiling hot. "Brie, let me help you."

As I used my supernatural strength to help her up, she didn't protest. She was too busy gritting her teeth. Ducking beneath her arm, I leaned most of her weight on me and made for the door. Kolton held it open for us, then followed us outside like a silent sentinel. We'd barely made it into the woods when her legs gave out.

She groaned as I held her upright, muttering, "Something . . . doesn't feel right."

"I'm so sorry, Brielle. I know it sucks. It'll get easier with each shift, I promise." I looked to Kolton for help.

Without a word, he eased forward and took Brielle from me. She didn't object this time as he lifted her up and strode through the trees. We were almost to the pond when Kolton murmured, "She's too hot."

Alarmed, I rushed to say, "Then let's hurry and get her in the water. It should—"

Brielle suddenly stiffened in Kolton's arms and released a blood-curdling scream. At the awful sound, Kolton froze in his tracks, then carefully lowered her to the ground.

"What are you doing?" I cried, rushing forward to pick her back up. "The water is only feet away. She needs to cool off."

Before I could touch her, Kolton said one word. "Don't."

Brielle's back arched off the ground and she screamed again, so loudly that my blood turned to ice.

"What do you mean *don't?*" I shouted at Kolton, my worry quickly turning to anger at his odd behavior. "Water helps with the transition. You said so yourself. Why are you doing this?"

He clenched his jaw, refusing to meet my eyes as he replied, "Water won't help her. Anything that touches her skin will cause her excruciating pain. I'm sorry, Nora. Her body is rejecting the toxin. There's nothing I can do."

It was like someone had opened up the ground beneath me. I could feel myself falling, pinwheeling out of control. I'd never seen it happen before, but I'd heard about what he spoke of. Not all humans infected with werewolf toxin survived the transition. Sometimes, the human part of them fought back, treating the toxin as a virus. When that happened . . .

"No!" I snapped, shaking my head. "She's not going to die."

"Nora," Kolton quietly said, reaching for me. I shoved his hands away and stood.

"Jagger!"

I didn't know why I called his name, only that I needed him here.

Brielle screamed again, the sound filled with so much pain that tears pricked my eyes. Fiercely blinking them away, I threw back my head and roared as loudly as I could, "JAGGER!"

When I heard crashing through the trees a few seconds later, Kolton surged to his feet. He reached for me, but I batted his hands away again.

"*No,*" I barked, not caring how rude I sounded. "I don't need protection right now. So unless you can help Brielle, don't come any closer."

I could have sworn I felt his hurt through our bond, but I kept my focus on the male racing toward us. He burst through the trees moments later, carrying what looked like a normal-sized gray wolf. At the sight of Brielle writhing on the forest floor, Jagger strode toward Kolton.

"Take her," he said, shoving the squirming wolf into Kolton's arms. Kolton took the wolf from him without comment—the wolf being Melanie, I now realized. When he approached Brielle, Kolton didn't stop him.

"Her body is rejecting the toxin. You have to help her," I begged Jagger as he knelt beside her. He watched her moan and writhe for a moment, then reached out to touch her.

The second his skin made contact with hers, she released another blood-curdling scream. He curled his hands into fists, helplessly watching her body shake.

"*Please*, Jagger," I cried, feeling my heart start to break. This wasn't supposed to happen. Not to Brielle.

When her screams ended, Jagger said, "We need Griff. He has the most experience with this."

"There's no time," Kolton replied, still holding a wiggling Melanie. "She has minutes left."

Minutes? My legs weakened, and I sank down beside my friend.

Jagger continued to helplessly stare at her, opening and closing his fists as if debating whether or not to touch her again. When she suddenly started to convulse, he threw caution to the wind and grabbed her arms. She violently bucked against his hold, shaking so hard that her head repeatedly struck the ground.

"*Brielle!*" he bellowed. I'd never heard him sound so panicked.

Seconds later, the convulsing stopped. *Everything* stopped. Jagger leaned down and placed his ear to her mouth.

"She's not breathing."

"Brie, *no*," I whimpered, in too much shock to move.

Jagger swiftly turned his head and pressed his mouth to hers. Expelling his breath into her lungs, he straightened and began CPR. All I could do was watch, wringing my hands as her complexion grew paler and paler.

"Come on, Brielle. *Come on*," Jagger growled, his movements growing frantic.

"Jagger," Kolton said. "Let her go. She's gone."

"No." Jagger shook his head, continuing to compress her chest. "No, she can't be gone. She's my mate. My *mate*."

I covered my mouth, shocked and heartbroken over his confession. "Brie, please wake up," I whispered, barely able to see past my tears.

Heal her, Storm's voice suddenly filled my head.

I blinked, startled by her words. *What?*

The four elements that make up all of creation thrum in your veins. Use them. Save your friend, Nora.

Renewed hope surged through me.

I scrambled forward to touch her, but Jagger snatched her away with a growl.

"*Jagger.*"

At Kolton's barked command, I held up a hand. "No, it's okay. I won't take her away from you, Jagger. I promise. I just need to touch her."

I reached for her again. When he didn't pull away, I laid my hand on her arm, then closed my eyes and focused on the magic inside me. Not giving myself time to doubt my abilities, I willed it to aid me. To fix whatever had caused my friend's breath to stall and her heart to stop. I had seconds. *Seconds* to save her before she was gone forever.

"*Please*, Brielle," I breathed, pushing my magic toward her. "Please accept the toxin. It's the only way you'll live."

Making my intentions crystal clear, I let the magic bleed from me and into her. After a moment, I heard Jagger suck in a quiet breath. Taking that as an encouraging sign, I gripped her arm tighter and continued to pour healing energy into her.

"Breathe, Brielle," I fiercely said, digging my nails into her skin. "*Breathe!*"

A loud gasp reached my ears. I opened my eyes just as Brielle jerked awake. She continued to gasp for air, wildly looking about until her gaze found Jagger. When she weakly whimpered his name, he squeezed his eyes shut and released a trembling breath.

Suddenly lightheaded, I leaned back, so far that I almost tipped over. A strong pair of arms immediately surrounded me from behind, offering their support. I knew who it was without looking but glanced back in search of Melanie. Her wolf was a short distance away, busily digging a hole at the base of a tree.

"I'm sorry for snapping at you," I whispered to Kolton, refocusing on my best friend. She'd closed her eyes, but her chest continued to rise and fall, slowly returning to a normal rhythm.

Sighing, Kolton replied through our bond, *You have nothing to be sorry for, sweetness. I deserved to be yelled at.* My breath caught as our connection burst awake. Remorse hit me hard, along with a slew of other emotions. *I failed you again. I can't even begin to apologize for my poor behavior this past week.*

I shook my head, leaning more fully against him. *I know why you acted the way you did, and I don't need you to apologize. All I need is for you to let me in.*

But—

But you're scared for me to see your darkness?

Surprise flickered through our bond.

News flash: I've already seen it, Kolton. Maybe not all of it, but I'm well aware that it exists. You keep trying to protect me, and I love you for that, but I don't want you to protect me from yourself. If Brielle's near-death experience has taught me anything, it's that life can be snatched away from us in an instant. We're all a breath away from death's door, even me.

He tensed, but I forged ahead before he could speak.

I know you don't want to accept that, but the sooner you do, the sooner you can make peace with it. This darkness inside you isn't just your fear of losing me. It's your fear of losing yourself. You can't keep hiding from the darkness as if it's a terrible beast. This pain is a part of you, and you need to feel it. To face it. Only then can you truly begin to heal.

His arms tightened around me. He didn't respond right away, but eventually, he said, *You're kind of incredible, you know.*

I watched my friend continue to breathe in life-giving air and allowed myself a small smile. When she groaned, my smile slipped.

"She's okay," Jagger said, then slowly stood with her in his arms. "I've got her."

We watched him turn toward the pond. Still fully clothed, he carried her into the water, each movement careful and attentive. I flinched when she cried out in pain, but Kolton only held me closer, whispering aloud, "He'll take good care of her."

"But what if she stops breathing again?"

Kolton kissed the top of my head. "She won't. You saved her, just like you continue to save me."

I let myself relax again, allowing a comfortable silence to settle between us as Jagger tended to Brielle's transition. I suddenly straightened with a gasp. "Mate. He said she was his mate. Do you think they're . . . ?"

Kolton softly laughed. "Yes, sweetness. I think they're soulmates."

CHAPTER 23

NORA

The next few days passed in a blur as Brielle grew accustomed to being a full-fledged werewolf. We took turns running with her, guiding her wolf so she wouldn't stray too far. Her coat was a rich brown, darker than Griff's tawny hide by several shades. She was smaller than Storm by at least a foot, but what she lacked in size, she made up for in ferocity.

Jagger's black wolf was huge compared to hers, but that didn't stop her from testing him more than once. Every time he got too close, she'd snap at him, putting him in his place. He could have easily pinned her down and forced her submission, but he didn't. He allowed her to express her dominance, never straying too far from her side.

Even when she shifted back each morning, disoriented and drained from hours spent in her wolf form, he kept a close eye on her. On the second morning, as we were watching her struggle to transform back into her human skin, he quietly said three words to me. Three words that sat like an elephant on my chest.

"Don't tell her."

I immediately knew what he was referring to. My first instinct was to question him, but I could sense he wasn't ready to talk. I hadn't said a word, even though keeping a secret like this from my best friend would be the worst kind of torture.

My soulmate bond with Kolton was the best thing that had

ever happened to me, but I hadn't felt that way at first. It had been confusing and downright terrifying. If Jagger needed time to process it, then I completely supported his decision. Hopefully he wouldn't take too long though. Living in the same house would only encourage the bond to grow stronger. It was only a matter of time before Brielle became aware of it as well.

When the moon finally lost its pull and we settled back into a sense of normalcy, Kolton dropped the mother of all bombs on us.

"I think it's time we revealed who we are."

Everyone stopped what they were doing to gape at him. Even Melanie looked up from her schoolwork to eye him quizzically. Brielle had expressed a desire to feel "human" again, so Vi and I were in the middle of doing her hair and nails. I paused in my task to sift through Kolton's emotions. Ever since Brielle had almost died, he'd kept our connection wide open. But we'd been so busy the past few days. I was as shocked by his announcement as everyone else.

I'm sorry. I should have said something to you first, he said through our bond, correctly reading my emotional response. *I've been preoccupied lately.*

It's okay, I got out before the others interrupted our silent conversation.

"Say *what* now?" Griff asked, setting down the glass of water he'd been guzzling. He and Jagger had taken a morning run and were still sweaty and shirtless. I'd noticed Vi and Brielle sneaking glances at their ripped torsos more than once. I mean, who wouldn't? You'd have to be blind not to appreciate all those muscles.

"Ever since Keisha left Nora that message," Kolton explained, "I've been realizing how vulnerable we are. For twenty years, I've hidden who I truly am. We've *all* been hiding, afraid of what the werewolf community would do if they found out. But keeping our

222

unique abilities a secret is becoming too dangerous. We need more protection. If Keisha is planning to gather new allies, then we should do the same."

None of us spoke for a long moment, trying to digest his words. He really wanted us to *expose* our abilities to normal werewolves?

Leaning against the kitchen island with his arms crossed over his chest, Jagger was the first to speak. "What do you suggest we do, boss?"

"I think we should host a meeting. An Alpha Meeting."

Vi shot off the couch. "An Alpha Meeting? *Seriously*, Kolton? That would expose us to hundreds. *Thousands*. Every single werewolf on this planet would know that we're different. Are you out of your *mind?*"

I growled, earning me several surprised looks. I too was surprised. I'd never growled at Vi before.

Her expression grew apologetic. "I'm sorry. Poor choice of words. I didn't mean it like that."

I nodded, glancing at Kolton when I felt how pleased he was by my reaction.

Later, he whispered through our bond before turning to Vi again. "Apology accepted. I know an Alpha Meeting is risky, but it would even the playing field. We're not the only werewolves in the world who are different. For all we know, other packs have been attacked too and need help. Exposure would allow us to unite with the werewolf community in a way we never have before."

"But you would have to invite *all* of the alphas, including Arrow. If he came, he would have diplomatic immunity."

Kolton took his sister's argument in stride, remaining calm as he replied, "That's a chance we'll have to take. If we're willing to expose our own secrets, then his leverage over us will be moot."

"Not *all* of his leverage." Vi darted a pointed glance at Melanie, who still didn't know that her mother was alive. Arrow had proven himself capable of malicious deeds, and he could still reveal what he knew of Charlotte's condition if given the opportunity.

At the risk of sounding stupid, I asked, "What's an Alpha Meeting?"

Hendrix had never held one or spoken of one, to my knowledge.

"It's a chance for every pack alpha around the world to congregate in one place and discuss important topics without the worry of challenges breaking out," Kolton explained. "They're allowed to bring their mates and up to five dominant pack members. Fighting isn't allowed during the event—physical ones, anyway. If I host the meeting, it'll be held on Midnight Pack land where I can best protect you. Even if the alphas react poorly to what I reveal, they can't touch any of us."

"But they can at a later date," Vi continued to argue, clearly not on board with this plan. "If they feel threatened by who we really are, they might work together to challenge you. You might be stronger than them with Shadow's help, but they could overwhelm you with numbers."

Sensing her underlying fear, Kolton's expression softened. Still, he firmly replied, "Then we'll have to win them over. I'm sorry, Vi, but we need help. I was too stubborn to admit that before, but having a pregnant mate changes everything. I need to protect my family, and hiding in this cabin isn't going to solve anything. Gaining allies is the best way to keep you all safe long term, and revealing our secret to the werewolf community is the cost."

They stared at each other for a long moment, but eventually, Vi submitted with a resigned sigh. "I hope you know what you're doing, big brother."

He could have hid from me then. Could have kept me from feeling his inner turmoil. But he didn't. I felt every tumultuous emotion as he replied, "Yeah. So do I."

Before any of us were ready, the day of the Alpha Meeting arrived.

Kolton had spared no expense for the event, overseeing every little detail to make sure it was perfect. Vi had spent hours sending out invitations and securing venues. The famous Lake Placid Lodge had been reserved for the occasion, and the entire resort was now filled with dominant werewolves.

Only a handful of submissive wolves were in attendance this evening to handle the catering, the regular human staff dismissed for obvious reasons. I could only imagine how many strings Kolton had pulled to make this event possible, but being a billionaire definitely helped. He'd even paid for travel costs, ensuring everyone arrived with ease. The Rivers' private jet had been flying back and forth all day, along with a few helicopters.

Hosting an Alpha Meeting was a monumental task, which explained why it didn't happen very often. Most alphas wouldn't be able to afford the cost, let alone accommodate everyone. Several alphas had come alone, but many more had brought their mates and a few dominant pack members. Not every single alpha would be in attendance tonight, but Vi had said at least seventy-five had RSVPed. Seventy-five powerful male and female alphas, plus their mates and strongest pack members, all under one roof.

What could possibly go wrong?

Do you think we're doing the right thing? I asked Storm, fiddling with my hair for the umpteenth time. I'd had it professionally done with Vi earlier today, but I wasn't used to having it up like this. The hairdresser had miraculously tamed the unruly mass to look elegant and effortless, leaving a few curls to frame my face and trail down my neck. Feeling whimsical, I'd asked Vi to help me secure daisies in the curly tresses. They didn't exactly match my dress, but I didn't care.

It's hard to say, Storm replied. She'd been alert all day, no doubt in response to the growing number of dominant werewolves, but I hadn't sensed any misgivings from her. *Angels have always respected each other's differences. We each have our own purpose, no matter how great or small our abilities are. But I've noticed that creatures on the earthly plane often fall prey to politics. They are easily threatened by ideals that are different from their own. Instead of celebrating each individual, they condemn them.*

I snorted. *True. Humans and supernaturals alike often treat each other like angels and demons do.*

Storm paused in thought. Then said, *Not all. I no longer see the glaring differences between me and—*

When she didn't finish, I slowly grinned. *Shadow? Is that who you were going to say?*

As if I'd summoned him, Shadow's deep voice suddenly filled my head. *Are you two having a conversation without me? Rude. I can't listen in on Kolton's conversations and yours at the same time.*

I snorted again. *I never thought a demon would have FOMO.*

All part of my charm, little one. I don't want to miss a thing, especially anything that involves drama and sex. Even better if it's both at the same time. Back in Hell, I used to create chaos among the nobles, all so I could rile up the females and—

Shadow, you are not *sharing that story*, Kolton interrupted with a growl.

Shadow released a long-suffering sigh. *You're always so uptight.*

Probably because you've never indulged in an orgy. I used to—

Shadow, Kolton barked.

I laughed, feeling some of my earlier tension fade. If the four of *us* could coexist, then maybe this meeting would have a positive outcome.

Knowing it was almost time to head down, I slipped on my midnight blue heels and secured the straps. Their color matched my dress, which was a floor-length mermaid cut with a one shoulder neckline, leaving the other shoulder bare. The lace and sequined material clung to my curves, showing off the tiniest of baby bumps. It was so small that only a keen observer would notice, which was probably everyone in this building. I was already prepared to receive lots of attention the moment I stepped outside the suite Kolton had reserved for us. News of my pregnancy had no doubt spread beyond Midnight Pack's borders, especially over the past few days as curiosity over this Alpha Meeting had risen up.

Kolton hadn't explained his reasons for holding the meeting, so rumors had grown rampant. The invitations had been sent out less than a week ago, but the phone calls had been endless. The sooner we spilled the beans, the better. We hadn't heard a peep from Keisha, but the clock was ticking. The farther along in my pregnancy I got, the more Kolton worried over my safety. I was in my second trimester now, according to the werewolf gestation period. In less than three months, I'd be at full term.

When I heard footsteps approach the suite, I straightened and faced the door. Jagger was just outside standing guard, so I wasn't worried, but I wanted to remain vigilant all the same. Fighting might not be allowed tonight, but these were uncertain times. I needed to be ready for anything.

As the door opened, I immediately relaxed. Kolton's broad frame filled the doorway, looking devilishly handsome in a midnight blue tux. His dark hair was neatly swept back off his forehead, and the beard he'd been sporting lately was once again reduced to a sexy five-o'clock shadow. When his gaze landed on me, I instantly blushed at his bold perusal. Top to bottom, his eyes didn't miss an inch. Admiration pulsed through our bond, and my blush deepened.

Closing the door, he approached me on silent feet. I held still, letting him look his fill. He greedily eyed my curves, walking right past to slowly circle me. When he released a pleased rumble, my toes curled.

"Never have I seen a more beautiful creature," he purred in my ear, pausing to nuzzle his claim spot and kiss my bare shoulder. "But something's missing."

When he came around to face me once more, I raised an eyebrow indignantly. "Really? All of this isn't enough for you?"

His mouth curved into a wicked grin. "Oh, it's more than enough for me, my sweet flower."

I stared at him in confusion. "Then what could possibly be missing?"

With a flourish, he pulled a blue velvet box from behind his back and handed it to me. "This."

I bit my lip and accepted the offering, suddenly excited. I'd never been one for expensive jewelry, but if Kolton wanted to shower me with trinkets, I wouldn't complain. Opening the box, I expected to find a necklace inside, but that wasn't what I found. "A crown?"

Holy hell, was this thing *real*? It had to have cost a fortune.

Kolton removed the diamond-and-sapphire-studded headpiece. It was more of a tiara than a crown, delicate and slim. "Fit for a queen," he said.

"But I'm not a queen," I protested, though I didn't stop him from carefully sliding the prongs into my hair, making sure the crown was secure on my head before letting go.

"You might have only been the alpha of Midnight Pack for a day, but you will always be its queen. *My* queen. And I want everyone here tonight to know it."

Tears welled in my eyes. God, I loved this man. "You're going to ruin my makeup," I whispered, overcome with a sudden need to kiss him.

A sweet smile ghosted his lips. He leaned forward and brushed a featherlight kiss to my mouth. "I have every intention of ruining your makeup, hairdo, and this sinfully sexy dress," he rumbled back. "But it'll have to wait till after the meeting. Most of the alphas have arrived, and it's time for us to make our appearance. Are you ready?"

I nodded, suppressing a disappointed whimper when he pulled back. "Are you?"

I expected him to nod in return, but he surprised me once again by openly admitting, "No. I'm terrified that this will blow up in our faces, but it was the only thing I could think of to ensure our future survival."

Knowing he needed reassurance, I replied, "It's a risky plan but a solid one, and I'm proud of you for suggesting it. I know it wasn't easy for you."

His throat worked. "Easier than sitting back and waiting for my wife and child to be taken from me."

"Oh, Kolton." I reached out and found his hand. When I discovered that it was shaking, I squeezed his fingers tightly. "I won't let anyone tear us apart, remember? We're going to leave this room and secure our future *together*. Okay?"

A slow smile curved his mouth. Lifting our hands to his lips, he kissed my knuckles and murmured, "Okay, sweetness. Together."

CHAPTER 24

NORA

The energy saturating the room was almost suffocating.

No wonder Alpha Meetings were few and far between. The air practically hummed with power. As we entered through the open doors, I took a moment to appreciate the decor. Tree trunk columns, moss-green carpet, and stone wall facades almost made it feel like we were outside. Fresh flowers and crystal were draped over every surface, making the room look like a fairytale oasis. The french doors leading to the expansive terrace overlooking Lake Placid and the mountains beyond were open, allowing in much-needed fresh air.

"Do you see Arrow?" Vi whispered from behind me, not able to hide her worry. Besides her and Jagger, we'd also included Griff and Carter in our entourage for the evening. Nervous about leaving Brielle and Melanie unprotected at the cabin, Kolton had asked Buck to stay with them. Jagger hadn't argued with the arrangement, but when he'd seen Brielle smile at the brown-haired male, he'd left the cabin in a hurry.

"I don't see him," Kolton replied, able to see over the crowd better than the rest of us.

Arrow hadn't RSVPed, but that was because Vi had "accidentally" forgotten to send him an invitation. It was against protocol, but no one had said anything.

Knowing it was important that the rest of Midnight Pack be a part of this meeting, Kolton had personally invited Carter to attend.

The influential male had held off questioning him further about the event thus far, but I could tell he was thirsty for answers like all the others in this room.

It didn't take long for the crowd to realize that their host had arrived. Face after face turned toward us, each one distinctly different. Practically every nationality was here tonight, as alphas from around the world had come to represent their pack. Some countries housed more werewolves than others, but almost every single one had at least a few.

New York held the largest pack in America, but there were dozens of smaller packs in Canada and Russia. If the land wasn't so vast, a powerful alpha could have united the smaller packs into one, but none had attempted it. More and more, I could understand why. Being the alpha of a large pack was stressful. Not only were you responsible for protecting each member, but you were constantly under a spotlight. Coming from a small insignificant pack, I might not have known much about Kolton before I'd met him, but he was clearly recognized among this group.

His hand slid around me and gripped my hip as he moved forward to greet his guests. Soon, I was in the spotlight as well, being introduced to dozens of names that I soon forgot. Male and female alphas alike congratulated us on the pregnancy, introducing us to their mates and entourage.

Although their words were friendly, their eyes watched us keenly, especially me. Most of them had met Kolton before in past Alpha Meetings, but I was fresh meat. They were curious and more than a little eager to test me. I couldn't blame them though. It was the way of wolves. But every time one of them got too close to me, Kolton was there to warn them away with a stern look.

I pressed closer to his side, doing my best to comfort him. He was doing amazing though, all things considered. And after he'd introduced me to each and every alpha, he even allowed me to leave his side. I didn't go far, staying where he could see me, but the press of bodies and stifling energy was making me lightheaded.

Walking out onto the terrace with a glass of water I'd taken from a passing waiter, I greedily inhaled the fresh air. The sky was perfectly clear tonight, hosting hundreds of twinkling stars and a brilliant waning moon. As I looked out onto the water, I heard someone join me on the terrace. Instead of turning, I stood tall and held my ground.

We weren't among enemies tonight. Tomorrow was a different story, but no one would dare touch me this evening.

Words were a different matter though. Alpha Meetings prohibited physical altercations, but free speech was encouraged. And the male who approached me was taking that to heart.

"My, oh my, Kolton sure found himself a looker." When he whistled quietly in appreciation, I stiffened and turned to face him. Then froze in surprise.

"Mace!"

The male turned just as Vi hurried across the terrace and threw herself at him. He laughed and twirled her around, looking and sounding so much like Griff that I gawked like an idiot.

"When did you get in? I didn't see you earlier," Vi gushed, pulling back to grin up at him.

"You know how I like to be fashionably late," he told her, then paused to eye her up and down. Her hair was loosely curled, framing her pretty face, and the amethyst gown she wore showed off more than a hint of cleavage. "Wow. Little Violet is all grown up. You look stunning. Wouldn't you agree, baby bro?"

My eyes widened as Griff joined us on the terrace, looking more than a little pensive. His gaze darted to the male's hands on Vi's arms, then to his face. A face that looked so much like his that they could be twins. Same smile. Same puppy brown eyes. The only difference was their hair. Griff's was spiky and blond, whereas Mace's was a darker shade of blond and curling against his forehead.

Since when did Griff have a *brother?*

Before Griff could respond, his brother released Vi and turned back to me. "Where are my manners? I'm Mason O'Neal, the alpha of Moon Bay Pack, which just happens to be Canada's largest pack," he said with a wink. "And you must be Nora, Midnight Pack's new alpha female. Kolton's one lucky bastard. I'm not surprised to see that he impregnated you so quickly. If you were my mate, I definitely would have."

"*Watch* it, Mace," Griff snapped, his eyes flashing bright yellow. "That's my alpha female you're speaking to."

Mason smirked at Griff. "Careful, baby brother. You don't want anyone to see what a special snowflake you are. Plus, fighting isn't allowed tonight. You wouldn't want to be *banished* from all future Alpha Meetings. I'm actually surprised to see you here. What are you, the pack's *third* in command? How does it feel to be passed up for the number two spot? It's gotta sting, especially since the position was given to an outsider. You were Kolton's best friend first, after all."

When Griff's hands balled into fists, Vi stepped between them. "Seriously, Mace? You can't give it a rest for one night? It's been *six years* since you've seen your brother. Give him a break."

Mason looked between them, then shook his head with a laugh. "Oh, I see. He's still your obedient little whore, crawling to you every time you go into heat. Isn't that right, baby—"

Griff lunged at his brother with a growl.

Vi raised her hands and barked, "*Enough!*" When Griff immediately stopped, Mason laughed again. Vi threw him a withering glare. "*Grow up*, Mason."

Still smirking, he drawled, "Well, I guess that's my cue to mingle." Tossing me another wink, he left the terrace and sauntered into the crowd.

Everything okay? Kolton asked through our bond.

I found him in the crowd and nodded. *Just some family reunion drama.*

His worry faded. *Call me if you need help.*

Thanks, I will. I focused once more on Griff and Vi.

They were clearly both upset, and I felt like an awkward third wheel just standing there. Before I could tiptoe away though, Griff heaved a sigh and said, "I can't do this anymore."

Ah hell. I should *not* be here for this conversation.

"I have to say something, Vi," he continued. "Something I should have said a long time ago. I—"

"I know," Vi quickly interrupted. "You don't have to say it. I can't do this anymore either. I never should have let you help me when I was in heat. It crossed a line, and I value our friendship too much to keep letting it happen. I—" Her breath hitched. Ducking her head, she whispered, "Excuse me."

Griff watched her hurry away, then quietly swore and shoved both hands through his hair. When he turned to me, I gave him a sheepish look.

"Sorry. I didn't mean to eavesdrop."

"It's okay," he said, his voice flat. Nothing like his usual chipper tone. Sighing again, he joined me at the terrace railing and blankly stared out into the night.

Sipping my drink in thought, I finally settled on saying, "I didn't know you had a brother. He makes quite the first impression."

Griff barked a dry laugh. "Yeah, he was just trying to get under my skin. We're only a year apart. He left the pack shortly before Kolton became alpha, and I haven't seen him since. As you just witnessed, there's a reason I don't talk about him. We don't exactly get along."

I mulled over his words, then said, "He's wrong, you know. Vi doesn't see you that way. She cares about you. A lot."

Griff gave me a sad smile. "Thanks, Nora. I care about her too."

Not wanting to overstep, but desperately wishing to help my friends, I gently replied, "Then maybe you should tell her how you feel."

His smile faded. "She will always see me as her brother's best friend, nothing more. Maybe she did us both a favor tonight. What we had was never going to last."

With that, he turned and headed back inside.

CHAPTER 25

KOLTON

As the night wore on, Shadow's impatience increased.

Unlike everyone else, he didn't have a single qualm about exposing himself. He *wanted* the world to know of his existence. If it were up to him, he would have flooded social media with videos of him shifting into his true form.

The thought of mass hysteria didn't concern him. He relished the idea of striking fear into the hearts of every living soul on this earth.

Good thing we had an agreement.

An agreement that had *mostly* held firm for two decades. I'd given him countless "human" life experiences, and in return, he'd followed my lead. The arrangement had worked well for us, keeping me safe and him satisfied.

But the tables were about to turn.

Keeping him hidden was no longer to my benefit. Although exposing him to the entire world would mean certain death, revealing him to the werewolf community might not. We all shared a mutual secret, and I'd proven my worth to the community on several occasions. My goal may be to better protect my pack against future witch attacks, but I had every intention of returning the favor should another pack need help.

Wolves were only as strong as their pack, and it was about time we considered *every* wolf a pack member.

That's what I'm talking about, Shadow purred, blatantly listening in on my thoughts. *Werewolves are always talking about how united they are, but they fight over territory like scraps of meat. We demons come together in hordes to defeat our enemies. Only when they're dead do we squabble over petty differences.*

I stifled an eye roll at his haughty words. He was right though. Despite their claims of neutrality, werewolves got caught up in rules and politics the same as any other species on this planet. If it wasn't for Nora, I would still be one of them. Still be neck-deep in protocols, determined not to rock the boat.

But I couldn't do that anymore. Couldn't keep quiet in the name of protecting my own. I could ruin everything by opening my mouth, but I could *lose* everything if I didn't. This was bigger than my fears. Bigger than I could handle on my own.

I focused on the woman beside me, on the female who'd bravely agreed to face life's challenges by my side. She'd already done more than I could have ever asked for. Filled my shoes when I couldn't. Pulled me from the abyss again and again. She was proof that change needed to happen. That risks were worth taking. That fear could be overcome.

She was my Midnight Queen, and I would do anything for her. Our future, our children, and our love that continually brought me to my knees needed to be protected at all costs.

So I finally gave Shadow what he wanted. Finally loosened my white-knuckled grip on control and allowed him to rise to the surface. He gladly surged up, happy that I'd given him free rein. But he didn't take over. I'd been counting on that. On the fact that he enjoyed making a grand entrance. We didn't have everyone's attention yet, and he was looking forward to seeing the entire room's reaction to his presence.

Sensing the change through our bond, Nora peered up at me in question. Her blue eyes were bright, made all the brighter against the midnight color of her dress. My breath caught at her staggering beauty, and I took a moment to drink it in. To gain strength from her unwavering gaze.

The Universe had outdone itself when creating this magnificent female.

Whatever happened next, I would always be grateful that fate had chosen me to be her mate.

"I love you," I whispered, bending down to softly kiss her lips.

Okay, loverboy, get on with the show already, Shadow interrupted the moment. *I'm ready for my closeup.*

Nora stood on tiptoe to deepen the kiss, then murmured against my lips, "You got this."

I kissed her one last time and pulled away, using her confidence to fuel my own. Moving to the stage a few feet away, I strode onto it and faced the room. As soon as I did, the crowd quieted. They'd been waiting. Waiting for this moment. I scanned their faces, making sure to meet the eyes of every single one. These people would either become my greatest allies or greatest enemies. I needed them to see. To *know* that siding with me was in their best interest.

Shadow practically clapped his hands with glee. Being surrounded by this much power invigorated him. He wasn't in the least bit intimidated by it. I used his confidence as well to stand tall and keep my hands from shaking. If they detected even the slightest hint of weakness, I would lose them in an instant.

"Thank you all for coming today. I invited you here for a very important reason," I began, relieved when my voice held steady. "A coven of witches has been attacking Midnight Pack. It's why we're meeting here tonight and not at my family's estate. They burned it to the ground." Surprised exclamations rippled through the crowd, but I forged ahead before any of them could start asking questions.

"We defeated the coven a few weeks ago, but the leader managed to escape. She is a powerful Oracle and has sworn to gather witches from around the world to aid in her cause. Since then, she has brutally killed a mated pair from my pack and revealed her plans to take my wife and unborn child from me. Her threats aren't idle. She will stop at nothing to get what she wants."

"What does she want?" a male alpha from China asked, drawing the crowd's attention. "Why is she obsessed with werewolves?"

"She isn't," I said, carefully watching my audience. "Not with normal werewolves, anyway."

Confusion lit many of their faces, but not all. Hope welled in my chest.

"*Normal* werewolves?" a female alpha from Russia questioned. "I do not understand what this means."

"Many of you don't," I replied, "but some of you do. Some of you know exactly what I'm referring to. You've known, but you've kept it secret, just like my father did. Like *I* did. But the secret's out. By now, dozens, possibly *hundreds* of witches have been made aware of it. I can't claim to know everything about their kind, but I do know that they aren't happy. They don't think wolves like me should exist. They think I've stolen something sacred from them, and they want it back."

"Wolves like *you*? What's going on, Alpha Rivers?" demanded the alpha from China.

"He's an *abomination*," called a male from the back of the room.

At the sound of his voice, I stiffened. Darting a quick glance at my pack, I found Nora and Vi frozen with shock. Carter appeared curious, while Jagger and Griff looked ready to bodily remove our unwelcome guest if given the signal. But, as the crowd allowed him to push forward, I didn't say a word. Speaking now would only make me look defensive, like I was hiding something. When he reached the front, he brazenly hopped onto the stage beside me and faced the crowd.

"Apologies for my late arrival," Arrow magnanimously said. "My invitation must have been lost in the mail." His gaze found my sister, as if he knew she'd been responsible. She glowered back at him. "Looks like I made it just in time for the big reveal though. Our illustrious host was going to share why the witches are targeting him and his family. But I should warn you that he thinks of himself as the *hero* of this story. In reality, he's the worst of all villains."

Arrow's voice had almost risen to a shout, but I forced myself to remain silent. Even Shadow kept perfectly still as the male continued to spout off his hatred.

"In reality, he doesn't belong up here on this stage. He doesn't belong anywhere but in the filthy pit he crawled out of. He corrupts everything he touches, especially the female he mated. She was pure and innocent before he got his hands on her. Now, she is *polluted*. Forced to carry his wicked spawn. And *that*," he yelled, pointing at Nora's stomach, "is the greatest of all abominations. The *ultimate* abomination. It—"

With a bellowing roar, Shadow surged to the surface. I allowed the change. *Encouraged* it. Inflamed with fury, I shifted into Shadow's demonic form in record time. Up, up, up, I rose to tower over Arrow. My tuxedo shredded to ribbons, unable to contain my larger frame. Black, dagger-like claws scraped off the ruined clothing to expose a massive body covered in dark fur. When the transformation was complete, I settled back and let Shadow have his moment of glory.

"At last, we meet," he growled down at Arrow, his voice rumbling like an avalanche. "You don't seem so powerful to me from up here. In fact, you look like an insignificant bug. I would squish you right now if it weren't for the respect and loyalty I feel toward my earthly family. But someday. Someday soon, I will eviscerate you for threatening and insulting what is mine. If that makes me the villain, then fine. I'll play that role with relish."

Arrow stumbled back as if he'd been struck, but shockingly, Shadow hadn't even touched a hair on his head. He was behaving. Honoring the code set forth for this evening. Destroying Arrow would provide us both endless satisfaction, but despite the damage he'd just caused, killing him would only prove his words to be true.

Save it for later, big guy. It's time to let Kolton finish his speech, a feminine voice floated through our minds, one that instantly soothed our rage. Nora was suddenly beside us, placing her hand on Shadow's powerful bicep. When he turned and wrapped his massive arms around her, the room erupted into chaos.

As the shouts escalated, each one vying to be heard, Shadow inwardly snickered. *I think the reveal was a success. What do you guys think?*

I think they're going to start running for their lives if Kolton doesn't say something soon, Storm tartly replied.

I agree, Nora chimed in. *We need to do damage control after all the awful things Arrow said. Maybe I should shift too.*

No, I said, relieved when Shadow backed me up by tightening his arms around her. *The only one who needs to expose themselves tonight is me. The more their focus is on me, the better.*

Nora craned her neck back to look Shadow in the eye, but I knew the suspicious look was directed at me. *Was this your plan all along? To expose only yourself in case things went south?*

When I didn't answer, she pursed her lips and shoved at Shadow's arms. He loosened his grip on her, and she pulled away to face the crowd, roaring, "*Enough!*"

The crowd immediately quieted, blinking up at the pregnant female in surprise.

Nora, what are you doing? I quietly growled, itching to pull her back into Shadow's protective embrace.

Like hell am I allowing you to sacrifice yourself for the rest of us, she growled back, reaching up to straighten her crown. *Those days are over, Kolton. We do things* together *now.*

Before I could stop her, she conjured a ball of magic to her fingertips. Her captive audience gaped at the magical display, their mouths open like fish out of water.

"As you can see, my husband and I aren't normal werewolves," she began, holding the bright magical ball steady as she spoke. "We were *born* this way, along with a few others in our pack. We invited you all here today because we believe there are more like us. More werewolves who were born with spirit familiars inside them."

Shocked whispers swept through the crowd, but she didn't stop.

"With the help of our familiars, we can shift at will and perform magic. *This* is why witches are targeting werewolves. They believe that spirits should only bless *them*, that werewolves have no business connecting with the celestial plane. Well, I say to hell with that. The spirits *chose* us, and we have every right to their power. Witches need to be put in their place. They need to learn that werewolves aren't going to roll over and submit to their demands.

"These differences don't make us abominations. They make us *strong*. Even stronger when we join forces. So we're asking you to join with us. To rise up against the witches and anyone else who would threaten our kind. Because, at the end of the day, we're all the same. We're all just creatures trying to survive. To live life without being persecuted for who we are. I encourage you all to remember that. To put aside what you've been taught and allow your perspectives to change.

"We need your help. Our family is growing, and we want more than anything to keep it safe. You might not have known that werewolves like us exist, but we're here to prove that we can coexist. We *have* been coexisting. Some of you just weren't aware of it. Those who've known might be secretly harboring wolves like us in their own pack, wolves that they've kept hidden for their protection. Better yet, maybe some of you in this room *are* those wolves."

Shadow quietly chuckled as the room erupted again. He was enjoying this open exchange immensely. He never liked that I'd kept him hidden from the world.

Your mate gives better speeches than you, he said, keeping a close eye on the restless crowd. When a male bumped the stage, Shadow reached out and pulled Nora back into his arms. She accepted the protective move and extinguished her magic.

I know, was all I said, too busy brimming with pride and scanning the room for possible threats. So far, our audience seemed more alarmed than hostile. Even with Arrow's condemning words and Shadow's fearsome appearance, they didn't look at me or Nora with fear. More like . . . awe.

"*Lupus Deus,*" I heard someone say.

"Apollo and Artemis," another said.

Storm started to groan, but the sound was cut off by a resounding belly laugh. Thankfully, Shadow stopped himself from laughing aloud. But he didn't hesitate to croon at the irate male still standing beside us, "How do you like me now, *Zuriel?* They think I'm a god."

Really, Shadow? Nora and I both scolded at the same time.

His mouth stretched into a wolfish grin. Arrow didn't respond, but his fists shook with silent rage. When Shadow opened his mouth again, Arrow jumped from the stage and stormed off.

"Pity," Shadow said, watching him shove through the crowd and exit the room. "I was just getting started."

He'll be back when another opportunity presents itself, Storm quietly said. *We haven't seen the last of him.*

Shadow grinned again. "Good, because I haven't officially met Zuriel yet. I want to look that bastard in the eyes before I wipe the floor with him."

Storm didn't comment.

I was just about to ask Shadow to give me back control when the room suddenly shook and swayed.

Nora stiffened in Shadow's arms. "Did you feel that? It—"

The stage groaned and cracked, then split open beneath our feet.

CHAPTER 26

NORA

It all happened so fast.

We went from standing on solid ground to falling within seconds.

The earth simply opened up and swallowed us whole.

As we fell, Shadow curled himself around me like a living shield. He grunted as huge chunks of rock and earth pelted him, but didn't loosen his grip on me. When we hit solid ground again, he rolled us out of the way just as a slab of cement came crashing down.

Nora! Kolton shouted through our bond, his voice filled with fear.

Choking on a mouthful of chalky dust, I replied, *I'm okay.*

The baby?

Fine. We're both fine.

More rocks tumbled down, but Shadow's massive body continued to shield me. When there was a lull, he started to stand.

Shadow, give me control, Kolton demanded. *I need to protect her.*

Let me do it, Shadow replied back, surprising us both. *Let me protect your mate. We have more strength in this form.*

I could tell that letting Shadow take charge was the *last* thing Kolton wanted to do, so I was doubly surprised when he said, *Fine. My world is in your hands, Shadow. Keep her safe at all costs.*

Oh, I will. I'll destroy anything that tries to touch her. He managed to sound dead serious and excited at the same time, clearly pleased that Kolton trusted him to protect me.

Wiggling an arm free of his tight hold, I willed magic to my fingertips. The bright light illuminated the dark space, allowing me to see even better through the dust and gloom. "We need to find the others. They could be injured."

Or worse. Werewolves were strong, but being crushed beneath tons of rock and cement could still kill them.

Shadow started to move, keeping one arm secured around me as he did. I went along for the ride without comment, knowing that now wasn't the time to assert my independence. Even if I asked Storm to shift into her angelic form, Shadow's hulking body was the best protection for both me and the baby. Our safety was more important than needing to look strong and capable.

Sure enough, another rock came crashing down and Shadow threw up his free arm to stop it from hitting me. I winced as he grunted in pain again.

"You okay?" I asked, peering up at him.

His blood red eyes met mine. "Just a flesh wound."

I blinked. "Did you just quote *Monty Python?*"

Despite the circumstances, he gave me a wolfish grin. "Demons have hobbies too, little one. I also like *The Princess Bride.* Anybody want a peanut?"

I took a moment to stare at him in wonder. He was the scariest thing I'd ever seen, yet here he was, using his body to protect mine and quoting movies. The old saying "Don't judge a book by its cover" most definitely applied to him.

A shout suddenly reached our ears.

"Vi!" I shouted back, relief filling me when she called, "Over here!"

Shadow surged toward the sound of her voice, using his clawed hand to climb over slabs of cement and shove aside debris. Every time rocks rained down on us, he paused to shield me from harm.

I guided the way with my ball of magical light, and soon, we saw movement up ahead.

"Help me!" Vi yelled, struggling to lift a massive cement slab. "It's Griff. He's trapped."

Shadow hurried his pace. When he reached Vi's position, he carefully set me down on the uneven ground. "Don't move from this spot," he ordered.

"But I can help," I argued, trying to catch sight of Griff underneath the rubble.

"You're with *child*," Shadow sternly said. "You can help by keeping him safe."

Oh. Well, I couldn't really argue with *that*. Maybe I wasn't useless here after all. I had a baby to protect.

Nodding, I stayed put as he turned to help Vi with the slab. One giant heave and he lifted it off the ground. Not surprising, since he'd been able to break down a steel door capable of withstanding a *bomb*. Vi scrambled beneath the slab and quickly pulled out a body covered in dust.

Griff. I'd recognize that spiked hairdo anywhere.

His chest was so still that, for a heartstopping moment, I feared we were too late. He suddenly jerked upright with a sharp inhale, the sound closely followed by a violent coughing fit.

"Griff," Vi whimpered, then threw herself at him. He caught her with a groan, still struggling to breathe. "I'm so sorry. I tried to hold on. It's all my fault."

He started to laugh, but only ended up coughing again. "This isn't . . . your fault. Thanks for . . . finding me. Couldn't breathe."

In reply, she hugged him harder. Sighing, he closed his eyes and held her back.

Seeing them both safe, I longed to savor the moment, but we

couldn't stay here. It was too dangerous. I was pretty sure the entire building had collapsed. Debris was everywhere, and water was pouring down from broken pipes. The area could flood, or the remains of the building could shift and bury us alive.

"We need to go. Have you seen Jagger or Carter?" I questioned.

Vi pulled back to shake her head. She had a nasty gash on her arm that was still leaking blood, both otherwise looked unharmed. "It happened so fast. I only had time to grab Griff's hand, and then we were falling."

Grimly nodding, I called out, "Jagger! Carter!"

Through the sounds of trickling water and shifting debris, I heard a few voices call back. None were Jagger or Carter though.

"We can help the others, but we need to find Jagger and Carter first," I firmly said, picking up my skirt. I'd only walked a few steps when massive arms surrounded me once more. I didn't protest, allowing Shadow to pick me up as if I weighed nothing. Vi and Griff followed in our wake, the latter regaining his wind with each stride.

I strained my ears, listening for any sound of our missing pack members. More voices reached us, but not the right ones. Just when I started to worry, we heard a cough.

That's Jagger, Kolton immediately said, relief evident in his tone. *To the left and up above.*

"Hold on," Shadow said, right before he crouched on his hind legs and launched us upward. I extinguished my magic and gripped his arm tight as he scaled the debris with surprising strength, only using one hand to steady our swift ascent. Within seconds, we were ground level.

Furniture littered the surrounding area, the suites on the second floor now a pile of unstable rubble at our feet. I called out to Jagger again and received an answer this time. Shadow climbed over broken beds and dressers, ducking under jagged beams of wood until a familiar shape materialized through the swirling dust.

As we approached, he didn't move. He simply stood there with his head lowered.

"Jagger?" I called one more time, wiggling to be let down. Shadow paused to set me on my feet but kept one step behind me as I picked my way forward.

Jagger raised his head, only to lower it once more. As soon as I got close enough, I understood why. "I couldn't stop it in time," he said, his voice hushed. "It came out of nowhere."

"Carter," I whispered, placing a hand over my mouth. He was laying on his back with a thick wooden beam sticking out of his chest. His *heart*. His eyes were still open, vacantly staring up at the sky.

No, Kolton quietly groaned as Shadow came to stand behind me.

He might have survived if the beam had been smaller, but the thickness of it must have destroyed too much of his heart.

Vi and Griff joined us, reacting similarly.

"How could this have happened?" Vi said, helplessly looking around at the wreckage. "I don't understand."

We need to search for survivors. There could be more trapped like Griff was, Kolton said, setting aside his grief for later. I struggled to do the same, relaying his message to the others. Nodding, they dispersed, slowly picking through the rubble. I took a moment to crouch beside Carter's body and gently close his eyes.

"I'm sorry," I whispered, not knowing what else to say. Despite all of his unanswered questions, he'd remained loyal to the Rivers' family until the end. I didn't even get the chance to thank him for everything he'd done to keep the pack from falling apart.

When I stood again, Shadow was a short distance away, helping someone crawl out from beneath what looked like the remains of a stone fireplace. I moved to help, only to freeze solid as I felt an invasive presence tap at my mental shields. It felt like the tip of a pointed nail, poking at my mind to be let in. Alarmed, I slammed my shields down. In retaliation, the nail scraped down the shield's outer wall, making me wince and grab my head.

Keisha. She was trying to penetrate my mind!

Storm rose up, growling as she sensed Keisha's presence. *Don't let her in!*

I'm trying not to, I cried, still clutching my head. *But it hurts.*

We have to find her, Storm urgently said. *She has to be nearby for her strength to be this great.*

I stopped breathing. *Nearby? She's here?*

A sudden flash of light blinded me, and I squeezed my eyes shut. When I opened them again, it was to find a hand reaching out to grab me. Before I could react, a deafening roar pounded my ears. The hand jerked away, but it was too late. A massive form whooshed past me and I heard a scream. A scream that abruptly cut off. The bright light winked out, allowing me to clearly see what had happened.

Shadow had his jaw clamped down on the throat of a man. No, a *warlock*. He was still alive, his mouth opened wide in horror. He looked at me as if to plead for help, but a second later, Shadow bit clean through his neck, severing his head from his body.

I looked away as blood sprayed, the head hitting the ground with a meaty thunk. As I did, a cerulean blue light lit up my peripheral vision. I whirled, just in time to see Keisha standing just beyond the wreckage.

"Keisha!" I screamed, stepping toward her.

Still wearing a black cloth around her eyes, she simply grinned and slipped inside her portal. In an instant, she vanished.

The next several hours were a flurry of activity.

Three other werewolves had been killed by the magic-induced collapse. Griff's brother had made it out unscathed and had stuck around to help us find others who'd been buried alive, but I'd overheard him mutter to Griff, "You should have convinced him this was a bad idea. The alphas won't lend their aid. Not after this."

We hadn't been the only ones to witness Keisha leaving the scene, along with several other witches who'd portalled away before we could stop them. The decapitated warlock was undeniable proof of their presence, but it was clear that many of the alphas blamed Kolton for the catastrophe. He'd shifted back into his human form, making himself more approachable, but the awe from earlier was gone. Most left with their entourages as soon as they were free of the rubble. Only a few stayed to help us clean up the mess before humans caught wind of what had happened.

They would want answers as to why the famous building had collapsed. Unlike the Rivers' estate, we couldn't hide this disaster from them. Local authorities would comb the wreckage, so we couldn't leave anything for them to find. Even our DNA needed to be scrubbed clean of the site.

"We need to set it on fire," Kolton solemnly told us when the last werewolf had been accounted for. "There's too much evidence. Too much blood."

The others nodded without comment.

I was about to ask how we would start a fire when Kolton raised a hand engulfed in dark purple flame. Vi, Griff, and Jagger did the same, the colors varying depending on their magic.

Shaking his head, Mason turned and silently left.

I glanced around, noting that we were the last ones here. Carter's wrapped body had been placed a safe distance from the wreckage, but the others who'd died had been carried away by their packs.

You're an Elemental, Storm suddenly said to me. *You have the ability to produce fire as well. A fire greater than all of theirs combined.*

I blinked. *Really?* I shouldn't be surprised, but I was. I was still getting used to the idea of having magic.

Try it. Think of the element you wish to conjure.

Will you help me?

You don't need help. You're a natural.

I felt myself smile a bit at her compliment. I looked up and caught Kolton staring at me. He raised an eyebrow, as if waiting for me to join their magical light display. Smiling a bit more, I focused on my magic. On willing *fire* to my fingertips.

With a *whoosh*, white-hot flame covered my hand. It was stronger than the usual glow. Wilder. As it danced in place, I marveled at how the heat didn't scorch my skin. Emboldened, I willed the fire to burn brighter. *Hotter.* So hot that it turned blue.

I glanced up again to find them all staring at me now, their expressions identical. At the wonder on their faces, my cheeks heated. It wasn't *that* impressive. Was it?

Everything about you is impressive, Kolton murmured through our bond, making me blush harder. Aloud, he said, "Whether or not the werewolf community accepts us, never forget that you're a miracle, Nora. Now, show us what you can do. Show us what you're capable of."

Biting my lip, I decided to let instinct take over. Instead of throwing the ball of fiery magic at the rubble, I flattened my hand and blew on the flames. At the same time, I focused on another of my elemental abilities. A gust of air pushed the fire forward, so forcefully that it shot from my hand in a stream of deadly blue flame. I continued to blow on the fire, directing its path until several pieces of furniture were ablaze.

"Show off," Vi said with a snort, casting her own ball of magic into the wreckage.

Griff and Jagger followed suit, but Kolton paused for a moment, gathering more magic to his fingertips before whipping his hand out. Tiny bolts of purple flame shot into the rubble like bullets. At their impact, several explosions sparked into the air, making us all take several steps back.

You're quite impressive yourself, I told him, watching as our joint effort devoured the once beautiful lodge like a starving beast.

With a tired sigh, he reached out to grasp my hand. *Perhaps, but it wasn't enough to stop this tragedy from happening. Instead of gaining allies, we lost one of our own. I don't . . . I don't know how to fix this.*

I squeezed his hand, the only reassurance I could give him. "Maybe not," I whispered, "but we'll figure it out together."

CHAPTER 27

NORA

I was still in bed late the next morning when I heard Kolton's raised voice. Opening my eyes, I listened for a moment, realizing that he must be on the phone.

Not surprising.

Ever since we'd arrived back at the cabin earlier this morning, he'd been on the phone. We'd personally delivered Carter's body to his family but had only told them what they needed to know. The witch had attacked again. The rest would have to wait until we could gather the entire pack together.

Exhausted, we'd headed back to the cabin to clean up and get some rest, but I could see now that Kolton had never come to bed. Still tired, I dragged myself out of bed and went in search of him. I didn't have to go far. When I softly knocked on the hallway bathroom door and opened it, Kolton wrapped up his conversation and ended the call.

"Sorry, did I wake you?" he asked, setting his phone on the counter.

"It's fine," I replied and slipped into the bathroom to hug him. "You didn't come to bed."

He sighed and folded me into his arms. I immediately felt some of his tension drain away. "I tried. Several times. But I keep getting calls I can't ignore."

"Anything new?" I asked, snuggling against him.

"Just pack members and now alphas from around the world calling with a million questions. Some sound understanding and even supportive."

"Well, that's good."

"While many more are angry and blame me for everything bad that has happened recently."

"You aren't to blame. You've only been trying to protect us."

"Say that to the wolves who died. To Carter."

I pulled back to look up at his guilt-ridden face. "You can't stop every bad thing from happening, Kolton. You're only one man."

A muscle thrummed in his jaw. "But I can't seem to stop *any* bad thing from happening."

"You stopped that warlock. You thwarted Keisha's evil plan to take me and our child."

You mean me, right? a voice in our heads interjected. *I swooped in like a wrecking ball and saved the day.*

"Butt out, Shadow. This is a private conversation," I chided.

He huffed, but fell silent.

"He's right, though," Kolton said. "If he hadn't been there, I might not have gotten to you in time. I was distracted by—"

I placed my finger over his mouth, stopping him from saying more. "No what-ifs. We're safe, and that's all that matters right now."

"But—"

"Take a break, Kolton," I gently interrupted him. "Take time to rest."

He opened his mouth again. Before he could say a word, I slid my other hand between us and grabbed him through his jeans. He expelled a harsh breath against my finger.

"That's a good boy," I whispered, slowly squeezing his length. It swelled beneath my fingers, drawing a soft moan from him.

Encouraged, I brought my other hand down to undo his button and zipper.

"The door's still open," he said, then grunted when I slid my hand inside his pants and gripped his growing erection.

"I'll be quick," I breathed, pulling out his shaft so that I could stroke it.

Leaning back against the counter, he gave in and closed his eyes. As I pleasured him, he slid his hands beneath my short nightgown and gripped my bare butt.

At the discovery, a pleased rumble vibrated his chest. "I love when you're not wearing underwear."

"I thought you liked ripping my underwear off?"

"I love that too."

Humming, I rose up and nipped at his bottom lip. He opened for me, and I darted my tongue into his mouth, instantly growing wet when I tasted him. He raised a hand to grasp the nape of my neck and deepen the kiss.

I sighed into his mouth, pumping him faster. The kiss turned passionate. Feverish. I brushed my thumb over his swollen tip and found it wet with his arousal. He gripped my butt harder, kneading the flesh. Drawing me closer to him. Encouraging me to impale myself on his—

"Oh, *come on*. I did *not* need to see that," a voice from the doorway groaned.

Startled, I broke the kiss and tried to pull away. Kolton held me fast, growling at our intruder, "Shut the door, Griff. We're not finished yet."

"*Finished?* Yeah, I can see you're not finished. You'd better not leave a mess on the floor. We all have to use this bathroom, you know."

My face burst into flames.

"*Griff,*" Kolton barked, still gripping my butt. When I started to release his dick, he growled through our bond, *Don't.*

Oh my. Someone was desperate for an orgasm.

Yes, I am. And you're going to give it to me right now, he continued to growl. Aloud, he snarled, "You have one second to shut that door, Griff, or I'm going to—"

The door slammed shut.

"Continue, wife," he ordered, his cock swelling once more.

Struggling to control my laughter, I obeyed, not wanting to make him any more grumpy.

"I'm not grumpy." His words ended in a groan as I picked up where I left off, rapidly pumping his shaft.

"Oh, you are," I replied with amusement, "but I think it's cute."

He huffed but didn't argue further, too focused on what I was doing. His need for release was a total turn on. He didn't even care that Griff had caught us red-handed. Literally.

When he came less than a minute later and made a show of loudly moaning, arousal was practically dripping down my thighs. As soon as he was finished, he stripped us both naked and turned on the shower, then proceeded to pleasure me senseless.

If I made too much noise, I wasn't aware. My only awareness was the utter joy and relief I felt to be sharing this moment with my mate. We'd narrowly survived another brush with death, and although our future was more uncertain than ever, at least we were both still alive.

Over the next several days, everything felt . . . tense.

Not just with Midnight Pack and nearly every alpha in the entire world, but with our inner circle as well. Besides all the trauma we'd recently endured, there were certain topics that everyone was clearly avoiding. Namely, anything that had to do with their current relationship status.

Even Melanie could feel the tension and had commented more than once on how weird everyone was being.

Normally the one to lighten the mood, Griff had been exceptionally quiet this past week. At first, I thought it had something to do with his almost being crushed to death, but it was his subtle glances at Vi that clued me in.

He wasn't happy with how things currently were between them.

Vi usually scolded and bossed him around on the regular, but she'd been rather formal and distant with him ever since we'd returned to the cabin.

And then there was Brielle and Jagger.

Although Brielle was still mostly aloof toward him, Jagger had become increasingly more agitated. He was spending more and more time away from the cabin, either running errands or taking long walks through the woods.

I was pretty sure that if this pattern continued for much longer, we were all going to explode, including myself. I desperately wanted to help my friends fix their problems, but I didn't think my input would be welcome. I needed something else to focus on so I wouldn't accidentally blab my mouth and make things worse.

Despite how busy he'd been with trying to calm the pack, making amends with the alphas, and keeping his billion-dollar business running, Kolton had picked up on my stress. When he'd asked me about it, I'd simply replied, "This cabin is too small."

He'd mulled over my words that evening, but bright and early the next morning, he'd announced at breakfast, "Okay, everyone, change of plans for today. Clear your schedules because we're going out."

"Out where?" Vi asked dubiously.

"To the estate. I hired a crew a couple weeks ago to clear the wreckage, but they haven't quite finished yet. Since we could all use a change of scenery, I told them that we would finish the job for them."

His statement earned him several groans.

"This isn't up for debate. We're all going," he firmly said.

"What about the witches?" Jagger asked. "There's not much protection out there."

"If they show up, we'll see them coming from a mile away. Besides, there's nothing left for them to burn down or destroy."

"Just our bodies," Griff muttered.

Ignoring Griff's comment, Kolton stood from the table. "Meet me out front in half an hour. Anyone who's late gets dragged out."

I blinked at his brusque tone but didn't say a word. Despite the risks that leaving this cabin posed, we all needed a distraction. A little physical labor might be the perfect thing to take our minds off our problems.

An hour and a half later, we pulled into the estate's roundabout. At a glance, I could already see the difference the cleaning crew had made. The giant, smoking pile of rubble was nearly gone. Most of the remaining debris was broken slabs of foundation and crumbling stone facade. A huge metal dumpster sat beside where the mansion used to be, filled to the brim with our scorched belongings. We hadn't bothered to pick through the wreckage, but I doubted anything had survived the fire.

"I started working on the blueprints for the rebuild," Kolton told me as he parked the truck and killed the engine. A huge cooler stocked full of food for the day was in the backseat, so the others had driven in Vi's Jeep. "I was thinking we could add an attached greenhouse to the back just off the kitchen, since that side of the house gets such good sunlight."

Tears of joy instantly sprung to my eyes. I turned to him, grinning a mile wide. "Seriously? You would really do that?"

He blinked, as though surprised by my reaction. "Of course. You're my wife, Nora. I want to see you happy."

"I *am* happy. You've given me everything I've always wanted and so much more." At the look on his face, my grin faded. "What's wrong?"

He broke eye contact to blankly stare out the front windshield. "This isn't the life I wanted for you. A life filled with constant fear and danger. I know I married you to ensure my family's safety, but all I want now is to ensure *your* safety. I would give my life for you in a heartbeat, but I'm afraid even that won't be enough."

My pulse quickened. "What are you trying to say, Kolton?"

He clenched his jaw, then blurted, "Maybe it would be best if you went into hiding. Just until the baby's born. Or maybe a little longer."

A gaped at him with growing horror. "*Without* you? Is that what you're saying?"

"I can't *protect* you, Nora," he said, his voice rising. "Not when I'm constantly worried about you. Even when I'm drowning in my responsibilities, all I can think about is you and our baby's safety. I'm distracted and keep making poor decisions. Maybe the solution is to hide you away where no one can find you. That way, no one can hurt you."

I continued to gape. "You want to *send* me away?"

He sucked in air through his teeth. "Don't say it like that, Nora. I don't want to. I *need* to. I don't know how else to fix our world so that it's safe for you."

"That's because you're trying to fix it all by *yourself* again," I shouted. The others could probably hear, but I was too upset to care.

"That's your biggest problem, Kolton. You try to carry the whole world on your shoulders, sacrificing *all* that you are, just so the people around you don't have to. But *guess what?* We *want* to carry some of that weight. We want to *sacrifice.* You taught me that families help each other. You *married* me so that I would help this family, would help *you,* and now you want to take that away from me? Screw that. I promised you I wasn't going anywhere, and like hell are you going to make me break that promise."

"Nora!" he called, but I was already out of the truck and storming away. The others silently watched as I skirted around them and kept going, aiming for the wide patch of grass between the destroyed house and still-intact garage. As soon as I hit the grass, I knew exactly where to go. I picked up the pace and charged toward my destination, suddenly needing it more than oxygen.

It had been too long. *Too long* since I'd visited my place of solace.

Second place. Kolton was my first place, but I kind of wanted to punch him right now. Purely to knock some sense into him, of course.

I knew he couldn't just push a button and stop worrying about me, but sending me away to *hide* until the danger had passed?

Hell, no.

My days of running and hiding were over. I didn't like living in constant fear, but I would rather endure that than be separated from the people I loved. I no longer wondered where I belonged. I was no longer afraid that I didn't *fit.* I knew my mule-headed mate understood that, but he kept getting in his own way. Kept forgetting that we were supposed to be doing everything *together* now.

We were *one.* One body. One mind. One soul.

So why did it feel like he was constantly trying to split us in two?

"You can't keep taking on all of life's problems by yourself," I grumbled aloud, marching past the neglected swimming pool and toward my little slice of heaven. "I know you're a big strong alpha, but so am I. Let me *help* you. Let me *breathe*. I know it's scary, but that's life. We're not guaranteed a tomorrow, only today. So I want to live it. *Live it!*"

I was shouting again like a lunatic, but I'd officially reached my limit. It was time to release all of my pent-up emotions. Time to put my foot down and say my piece. And it felt *good*. I'd been tiptoeing around Kolton for weeks now, afraid that speaking my mind would send him spiraling again, but I couldn't keep living my life that way.

It wasn't fair to me, and it wasn't fair to him either.

If he continued to hide me from the world, I'd eventually grow to resent him. I'd been raised that way by my old pack, and he knew it. Knew that I'd been stuffed into a tiny box and told to stay there.

But I couldn't do it. Even for the sake of his sanity, I couldn't become that weak, helpless girl again.

"I'm sorry, but I can't," I whispered as sudden emotion tightened my throat. I didn't want to hurt him, but I couldn't be trapped again. Couldn't be a *prisoner*. I needed space to grow. Space to be me.

We were one, but I still had dreams and desires of my own. Still had a burning need to become a better, stronger version of myself. That version wasn't foolishly reckless like my old self. It thought first and planned. It considered the well-being of others and myself. But it didn't shy away from living life just because it was dangerous. I could still live out loud without being reckless. Could still make the most of my time here on earth, however long that may be.

More than anything, I wanted to spend every second of that time with Kolton. To build countless memories and share moments of joy. And when things got difficult, I wanted to spend that time with him as well. No matter how hard life got, I was greedy to share it all with him.

He'd said he didn't want this life for me, but despite the dangers, this was the only life I wanted.

So I couldn't allow him to lock me away.

He'd admitted that losing me would destroy him, but being separated from him would destroy *me*.

As I reached the gardens, I felt a little better, but not much. I hated that we weren't on the same page. Hated that he was over there and I was over here. Hated that our family was at odds. Hated that our pack had begun to doubt us. Hated that some of them had died. That the Alpha Meeting had ended in failure. That Arrow was still trying to tear our family apart. That Keisha was still out there and gaining new allies. That her stupid premonition wouldn't stop replaying in my head over and *over* again.

Maybe Kolton wasn't the only one trying to carry the weight of the world on his shoulders.

Sighing, I threw myself into the task before me instead of dwelling on all my doubts and fears. Before long, I heard noises coming from the house. Or rather, from the wreckage. We'd brought hand tools to help break up the larger pieces but no heavy equipment. As werewolves, we didn't need it anyway. After several minutes, I glanced up and easily found Kolton. Even from this far away, I could see that he'd removed his shirt, his deep olive skin already glistening with sweat.

I tore my eyes away before I could do something stupid, like drool. Even when I was mad at him, I still desired him. I was a hopeless Kolton addict, that was for sure. A few minutes later, Melanie joined me, saying that the boys wouldn't let her help.

At the adorable pout she gave me, I smiled and said, "That's okay. You can help me instead. I've been wanting to try something, and you can be the first to see me do it."

Her dark amber eyes brightened with interest. "Can Princess watch too?" She squeezed her blue unicorn, so hard that I feared its head would pop off. The stuffed animal had never been far from her side this past month. I was pretty sure she was afraid of losing this one too.

Sad that the six-year-old had to worry about such a thing, I lightly tugged on one of her pigtails and replied, "Of course she can. Whenever I do this, she's always welcome to watch."

Melanie smiled, revealing her two missing front teeth. The adult teeth were slowly growing in though, making her look "like a big girl," as she put it.

"You see these roses?" I asked her, pointing to the bush I'd been working on. "Several of them have begun to die, and that makes me sad."

The girl reached out and patted my shoulder sympathetically. "Don't be sad, Nora. You're so pretty."

At her childlike logic, I stifled a laugh. "Thank you, Mellie. You're pretty too. So is Princess."

She smiled again.

Focusing on the bush, I eyed the white flowers and pinched one off. By tomorrow, it would be dead and shriveled up, but I looked back at Melanie and said, "Do you think this rose is pretty?"

She scrunched up her nose, then shook her head.

I conjured magic to my fingertips, willing it to bleed into the rose's stem like water. Within seconds, the wilted flower began to transform. The wrinkled petals smoothed out, becoming a pearly white once more. Full of new life, they fanned open, making Melanie squeal and clap her hands with glee.

"Is it pretty now?" I asked, smiling wide.

"Yes! Can I have it?"

I handed it to her, and she took it, scampering off to show the others.

I was wondering when you would try that, Storm spoke in my mind. She almost sounded pleased. Maybe even proud.

"Earth magic is your affinity. Plus, you're the Goddess of Wild Nature. I wanted to see what all the fuss was about."

She huffed a laugh. *Yes, that used to be me. Now, it is us.*

I tilted my head to the side. "Us?"

Those abilities are no longer mine. At least, not fully. Even when my spirit leaves you someday, I will never regain them completely. A part of them will always belong to you. I'm starting to believe that might be why Zuriel wanted me to come to Earth.

"So that when you returned to Heaven, your power would be diminished?"

Yes.

"Oh, Storm. I'm so sorry. But I hope you will stay with me for a long time."

She was silent for so long that I worried she didn't feel the same. Then, *Because of your human soul, I am unable to extend your life beyond that of a mortal one. I will live far beyond your lifespan, but wherever I go next, I know that I will miss this time I had with you.*

I sniffed back tears. "Aww, Storm, you're going to make me cry."

Not surprising.

A laugh burst from me. "Right? These pregnancy hormones are no joke."

We chatted for a bit more, then fell into companionable silence while I resumed my task. Roughly an hour passed before I heard the approach of footsteps. Knowing who it was without looking up, I kept my focus on the weeds I was pulling.

He stopped in front of me, but when I still didn't acknowledge him, he crouched to my level. A hand slid into my line of sight, and I paused when I saw a pathetically drooping daisy resting on his palm.

"Can you fix it?" Kolton quietly asked me.

Suddenly emotional all over again, I bit my lip to keep it from trembling. Instead of answering, I reached out and touched the delicate flower. Moments later, my magic breathed new life into it. I risked a peek at Kolton's face and found it lit with wonder. Swallowing roughly, he lifted the daisy and tucked it into my hair.

When I started to drop my gaze, he gently grasped my chin. "I heard most of your thoughts earlier. I'm sorry, Nora. You're right about everything. We're soulmates, but we're more than that. We're equals. A *team*. And that means we work better together. I won't send you away. I'll never send you away. It's time I accepted that I can't control our fate. All we have is right now, and I *desperately* want to spend it with you."

A tear slid down my cheek, and he caught it, gently brushing it away.

"Forgive me, sweetness. Please forgive me," he whispered.

Unable to speak, I simply nodded.

Closing his eyes in relief, he breathed, "Come here. I need to hold you."

Hungry for his warmth and comfort, I fell into his waiting arms, letting my tears freely flow.

He held me for a long moment, soaking up my closeness as I soaked up his. Then said, "You're going to be an incredible mother, you know. Mellie adores you."

I smiled against his chest. "Do you really think we're having a boy?"

"I do."

My smile widened. "What should we name him?"

"Hmm. I'm open to suggestions. Nothing crazy like celebrities are naming their kids these days though."

I laughed.

"Boss, we've got company!" Jagger suddenly hollered.

Just like that, our little moment of peace vanished.

Kolton stood up, bringing me with. He practically jogged toward the others, each step more urgent than the last. When we reached their location and spotted a sheriff's car in the roundabout, Kolton started to relax.

Until two men stepped out and faced us.

He immediately pulled me against him and growled a word. One word that filled my veins with ice.

"*Witches.*"

CHAPTER 28

NORA

"Whoa. *Buddy.* Calm down." The younger of the two men raised his hands, then immediately realized his mistake when both Griff and Jagger growled too. "Okay, okay, I'm lowering my hands. Seriously, we just came to talk. Also, *warlock*, if you please. I'm not too keen on being called a witch."

"Noah, let me handle this," the older man said, slowly rounding the SUV. He was broad, blond, and blue-eyed. So was the younger man, but with longer hair tied back in a manbun. They looked enough alike that I guessed they were related. "Forgive the intrusion, but we're here to speak with Kolton Rivers."

"You found him," Kolton replied testily, still gripping me tight. "This is private property, so unless you have official police business, I'll ask you to leave."

The man blinked, then looked down at his brown leather jacket and jeans.

"The car, Dad," the younger man said with a slight eye roll.

"Oh, right. I'm Sheriff Andrews from Rosewood, Maine, but I'm not on duty right now, so you can call me Bill. I'm actually here on behalf of the SCA."

"SCA?" I couldn't help but question.

"Supernatural Containment Agency." He eyed me skeptically. "Surely you've heard of us. You're all werewolves, right?"

"I've heard of you," Kolton responded, still rigid as if he expected the warlocks to attack at any moment. "The SCA is like the police force for supernaturals, making sure we all behave. Well, I can assure you that we haven't harmed any humans, so you can leave now."

Bill assessed Kolton for an uncomfortably long moment, then reached back to knock on the SUV's hood. "You can come out now, Victor. You too, Reid."

The back doors of the SUV opened, revealing two more men. Unable to see them through the dark-tinted windows earlier, Kolton tensed even more as they stepped from the vehicle. But, as the older man turned toward him, he said in surprise, "Alpha Zimmerman?"

The middle-aged man with graying black hair nodded. "Sorry for barging into your territory without an invitation, Alpha Rivers, but the SCA didn't want me to contact you ahead of time. You might remember meeting my nephew Reid at the Alpha Meeting." He waved the younger man over. "He's my second and is training to take my place someday, probably sooner than later," he finished with a gravelly laugh.

Reid looked to be a year or two older than me, with light brown skin and spiky dark brown hair. As he came to stand beside his uncle, he gave us all a friendly smile, one that crinkled the corners of his golden hazel eyes. He immediately put me at ease. The others seemed to relax a little as well. Well, everyone except Kolton. He was still on edge, trying to gauge if they were a threat or not.

"What's the reason for your visit, gentlemen?" he asked, not bothering to hide his wariness.

Victor glanced at Bill, who gestured for him to proceed. "Well, after what happened at the Alpha Meeting," the alpha began, "we've been debating if the SCA should be involved."

"We?" Kolton questioned.

"Reid and I. My nephew has a few personal connections within the SCA, one of them being the Andrews family. He went to school with Bill's daughter, then later with her best friend. They're both vampires now, but he still stays in touch with them."

"Did you just say *vampires?*" Griff interjected. I looked over to see Vi about to elbow him into silence, but she stopped inches away from touching him and dropped her arm.

"One of them is a hybrid, actually," Reid said. "Half vampire, half witch."

Well, *that* got our attention.

"How is that possible?" Kolton asked, clearly not ready to believe him just yet.

He shrugged. "Probably the same way you're able to shift without the full moon and perform magic."

Our gazes shot to the witches—I mean, warlocks. They didn't seem at all surprised by the news. Even more, they didn't look angry.

"The reason why Victor decided to contact us is because he knows we're aware of species that aren't supposed to exist," Bill said, making it clear that he already knew *we* were one of those species. "And because we know a lot more about what's currently going on than you do."

I glanced up in time to see Kolton raise an eyebrow. "Is that so?"

"As warlocks, we keep close tabs on the witch community," Noah said next. "Over five years ago, we were partly responsible for disbanding the elders and excommunicating them. But lately, we've been hearing rumors that they're banding back together."

Oh, crap. That didn't sound good. I knew little about witch politics, but I knew that a dozen or so powerful witches and warlocks called elders used to rule the community as a whole, despite there being hundreds of covens scattered around the world.

"And you believe these rumors?" Kolton asked.

"We think some of the elders were responsible for the attack at your Alpha Meeting," Bill replied.

Jagger quietly swore.

Kolton mulled over this terrifying bit of news, probably still debating whether to believe them or not.

I think they're telling the truth, I said through our bond. *And I don't think these warlocks are in league with Keisha.*

A resigned sigh fled him. *I think you're right.*

Maybe they can help us.

Maybe. The SCA isn't to be trifled with though. If they think we're a danger to the public, especially humans, we'll never see the light of day again.

A shiver of dread worked its way up my spine.

Noah suddenly snorted, drawing our attention to him. "Let me guess. Soulmates?" He flicked his fingers at me and Kolton. "I can tell when soulmates have their little *mind* conversations. My sister's best friend has a soulmate and they do it all the time. So obnoxious."

I darted a glance at Jagger and noted the way he carefully avoided looking at Brielle.

"So what's the plan?" Kolton asked instead of answering Noah's question.

Bill crossed his arms over his broad chest. "Currently, we don't have one. The SCA usually stops skirmishes between supernaturals when they're small and can easily be handled. But this matter is neither small nor can easily be handled. A growing number of supernaturals have been made aware of your existence, and many of them will wish you harm."

"We're aware," Kolton dead-panned.

"Which is why," Bill went on as if he hadn't spoken, "we've contacted our allies about the situation."

"Allies?" I questioned.

"The vampire king and his family. He's invited you all to his castle."

My mouth fell open.

"No, thanks," Kolton immediately replied. "Werewolves and vampires don't mix very well."

Reid snorted, as if in agreement.

"Apologies, I worded that poorly," Bill said, his stern gaze brooking no argument. "You've been *summoned* by the vampire king. No one ignores his summons, not even the alpha of Midnight Pack."

Ah, hell. What had we gotten ourselves into now?

Instead of driving to Maine, we took the Rivers' private jet. Although flying cut down travel time by several hours, I was pretty sure efficiency had nothing to do with it.

"Male pissing contest," Vi had muttered to me with an eye roll as she'd boarded the plane.

Yup. I wasn't the only one thinking it.

The big bad alpha didn't like being summoned by the big bad vampire king.

Despite his clear misgivings, Kolton had agreed to go. We'd stopped at the cabin to pack some belongings, then had headed straight for the airport. Bill, Alpha Zimmerman, and Reid had joined us, but Noah had remained on the ground to drive his dad's SUV back to Maine.

This was my first *conscious* flying experience, and I was both nervous and excited as I boarded. Mostly nervous though, considering the reason for the trip. I'd never met a vampire in person before, let alone the vampire *king*. Would he take one look at us and order his subjects to drain our blood? Werewolves were fast, but vampires were faster. Would we even be able to stop them if they tried?

They're not going to drain our blood, Kolton lightly chided me through our bond. *They have rules the same way we do.*

I grimaced at having been caught with such panicked thoughts. *Sorry. Didn't mean to think that so loudly.*

I was about to choose a seat when Kolton grabbed my waist and sat, depositing me squarely in his lap.

"Um, don't I need to wear a seatbelt?" I asked, not that I was complaining.

"I think you need my comfort more," he whispered in my ear, then nuzzled the side of my neck. At the way his stubble tickled my sensitive skin, I stifled a giggle.

"*Behave* yourselves," Griff said, throwing himself into the seat across from us. "No dick grabbing on this flight. I don't need to see that more than once."

Mortified, I turned about fifty shades of red.

Kolton ignored him and slid his hand underneath my skirt to grip my thigh. We'd decided to dress up for the occasion, but I was wishing for a pair of jeans right about now. This was going to be a *long* flight if Kolton kept me on his lap the entire time.

When we were finally ready for takeoff, my nerves were so bad that I no longer cared what Griff or anyone else saw. Kolton seemed to realize this and took full advantage, inching his hand up my thigh. I didn't stop him, welcoming the distraction as the jet taxied down the runway.

Catching on to what Kolton was doing, Griff groaned something about "raging pregnancy hormones," and faced the window.

Kolton quietly chuckled and inched his hand higher. *Does this help soothe your nerves, wife?*

The plane suddenly picked up speed. Instead of answering, I gripped the armrest and squeezed my eyes shut.

Relax, sweetness, he purred, sliding his hand between my thighs. *I've got you.*

Just as the jet lifted into the air, his fingers brushed over my clit through my panties. I stopped breathing, determined not to make a sound. It was one thing for Griff to know what we were doing, but quite another for everyone *else* to know.

Kolton didn't seem to care either way, too focused on calming my nerves. His fingers expertly moved over my center, undeterred by my clothing and awkward position. I tried to steady my breathing, but he was making me feel too good. I was in the clouds, literally and figuratively, flying higher and higher with each passing second.

When he suddenly pushed aside my underwear to touch my bare clit, I bit my tongue to stifle a moan. Gripping the armrest for dear life, I struggled to keep quiet as my pleasure began to build. Kolton's fingers continued to work me, targeting all the right spots as though determined to break me. To make me come apart in front of everyone. *Loudly.*

Nope. Not going to happen. I'd bite my tongue off before I allowed myself to be embarrassed like that.

Clearly catching my thoughts, Kolton sucked my earlobe into his mouth and bit down. The added pleasure-pain was almost my undoing, and a small gasp escaped me before I could stop it.

You suck, I moaned through our bond.

He chuckled, continuing to nibble on my ear. *The plane has a bathroom. I could suck on you in there next.*

The thought of him eating me out in an airplane bathroom shouldn't have turned me on, but it did. So much so that it brought me to orgasm. Throwing my head back, I gave in to the pleasure, desperately hoping that I wasn't making any noise. Kolton continued to stroke me, prolonging the length of my climax. When I eventually went limp against him, he fixed my underwear and pulled his hand out, placing a kiss just below my ear.

Sighing, I snuggled against him and chanced a peek out the window. Wow. We were *really* high up. If I wasn't still floating on a blissful high, that might have freaked me out.

"Let me know if you get nervous again," Kolton whispered out loud. "I'm here to help."

Griff groaned, and I didn't stop myself from laughing this time.

CHAPTER 29

KOLTON

My knowledge of Ambrose D'angelo, king of the vampires, was mostly based on rumors.

I'd never met him and never planned to. It wasn't an exaggeration when I'd said that werewolves and vampires didn't mix very well. At our core, we were both predators, creatures of the night. We might have the ability to look like humans, but our instincts were far more primal. Forcing the two species together often resulted in territorial fights and hierarchy battles.

It was bad enough trying to make several alpha werewolves in the same room play nice. Now, I was expected to bow to the whims of a pompous vampire. The only reason I'd agreed to this summoning was because I couldn't afford to make another powerful enemy at this time. Werewolves were the physically stronger of the two species, but vampires were faster and possessed the ability to thrall. Strength was useless if you were *compelled* to submit.

Shoving down the growl in my throat, I focused on our surroundings. On anticipating even the slightest threat. We'd arrived in Rosewood, Maine just as the sun had set, then had traveled by car to a large island, one that the vampires had dubbed Sanctum Isle. As we crossed the only bridge leading to and from the island, it was clear that trespassers weren't welcome. Guards stopped us at a gated checkpoint, only allowing us to pass after a lengthy conversation with Bill Andrews.

I was still surprised that vampires were working with witches. More specifically, the SCA. Out of all the supernatural species, vampires attacked humans the most. How well their alliance was holding up, I had no idea. Werewolves tended not to get involved with any other species but their own. Which was why this summoning was so odd and had me on edge.

What did vampires care that werewolves were being attacked by witches?

Once we'd passed through the gated checkpoint and what looked like a town completely populated by vampires, it took another hour to reach our destination. The secluded road had stretched for miles, winding through dense woods made up of mostly pine trees. But when we'd neared the rocky coastline of the island, the landscape had opened up to reveal a giant limestone castle six stories high.

From the seat behind us, Brielle oohed and aahed. "I can't believe there's an actual *castle* here. Do you see all the rose trees and bushes, Nora Bora?"

Well, at least one of us was excited.

"They take such good care of them," Nora replied, sounding impressed. I glanced over to see her face practically smooshed against the glass.

Okay, make that two.

We'd taken two SUVs for this trip. Jagger, Griff, and Vi were in the other one with Alpha Zimmerman and his nephew. I didn't know much about the alpha's personal life, but I knew that Reid had been playing professional football for the past couple of years. I didn't know how he managed during the full moon, but he was a bit of a celebrity in our community. Both males seemed decent enough, but so had Arrow Pemberton when we'd first met him.

Ever since becoming alpha, I didn't easily lower my guard, even among my own kind. I had too much to lose.

I wasn't going to fault the girls for their excitement though. I knew Nora hadn't been allowed to travel much, so this probably felt like a wild adventure to her. Even Mellie was riveted by the castle, whispering to her stuffed unicorn, "Look, Princess. It's just like the fairytales."

I wondered how Vi was faring. I hadn't failed to notice the change in her ever since the Alpha Meeting. Nora had explained to me what had happened between her and Griff, and I wasn't surprised to find out that Mason had been the catalyst. He was a sore spot for Griff, and it didn't take much for his older brother to push his buttons. When Vi had gone into her first heat shortly after Arrow had broken off their betrothal, the two brothers had vied for her attention. When Griff had won, Mason had left the pack to strike out on his own.

Assuming Vi and Griff would become a mated pair, I was surprised when years passed and their relationship had never grown. Both seemed intent on keeping things casual, a notion that I understood all too well.

Until recently. Until Nora.

Now, I was saddened that they hadn't given their relationship a fighting chance. Neither of them seemed ready to talk about it though, so I hadn't said a word. Neither had Nora, although I could tell it was bothering her to keep quiet. Not just about Vi and Griff, but about Brielle and Jagger as well.

This trip wasn't exactly my idea of an exciting adventure, but at least it would take our minds off things. We had much bigger problems than relationship woes. A six-story castle full of powerful royal vampires, to be precise.

Unlike Feltore—the less powerful vampires who'd been made rather than born—the vampires living within these walls weren't deterred by sunshine. They were Venturi, the elite of their species. Most of their nobles and council were also Venturi, except for a select few. I knew they had the ability to bind lesser vampires to them, a blood ritual that allowed them to share power. One of the Venturi princes had a drothen, I knew that much.

Other than that, I knew little about their lives. Even less about them as individuals. Whether they planned to help us or harm us, only time would tell.

As the SUV pulled around the circular drive and rolled to a stop, I quickly exited the vehicle to assess our surroundings. It was fully dark now, but several old-fashioned street lamps lit up the area. Not that either of our species needed the extra light. I assumed it was for show, or maybe for Bill Andrews, since witches and warlocks didn't have night vision like we did.

When the girls started to open their doors, I held up a hand, making sure the coast was clear before signaling that it was okay to emerge. The salty sea air was crisp and clean, devoid of any traces of magic. But as I rounded the vehicle to open Nora's door, my keen hearing picked up three new heartbeats.

I hadn't even detected their presence until now, which put me on even higher alert. If it wasn't for their heartbeats, they could have easily sneaked up on us unaware. Lifting my gaze, I found them at the top of the steep stairs leading to the castle's front entrance. At the sight of three virile male vampires staring back at me, my instincts roared to the surface, along with Shadow.

I can take them, he confidently purred, more excited than intimidated. *Just say the word, and I'll show those little vamps how powerful we really are.*

Settle, Shadow, I sternly ordered him, looking away so I could focus on the other SUV. As they hopped out, both Griff and Jagger caught my warning glance and immediately corralled Vi toward our location. I did the same with Nora, Mellie, and Brielle, making sure I was between them and the eerily quiet vampires.

They were anything but little, the largest one with caramel-colored hair and deeply tanned skin close to my own size. The other two were darker with jet black hair and leaner builds but equally as tall. Based on how similar they looked and the way they carried themselves, I assumed they were the princes. The largest vampire must be the drothen I'd heard about.

When he caught me eyeing him again, his broad mouth formed a wicked smirk, one that said he knew how intimidating he looked and it greatly amused him.

"Looks like you already made a friend," Jagger muttered under his breath as he came alongside me.

As if he'd heard, the big vampire's smirk turned into a full-fledged grin.

"Hey, Bill," he called down when the burly sheriff emerged from the driver's seat. "I didn't realize you were such a dog lover."

The comment threw us all for a loop. It would have been insulting, but the vampire's expression was so openly amused that it made him look like an innocent kid.

"Tone it down, Kade," Bill called back up, gesturing us to follow him as he made for the stairs. "They aren't prepared for your special brand of humor."

The big vampire laughed. "Just trying to break the ice. They all look like you just stole their favorite chew toys or something."

Bill grumbled incoherently and began to climb the stairs. Alpha Zimmerman and Reid joined us, the latter throwing us an apologetic glance. "Ignore Kade. He's harmless."

Harmless? I doubted that very much.

Without a sound, I told Jagger and Griff to go first so I could bring up the rear, allowing me to keep an eye on my entire pack. I wrapped my arm around Nora, my hand firmly gripping her hip as we ascended. But my gaze didn't leave the three vampires. They silently watched our approach, assessing us as we assessed them. The prince in the middle with black hair falling into his dark eyes scanned our group with an aloof expression.

His gaze suddenly rested on Nora. Namely, her stomach. The thin material of her dress didn't hide her small, yet noticeable baby bump, and he clearly realized she was pregnant. When his gaze lingered for several seconds, I couldn't hold back a quiet growl. His attention immediately snapped to me.

Time stood still as we shared a look, one filled with challenge and primal, protective energy. I didn't look away and neither did he. Heat practically billowed from our silent powerplay. With a single look, I knew we were equally matched for dominance. He knew it as well, his eyes narrowing for a moment, then slowly filling with . . .

Understanding.

I blinked when he abruptly nodded and looked away, purposefully backing down. Before I could mull over his reaction, we reached the top of the stairs.

"This way," the other prince with close-cropped hair and a no-nonsense attitude said, turning on his heel and heading for the castle's open doors.

We fell into step behind the three vampires, consciously keeping the girls clustered in the middle. When Bill moved ahead to speak with the vampires, I came alongside Reid and whispered, "I thought you were friends with them."

They hadn't exactly greeted him with a warm welcome.

He huffed a quiet laugh. "I'm friends with their *mates*. With them, not so much. We tolerate each other, but there's too much male testosterone, if you know what I mean."

Nora snorted. "I guess that's one thing werewolves have in common with vampires."

Reid grinned. "Yeah. They might even be more protective of their mates than we are."

"Doubt it," she said, and he laughed.

As I stiffened at the easy way he joked with her, I couldn't help but agree with Nora. I doubted vampires could rival werewolves for overprotectiveness.

We fell silent as we entered the huge foyer of the castle. I spotted a few guards, but the king was nowhere in sight. While still keeping a sharp eye on the three vampires ahead of us, I scanned our new surroundings. Only one word came to mind when I saw the blatant display of power and wealth everywhere I looked: overcompensation.

"Pretty!" Melanie said quite loudly, earning her a look from the golden vampire. I bristled and started to reach for her, then paused when his sky blue eyes softened.

"I can't wait for the twins to be that age," he said, watching as Mellie took in all the crystal, gold, and jeweled furniture with childlike wonder. "Walking and talking like mini adults instead of drooling everywhere all the time."

"Kade," the prince beside him quietly warned.

"Chill, Lochie. I doubt werewolves eat babies. Right?" He shot me a concerned look, but I didn't miss the mischievous twinkle in his eye before he turned back around.

"Only when we're fresh out of virgins," Griff chose that moment to open his mouth.

Vi poked him in the back. *Hard.*

Kade's loud guffaw drowned out Griff's surprised yelp.

"See? This is why you guys need me around more often," Kade drawled to the princes. "You could learn a thing or two from my diplomacy skills."

The no-nonsense prince snorted. "I'm sure Isla would like that. After eight months of being married to you, I bet she could use a break."

Bill made a sound that resembled a laugh.

"Et tu, father-in-law?" Kade sighed. "I'll have you know that your daughter is still *very* happy with me, especially in the bedroom. I doubt she'll want to get rid of me anytime soon, not when I know exactly how to please her and do so consistently several times a—"

"Kade Carmichael, don't you dare finish that sentence!" a female voice from down the long hallway shouted.

"You're in for it now," the prince walking beside Kade murmured with amusement.

"Thanks, Lochie. I appreciate your supp— Hey, shortcake! I was just talking about you," Kade said as a short and curvy blonde with the ends of her hair dyed pink came storming toward us.

"Yeah, I heard. The whole *castle* probably heard," she snapped, then ground to a halt when she spotted us. "Oh, they're here. Seriously, Kade? You talked about our love life in front of our *guests?* Hi, Daddy. Sorry you had to hear that."

She started forward again, and Kade held open his arms. Instead of walking into them, she brushed right by him and hugged Bill.

The no-nonsense prince snorted again.

"That's okay, sweetheart," Bill said to who I assumed was his daughter, the one who'd been turned into a vampire. "I'm used to it by now."

She turned her head to glower at Kade, but he just shrugged his broad shoulders unapologetically.

"Have these goons been welcoming enough?" she asked, pulling back from the hug to focus on us once more. "I know this is probably all rather shocking."

When all I said was, "They've been fine," she sighed in frustration.

"I'm so sorry. I wanted to go with my dad and brother to properly greet you, but I can't travel during the day. The sun"—she waved her hand in the air—"doesn't agree with me these days."

Before any of us could reply, she caught sight of Reid and greeted him like a long-lost friend. "Reid!" She skirted around the group and enveloped him in a huge hug.

"Really?" Kade muttered. For a split second, I could have sworn Isla grinned like a fiend.

The bubbly female focused on Nora next, saying, "Hi, I'm Isla. Your hair is *gorgeous,* by the way. I've always wanted curly hair."

Nora touched her hair self-consciously. "Thank you. I'm Nora, and I've always wanted straight hair."

I glanced down at her in surprise. *Really?*

She peeked up at me and replied back, *Curly hair requires a ton of maintenance. It's why I almost gave up and cut it.*

I reached over and gently tugged on one of her fiery curls. *Please never cut it. I'll happily maintain it for you if you need me to.*

Isla's hands suddenly flew to her mouth and she whispered, "Oh my goddess, you're soulmates. And *pregnant!* Oh, you need to meet my best friend Kenna right away. You have so much in common with her!"

Overwhelmed by her exuberance, I tightened my arm around Nora.

"Mate," Kade quietly called. That one word instantly caught Isla's attention. Excusing herself, she moved toward him. This time when he held his arm out, she walked right up to him and snuggled into his side. The big vampire heaved a contented sigh and kissed the top of her head.

The sight gave me pause. I knew that werewolves weren't the only species to have close family ties. Still, I was surprised to discover that the creatures before me were just that. A family. A devoted one, by the looks of it.

Suddenly, I wasn't as on edge as I was a moment ago.

They might drink blood and have the ability to control people's minds, but these vampires weren't at all what I thought they would be.

"I know exactly how you feel," Reid whispered beside me. "They're a lot, but they're good people. For vampires, anyway."

"I heard that, Reid," Isla sang, twirling out of Kade's embrace to lead the way toward a flight of stairs. He followed her as if in a trance, staring at the way her white skirt swished against her thighs. The rest of us started moving again as well, and I could sense that they too were feeling a little less tense.

There was still one person we hadn't met though. The vampire king. Something told me that meeting him wouldn't be this easy. He'd maintained his reign for hundreds of years, after all. I doubted he was all sunshine and smiles like Kade and Isla.

Sure enough, when we'd reached the second floor and passed through a hallway lined with golden-framed mirrors to enter what looked like a massive throne room, a single man sat at the far end. I instantly knew that this was King Ambrose. He looked like a slightly older version of his sons with the same jet black hair, neatly swept off his forehead. He was casually draped over his gold velvet-cushioned throne, yet he was impeccably dressed in a black suit and burgundy shirt.

"Come, come," he said, beckoning us forward. "Don't be shy. Let me have a look at you."

At the arrogant way he ordered us around like *dogs*, my hands began to tremble. Nora pulled away so she could grab my hand and squeeze it tightly.

It's okay, she calmly said through our bond. *He only wants to test us. I've dealt with dickheads like him many times.*

I would have laughed if I wasn't so angry.

As we pushed forward, I gestured at the others to move behind us. The vampires went to stand along the wall, which put me more at ease. This way, I could still keep an eye on them.

Should we bow? Nora questioned, handling the situation far better than I was.

No, I immediately answered. *He might be a king, but he's not our king.*

I could sense that she wanted to say more, but she fell silent when we stopped several yards from the dais. When I made it clear that we weren't going a step further, Ambrose's lips curved into a half smile.

"I've never had so many werewolves grace my halls before," he said, placing his elbows on the armrests so he could steeple his fingers. "To be honest, I'm not really a fan of your species. Werewolves rarely concern themselves with anything outside their little packs, and I'm not overly fond of how their blood tastes. In fact, it wasn't even my idea to invite you all here today."

It took everything in me not to growl at him. If it wasn't for Nora's calming presence, I would have surely lost it. "Then why, pray tell," I said, my words clipped and dangerously soft, "have we been summoned here?"

Despite the clear warning in my tone, that cocky half smile didn't leave his face. "You've been summoned here because my daughter-in-law has a bleeding heart, and because she's given me two beautiful grandbabies. If it wasn't for her, no one here would think twice about helping you. We have our own drama to deal with."

Out of the corner of my eye, I saw the two princes shake their heads. The golden vampire tipped his head back to stare up at the ceiling, but no one refuted Ambrose's words. I had the impression that contradicting the vampire king wasn't recommended.

"Where *is* McKenna, by the way?" Ambrose said before I could formulate a response to his insulting words. "This was her idea, after all."

"Feeding the twins," one of his sons replied.

"Well, tell her to let my wives take over. I wasn't prepared to actually *speak* with the werewolves today."

Wives? Nora asked in surprise.

I was too incensed to answer her question, disliking the vampire king more and more with each passing second.

This trip had been a huge mistake. What had I been thinking? I didn't know why I thought, even for a second, that *vampires* would want to help us.

I was just about to call this whole thing off when I heard a side door open and a feminine voice say, "I'm here. So sorry I'm late. Did I miss anything?"

The prince I'd locked eyes with earlier left the others to meet the newcomer. In a few swift strides, he erased the distance between them and wrapped her securely in his arms. The young brunette looked up at him, and he kissed her full on the mouth as if they were the only two people in the room. I immediately knew what he was doing. Staking a claim. Showing the other males in the room that this female was *his*.

"Okay, Loch, we get it," his brother impatiently said after a moment. "You're obsessed with your mate and want everyone here to know it. Can we get down to business now? I'm hungry."

"The scary vampire is hungry," I heard Griff mutter under his breath. "Not a good sign."

"*Griff*," Vi hissed. "He's going to eat *you* if you don't shut up."

"I probably wouldn't taste very good. Bill over there looks much more appetizing."

"We don't feed off our guests," Ambrose said, proving that vampire hearing was on par with ours. "Unless they want us to, of course."

His burnt umber irises flashed bright red for a moment, making me tense all over. "Is that what the humans in your castle are for?" I asked before I could stop myself. I'd seen several scurrying about the halls, and I doubted they were simply here to keep the castle clean.

Ambrose chuckled lightly. "You're direct. I admire that in a leader. Not many would dare ask me such a bold question, and for that I'll give you an honest answer. Yes, they service our needs. No, they are not here against their will. We do not thrall them and we do not have to. Most of them have been raised here and don't wish for any other life. Now, let me ask *you* a direct question. How is it that a strong leader such as yourself can't properly defend his subjects against a few measly witches?"

At that, even *Shadow* took offense. *Let me at him. I want to rearrange that smug handsome face of his.*

When I almost let him take control, Nora squeezed my hand until it hurt. *Don't let him bait you. That's what he wants.*

"Father, enough," the prince called Loch quietly said, still holding the brunette in his arms.

Ambrose pushed to his feet, continuing on as if his son hadn't spoken. "I'm starting to think that the notorious alpha of Midnight Pack isn't as powerful as everyone says he is. Maybe the witches are on to something. Maybe they sense weakness and simply wish to flush it out. As predators, it's in our *nature* to eliminate weakness. Who are we to stand in their way?"

My entire body trembled, barely able to contain the combined rage of myself and Shadow. I didn't care if the male before me was a king. He'd just stepped over a line. Every inch of me *demanded* I put him in his place.

I was just about to release Nora's hand so I could challenge the bastard when he became a sudden blur. In less than a blink, he was shooting toward me like a bullet. Before I could finish bracing for the inevitable collision, a bright light blasted him back.

He flew through the air and struck his gaudy throne, so hard that it toppled over backward, him along with it. The princes rushed forward to help him, but he popped back up a second later and waved them off.

"I'm so sorry," Nora said in a panic, still holding out her hand. The hand that had thrown the king back with magic. "It was an accident. No, wait. It wasn't. You were about to attack my husband, and I couldn't let you do that. But I'm still sorry, Your Majesty. Sir. I meant no disrespect."

A feather could have dropped, and we would have heard it. Everyone gaped at her, and I couldn't blame them. I wanted to gape myself, but I was too busy preparing for the vampires' retaliation. We probably couldn't outrun them, so there would be no avoiding a physical altercation. If we shifted right now, we might stand a fighting chance of getting out of this alive.

Get ready, Shadow, I said, bracing my body for the shift.

Any second now. Any second, and they were going to—

Ambrose made a noise. A strangled sound between pinched lips, like he was trying really hard not to—

He suddenly threw his head back and roared with laughter. Roared and roared, clutching his stomach.

After a few stunned moments, the other vampires joined him. They laughed their heads off, as if seeing their king get blasted by a fiery-haired pregnant female was the funniest thing they'd ever witnessed. Griff started to snicker, and I cut him off with a quick hand gesture.

When the laughter eventually died down, Ambrose wiped a tear from his eye and focused on Nora. Instead of malice, intense interest filled his gaze. Slowly, he smiled and purred, "Well, aren't you a fascinating creature."

CHAPTER 30

NORA

Holy hell.

If I wasn't so used to holding Kolton's gaze, I would have had to look away from the vampire king. It was like he could see straight through me, slowly peeling back all the layers of who I was like an onion.

"I admire females who fiercely protect their mates," he said, sweeping his garnet gaze over me. "My intention was to flush out a *wolf,* but that unexpected display was confirmation enough. A werewolf with magical powers is truly fascinating. Do the rest of your companions share this ability?"

Swallowing nervously, I decided to go with honesty. I'd just attacked the vampire king in his own home, after all. "Yes, Your Majesty. All but one."

His grin widened. "And here I thought a vampire witch hybrid was the strangest thing I'd ever see. I've been around for a very long time and have never heard of hybrid werewolves until now. I didn't believe it at first, but here we are." Bending over, he righted his throne and sat once more. "You have my full attention. Please. Tell me more."

Holy crap, was this really happening? I thought for sure he would be livid with me. Instead, he appeared to be nothing but genuinely interested in what I had to say.

"Umm . . ." I started, not sure how much I should tell him.

Tell him everything.

I blinked at Kolton's quiet command. *Everything?*

Yes, sweetness. I don't think he was actually going to attack me. I think you were right. All of this was a test.

Well, now I feel even worse about blasting him.

Don't be. It was sexy as hell that you protected me. None of them are mad at what you did. I think it made them respect you. So go ahead. Tell him everything.

Oh, wow. This was huge. Kolton was putting his trust in *vampires*, ones he barely knew. The very least I could do was trust his judgment, especially after I'd almost ruined everything.

So, I stood tall and told them the whole story, starting at the beginning. By the time I was finished, more than one vampire had their mouths open in shock.

"An *entire* spirit?" the big vampire called Kade incredulously said. "Crammed inside a single mortal body? Even the little girl has one?"

"I'm the only one who doesn't," Brielle spoke up for the first time, almost sounding bummed. "I'm just the alpha female's best friend. I used to be human, actually, but here I am."

Isla, the blonde-haired vampire, gave her a sympathetic look. "I used to be human too, and I'm also 'just the best friend.'"

"Me too," Kade said.

The newest arrival, the pretty brown-haired female with silver-gray eyes, shook her head with a sigh. "*None* of you are 'just the best friend.' You're all invaluable, and don't forget it. Also, Silver has confirmed that the werewolves do indeed carry celestial spirits. She can sense them."

"Silver?" I questioned, not recalling having heard that name before.

"Oh!" she said, looking sheepish. "Sorry, I haven't properly introduced myself. I'm Kenna, and this is my familiar, Silver." She gestured at her feet, and it was then that I saw a pair of pale blue eyes staring at me from between her legs.

My mouth formed a large O as the eyes slowly moved out into the open, revealing a silver and white fox with large black-tipped ears. She was *beautiful*.

Storm rose up, clearly intrigued by the animal familiar. *She's an angel. A powerful one.*

I smiled at the little fox, feeling a sudden urge to pet it. *Do you know her?*

No. There are thousands of angels. Most are too busy to mingle outside their designated circles.

She's adorable, Shadow interrupted. *I'd like to chase her.*

Storm made a noise, one that sounded a lot like a warning growl.

Don't worry, angel baby. I only have eyes for you. She's just so cute and cuddly-looking, like a fluffy chew toy.

I gasped. *You can't chew on her, Shadow. That's bad. Bad boy!*

He barked a laugh.

"What is happening right now?" the grumpy-looking prince who I still didn't have a name for asked. "Are the spirits talking to each other or something?"

"My familiar has a telepathic connection with my husband's familiar," I explained, "but they can't verbally communicate with other familiars."

"It's a shame, because Silver would love to speak with them," Kenna said. "She's especially surprised that fate brought two soulmates together who house an angel and a demon."

I smiled wide. "Me too. It's been an adjustment, but we're making it work."

She smiled back. "I can see that. I'm so glad you all decided to come here. As a vampire witch hybrid, I have a little experience with being different. When we were informed about your situation, I right away assumed you were being targeted for the same reason I was five years ago. You'd think it would be easier to fit into the supernatural world when you're different, but that's just not the case."

"Exactly!" I said, a little too excitedly. We were two completely different species, and yet, we shared so many similarities. I couldn't wait to learn more about her.

"Anyway," Kenna went on, "the king has graciously agreed to let you all stay here while we figure out how best to help you. No one can portal inside these walls, not unless they've been here before, so you can rest assured that no witch or warlock will get to you."

"That's very generous of you," Kolton spoke before I could, "but we can't stay here. We've just lost our third pack member to these witches, and the rest of them are counting on us to keep them safe. We can't do that from here."

"But you can't protect them in your own territory either," the king countered, steepling his fingers once more. "I've personally had dealings with a witch elder, back before they were banished. I'm embarrassed to say that she was almost my undoing. A single witch almost single-handedly destroyed a five-hundred-year old Venturi vampire. I share this with you now because witches are conniving opportunists—no offense, Bill."

"None taken," the sheriff replied.

"They don't fight like we do," Ambrose went on. "Instead of using brute force, they play mind games."

"Don't vampires play games too?" Kolton challenged. "You have the ability to control minds with thrall."

The king smiled. "True. But we have rules about how to use thrall. Those rules have only become more stringent since we've allied with the SCA. Witches, on the other hand, have been without rules for a long time now. And the elders who were supposed to enforce order among the covens turned out to be corrupted, only interested in gaining more power. They tried to take McKenna, and I paid a steep price to keep her from them. They want their power restored and will stop at nothing to make that happen. Once they set their sights on something, you can't reason with them or make a deal that will end in your favor. If you wish to best protect your pack, you'll need to make sacrifices of your own."

"I already have," Kolton said. "I risked my family's safety by revealing the full extent of who I am in front of dozens of powerful alphas, asking them to look past our differences and stand united. But you were right about werewolves rarely getting involved in anything outside their packs. Since the attack, only Alpha Zimmerman and his nephew have had the courage to show their faces to us."

"Vampires haven't always been united either," Ambrose replied. "You might be surprised to know that not all of my subjects are happy about the alliance I made with the SCA. It was necessary, though, for the preservation of our kind. I've ruled this kingdom for centuries, and if I want to pass down that reign to my children and grandchildren, I have to know when change is needed."

Kolton slowly nodded. "So you're saying that it's time for me to look beyond my own kind for help."

The king inclined his head. "Help can come from unexpected places, even from those you'd once considered your enemies." He looked over at Kenna with fondness, making me even more curious about their backstory.

"We know you have no reason to trust us," Kenna said, "but we've been where you are. We've had to put our faith in others outside our circle in order to find a semblance of peace in this life. When we were at our most desperate, I called on Reid for help. He and his pack answered the call despite the risks, and that's why I asked the king to summon you all here today. Werewolves came to our aid when we needed it most, so we'd like to repay the favor. If you'll have us, that is."

I glanced at Kolton, and he met my gaze. Without a word spoken between us, I felt us align. Felt us come to the same conclusion. He turned to the others, sharing looks with each member of our pack. Our family. No one said a word, but each look was identical. We were of the same mind.

We were *united*.

Turning back to face the vampires, he said with absolute certainty, "On behalf of my pack, I thank you all for your offer of help. We've decided to accept it."

None of us were prepared to find a place of solace in the home of the world's most powerful vampire family, but that's what happened.

Little by little, day by day, I saw the constant stress Kolton was under slowly melt away. Not completely, but our new allies made it possible for him to focus on one task at a time instead of a hundred things at once.

With the combined help of the SCA, they had far more resources than we did. They had an actual finger on the *pulse* of the supernatural world, one that spread to nearly every community, be it vampire, werewolf, or witch. They had eyes and ears everywhere, and as soon as we'd said yes to their help, they'd started to make plans to find the witches responsible for the Alpha Meeting attack, including Keisha.

We'd also told them about Arrow and the part he'd played in all of this, but we'd decided to focus our efforts primarily on the witches.

We'd deal with him and his underhanded betrayals soon enough, but finding those witches needed to be our main priority. There had been no new attacks on the pack, but it was only a matter of time. Who knew how many allies Keisha had rallied to her cause by now.

The witch community was unstable. Leaderless. Many of them might be desperate enough to believe her fanatical promises of a better future. To aid in her attempts to capture werewolves like us, hoping to harness that power for themselves.

Crazier things had happened throughout history. A convincing enough leader could make their flock believe just about anything, a scary but true fact.

It had taken some convincing, but Kolton had agreed to remain at the castle longer than planned in order to build a stronger relationship with our new allies. He'd been about to call Carter and explain our current situation before remembering that he was no longer with us. His guilt over the losses we'd suffered still plagued him, but he seemed more and more confident that we'd made the right choice in coming here.

On our fifth night at the castle, as we were readying for bed, Kolton confided in me, "I'm not sure who to appoint in Carter's place. He was the most dominant of the influential pack members, and I've always entrusted him with pack news first."

"What about Rebekah?" I suggested, slipping on my white satin nightgown. Not the one I'd worn on our wedding night, but one that accommodated my steadily growing belly. I was almost to the halfway point in my pregnancy now, and there was no mistaking my baby bump any longer.

"Rebekah is a strong female, but she would have her work cut out for her dealing with ten dominant males on a regular basis."

I shrugged. "I would at least let her try. There aren't enough strong females higher up in the ranks. At the Alpha Meeting, eighty percent of the alphas were male."

"True. Physical strength is an important factor in werewolf hierarchy, and not all females want to test their strength against a slew of testosterone-driven males."

Snorting, I smoothed the thin satin fabric over my swollen stomach and glanced at my reflection in our bedroom's full-length mirror. "Well, now that our secret is out, maybe we'll discover a few females like us who want to take their chances. Being able to shift at will has its benefits, especially during a challenge."

"That would be great. Maybe when all of this is over, the SCA can help us search for more wolves like us."

I frowned and turned sideways. "Yeah. We seriously can't be the only ones with spirit familiars."

"I'm sure there are many more, but they're still too afraid to expose themselves, especially after what happened at the Alpha Meeting. I—what's wrong?"

"Hmm?" I glanced up in the mirror's reflection to find him watching me. My cheeks started to warm. "Oh. Nothing. I'm just . . ."

When I didn't finish, he tossed his shirt on the bed and moved toward me. "You're just what, Nora?"

I dropped my arms to my sides, looking everywhere but at him. "Really, it's nothing. I just . . . I look *different*, is all."

"Different?" he questioned, still coming toward me. Our room was large, and every step he took toward me made my cheeks flame hotter.

Feeling self conscious, I snipped, "Yes, *different*. I'm round like a bowling ball. I doubt you find that attractive."

I felt more than saw Kolton's shock. "Nora."

I bit my lip, refusing to meet his gaze in the mirror. "No, it's okay.

I'm being pathetic. I know I won't look like this forever."

"Nora, look at me."

Sighing, I did as he instructed, watching as he came to stand directly behind me.

"You don't think I find you attractive?" he quietly asked. When all I did was shrug, his gaze darkened. "Then I haven't been doing my job properly, and that makes me upset."

I blinked. "Job?"

"Yes. The incredibly important job that I alone have been tasked with. The job of proving to my wife that she is the hottest, sexiest, most desirable creature I've ever laid eyes on. Even when you're like this, swollen with my child, I am filled with lust for you. In fact," he said, his voice lowering to a seductive purr, "I've never been more attracted to you than I am right now."

I pressed my lips together to keep from laughing, even as my core fluttered at his words. "So you're horny for pregnant women?"

"I'm horny for *my* pregnant woman," he corrected, slipping an arm around me to cup my belly. "I think she's more radiant than the sun." His other hand came around me to cup my left breast, another part of my body that had started to swell. "I think her beauty is unmatched in whatever form she takes." One hand squeezed my breast, while the other stroked my belly before slowly moving south. "And I think she deserves to watch her body be worshiped by her devoted, hopelessly smitten husband."

My eyes nearly bugged out. "Watch?"

"Don't look away, sweetness," he crooned, ducking his head to nuzzle his claim spot. "Watch while I prove just how attracted to you I am."

Before I could say a word, he slid his hand between my legs and stroked me through my nightgown.

"Oh," I breathlessly gasped, my lashes fluttering as I watched his hand move.

"Don't close your eyes," he softly commanded, then slipped his hand inside the top of my nightgown to grip my bare breast. When he groaned, butterflies erupted in my stomach. "I love how full your breasts are. They're a pleasure to look at and play with. Even more so to suckle on."

Holy hell, this was *so* doing it for me. I could already feel myself growing wet.

"Your body's my temple, one I wish to pay homage to day and night. Nothing compares to it, and I am honored to be its caretaker."

My breathing grew unsteady as he continued to whisper sweet nothings against my skin, using his hands to awaken my flesh. I watched as he enjoyed my body, exploring different ways to heighten my pleasure. When he started to remove my nightgown, he did so in a way that didn't make me feel self conscious. I felt *desired* and incredibly turned on.

A pleased rumble left him when he found me pantyless, and he took a long moment to caress my naked body with his gaze.

"Breathtaking," he whispered, then came around me to worship my body with his mouth.

Keeping my eyes open became a challenge, but I didn't want to miss out on this loving gesture he was gifting me. As he began to hungrily devour my breasts, I could barely focus, let alone stand. He gripped my hips to steady me and continued his exploration without pause, filling me with euphoria. I moaned when he feverishly sucked on my skin. Trembled when he nipped at it. Forgot how to breathe when he knelt before me and gently kissed every inch of my swollen stomach.

"I bow to no one," he whispered against my skin, kissing just below my navel, "except for my queen. I will always bow for my queen."

And then he delved between my thighs, lighting up my core as his tongue found my center. Curling forward, I gripped his hair and groaned, overcome by a powerful wave of ecstasy.

Eyes on me, wife, he ordered through our bond, and I peeled my eyes back open to watch him pleasure me. Unable to properly see him over my baby bump, he angled us so that I could view what he was doing in the mirror. The sight of his strong tongue greedily stroking my flesh was almost more than I could take. It turned me on so much that I started to make pathetic little whimpering noises. He chuckled against my sensitive skin, nearly making me come. *Not yet, sweetness. Enjoy the show for a little while longer.*

I would have snorted if there was any oxygen left in my lungs.

The exquisite torture lasted for several minutes. Every time I was on the verge of orgasm, he would repeat the same phrase.

Just a little while longer. A little while longer.

I held on, practically pulling his hair out as I gripped his head for dear life. When my whimpers became loud, panting moans, he finally put me out of my misery.

Come for me, my sweet flower, he breathed, swirling his tongue against my clit so fast that I had no choice but to obey.

Throwing my head back, I screamed out my release, completely forgetting where we were. Kolton's amusement flickered through our bond, but I was too blissed out to care that half the castle had probably just heard me orgasm. When the last of my fluttering aftershocks faded, Kolton rose to his feet and scooped me up. Sighing, I melted against him as he carried me to the bed, then tucked me under the covers.

As he turned off the lights and joined me, I reached for him and immediately found his hard erection.

He groaned, clearly in need of relief, but instead of letting me pleasure him in return, he placed my hand on his bare chest and tucked me against him. "Later," he whispered, kissing my forehead. "You're growing our strong alpha boy. You need your rest."

Suddenly too tired to argue, I closed my eyes and snuggled into his side.

I was just starting to drift off when he said, "I think we should stay here."

My eyes popped open.

"Just until the baby's born or until the witches are taken care of. Whichever comes first," he continued. "Bill has offered to help us keep an eye on my mother during the full moon, and he's already stationed a few SCA operatives near the area. And Brielle has been given permission to use the woods on this side of the island while she wolfs out."

I blinked, still trying to digest his words. "You really want to stay here?"

He huffed a quiet laugh. "Don't sound so shocked. It was Loch's idea, actually."

At the casual way he said the vampire prince's name, I smirked. "You two have been talking quite a bit lately."

"He understands what it feels like to have a soulmate you're constantly terrified of losing."

I slipped an arm around his waist and hugged him. "Kenna has been very helpful to me as well. She didn't fully know who she was either until recently."

"I think we can learn a lot from them, which is something I never expected to say. I've been so used to being in control and worrying about every little thing that it feels kind of nice to take a step back."

I jerked my head up to gape at him. "Who are you and what have you done with my husband?"

He chuckled and lifted his head to softly kiss my lips. "So, do you want to stay?"

I smiled and whispered back, "Yes, husband. I want to stay."

CHAPTER 31

KOLTON

I awoke to fingers gripping my morning erection.

They were wholly familiar. Soft, delicate, yet surprisingly strong.

When they squeezed me, I groaned sleepily and reached for Nora on the bed beside me. My hand caught nothing but air.

Rubbing my eyes, I peeled them open in search of her. She was no longer beside me but on her knees between my legs, stark naked. So was I. One glance and I found my stiff cock firmly grasped in her hand.

"Happy Birthday, dear husband," she sang, her voice seductively low. My cock twitched in response. She smirked and began to stroke it.

Groaning again as pleasure rolled through me, I threw my arm over my eyes and murmured, "Best birthday ever."

"Oh, this is just the beginning. I have a full day planned for you."

"A full day of *this?* I accept."

She scoffed, continuing to stroke me. "The others might feel left out."

"Too bad. It's my birthday and this is what I want. All. Day. Long."

She laughed. "You want *this* all day long?" Leaning forward, she licked my swollen tip. When I shuddered and softly moaned, she did it again. "And this?" She swirled her tongue over the whole tip, filling me with bliss.

"Yes. A full day of this. It's the only present I need."

Humming, she placed the entire head into her mouth and began to suck.

"God, Nora," I breathed, my thighs tensing. She sucked and stroked me in tandem, making me the happiest man on earth. When I went rock hard, seconds away from orgasming, she pulled her mouth and hand away. I blew out a pent-up breath and lifted my arm to glare at her, though the glare was filled with desperation. "Cruel woman."

She grinned and crawled forward to straddle my hips, drawing my gaze to her ample chest. Two months had passed since we'd arrived at the castle, and Nora was now weeks away from giving birth. Her belly was full and round, and so were her breasts. They may be preparing for the arrival of our son, but I had taken full advantage of them these past several weeks.

The sight of them gently bouncing was too much of a temptation, and I gave in, reaching out to cup them. They filled my hands and then some, and I growled with satisfaction.

Still hard and aching for release, I was about to take charge of the situation when Nora slowly lowered herself on top of me. I tensed, anticipating the feel of my dick sliding into her wet pussy, but she stopped when my swollen tip brushed her opening.

I growled again, this time in warning. "I want my present, wife. Give it to me."

She teasingly circled my tip around her entrance. "So demanding. Say please."

"*Please*," I growled, tweaking both her hard nipples as punishment. She gasped and sank onto me. My dick slid an inch inside her, making me sigh with relief. When she robbed me of my pleasure by lifting up again, I rolled her nipples between my fingers, eliciting another gasp from her.

It was like her nipples controlled her pussy because she sank down on me like last time, just enough to wet my head. A wicked smirk tilted my lips. I tweaked her nipples again, gratified when she took more of my cock. I kept doing it, massaging the sensitive nubs until she was trembling and moaning, rocking her hips against me.

I closed my eyes, a pleased grin plastered across my face as she rode me. Every time I played with her nipples, her walls would deliciously tighten around my throbbing cock. I continued to do this until we were both panting, our bodies drowning in sensation.

Nora suddenly dug her nails into my chest and stiffened all over, her walls mercilessly squeezing me as she orgasmed around my cock. The vicious spasms sent euphoria shooting up my shaft, and I spilled my release inside her with a loud groan. She rode me for a moment more, milking both of our pleasures, before collapsing onto my chest.

Her round stomach pressed into mine, and I gently rolled us so that she could more comfortably lay beside me.

"That was . . ." she breathlessly started.

"The perfect birthday gift," I finished for her, cupping her cheek to press a lingering kiss on her lips. "Now give it to me again."

She huffed a laugh. "Greedy bastard. I'm too big to ride you like that again. At least this soon."

Chuckling, I rolled her beneath me. "No problem. You just lie there, and I'll do all the work this time."

She stuck her bottom lip out. "But my job is to make sure you don't work today."

"But this is pleasurable work. The best work there is. My body loves this kind of work. Craves it. I—"

"Okay, okay," she interrupted me with an eye roll. "I still can't believe you want to have sex with me when I'm like this."

"When you're like what?" I asked, dipping down to nuzzle the spot between her neck and shoulder. "When you're a fierce pregnant goddess?"

I placed my hand on her swollen belly and was immediately rewarded with a kick. Smiling against her neck, I tenderly stroked the spot.

"I think our son likes it when we have sex."

She sputtered out a laugh. "I think it's the movement that he likes."

"Well, he's about to experience more of it."

With one smooth thrust, I slid inside Nora balls deep. We both moaned at the sensation, a sensation that never failed to make me feel like I was coming home. We'd been mated for three and a half months now, yet each time we had sex felt like our first. Soon, our lives would become even more hectic with a newborn child, but I would continue to prioritize these moments with my mate. Our intimacy was more important to me than oxygen.

It fed me. Nourished me. *Healed* me as nothing else could.

These moments with Nora gave me life, and I hadn't been joking when I'd said that it was the perfect birthday gift. Filling myself up on her for hours on end sounded like heaven. I'd done so as often as I could the past few months, never sure when we'd get the news that there'd been another attack or the SCA had found the witches. But all had been quiet. Not a single attack or sighting.

I'd wanted to believe that meant the witches had decided to leave us alone, but I'd be lying to myself if I did. The more pregnant Nora became, the more often I woke up drenched in sweat, fighting off the remnants of a nightmare. But, as our soulmate bond continued to strengthen, the perks of our connection had grown. During almost every nightmare, Nora had been there to soothe my fears. Our dreamwalking happened nearly every night now, making it possible for us to remain close even in slumber.

That wasn't the only perk though. Loch, the vampire prince who'd slowly become my friend, had taught me a new trick—one that he used often to check up on his mate. On the days when Nora and I were separated for hours, each of us tending to our own responsibilities, I'd learned how to seek her out with my mind. Still fully awake, I'd close my eyes and focus on my senses. On finding her through scent and taste and the sound of her voice. I'd surround myself with her essence until I felt a tug. An *urging* through our bond.

This way, it seemed to say. *This way to your mate.*

I'd follow the tug with my eyes still closed, my body frozen in place as my mind stretched outward in search of Nora. The castle walls didn't deter me, becoming mere obstacles that my mind could easily slip through. The harder I focused, the faster my senses picked up on her trail like a bloodhound. Within seconds, I could pinpoint *exactly* where she was. Not only that, I could mentally see her. Mentally *touch* her. Even speak with her face-to-face as if we were in the same room.

It was like being a ghost. A ghost that could feel the warmth of its mate's flesh as it reached out to touch her.

I'd practiced the ability often, needing the reassurance of knowing where she was. Of knowing she and our baby were safe. Despite the vampires' promise that neither Keisha nor the elders could infiltrate the castle, I still hadn't forgotten the premonition.

I will take him from your womb, she'd told Nora. *You will die while giving him to me.*

Those words had seared themselves into my brain. Had taken root to wreak havoc on my waking and sleeping moments, growing stronger with each day that passed. Months had gone by with no more news. It was like the witches had vanished into thin air. Like they'd become *ghosts*. Nora had assured me that Keisha hadn't tried to contact her through astral projection, but I still worried the Oracle could see her somehow. Could *reach* her.

They shared a bond. Not like ours, but their blood connection was like a gaping wound that wouldn't heal. Keisha could sink her claws into it at any moment.

I thrust into Nora with renewed vigor, silently cursing myself for allowing my troubled thoughts to invade our intimate moment. I was twenty-six years old today, my first birthday as a husband and soon-to-be father. For the sake of my beautiful mate who wished to make this day special, I would set aside my worries for later. She deserved nothing less than my full attention, and I was going to start by making her orgasm as many times as I could before she insisted we leave this bed.

A few hours later, we finally came up for air. Only to spend another hour in the bathroom having shower sex. I was on the best of highs and made sure Nora knew it. She smiled, happy to see me enjoying my birthday so far. As long as I got to spend the whole day with her, I would enjoy every single moment.

By the time we left our room, it was almost noon. Instead of joining the others for lunch, Nora led me down to the kitchens and proceeded to prepare me a meal. I couldn't take my eyes off her, adoring the way she unconsciously rubbed her belly. Pride warmed my chest at how well she bore this pregnancy. Even when she'd started to waddle a bit like a penguin, I couldn't get over how radiant she looked. How *perfect*.

She suddenly turned from the stovetop where she was making grilled cheese sandwiches with bacon and extra cheese to point a spatula at me. "Don't even think about it."

From my spot at the massive wooden table that passed for a kitchen island, I blinked at her innocently. "Don't think about what?"

"I know where your mind is at. You want to get me *pregnant* again as soon as I pop out this baby."

I threw my head back and roared with laughter. When I could speak again, I said, "Might be hard to control myself now that I know you have a breeding kink."

She quietly swore and turned back to the stove.

I barked another laugh, watching as she rubbed her belly once more. "Is it uncomfortable?"

She flipped the sandwich before answering, "Is growing another life form inside me that wants to squirm around and kick my ribs all night long uncomfortable? No, not at all."

"Did you seriously just ask your *very* pregnant wife if she's uncomfortable?" Vi said with an exasperated sigh, strolling into the kitchen with the rest of our pack.

"Right after you railed her all morning?" Griff smirked when his comment received several verbal complaints. "Hey, this place might be huge, but the walls still have ears."

"So do innocent little girls," Jagger said with a pointed look at Melanie.

"That's why I used the word *railed*. She has no idea what I'm talking about."

I listened to the familiar bickering with a small smile on my face. Staying here these past two months hadn't just been good for me and Nora. The easy comradery that Vi and Griff had always shared was almost back to normal. Even if they never became a mated pair, I was relieved that they'd found a way to keep their lifelong friendship intact.

Unfortunately, Jagger and Brielle weren't getting any closer. Even now, I watched as Brielle went to stand beside Nora at the stove, oblivious to the way Jagger silently watched her. She'd grown close to Isla though. Their transition from human to supernatural being was similar, and I could tell that Brielle took comfort from that. She'd shifted into her wolf twice since we'd arrived here, and although she'd braved the painful transformation both times, I'd sensed her fear.

None of us could blame her though. She'd nearly died the first time. Her starry-eyed view of becoming a werewolf had been squashed the second it had tried to take her life. Maybe even before that. Things were still tense between her and her parents. As soon as it was safe to do so, we'd plan her official pack initiation. Hopefully that would help her feel less untethered.

I'd just taken a huge bite of the gooey, crispy bacon and grilled cheese sandwich Nora had made for me when Vi kissed my cheek and sang, "Happy Birthday, big brother. Now finish up and leave so we can bake your cake."

"Did someone say cake?" A golden head popped around the corner of the kitchen entrance. "What kind?"

"Red velvet," Nora answered Kade, turning from the stove with her own grilled cheese sandwich. "It's Kolton's favorite."

Kade made a face. "Red velvet cheesecake would be better. With strawberries on top, of course."

"Gross," another voice said. I nodded at Loch as he entered the quickly-crowding kitchen. "Although, that sandwich smells good."

Nora lowered her sandwich to say, "I could make you one."

"Oh, no thanks," the prince quickly replied. "I've already . . . eaten."

From behind him, Kade smiled like the Cheshire cat. "You can just say it, Lochie. We all know you enjoy snacking on your wife."

Griff guffawed. "Good one, man."

"Kade, I'm *right* here and you know it," another voice said, this one feminine. Kenna walked in, a baby perched on each hip. Silver was absent, but I'd learned that the fox familiar often liked to find a quiet corner to curl up in. As Kenna entered, Loch reached out and took the boy. Kade did the same, plucking up the ten-month-old girl to twirl her around. She belly-laughed, making everyone in the kitchen smile.

"Can I hold her?" Mellie asked, making grabby hands at the baby.

"Sure thing, squirt," Kade said.

"Kade," Loch quietly warned.

"Don't worry. I won't let Zo-Bee suck the little werewolf dry," the big vampire said with a wink. Mellie giggled as he scooped her up one-handed and placed her on the stool beside me, then settled the baby onto her lap.

"Remember, don't touch Zoey's skin," I reminded Mellie, who nodded seriously as she carefully held the baby's pudgy waist.

Two months ago, I wouldn't have allowed my baby sister anywhere near a hybrid who could suck the werewolf toxin from her DNA with a single touch. I'd been shocked to discover what kind of witch Kenna was and even more shocked to learn that she'd passed down her abilities to both her children.

But trust was a two-way street. Even Mellie could turn into a dangerous creature at a moment's whim. The vampires had risked a lot by allowing us to remain in their home, so I'd made a few sacrifices of my own, one of them being the tight protective grip I had on my family.

As I watched my little sister interact with the baby, my heart warmed. By the end of the month, she would have a new baby to hold.

"Did I miss the party?" Isla asked, sounding disappointed as she stepped into the kitchen.

"No, we were just about to make Kolton's red velvet cake," Brielle answered, claiming a spot at the island.

"Oh, fun! I could help you turn it into a red velvet cheesecake."

Kade looked at his mate with pride. "That's my girl."

Yet another body joined us in the kitchen, this one Everett, the king's eldest son. He took one look at the crowded room and muttered, "Nope."

Jagger snorted as the prince exited as quickly as he'd entered.

When we all settled in with no plans to leave, Vi simply huffed and got to work pulling out ingredients. In no time, we were all chipping in, making a mess of the massive pristine kitchen. It was chaos, but I enjoyed every minute of it.

Moments like this made me feel the most like myself. I wasn't worried about the glaring differences between our two species. Wasn't concerned for the safety of my pack. Moments like this were easy. Simple. We were just two families celebrating another year of life.

The day flew by way too quickly, but I spent the majority of it with my family and our new friends. The only downside was that the rest of Midnight Pack couldn't be involved. I was used to answering the front door at all hours of the day as yet another pack member arrived with a gift and birthday wishes. The day wasn't the same without them, but I took solace in the fact that they were safe. That none of them had encountered a single witch in the past two months.

After indulging in way too much red velvet cheesecake, Nora and I said goodnight to the group to enjoy some alone time.

"Let's not go to bed just yet," she said, snuggling into my side as we strolled along the castle halls. "Although, I do have a surprise waiting for you in our bedroom."

"Oh?" I raised an eyebrow. "I hope it's lacy and semi-transparent."

She laughed softly. "Even better than that. I promise."

I teasingly hummed my skepticism, but she simply rested her head on my shoulder with a secretive little smile. Deciding not to press further, I tightened my hold on her and let a comfortable silence settle between us. She too seemed content with letting the silence linger, especially after the full day we'd had.

Without planning to, we ended up in the front foyer. The guards at the entrance nodded at us, then opened the double doors so we could continue our stroll outside. The moment we stepped onto the stone pathway, something cold and wet plopped onto my nose. I glanced up to see a flurry of fat snowflakes falling from the night sky.

Shadow immediately surged to the surface like an overeager puppy. *Snow. My favorite! Let me out so I can play. Pretty please? It's my birthday too.*

I snorted. *No, it's not.*

Well, it's my mortal birthday.

You're not mortal.

Fine, be a spoil sport. I still want to romp around in the fresh snow with my angel baby. She looks so beautiful surrounded by all the sparkling white. I imagine that's what she looked like in Heaven.

I was about to shake my head when Nora said, "Storm wants to play too. I don't mind if they do."

My gaze went to her stomach.

She touched it before saying, "You know that shifting doesn't harm the baby."

"I know. I still worry though. You only have a couple weeks left. The excursion could put you into early labor."

"Good."

I glanced up to find her smirking at me.

"Come on. Our baby will be fine," she prodded, reaching for the top button of my shirt to undo it. "Let Storm and Shadow have some fun."

When she winked, the full meaning of her words sank in. Our familiars had been growing closer, and despite how unconventional it was, a relationship was starting to bloom between the angel and demon. Storm had even confided in Shadow about her fear of being a Fallen. Nora had been shocked when the angel spirit had decided to open up, then had later told me that she'd known for a while now.

Shadow had reacted by adamantly saying that there was no way his perfect angel baby had fallen from grace. Since then, Storm had been rather *receptive* to his flirtatious advances—both through the mental bond and while they were in wolf form.

When I'd teased Nora that their relationship could very well become intimate, she'd been quiet for a long moment. Then said, "If it happens, it happens."

While Nora continued to unbutton my shirt, I could feel how excited Shadow was. Knowing how colorful his past was, he'd been quite the gentleman where Storm was concerned. He definitely wanted her, but he'd let her come to him more often than not. Based on how excited he was right now though, I was pretty sure he hoped to get lucky tonight.

Be gentle, I quietly warned him, and left it at that.

Oh, I'll handle my fair lady with kid gloves, he crooned, making me roll my eyes.

"Do I even want to know?" Nora asked, catching my eye roll.

I chuckled. "Probably n—"

"It's about time you two crawled out of your den," a deep voice interrupted, one that immediately sent heat shooting through my veins.

Pushing Nora behind me, I whirled toward the woods closest to us. As a lone figure emerged from the shadows, a growl tore from my throat, made all the louder by Shadow.

Arrow stopped and raised his hands. "Easy, Rivers."

"How are you here?" I barked, keeping my gaze locked on him as I cast my senses out to search our surroundings. I could only scent him, but that didn't mean he was alone.

"We don't have time for chit-chat. I came to offer you two choices. Give Nora to me now, or fight me and lose her to the witches. I personally think the first option is better."

"Arrow, get out of here now before I scream and alert the whole castle to your presence," Nora said, her voice eerily calm. "Have you ever tried to run from a vampire? News flash: it won't end well for you."

At the sight of Nora, Arrow's nostrils flared. I tucked her behind me again, but I knew he'd seen her swollen stomach.

"What will it be, Rivers?" he said, his blue eyes flashing dangerously bright.

"This is your last chance to leave," I warned him, reaching up to slowly remove my shirt. "Run away with your tail between your legs like the coward you are, or I'm going to rip you limb from limb like I've wanted to for a very long time."

He clenched his jaw, then hissed, "*Fine*. Option two it is. Kolton Rivers, I challenge you for alpha, just as my father challenged yours. Like him, I will defeat you, and you will lose *everything*."

Shadow crowded to the surface, filling my body with power. It rippled over my bare arms and chest, engorging my muscles and peppering my skin with dark fur. "Challenge accepted."

"Kolton, no!" Nora screamed, but I was already charging. Already racing toward my nemesis with an unearthly roar. He roared back, shedding his own shirt as silver fur sprouted over his engorged muscles.

We met in a clash of fangs and claws, using our bodies as battering rams. As weapons meant to maim. To *kill*. There could only be one victor in this fight. One male left alive.

For a terrible moment, the memory of my father's final fight invaded my mind. The night had been so similar to this one. A celebration interrupted. A pregnant mate swollen with child. A husband desperate to protect his family.

History was repeating itself. Right here. Right now.

I'd always feared it would come to this, and it had. My worst nightmare was unfolding before my very eyes. If I lost this challenge, my family would pay the price. I could only imagine what Arrow would do to them.

For a terrible moment, the terror almost consumed me. Almost made me lose my concentration, just as my father had lost his.

But as Arrow tried to grab my head and snap my neck, defeating me the same way his father had defeated mine, an extra burst of strength surged through my veins. Strength that wasn't mine or even Shadow's. It was Nora's. She'd used our bond to give me what I needed, helping me as only she could.

With a roar, I broke Arrow's hold on me and shoved him back. He hit the ground and crashed through the snow. I lunged after him, still on a high from the boost of extra strength. But as he skidded to a stop, he didn't focus back on me right away. It was only a split second, but in that second, he looked at Nora.

Dread immediately filled me.

Whirling, I turned just in time to see a portal burst into existence right behind Nora.

Everything slowed. I saw the next few moments with terrifying clarity. Saw hands reach for my beloved wife. Saw her pulled into the swirling circle of magical light. Saw her eyes wild with fright. Saw my whole world start to vanish.

I ran toward her. Screamed her name at the top of my lungs. But I couldn't stop it. Couldn't stop the portal from closing. Couldn't stop my mate from disappearing. In a flash of sparks, she was gone.

"NOOOOOO!"

The frozen ground beneath me quaked as I bellowed my agony. On the verge of collapse, I searched for Arrow, but he was gone too.

CHAPTER 32

NORA

The first thing I felt was pain.

When I whimpered, a hand lightly stroked my hair.

I ducked away from it, confused and disorientated.

"Shhh, it's okay," a male voice whispered. The hand continued to stroke my hair. "This will all be over soon, I promise. They said I could have you once that thing is removed from your body."

Struggling to breathe through the pain, I cracked my eyes open and saw a blurry face hovering above mine. I blinked a few times, and the face sharpened into focus. My heart sank. "Arrow," I said, the growl I'd intended turning into a pained groan. "What . . . have you done?"

"What I needed to do. You weren't cooperating, so I was forced to make a deal with the witches."

"You're sick. *Sick.*" I moaned and tried to rise, only for Arrow to gently push me back down. I was on a bed in a cozy little room with dark wood paneling on the walls, very much unlike the last prison I'd woken up in. "Why . . . why am I so . . . so weak?"

"You were injected with liquid silver so you could be transported here safely. They said it won't harm that *thing* inside you, if that's what you're worried about."

The meaning of his words finally penetrated the fog in my brain. "You mean my son? It's a *baby*, Arrow. A helpless, innocent baby."

"I know you feel that way right now, but you've been blinded.

Tricked. You're not carrying a baby. You're growing the spawn of the devil inside you."

A slightly unhinged laugh burst from me. "The only devil in this room is *you.*"

His lips thinned. When he reached up to touch my hair again, I jerked my head away. Sighing, he said, "Everything will become crystal clear soon. When you're with me, you'll no longer be confused."

"I would rather *die* than be with you," I spat, struggling to rise once more. He pushed me into the mattress again, harder this time.

"Don't test me, Nora," he said, in a voice that gave me pause. I focused on his eyes and found them glowing bright blue. Zuriel. "Once you see how truly powerful I am, you'll be begging for my forgiveness. Even in this state, I've managed to drive that demon husband of yours into hiding. His own pack is falling apart around him, all thanks to me. Instinctively, they recognize that I'm the far superior leader. First Jasmine, then Hugo. Learning your whereabouts these past few months was *easy.* The Alpha Meeting. The castle. My intel made me invaluable to the witches, and they couldn't wait to strike a deal with me."

My heart sank even more. Hugo, one of Midnight Pack's most influential members, had betrayed us? The news would devastate Kolton. "They're going to kill you," I told Arrow, focusing my energy on waking Storm. My body was alarmingly weak, and I desperately needed her to help me escape this madman. "Either my family or the witches will end you, Arrow. You know they won't let you live after this."

The bright glow of his eyes only intensified, almost as if he was excited. "I'm no fool. I know they'll try. They'll *all* try. But they won't be able to. Not after you heal me."

I blinked. "*Heal* you?"

He barked an incredulous laugh. "You haven't figured it out yet? I *need* you, Nora. I need the precious magic pumping through your veins like life-giving water. Only you can cure what ails me. Only you can restore my power to what it once was. It's why I've fought so hard for you. You're my salvation. My *redemption*. With you by my side, no one will be able to defeat me, to even *touch* me. As soon as you're free of the devil's spawn, we will rule this earth like gods."

I was silent for a long beat, overcome with shock. My mind whirred a million miles an hour, the pieces finally coming together. It suddenly all made sense. Every single crazy thing he'd done made perfect sense.

"You're a Fallen," I whispered. "*Zuriel* is a Fallen."

His description of fallen angels—violent mood swings, selfish deeds, unstable power. That was *him*.

Anger. *Rage* bled into his burning gaze. "It's a mistake. *Heaven* made a mistake. I was never supposed to be sent here. I was the leader of the largest legion of archangels, revered and adored. I never failed to perform my duties. I was *flawless*."

Despite my pain, I scoffed at him. "Flawless? You were jealous of Seraphina's power, *Zuriel*. You tried to send her to Earth so you would be revered and *adored* again. So you would be the number one honcho. You're not flawless. You're just a dick."

Arrow's lips pulled back in a sneer, one that was decidedly Zuriel's. "She was the one who forgot her place. I made her great, but being second in command wasn't enough for her. My punishment was fair, and she chose to disobey me. If anyone deserves to fall from grace, it's Seraphina. But she can redeem herself by healing me and following my lead once more. All will be forgiven, you have my word."

Holy hell, Zuriel was even crazier than Arrow. I couldn't help but wonder if the fallen angel had been pulling the strings all along. If

Arrow was just a hapless pawn in all of this. I couldn't think of him as the victim though. Not when he would allow the witches to take my child from me. Not when he would help Zuriel destroy my family.

A familiar warmth suddenly stirred awake inside of me. Unable to wait for Storm to fully gain consciousness, I made my move. Arrow's eyes widened as my hands shot up and gripped his face. When magic pulsed from me and into him, he bellowed and jerked away. That didn't stop me. I flung a magic ball at him, then another and another, forcing my weak body upright in bed.

"I will *never* heal you!" I shouted, using every last ounce of strength I possessed to back him into the room's corner. "I will only ever use my power to *defeat* you."

"Elders!" Arrow roared, covering his face as I continued to lob magic at him purely intended to harm.

The bedroom door burst open, and in walked a witch I didn't recognize.

"I, Tallulah Sharpe, respected Cosmic elder, bind your magic," she loudly said, her voice ringing with authority. From my peripheral, I saw her toss two shiny objects into the air. When the objects suddenly shot my way, I tried to dodge them, but they were too fast. They latched onto my wrists like bracelets.

The worst feeling came over me then. It was like a part of my soul was being sucked out of me. It made me feel so wretched, so *empty*, that I started to scream. But I wasn't the only one. Storm rose up and howled in agony, the sound melding with mine. I collapsed onto the bed and curled into a ball as a wave of debilitating weakness crashed over me. I tried to pry the bracelets from my wrists, but they immediately burned me. The silver seared my flesh, adding to my misery.

Storm. Storm, help! I called out to my familiar, but she couldn't hear me. She continued to howl, writhing inside of me as if the pain was unbearable. As if the bracelets were sucking the very life out of her.

Through the tears blurring my vision, I looked up and found Arrow. The witch was nowhere to be found. "Please," I whimpered to him, holding out my wrists. "Please, take them off."

Genuine pity filled his gaze. "I'm sorry, Nora. Truly, I am. They'll unbind your magic once your memories have been wiped. It'll be like the horrors of the past six months never happened."

Barely able to register his words through the pain, I sobbed, "No. Not my memories. They can't take my memories. *Please*, Arrow. I beg you. Tell them I'll cooperate. I'll *heal* you. Just . . . just don't let them take my memories away."

He sadly shook his head. "I'm sorry, but this is for the best. Your mind needs a fresh start. When the bad memories are erased, you'll gladly help me purge the world of demons again, starting with the one who sullied you. Once he ceases to exist and you're finally free of him, everything will make sense. You'll see, Nora. You'll . . ."

My vision darkened as the pain became too much. My last terrifying thought was that I'd wake up to emptiness. To a world devoid of Kolton and everything beautiful he'd brought into my life.

CHAPTER 33

KOLTON

The moment my world was taken from me, I forgot how to breathe.

Blood pounded in my head, keeping time with my thundering heart. My bleak existence yawned before me like an endless pit of nothingness.

I lost her, I lost her, I lost her.

The darkness inside of me swelled, threatening to pull me under. If it did, there would be no escaping it this time. No piecing myself back together. I would break apart and never heal. Never look forward to another day.

Not without her. Not without my wife. My soulmate. The mother of my unborn child.

I opened my mouth to scream, but no sound came out. There was nothing left in me. I was a useless shell. A dead man walking.

STOP! a voice thundered in my mind. *You're not going there again. Snap out of it, Kolton. Your mate needs you.*

I blinked, and some of the darkness lifted.

She's not dead. I would have felt it, the voice continued. *There's still time to save her.*

Air trickled into my lungs, allowing me to whisper, "Shadow."

That's right. I'm here for you, buddy. I won't let you do this alone. Now, pull yourself together, or I'm taking over.

More air filled my lungs, allowing me to think more clearly. To push down the darkness that wanted to consume me.

I was suddenly surrounded by faces. Faces lined with worry and fear.

"Kolton, what happened? Where's Nora?" Vi frantically said. Beside her, Brielle's face was white with terror as she took in the blood that streaked my chest.

Jagger and Griff clasped my shoulders, giving me a shake as I stared at them blankly.

"Gone," I managed to croak. "She's gone."

Their expressions fell.

"Everett, find Father," I heard Loch say. "Kade, contact Bill."

Little arms wrapped around my right leg, and I looked down to find Mellie. Without a word, I bent and picked her up. She buried her face in my neck and whispered, "Here. You can have Princess. She can help you find Nora again."

Tears blurred my vision, and I hugged her tightly, letting the tears fall unchecked.

Use your bond, Shadow said, pacing inside me like a caged beast. *Try to find her through your connection. You've been practicing.*

Hope took my breath away once more.

Passing Melanie over to Jagger, I burst into action.

"Princess. Take Princess!" Mellie shouted, and I reached back to accept the blue unicorn from her.

With the stuffed animal clutched in my hand, I raced toward the fourth floor. Several of the others followed me, but I didn't slow or bother to explain.

Hurry, hurry, hurry, my mind screamed at me.

I practically flew up the stairs, taking them three at a time. When I reached our bedroom, I yanked open the door and charged inside. Then came to a dead halt.

There. There on the bed. Was a nest.

She must have made it earlier today. Slipped away for a few minutes so she could later on surprise me.

The nest wasn't made out of soft blankets this time. This one was made out of my shirts. Shirts she'd taken from me and worn to bed the past few weeks. They were laid out similar to the old nest, carefully positioned to look like a blooming flower. There were also several fresh daisies tucked into the shirt folds, but the center remained empty, of course. It was for her to curl up in. To place our newborn child. Because she felt *safe* here.

At the realization, I crashed to my knees.

After all these months, she'd finally felt safe enough to rebuild her nest.

And now, she was gone. She was *alone*. Facing who knew what kind of horrors.

"Oh, Nora," I groaned, dropping to all fours and crawling toward the bed. "I'm sorry. I'm so sorry, sweetness."

When I reached the bed, I dragged myself onto the mattress and laid down beside the nest. Shielding it. Protecting it as I should have protected her.

But it was empty. So devastatingly empty.

Fiercely hugging Mellie's unicorn, I squeezed my eyes shut and focused on the only thing I could do. On that small sliver of hope Shadow had given me.

With the scent of Nora all around me, I cast out my senses and began the search for my wife and child.

CHAPTER 34

NORA

I'd fallen into the most beautiful dream.

Kolton was there, his warmth all around me as he whispered soothing words of comfort.

I found you, I found you, I found you, he kept saying.

I snuggled deeper into his warmth, too exhausted to reply back.

Hold on, sweetness. I'm coming for you.

Hurry, I managed to whisper back, but I didn't know why. I was content. I was *safe.* He was right here with me.

And then the dream began to fade, along with his warm presence.

Leaving me cold and terrified once more.

When I awoke, the pain was indescribable.

It wasn't just physical. I'd endured silver shackles before and knew that I could survive what it did to my body. But the bracelets on my wrists weren't simply shackles. Somehow, they'd managed to cut me off from a vital part of myself.

Silver only weakened me so that I felt human, but these bracelets hadn't just weakened me. They'd stripped away my ability to do magic.

I wasn't stuck in a cage or shackled to the floor, but this prison was so much worse.

The only word that could describe it was purgatory.

Purgatory is preferable to this, Storm said, her voice a weak whimper.

Storm! I struggled to sit up in bed, but my body was like a lead weight. *What did they do to us?*

The cruelest thing a magic-user can do to another magic-user. They bound our magic. I've never . . . I've never felt like this before, not even when I fell to Earth.

Frowning, I slowly peeled my eyes open and searched the room. Empty. We were alone. Not even Arrow was here. Wow, they were either cocky or simply knew I had no chance of escaping. Probably the latter.

I struggled some more and finally managed to sit up. Feeling woozy, I paused for a moment before saying, *Don't give up hope, Storm. I don't think you fell to Earth. Also, I'm pretty sure Kolton just dreamwalked with me.*

Expecting her warmth to surge through me, my heart broke when all she did was faintly whisper, *What?*

I had a lovely chat with Zuriel earlier. Apparently, the dickhead is a Fallen. It explains why he wanted us to join him so badly. Not because of the bond you two once shared, but because he needs your magic to heal his tainted soul.

She was silent for a long moment, then, *He thinks I can heal him?*

He seemed pretty confident about it.

Then he's a fool. I have the power to obliterate evil and restore light. I don't have the power to save a heart willingly lost to darkness. Not even the Maker can do that, not if His creation doesn't truly want to be rescued.

Wow. That's deep. So you think Zuriel only wants a bandaid fix so he can keep being a dickhead?

I believe so. Actions speak louder than words, as they say.

Very true. Which is why I don't think you're a Fallen. I think you were sent here.

Sent?

Like on a mission. I think you were sent to Earth to learn something. Or take out Zuriel. I haven't figured out which yet. Maybe both.

Storm wheezed out a weak laugh. *You've grown quite wise, Nora.*

Why, thank you.

And positive, considering our dire situation. I don't even think I can help you escape this time. The magic bindings prohibit me from controlling the shift.

Well, as I told you, I think Kolton dreamwalked with me. He said he's coming for us.

Which gave me much-needed hope, but I didn't know how long it would take him to get here. I couldn't just sit around in the meantime.

I started to scoot toward the edge of the bed, keeping an eye on the door as I did.

What are you doing? Storm asked, her voice laced with concern.

Figuring out where we are. If I'm going to be rescued like a damsel in distress, the least I can do is be aware of my surroundings.

Well, be careful.

I will. As I swung my legs over the bed's edge, a foot kicked at my ribs. I paused to rub my belly and silently croon, *It's okay, sweet boy. Mommy's got you.*

Normally, I liked to whisper to him out loud, but I was pretty sure that same witch was just outside the door. I didn't want to know what other horrors she could inflict on me. As quietly as I could, I placed my feet on the floor and stood. The world immediately tilted, and I grabbed onto the bedside table to keep from falling.

Nora, Storm cautioned. *You're too weak to be standing. Think of the baby.*

Gritting my teeth, I waited for the dizziness to pass before slowly straightening. *I am thinking of the baby. Don't forget what Keisha plans to do. I haven't seen her yet, but I know she's here. I just need to figure out where here is.*

Storm didn't argue when I released the table and carefully shuffled toward the room's only window. Dark blue curtains covered it, but even with my senses weakened, I could tell that it was still nighttime. Sure enough, as I peeked through the curtains, it was dark outside. Maybe around midnight. I squinted into the shadows, my vision greatly impaired by the silver. I couldn't see very far, but there were lots of pine trees similar to the ones near the castle. What's more, I was pretty sure I could hear the faint sound of crashing waves.

Were we still in Maine near the coast? Daring to hope a little more, I searched for more clues. Anything that could help me when it came time to run. Because I would. As soon as an opportunity presented itself, I was getting out of here.

Not through the window though. I was on the second floor, and I didn't know what a fall that great would do to me and the baby in my current condition.

Needing reassurance, I called out to Kolton through our bond. I didn't know how far the connection could stretch, but I had to try. Had to know if the dream had been real. If he truly was on his way.

I felt him before I heard him. Felt his abject relief. Felt his pain and joy at hearing my voice.

Nora. Nora, talk to me. Tell me you're okay, he said, his words tumbling over each other in a rush.

I'm okay. They bound my magic and weakened me with silver, but otherwise haven't touched me or the baby.

I'm going to kill them. Every single one of them. We're coming, sweetness. Just hold on a little while longer.

At the confirmation, my legs nearly gave out. Clutching the window's ledge, I replied, *Hurry, Kolton. I'm in a bedroom on the second floor of a house. I think I'm still in Maine.*

You are. They took you to Portland. You're in Northwood Pack territory, just off the coast on a little private island. Arrow has a home there.

Ah hell, I was in Arrow's *home?* This had better not be his bedroom.

The fact that he'd brought me here said a lot about his confidence that I would make him invincible or whatever.

Kolton, they plan to erase my memories. I don't know how much time I have left before—

"Enjoying the view?"

At the unexpected voice, my spine snapped straight.

Nora, what's happening? Nora? Nora!

I didn't dare answer him. Didn't dare do anything but lower the curtain and carefully turn around. At the sight of Keisha in the doorway, my legs almost gave out. All the pain, all the torture she'd put me through, came rushing back. I trembled from head to toe but managed to remain upright as I said, "How . . . how can you . . . ?"

"See?" she finished for me. A smile twitched the corners of her lips, slightly shifting the black cloth around her eyes. "I can't, no thanks to you. My third eye is what allows me to sense things on the earthly plane." The smile abruptly vanished. "But you *damaged* it the last time we chatted, which affected our special bond. I haven't been able to sense you from afar since then, so I had to hire a little help."

At the disdain that entered her voice, I assumed she meant Arrow, not the elders.

Growing weaker by the second, I kept her talking, not knowing what else to do. "I'm surprised you made a deal with him after all you told me. He wants to keep me for himself, you know."

She lifted one shoulder in a tiny shrug. "His usefulness to me and my esteemed companions is about to end, and so has yours." Her chin dipped until her line of sight was trained on my belly, as if she could *see* it. "I'd almost given up hope of avenging my coven after I was left injured and utterly alone. I was the last surviving witch who knew about you and your little family of abominations. The last witch who could see a greater future for her kind.

"But I'm not the only witch who's tragically lost her coven," she continued, playing with the end of a braid with her pointy nails. "Five years ago, the most powerful witches of our time were forced into isolation. I cried out to them in my sorrow, and they graciously answered my call. Since then, several more banished witches and warlocks from around the world have joined us. If I deliver to them what I promised, they've agreed to become my new coven. What's more, I will be sworn in as the newest witch elder."

My breathing grew ragged, not just from the pain and weakness, but from her terrifying words. "But the elders were cast out of the witch community," I said. "Their order has been disbanded. It no longer exists."

She laughed as if I'd said something funny. "Oh, little wolf, you are so stupidly naive. This world will always be ruled by those who *take* it. I have no intention of allowing this golden opportunity to slip through my fingers, and neither do the elders. The order will rise again. You, unfortunately, won't be alive much longer to see that happen. I was prepared to use *you* to usher in this new era, but the premonition I received changed everything. Your son will be a much greater reward. Children are so much more malleable. They're trusting. Giving. He'll give me everything I seek without question because I'm his *mother*. Because he *loves* me and wants to see his mommy *happy*."

My composure snapped. "I will *kill* you if you touch him!" I roared. White-hot rage gave me an unexpected surge of strength, and I rushed toward her. Before I could make it two steps, she jerked up a hand. I gasped as an invisible force slammed me back against the wood-paneled wall, pinning me in place.

Sudden warmth gushed down my inner thighs, making me gasp again. But Keisha didn't notice. Didn't have a clue that my water had just broken. The liquid trickled soundlessly to the carpet as she slowly approached, a wicked smirk twisting her lips. She came up to me all the way, invading my personal space without worry. Then slowly reached out and touched my stomach. When I felt her nails softly caress me through my white floral dress, tears burned my eyes.

"What were you saying?" she purred, continuing to stroke me. "You keep forgetting who has the real power here. Even your *wolf* can't help you. All magic has its limits, after all. I've reached the limits of mine, but I know I could be *twice* the witch I am now if I had my own spirit like you do. Last chance, little wolf. Last chance to give her to me."

I strained against her magical hold, murdering her over and over with my eyes, even if she couldn't see it. "Go to Hell."

She sucked on her teeth in disappointment. "What a waste. Now I'll have to send your wolf back to wherever she came from. Oh! But I do know. I'll tell you a little secret though," she said, then leaned closer to whisper in my ear, "I've always preferred demons."

With that, she turned and released me. "Tallulah," she called as I slumped against the wall, the last of my energy drained. "Wipe her memories. I'll be back shortly to perform the surgery."

My brain short-circuited. No, I needed more time. *Kolton* needed more time.

Storm, help me!

I felt her strain to reach the surface, to protect me in my desperate moment of need, but we were both helpless against the magic bracelets that bound us.

How do I get them off? I asked Storm, watching as Tallulah silently entered the room and closed the door behind her. I stayed where I was, slumped over in defeat. I was just a helpless pregnant woman. Helpless and harmless. I made myself as small and pathetic as I could, willing the witch to see me as weak.

Binding spells are powerful, Storm replied. *Breaking them requires a steep price. The only way to remove it is if the witch that performed the spell either willingly retracts it or is killed.*

Ah hell.

"You'll want to lay down for this," the thin, middle-aged witch said, eyeing me sternly.

I fluttered my lashes weakly. "I can't . . . I can't move."

She pursed her thin lips, then strode toward me impatiently.

Kolton, I need your strength, I shouted down our bond, praying he could hear me.

Nora, what's happening? he immediately responded, sounding out of breath. *We're almost there. Are you okay?*

No time to explain. I need your strength now, Kolton. Now!

The witch grabbed my arm, and I moaned, "Oooh. I think my water just broke. I feel so dizzy."

As I started to list sideways, forcing the witch to support my weight, adrenaline spiked through me. *Strength.* So powerful that I pushed past the pain and emptiness to lunge forward and grab the witch's head. Her eyes widened in horror, but I didn't hesitate. Didn't *think* as I used that surge of supernatural strength to twist her head sideways. So sharply that I heard a sickening *crack*.

Gasping in shock, I let go of her. She dropped like a stone to the floor, her head still twisted at an odd angle.

I stared at her, my heart thundering out of my chest. "Is she . . . ?" I whispered, unable to finish the sentence.

She's dead, Storm confirmed.

Bile surged up my throat, but I forced it back down, refusing to dwell on what I'd just done. Tearing my eyes from the lifeless body, I focused on my wrists. The silver bands looked the same, but I was starting to feel less empty. Less like one of my limbs had been cut off.

I reached for a bracelet.

Nora, Storm warned, but I was already digging my fingers under the silver object.

With a yank, I broke the binding and threw it to the floor. Then did the same with the other one.

Feeling Storm's concern, I rushed to say, "I'm fine. Just a few burns. Let's get out of here."

I was halfway across the room when the worst cramp of my life squeezed my midsection. Groaning, I clutched my stomach and stumbled to a halt.

Breathe, Nora, Storm urged. *It's just a contraction.*

Seriously? I wanted to laugh. To scream. To cry. Talk about bad timing.

"You need to take over," I panted through the pain. "I can't escape like this."

Yes, you can. You have to. Shifting during active labor could hurt the baby.

I whimpered but didn't argue, knowing she was right. It was my job to get us out of here. To *protect* us. A little labor pain wasn't going to stop me.

"Okay. Okay, I can do this. Here I go." Holding my stomach as if I could keep the baby from falling out, I waddled forward.

Nora, talk to me, Kolton said. *Tell me you're okay.*

I'm okay. I'm just in labor.

The baby's coming?

I couldn't help but smile a little. He sounded even more terrified than me. *Yup. Ready or not.*

All right. Just breathe, Nora. We're infiltrating the island now. They have no idea we're coming. Just stay where you are.

Sorry, no can do. Keisha's coming back any minute now to take our baby away. I'm coming to you.

When he colorfully swore, I almost laughed. Almost broke down in hysterics. He was so close to reaching me. *So close.* I just had to find him.

One step at a time, I told myself, silently moving toward the door. I strained to hear any sounds from the hallway beyond, but my senses were still weak from the silver. Deciding that time was of the essence, I carefully grasped the handle and twisted. It easily gave, allowing me to crack open the door. Pausing for only a moment to listen, I eased into the hallway.

Empty.

Normally, I would have taken an opportunity like this to run like a bat out of hell, but moving around while in active labor was no joke, even for a werewolf. I made it to the end of the hallway before another contraction hit. Gripping the corner of the wall, I breathed through the pain, forcing myself not to make a sound.

The moment the contraction started to fade, I was moving again. Down the stairs, each step careful and precise. My long skirt brushed the tops of my feet. My *bare* feet. If I had to guess, Arrow had been the one to remove my shoes, blech. I had no idea where he'd scuttled off to, but there was no way I was giving birth to my baby in his house.

It was a straight shot to the front door, but something told me that it was being guarded from the outside. I'd have to find another way out. I was just about to peer over the railing to make sure the coast was clear when I heard a shout, followed by a cry of alarm. I froze a handful of steps from the bottom, listening as two pairs of feet pounded across the front porch and off into the night.

Bingo. Now was my chance.

Throwing caution to the wind, I hurried down the remaining stairs and beelined toward the front door. Before anyone could stop me, I was outside and racing across the porch. My heart frantically pounded, telling me to go, go, go. It was so loud that I almost missed the faint sounds of fighting in the distance.

He's here. He's here!

My heart soared, and I changed course to head toward the fighting. My bare feet lightly skimmed over the snow as I picked up speed. I held my stomach with one hand and my skirt with the other, praying that I could make it into the protection of the trees before another contraction hit.

I should have known better though.

Pain viciously wrapped around my middle, squeezing the air from my lungs. As I stumbled and caught myself against a maple tree, an unearthly scream came from inside the house. Ice shot through my veins.

It was Keisha. And she was *mad*.

I tried to take off again, but the contraction wasn't ready to let me go yet. I dug my nails into the tree bark and forced myself to breathe. To push past the pain. I was still too exposed. Too *close*. Keisha could still sense where I was through her creepy third eye.

The contraction had just begun to fade when I heard a shout. A shout that was far too close.

"Nora!"

No, no, no. Not *him!*

I whirled and raised a hand, still gripping my stomach. "Don't come any closer, Arrow. I swear I'll kill you!"

He slowed, taking in my stooped posture and labored breathing. Then shook his head. "Running is useless, Nora. You can't reach them in time, and neither can they. My pack, a dozen witches, and several elders are standing between you and them."

I swallowed a whimper. "Let me go, Arrow. I'm begging you. I know that Zuriel is the one who wanted all of this to happen, not you. He's brainwashed you into believing that you want it too, but do you *really* think an innocent baby is evil? Do you *really* want to wipe my memories and make me your slave? Because that's what I would be. A *prisoner*. We aren't meant to be together, neither are Zuriel and Storm. So *please*, Arrow. Let me return to my soulmate."

He stared at me for the longest moment. We were frozen in time as the world moved on around us, oblivious to the turmoil stirring in Arrow's eyes. For a single moment, I thought I'd reached him. Thought I saw the person who'd been locked in a cage alongside me. Who'd been as desperate for freedom as I had. But his expression shuttered a second later, and with a sinking heart, I knew I'd lost him.

"Over here," he loudly said, impassively watching as my eyes widened.

Before I could take off running, an unseen force flung me back against the tree, pinning my arms to my sides.

"Why didn't you restrain her?" Keisha snapped, pushing past Arrow. "She could have gotten away."

Arrow shrugged. "I think she's in labor. She couldn't have gotten far."

"Still, her mate is fast approaching. I'll have to do this quickly. Go stall him with the others."

"But you assured me her memories would be wiped first. I need her compliant before you leave with that *thing*."

Keisha's lips twisted in a sneer, one he couldn't see. "We secured her for you, and now it's our turn to get what we want. Once the baby has been removed, I'll perform a quick forgetting spell on her. Now leave so I can work in peace."

I silently pleaded with Arrow one last time, but he was already moving away, leaving me alone with the psychotic witch.

"Keisha, don't do this," I said, struggling against her magical hold. Ignoring me, she hurried forward and bodily placed me on the ground. When she reached down and hiked my dress up, exposing my belly, true panic set in. Inhaling deeply, I screamed as loudly as I could, "KOLTON!"

NORA! he shouted back through the bond, his panic equalling mine.

Hissing, Keisha backhanded me, effectively shutting me up. "He won't be able to reach you in time, foolish girl. I'll have this baby out in seconds, and then I'll be gone. Scream all you want. No one is going to save you."

With that, she jabbed her pointy nail into my belly and began to cut. Cut and cut and cut. She sawed back and forth without mercy, filling me with pain and terror.

Storm pushed to the surface with a furious roar, but she was as frozen as I was. Neither of us was able to do a thing as the Oracle began to fulfill her wicked premonition, cutting my belly open with her bare hands so she could pry my son out and take him from me.

"Please!" I screamed into the night sky, but the world was deaf to my cries.

Pain and terror became my existence as the witch continued to cut.

And cut.

And cut.

CHAPTER 35

KOLTON

Pain exploded through me. *Nora's* pain.

Swift. Hot. Excruciating.

It drove me wild with terror, nearly making me lose my concentration. I barely avoided being impaled by a tree branch as an elder with Earth Elemental magic used the forest surrounding us for their personal arsenal. Before they could attack again, I was on them, my dagger-like claws raking through their neck with one brutal swipe. Blood sprayed me, adding to my already soaked skin and clothing.

I was still in my human form, needing the control it gave me, but Shadow was riding me hard. His desperation to reach Nora in time mirrored mine, and I'd never felt more in sync with the demon than I did right now. We were one mind, one *entity* as we plowed through the bodies separating us from our world. Anything that stood in our way received the same bloody end.

"Griff, with me!" I bellowed at my third in command, who'd just punched a big male werewolf out cold. But the others were even more in the thick of it. I hadn't expected Arrow's pack to be here as well. They'd caught onto our stealth attack sooner than we'd hoped, alerting the elders and at least a dozen other witches that Keisha had recruited. There were even a few animal familiars, one of them a hawk who kept screeching and dive-bombing to distract us. We currently had the majority of our foes surrounded though, keeping them heavily engaged so they couldn't run or portal away.

Several SCA operatives had responded to our call, and more were joining the fight by the minute. The majority of them were human, but they each held weapons designed to harm supernaturals, most coated in silver. The vampire princes and Kade were a blur among them, the latter wielding a wicked-looking silver sword. Jagger and Vi fought side-by-side in their demonic forms, dodging magic attacks and protecting each other's backs.

Bill and his son, Noah, were lighting up the woods with their bright Cosmic magic, freezing anyone who tried to run. The vampire king, along with Kenna, Isla, and Brielle, had stayed behind to protect the twins and Melanie. When Brielle had argued against being left behind, I'd had to sharply put her in her place. If we all made it out of this alive, I'd find a way to make it up to her later, but I couldn't worry about hurt feelings right now.

My mate was in trouble. In pain. In *agony*.

My only thought was on getting to her as quickly as possible.

When I glimpsed a familiar head of white-blond hair through the chaos, fresh rage trembled through me. Shadow fixated on the backstabbing male, but I quickly said, *Leave him. They won't let that bastard get away. Not this time.*

Using a sharp blast of magic to knock aside the last few people in my way, I was just about to take off when I heard a howl, followed by another and another. I glanced back and found that more allies had arrived to join the fight, but they weren't operatives this time. I spotted Alpha Zimmerman and his nephew, Reid. The three massive shapes *behind* them was what caught and held my attention though.

They were werewolves. Werewolves who'd shifted without the aid of a full moon. Wolves like *us*. And they'd come to help in our hour of need.

One of them found my gaze and paused. We shared a look that only lasted a second, but in that second, a world of understanding was conveyed.

Go. Go and protect your own. We've got your back, the wolf seemed to say.

I nodded my gratitude, then whirled and took off like a shot. Griff was right behind me, easily keeping pace with my loping strides as I partially shifted to cover more ground. I could still feel Nora's pain, but her agonized screams had abruptly cut off a few seconds ago. She was alive, but something was wrong. Terribly wrong. The invisible bond that connected us together felt frail. Not damaged like when I'd experienced my mental break, but *thin*. Threadbare. Almost translucent, as if it was fading away. As if *she* was fading away.

Shadow, I managed to utter through my panic.

I feel it, he replied. *Keep going, Kolton. We're almost there.*

And we were. We were seconds away. *Seconds*. But those seconds felt like minutes. Hours. *Days*. We were too far. Too *far*.

The trees started to thin when I caught the first whiff of her blood. My legs almost gave out, but I forged ahead, clenching my jaw so hard that it cracked. Soon, all I could smell was Nora's blood. Thick. Suffocating. Everywhere.

Too much. There was too much of it.

A bright burst of cerulean light was the first thing I saw. Immediately, I knew what it was. *Who* it was. I surged forward, willing my feet to sprout wings. A shape moved through the trees, heading straight toward the swirling light. I ran faster, faster than I'd ever run before.

Not this time, I silently vowed, crashing through the remaining trees to roar, "KEISHA!"

She paused, her back facing me as I slammed to a halt, spraying up snow.

One second. One *step* and she would vanish, just like she had last time.

"Turn around," I quietly growled, my entire body trembling as I forced myself to hold still.

An awful second passed. Then another. And another.

Just when I thought she would step into the portal and vanish into the ether once more, she slowly turned to face me. I stopped breathing when I saw what she held in her arms.

"He's mine," she said, her blood-soaked hands clutching a baby to her. *My* baby. My son.

He made a small mewling sound, and my heart broke.

"Keisha, take one more step with my son and you're dead," I said, my voice so soft that it was almost a whisper.

She smiled. "You mean *my* son? He will make me great. The greatest witch of all time. Together, he and I will usher in a new era for all witches. Our power will be legendary. You can't stop it from happening. You can't stop *me*. Not without hurting this precious baby."

She took a step back until one foot was inside the portal. Everything in me went silent. My racing mind. My thundering heart. Calm rolled through me. The deadliest calm I'd ever felt. It sharpened my focus. Sharpened my senses. Every single one of them was trained on her. On the witch who was threatening to take my world from me once more.

Not this time, I repeated.

With that victorious smile still stretched across her face, she started to lift her other foot. I whipped up my arm and sliced it through the air with deadly accuracy. Still smiling, she swayed, then started to fall. Her body fell backward, but her head tumbled off and struck the ground, splattering the snow with blood.

As her body, along with my son, started to vanish inside the portal, I lunged forward. Seconds. The portal would close in seconds, and I'd lose him. The swirling circle grew smaller and smaller, swallowing Keisha's body from view. All I could see now was my tiny, helpless son.

One second. One second more, and he would be lost to me forever.

I reached in and grabbed him, pulling him out just as the portal vanished.

As I tucked him against my chest, he belted out a lusty cry. I nearly collapsed with relief, cradling him close as I finally allowed myself to breathe. "I've got you," I whispered to him, swiftly checking him over for injury.

"Kolton."

At the sound of Griff's panicked voice, the rest of the world came rushing back in. I turned and immediately lost the ability to breathe again.

"Nora." For a moment that lasted an eternity, all I could do was stare at her. Stare at the blood saturating the snow around her. Stare at the damage Keisha had done to her body. She'd been brutally torn open, her child ripped from her stomach. And her face. Her face was so pale. Almost as white as the snow.

I moved toward her, unable to feel my deadened limbs. Her breathing was slow. Shallow. Our bond stretched thinner.

"Nora," I repeated, my voice cracking. Reaching her side, I fell to my knees in the blood-saturated snow.

Her eyes fluttered open. When they lifted and caught sight of the bundle in my arms, she smiled. It was faint but brilliant, filled with utter joy. "He's beautiful," she whispered, pure wonder encompassing each softly spoken word. "Just like his daddy."

"Oh, Nora," I croaked, watching as the bright spark in her aqua blue eyes started to dim. I shared a look with Griff. A helpless one. His mouth quivered, and he shook his head.

"You saved me," she continued to whisper, each word fainter than the last. "You saved us both."

When her eyes fluttered shut, panic wildly beat at my chest. Leaning over her so I could pass our son to Griff, I bent down and cupped her face, too afraid to do anything else. "Nora. Nora, look at me. You have to *fight*. You're strong. You've always been so strong. Please heal yourself, sweetness. I can't lose you."

She slowly lifted a trembling hand to touch my face. Cold. Her fingers were so *cold*. "I'm tired, Kolton. So tired."

"I know, sweet flower, but you can get through this. I'm here. I'm right here beside you."

She tried to smile again, but her lips barely moved. "Call him Luca. Luca Anthony Rivers. Tell him . . . tell him his mother loves him dearly. Tell him to live and to love as his parents did."

Tears fell from my eyes and onto her cold cheeks. "Tell him yourself. I'm not letting you leave me, Nora. You hear me? You *promised*. You said nothing would tear us apart. Don't go, sweetness. Please. Don't go where I can't find you."

I was crying. Sobbing. Pleading. *Begging*. But her eyes shut anyway. Her chest stilled, and her hand fell from my face. When her heart stopped beating, our bond snapped. Severed. As our connection shattered, I was immediately filled with unbearable loneliness. The agony of it was so great that I threw my head back and screamed. Screamed into the empty void of my existence.

When my voice grew hoarse, I gathered her into my arms and rocked her against me. Rocked and rocked, refusing to let her go.

"Come back to me. Please, Nora. I can't live without you."

I didn't know how much time had passed. Every second apart from her was a lifetime. The darkness rose up once more, offering to swallow me whole, but I refused it. Refused to break, no matter how much pain I was in.

Without her, I couldn't live, but a part of her still lived on. He was feet away, waiting for his father to protect him. To show him the warmth, love, and acceptance that he deserved. I wouldn't rob him of that. Wouldn't leave him to face the world alone. My soul would never be whole again, but I would live on. I would live on for our son.

Nora's cold body suddenly warmed.

"Kol!" Griff exclaimed, standing up to shuffle a few steps back. "Let her go. She's glowing."

Never. I would *never* let her go.

But, after a moment, the warmth grew hotter. Painful. I opened my eyes to a sea of blinding white. I desperately tried to hold on anyway, but I was suddenly blasted back. I crashed through the snow, then scrambled upright, prepared to rush back to her. But the sight of her body drew me up short.

It was no longer on the ground.

She was hovering several feet above the snow, her skirt and hair undulating in an unseen wind. The white light surrounding her pulsed and swelled, throwing out waves of heat. When I tried to approach, it shoved me back again.

Protecting her. It was *protecting* her.

The light continued to pulse and swell for several moments, growing so bright that I had to shield my eyes. It abruptly exploded, sending out a shockwave of heat that physically pushed me back. Regaining my balance, I looked at Nora again and gasped.

The protective glow that surrounded her was gone. In its place were wings. Angelic wings made of pure light.

CHAPTER 36

NORA

I hadn't wanted to leave. Everything in me had wanted to stay with my mate and newborn son.

Nora, heal yourself, Storm had begged me, alarmed at how much blood I was losing. Too much. Even a supernatural being needed blood to survive. Because of the silver still in my veins, my body's ability to swiftly heal had been compromised. Weakness stole over me so suddenly that using magic to heal myself wasn't even an option. *You can't leave your mate. You promised him.*

The reminder hurt something fierce.

I'm sorry, I told her, unable to keep my eyes open any longer. *I'm sorry we didn't have more time together. At least you can return to Heaven now where you belong.*

I don't care about that anymore, she snapped. *You have to stay. I'll make you stay.*

I tried to reply, but my time was up. The fight left me, and I inhaled my last breath. As I drifted off, all of my pain and sorrow melted away. I would miss this life, but I had to hope that something good awaited me on the other side. Maybe I would become an angel. And maybe, just maybe, I could return to Earth to visit my mate and child. Not as before. Not as Nora. But it would give me peace if I could watch over them, even from afar.

Time passed as I continued to float in a sea of nothingness. It almost felt like I was in limbo, waiting for something to happen. Oh no. Was I in some kind of purgatory?

How ironic would that b—

I was suddenly shoved back. Flying threw time and space. Hurtling toward some unknown destiny. I flew and flew like a shooting star, unable to stop my fast ascent. Or descent. Was I going to Hell?

As quickly as it began, I stopped with a jolt. It felt like I'd smacked into a wall, and all the air whooshed out of me.

Wait. I could breathe again?

I popped open my eyes and gasped when I found myself floating in the air. Was I having an out-of-body experience? Then where was my body? I glanced down and touched my stomach. I couldn't see it through my dress, but it felt whole. *Healed.*

And real. This felt *real.* I was moving and breathing and—

I looked to the side and saw something bright stretched out behind me. When I saw it on the other side too, my jaw dropped.

Wings. I had *wings.*

Before I could dwell on that impossibility, something pulsed inside me. Something achingly familiar. Something warm and accepting. Something intense and breath-stealing. Something that I'd terribly missed, if only for a moment.

Love. It was my soulmate's love for me, filling our bond so completely that I forgot about the wings and everything else. Like two magnets drawn together, my gaze found his. He was standing down below, looking up at me with awe.

I suddenly remembered everything. The unbearable pain of having my child ripped from me, of seeing the fear in my mate's eyes and being unable to comfort him, of leaving him and passing from this life into the next. I didn't know how I'd made it back, but I didn't care. All I cared about was reuniting with my mate.

The wings abruptly vanished, and I fell. Instead of collapsing to the snow, I hit the ground running. Kolton met me halfway, opening his arms so I could throw myself into them. When we collided, everything made sense again. Everything felt *right* again. He lifted me up, his arms holding me impossibly tight as he leaned down and kissed me. I grabbed his face and kissed him back, pouring every ounce of love I felt for him into it. His cheeks grew wet, and I wiped his tears away, overwhelmed to be given this second chance at life.

"How?" he whispered between kisses, showering me with so much love that my own tears fell. "How are you here? I saw you die. I *felt* it. Our bond broke."

I kissed him again before answering, "I don't know. I felt myself die too. Then I was hurtling back to Earth and thrown into my body. I feel great now. Healed. Almost as if—" I suddenly pulled back, breaking the kiss to gasp, "Storm."

Kolton's happy expression fell as he felt my panic. "What's wrong, Nora? Is she gone?"

Tears filled my eyes again, and he reached a hand up to gently wipe them away.

Before I could speak, an annoyed female voice spoke in my head, *You can't get rid of me that easily.*

I laughed and sobbed at the same time, overcome with relief.

Angel baby! Shadow exclaimed. *You scared the hell out of me for a second, which isn't an easy thing to do. What happened?*

She was silent for a long beat, then replied, *Nora was right. I was sent to Earth, not banished. The second she died, I was given a choice. Return to Heaven, or complete my earthly mission. I can see now that I was created for more than blind obedience. Being sent here wasn't a punishment but a second chance at life. I was meant for a greater purpose, so choosing to go or stay was easy.*

My lip trembled. "So you decided to stay? With me?"

With all of you, yes. But the decision came at a price. To return to Earth once more, I needed to give up another piece of my spirit.

"Oh, Storm," I whispered in dismay.

Do not fret, Nora. The piece belongs to you, a sacrifice I will gladly make again if the need ever arises. You've given me a home. A place to belong. I am blessed to share this life with you.

I started to cry again, wondering if I could die of joy. "I love you, Storm."

I love you too, Nora.

I love you too, my angel baby, Shadow chimed in. *I knew you couldn't bear to be parted from me.*

My eyes widened as Storm made a noise. A noise I'd never heard her make before. Holy hell, my moody familiar was *laughing*.

"Hey, guys?" a voice called. "Sorry to interrupt the happy reunion, but there's a little baby over here who really wants to see his mom and dad."

My eyes widened further. "Luca."

Kolton's expression softened. Setting me on my feet, he kissed the tip of my nose and turned toward Griff. As he walked away, I watched the line of his shoulders. Relaxed. They were relaxed. Positioned in a way that I hadn't seen in a long, long time.

It was then that I finally saw the round object in the snow not far away. A head. One covered in long black braids. Keisha. The black cloth around her eyes had been knocked askew, revealing dark empty eye sockets that would never see again.

Considering everything that had happened, her end was very fitting.

Completely forgetting about her the moment Kolton turned around again, I focused on the squirming baby in his arms. He was now wrapped in his father's bloody, tattered shirt, and for some reason, the sight filled me with peace.

Safe. He was safe. We *all* were.

When Kolton stopped before me, he looked down at our son and quietly said, "Luca Anthony Rivers, meet your mother. You don't know this yet, but she will protect you fiercely and love you completely. She doesn't do anything in half measures, and she will teach you the importance of strength and tenacity in the face of adversity. But even more than that, she'll help you without fail when you're feeling weak. She'll encourage you to face your fears and will even hold your hand while you do it. She'll be your biggest fan for *life*." He smiled softly, looking up at me. "Because that's who your mother is."

Trying not to cry again and epically failing, I whispered, "I love you."

"I love you too, sweetness," he whispered back, then gently placed our son in my arms.

"Oh," I quietly gasped as he blinked up at me and I saw his eyes for the first time. They were a bright aqua blue, just like mine. The rest of him was wholly Kolton though. Same deep olive skin and dark brown hair. He was undoubtedly going to break some hearts one day, which oddly made me want to smile.

It was from knowing that he had a future. From the *certainty* that he was safe and sound with his family. That he would always be loved, always belong, and would never question where he fit into this world.

I smiled wide, then leaned down to kiss one of his soft round cheeks. "I love you, Luca," I whispered. "I will remind you of that every day, and I will accept you always, no matter what."

He cooed softly, melting my heart.

I was suddenly lighter than air as Kolton scooped me up and cradled us both against him. I laid my head against his chest, more content than I could ever remember being.

"This is sweet and all," Griff said from beside Kolton as he headed into the woods with his wife and son held securely in his arms, "but what if the fight didn't end in our favor? Maybe we should be going the *opposite* direction."

"We're fine," was all Kolton said, continuing to where he'd left the others. "For the first time in a long time, we're actually fine, Griff. Although, if you want to run ahead and make sure my sister's in one piece, I wouldn't blame you."

I peeked at Griff. My heightened senses were back to normal, and I could easily see the deer-in-headlights look on his face.

"Griff," Kolton quietly chided, which made his friend's eyes widen further. "I don't often pry, but if you have feelings for my sister, don't let fear stand in your way. I almost let Nora go once, and it was the biggest mistake of my life."

Smiling, I pressed a kiss to Kolton's chest.

"Thanks, bro," Griff quietly said, clasping Kolton's shoulder. He didn't leave our side, but when we caught sight of the others through the trees, I knew he was searching for Vi. I found her a second before he did, back in her human form. It was a sure sign that the threat had been contained, allowing me to breathe easier. Griff beelined toward Vi, and when she saw his approach, she ran to meet him. Not even caring that she was naked, he wrapped her up in a bone-crushing hug.

Something in my chest loosened at the sight. I didn't know what the future held for them, but I knew they were going to be okay.

Kolton suddenly slowed, some of his tension returning. I glanced up and found his gaze locked on something. I followed his line of sight and immediately spotted his target. Arrow. My own tension returned. He was in cuffs, special ones designed to restrain supernaturals. They *all* were. His pack, the witches Keisha had recruited, and even the elders. Several bodies were scattered across the forest floor, souls who hadn't survived the fight, but I didn't recognize any of them. I blinked in surprise when I spotted three huge wolves though.

"Are those . . . ?" I started.

"Werewolves like us," Kolton finished, flashing me a grin. "They came for you. For us."

My mouth formed a large O.

Luca suddenly cried out, flailing one of his tiny hands. The sound drew several gazes, including Arrow's.

"Sounds like our son is hungry," Kolton observed, slowing even more.

"Hold on," I said, wiggling to be let down. "I need to do one last thing first."

He reluctantly set me on my feet, making a sound of protest when I placed Luca back in his arms.

"Trust me, Kolton," I said, meeting his eyes. "I have to do this."

He searched my face for a long moment, then sighed and nodded.

Giving him a grateful smile, I turned and headed straight for my target. Arrow looked me up and down as I approached, a fierce frown on his face. None of the others stopped me when I walked right up to look him dead in the eye. Slowly, his mouth formed a sneer. "What do you want, Nora? To *challenge* me?"

"No, Arrow. I want to heal you. I want to give you a second chance at life."

Victory flashed in his eyes, revealing the part of him that had been his downfall. The part that had corrupted his mind and heart. Even now, Zuriel was certain that I'd come to my senses and wished to join him after all. I let him believe it. Let him enjoy his final moment of arrogant disillusionment.

Then I placed my hands on Arrow's face and willed magic to the surface. Magic intended to *harm*, not heal. Magic intended to obliterate evil.

When my hands started to glow, Arrow threw his head back and screamed. Jagger and Griff held him steady as he thrashed against my grip, desperate to get away. Setting my jaw, I continued to burn the evil from him. The *taint* that had infected him for far too long. Piece by piece, I ripped Zuriel apart until he was nothing. Until his existence was erased, in this plane and the next.

I held on, making sure every last scrap of the fallen angel was removed from Arrow, then I let go and stepped back.

The male shook and gasped, barely able to stand as he adjusted to the shock of having his spirit familiar removed from his body. I watched him for a long moment, then said, "This is your chance, Arrow. Your chance to be a better person. Don't waste it."

Slowly, he looked up at me. I held his gaze as he continued to shake, not knowing what to expect. I'd been certain that Zuriel was the rotten part of him, keeping him a prisoner in his own body, but maybe I was wrong. Maybe Arrow couldn't be saved either.

I was about to leave him with a threat in case the evil still lingered inside him when he stunned me by saying, "Thank you, Nora. Thank you."

Blinking, I nodded, watching as his eyes brightened. Not with the glow of Zuriel's presence, but with gratitude. Genuine gratitude.

A great burden lifted off me, and I turned, heading back to my husband and child. When I reached them, I sighed, my heart overflowing with love.

Meeting Kolton's adoring gaze, I smiled and whispered, "Come on. Let's go home."

EPILOGUE

4 Months Later

NORA

Pounding footsteps alerted me to the intruder in my little oasis.

"They're here, they're here!" Vi said, a whirlwind of nervous excitement as she charged into my greenhouse. "Seriously, Nora? I know you're in here. Show yourself!"

"Jeez," I said, popping my head up. "What's a girl gotta do to get a moment of solitude around here?"

With a shrug, Vi beelined toward me. "I dunno. Hide better? Stop letting my brother impregnate you with babies?"

Snorting, I straightened and rubbed my growing belly. She had a point. At this rate, we were going to have a dozen kids before I turned thirty. Our new home was crowded enough as it was. Instead of hiring a nanny, I'd asked Kolton if my parents could stay and help out with Luca. Not permanently, but it was my way of handing them an olive branch. They'd gladly accepted the invitation, and had taken a room on the third floor.

The new mansion was bigger than the old one, sporting several new rooms for our "growing" family. I'd caught Kolton's meaning straight away, accusing him of treating me like his own personal baby factory. But when I'd gone into heat again a month after having Luca, neither of us could keep our hands off each other. We'd spent an entire week at the cabin, learning shortly after that I was pregnant again.

"Where are the others?" I asked Vi, wiping the dirt from my hands.

With the weather finally warming up, I was excited to start tending the outdoor gardens again, but having an attached greenhouse was a dream come true. Every time Luca needed me, I could easily hear him and slip away. He was extremely calm for a baby, so much like his father that I could barely stand the cuteness of it, but he was always hungry. I was pretty sure Kolton had become jealous of his son's constant access to my boobs. I'd caught him longingly eyeing my breasts quite a bit lately.

"Brielle is helping Miss Gabby get Mellie ready. Jagger and Griff are in the foyer. We received another housewarming gift from the pack, and they're trying to find a spot for it."

"Oh, what is it?"

Vi cringed. "An indoor fountain. It's so huge that Luca could learn how to swim in it."

I burst out laughing.

She pointed a finger at me. "Yeah, you think it's funny now, but they fully intend to visit soon. Not just Mrs. Bailey, but every single pack member. Now that everything's right as rain again, they want to show their support. But they also want to see their gifts prominently displayed. If they think we returned them, there'll be nonstop rumors over hurt feelings for weeks."

I shook my head, still chuckling. "At least they're supporting us. That's all I care about."

When we'd returned home, one of the first things we'd had to do was confront Hugo about his betrayal. Although fear had been his motivation for helping Arrow, a male in his position couldn't be allowed such a weakness. He'd been cast from the pack straight away, and Rebekah had become the new head of the influential members. Every time I joined Kolton for meetings with them, I was happy to see that the female was steadily holding her own in a room full of males.

Another big change we were still adjusting to was the frequent requests to see Kolton's "wolf." Not just from Midnight Pack, but from packs around the world. Word had spread like wildfire that we'd stopped the witches, along with a pack that had teamed up with them. Since then, werewolves everywhere were curious about the alpha who'd allied with vampires and the SCA to save his mate and child.

He was an enigma to them. We *all* were. But the acceptance had been staggering. After the Alpha Meeting, I'd expected a lot more hostility, even challenges. But the lengths Kolton had gone to to protect his family seemed to have struck a chord with them, a chord that every single werewolf possessed.

The most shocking part was when we'd get a surprise visit from a wolf like us. There were *dozens* of them. Maybe hundreds, but I doubted all of them would come out of hiding. Some had familiars who were similar to Zuriel, or narrow-minded like Storm used to be. Not all of them were thrilled to find out that Kolton had a demon familiar and I had an angel familiar, two beings who'd set aside their differences and chosen to accept each other. They were inseparable now, their fondness for each other growing each and every day.

As I moved to join Vi, I paused at a pot of daisies to pluck one and slip it into my hair. I'd barely seen Kolton all week as he'd traveled back and forth, making last-minute preparations for this day. He hadn't been this nervous in a while, and I couldn't wait to put him at ease. Being away from us hadn't helped, since we'd hardly been apart for more than a few hours these past four months.

We were all still recovering from the traumas we'd faced. Each day got easier, but we sometimes had to remind ourselves that Keisha was now dead, Zuriel was gone, and Arrow was safely locked inside an SCA high-security prison. I'd heard news from Bill Andrews that Arrow was being considered for a special program, one meant for troubled supernaturals who deserved a second chance. It was a new program, one that had begun shortly after I'd made that speech to Arrow.

I couldn't help but think that I'd played a small part in that, which gave me a sense of satisfaction. Even villains could turn their lives around, and I hoped that was the case for Arrow.

While everyone else in the house was preoccupied, I took the rare opportunity to speak plainly with my friend, quietly saying, "Things seem to be getting more serious with you and Reid."

Vi looped her arm through mine with a small laugh. "I guess. We're three states away, and he travels all the time for his football career, so we don't get to see each other nearly enough. Still, he's super sweet, ridiculously hot, and . . . it's just easy with him, you know?"

I nodded my understanding, even as I bit my tongue, refusing to say more. She'd moved on—or was trying to, at least—and I couldn't blame her for that. Griff hadn't pursued her further, and she'd obviously been feeling lonely. Reid Zimmerman was an amazing guy, and I wished them all the best—even if deep down, my heart was still hoping that Vi and Griff were endgame. I couldn't help it. I loved them both and didn't think either of them was completely over the other.

Something was still there. Something that continued to stand the test of time.

As we strolled down the hall, I smoothly segued into my next completely innocent observation. "Buck has been stopping by an awful lot lately. I couldn't help but notice how cagey Jagger gets when he does. I thought they were friends."

Vi snorted, her ponytail swinging as she shook her head. "They *are* friends. But friends in the male world become enemies when there's a female standing between them, if you know what I mean."

Why, yes. Yes, I did. I'd just wanted confirmation of my findings. Keeping quiet about Jagger and Brielle's soulmate bond had truly been torture, but maybe I wouldn't have to keep the secret for much longer. Not if things kept playing out the way they were.

"What are you two gossiping about?" Griff called from the foyer, making Vi roll her eyes.

"None of your business," she called back, then muttered under her breath, "I swear he gets more nosey every day."

"I heard that!"

"I don't care!" she yelled back.

Chuckling, I paused when I heard a car door slam. "They're here."

Vi snorted again. "That's what I said, Miss Mommy Brain."

Nudging her shoulder playfully, I waddled forward—it was only a *little* waddle—calling, "Mom. Dad. They're here!"

I heard an adorable squeal and clapping hands as my parents descended the left staircase with their grandchild. From his spot beside a ridiculously huge fountain, Jagger nodded at me as I waddled past to meet them at the bottom.

"Come here, sweet boy," I cooed, holding out my hands for my squirming son. He kicked his legs excitedly, gurgling as my mom passed him off to me with a smile. I smiled back. A genuine smile that had grown these past few months.

They'd really settled into life here as the newest members of Midnight Pack. The constant worry I'd grown up seeing on their faces was nowhere to be found, and they absolutely adored Luca. Even knowing that he would turn out different like his parents, they showered him with the love and affection I'd always dreamed of. Sometimes it hurt to see, but mostly, I was just grateful that we'd been given this second chance.

"Brie! Melanie!" I called up next, turning toward the front door. A sudden bout of nervous butterflies erupted in my stomach.

Not you too, a voice filled my head, making me grin a mile wide. *I'm counting on you to be the calm and stable one today.*

Only today, dear husband? As if I'm not calm and stable every day? I replied with mock offense.

He chuckled quietly. *Apologies, dear wife. You are a pillar of grace and strength. I don't know what I'd do if I couldn't lean on you.*

That came out slightly erotic, Shadow interrupted us with a purr. *You can do a lot more with a pillar than lean on it, you know. I can give you some pointers if you—*

Shadow, Storm groaned. *Now is not the time for this conversation. Or any time, for that matter.*

Oh, angel baby, I've missed you, he said, easily switching gears. *I feel like it's been forever since I've seen your bright blue eyes, milky white legs, and luscious fur. I've been dreaming of romping through the spring wildflowers with you and getting a little frisky—*

Shadow! Kolton, Storm, and I all yelled at once.

Fine, he sighed. *Shutting up now.*

Just in time too. The front door opened, and I slowed as Kolton's broad frame filled the doorway. The sight made my heart skip several beats. It didn't matter how much time passed. Every time I saw him, my heart went crazy with happiness. Spotting me just standing there in the entryway, gaping at him like a fish, a slow smile curved his lips.

"Come here, wife," he crooned out loud, crooking a finger at me. I hurried toward him, laughing when he stepped inside to pick me up and twirl me around. Still tucked against my side, Luca squealed, showing off his first baby tooth. "Hello, my beautiful mate," Kolton said, leaning down to kiss my lips until my toes curled. "Hello, my handsome son." He set me down to pick Luca up and blow raspberries on his belly, earning him another squeal. "Hello, my precious baby girl." He held Luca with one arm so he could reach down and lovingly caress my stomach.

I smiled at his antics. "Do you have gender radar or something?"

He shrugged. "It's a family skill. My mom correctly guessed the genders of all three of her children. Right, Mom?"

He stepped aside to reveal the woman behind him, and my smile softened.

She looks good. Really good, I said to Kolton through our bond.

All thanks to you, he replied, looking on as I moved forward to offer his mother my hand.

"Welcome home, Charlotte," I greeted her, relieved when she took my hand and squeezed it tight. Without hesitation, I nudged my magic toward her, something I'd done countless times over the past few months. Every time I did, she became more and more aware. More like the woman she used to be. Not whole, and far from being fully healed, but well enough to remember her children. Well enough to want a new life for herself with them.

Including the one she'd never met.

Tucking the premature streak of white hair behind her ear, Charlotte returned my smile with a nervous one of her own. "Where . . . where is she?"

Looking over my shoulder, I spotted Brielle coming down the stairs with a little girl tightly clutching a blue unicorn. I smiled at my best friend, who nodded and gently nudged the girl forward. At the same time, I released Charlotte's hand and stepped aside, allowing her a clear view of her youngest daughter for the very first time.

"Mellie," Kolton quietly said, his voice full of emotion as he watched their reunion, "this is your mother. Mom, meet Melanie."

"Hi, Melanie," Charlotte softly said, clasping her hands as they began to shake. Kolton reached out and gently squeezed her shoulder, offering his silent support.

Melanie stared at her mother with wide eyes. Simply stared and took her in. From the corner of my eye, I saw Vi place a hand over her mouth, as if she was afraid her sister wouldn't accept the woman before her. We'd hoped for and dreaded this day, unsure what the outcome would be. Keeping them apart all these years had been a tragic yet necessary evil, but we couldn't expect Melanie to simply embrace her mother after all this time.

Just when I'd started to think that Melanie wasn't ready for this introduction, she surprised us all by looking at her mother and saying, "Do you want to meet Princess?"

The collective sigh of relief around the room was audible, making me laugh. Making us *all* laugh. Even Charlotte. "Yes, Mellie," she said, blinking the tears from her eyes. "I would love to meet Princess."

As mother and daughter reunited after nearly seven years apart, there wasn't a single dry eye in the room. Yes, we were all still healing, but we were healing together. And that's what mattered.

Being together was *all* that mattered.

ALSO BY BECKY MOYNIHAN

WOLVES OF MIDNIGHT
Midnight Vow
Midnight Claim
Midnight Queen

A TOUCH OF VAMPIRE
Shadow Touched
Curse Touched
Fate Touched
Sun Touched (spin-off standalone)

THE ELITE TRIALS
Reactive
Adaptive
Immersive

GENESIS CRYSTAL SAGA
Dawn till Dusk
Fall of Night
Stars till Sun

ACKNOWLEDGMENTS

I can't believe Nora and Kolton's story is over already!! I've grown to adore these characters so much and will miss them dearly. But this doesn't have to be goodbye! If, like me, you're not ready to leave this world, there are a few beloved side characters who still need their happily ever afters. All you have to do is convince me to write their stories!!

I'll also be diving back into my vampire series with another standalone spin-off. I hope you enjoyed seeing those characters again in this book! I love how expansive this world is becoming and would be thrilled to continue writing in it. I've done a vampire and a werewolf series, so what should be next? Witches? Help me decide!

As always, thank you to my amazing beta readers, Morgan, Kate, Allie, and Melissa. I value you beyond words!

To my incredible ARC team, I am humbled by your dedication and enthusiasm for my books. Your excitement and kind words give me the confidence to keep writing. Thank you for supporting me and being my cheerleaders!

And to the rest of my readers, thank you so much for giving this series a chance. It's because of you that I will go on to write another and another. I hope you'll stick around for many books to come!

BECKY MOYNIHAN is a bestselling, award-winning author of paranormal romance and urban fantasy. Her books include the A Touch of Vampire series, Wolves of Midnight series, The Elite Trials series, and the co-written Genesis Crystal Saga.

When she's not writing, you can find Becky curled up on the couch in her North Carolina home, binge-watching shows and sipping Mountain Dew.

To stay up to date on new releases, sign up for her monthly newsletter: www.beckymoynihan.com/newsletter

www.ingramcontent.com/pod-product-compliance
Lightning Source LLC
Chambersburg PA
CBHW030552260626
47157CB00006B/2283